JOHNSON LOOKED BACK
THE COLLECTED WEIRD STORIES
OF THOMAS BURKE

The Hippocampus Press Classics of Gothic Horror Series

Edited by S. T. Joshi

Johnson Looked Back: The Collected Weird Stories of Thomas Burke
The Harbor-Master: Best Weird Stories of Robert W. Chambers
Lost Ghosts: The Complete Weird Stories of Mary E. Wilkins Freeman
Back There in the Grass: The Horror Tales of
Irvin S. Cobb and Gouverneur Morris
The Mummy's Foot and Other Fantastic Tales, Théophile Gautier
Twin Spirits: The Complete Weird Stories of W. W. Jacobs
From the Dead: The Complete Weird Stories of E. Nesbit
Frankenstein and Others: The Complete Weird Fiction of Mary Shelley

JOHNSON
LOOKED BACK

THE COLLECTED WEIRD STORIES
OF THOMAS BURKE

Edited by S. T. Joshi

Hippocampus Press

New York

Johnson Looked Back: The Collected Weird Stories of Thomas Burke
© 2018 by Hippocampus Press
"Introduction" © 2018 by S. T. Joshi

Published by Hippocampus Press
P.O. Box 641, New York, NY 10156.
http://www.hippocampuspress.com

Cover art © 2018 by Aeron Alfrey
Cover design and "Classics of Gothic Horror" logo by Dan Sauer,
dansauerdesign.com
Hippocampus Press logo designed by Anastasia Damianakos.

First Edition
1 3 5 7 9 8 6 4 2

ISBN: 978-1-61498-215-9

First Edition
1 3 5 7 9 8 6 4 2

CONTENTS

INTRODUCTION

"Few biographers are faced with such problems as he will be who aspires to be a late chronicler to our modern arch-entangler of truthful self-revelation, Thomas Burke."[1] So said John Gawsworth, who admired the work of his fellow Englishman but found himself frustrated by his inability to distinguish truth from exaggeration and, at times, outright fabrication in the life of Thomas Burke (1886–1945)—a task made more rather than less difficult precisely because Burke purported to chronicle his own life in a succession of books that are now seen to be more fiction than fact. These books have misled any number of critics—including such noted figures in our field as Richard Bleiler and Jessica Amanda Salmonson[2]—into accepting Burke's statements about his life at face value. Recent research, chiefly conducted by Anne Veronica Witchard,[3] makes it evident that in many ways Burke was his own most interesting fictional character.

Burke attained both celebrity and notoriety on the publication of *Limehouse Nights* (1916), a scintillating series of short stories set in the now vanished Limehouse district of London, heavily populated by Chi-

---

1. John Gawsworth, "Foreword" to *The Best Stories of Thomas Burke* (London: Phoenix House, 1950), 16.

2. Richard Bleiler, "Thomas Burke," in *Late Victorian and Edwardian British Novelists: Second Series* (Dictionary of Literary Biography 197), ed. George M. Johnson (Detroit: Gale Research Co., 1999); Jessica Amanda Salmonson, "Introduction" to Burke's *The Golden Gong and Other Night-Pieces* (Ashcroft, BC: Ash-Tree Press, 2001).

3. Anne Veronica Witchard, "Thomas Burke, the 'Laureate of Limehouse': A New Biographical Outline," *English Literature in Transition* 48, No. 2 (January 2005): 164–87; *Thomas Burke's Dark* Chinoiserie: Limehouse Nights *and the Queer Spell of Chinatown* (Farnham, UK: Ashgate, 2009).

nese immigrants; his book raised eyebrows both by its generally sympathetic portrayal of these immigrants (in spite of his use of terms such as "Chinaman" or "Chink" that are now regarded as derogatory) and, in particular, by its suggestion that young (in many cases underage) girls were attracted to older Chinese men. Burke, having discovered a winning formula, went on to write numerous other volumes about Limehouse, including *Twinkletoes: A Tale of Chinatown* (1917), which created the character of the young woman of the title, subsequently made famous by the 1926 silent film. Burke also wrote volume after volume that detailed facts (or fantasies) of his own life, especially as it related to his lifelong love of the inexhaustibly fascinating megalopolis of London. For devotees of weird fiction, however, his rare volume *Night-Pieces* (1935) is a choice treasure whose contents, until recently, have been a closed book.

Sydney Thomas Burke was born on November 29, 1886, at Clapham Junction, a suburb of London. In contrast to his frequent assertions that he was an orphan and that he spent "years of hell" at the Hardcress Home for Orphans, Burke in fact spent reasonably happy years at the London Orphan Asylum (actually in Watford, Hertfordshire). His father had indeed died early in Burke's childhood, but his mother was still alive. Leaving the orphanage in 1901, just before his fifteenth birthday, he took a position as an office boy with a stockbroking firm, Messrs. Stillwell & Co., in central London. At this time he lived at 4, Portland Place, Fulham, with his mother and a sister, Alice. Late that year he published his first short story in a magazine, *Spare Moments.* The next year he published a wide array of work—stories, poems, and articles—for various magazines and newspapers. During 1906–07 he worked during the day at a used bookstore in Clapham while working at nights on a London newspaper, the *Tribune.* It was at that bookstore that he discovered the work of Stephen Crane, especially the seminal work *Maggie: A Girl of the Streets* (1893), a searing account of a young prostitute that made Burke wish to portray the seamy but fascinating underside of London life and society, focusing on the underprivileged and the marginalised.

Burke then began work at The Literary Agency of London, where he developed an acquaintance with some of the leading writers of the day, including the novelist E. Nesbit and the literary critic St. John Adcock. He privately published his first book, a slim volume of *Poems* (1910), issued in an edition of 25 copies. Meanwhile, his sketches about London were appearing in prestigious magazines and newspapers of the day, including the *Idler* and the *Daily Chronicle.* These sketches led the publisher Stanley Unwin to commission him to write the book *Nights in Town,* published in 1914. Subtitled "A London Autobiography," it was the first of many books in which Burke fused his own life (or the persona he had already developed of the young, unconventional Bohemian exploring the obscure byways of the city) and that of London.

Unwin, in a later reminiscence, suggests that Burke had already written *Limehouse Nights* by this time:

> It must be remembered that the attitude towards books was much more squeamish and puritanical in 1914 than it has been since 1918. The three books I recall were George Moore's *The Brook Kerith,* Caradoc Evans' *My People* and Thomas Burke's *Limehouse Nights.* We were so impressed by the last that we at once commissioned him to write *Nights in Town,* which we published with success, and gave him a job in our office to tide him over temporary financial difficulties. He was the fastest typist I have ever known.[4]

It is not entirely clear that Unwin's recollections are sound, especially as regards the order of composition of *Nights in Town* and *Limehouse Nights.* Whatever the case, the publication of the latter—not by Unwin, but by Grant Richards—in 1916 created a furore. The book was reprinted in the United States in 1917 by Robert M. McBride, with evocative illustrations by Mahlon Blaine that highlighted the relationship between young British girls and Chinese men.

Limehouse was an extensive district in east London, now overtaken by the districts of Pennyfield and Docklands. As Chinese immigrants flocked to the area, it became a source of both fascination and trepidation on the part of Anglo-Saxons, who were then in the grip of the purported "yellow peril" menace. The very notion that lovely and underage white girls could be seized by—or, indeed, would willingly enter into the

---

4. Stanley Unwin, *The Truth about a Publisher: An Autobiographical Record* (London: George Allen & Unwin, 1960), 133.

embraces of—Oriental men sent a frisson of sexual terror through the British populace. Indeed, Burke himself was worried about facing prosecution for obscenity upon the publication of his book, but in fact no attempt at banning the book occurred. The book's popularity led D. W. Griffith to purchase the film rights for the immense sum of £1000; the film emerged as *Broken Blossoms* (1919).

Burke subsequently went on to write numerous volumes expanding on his account of Limehouse, including *The Song Book of Quong Lee of Limehouse* (1920), *East of Mansion House* (1926), *The Pleasantries of Old Quong* (1931; published as *A Tea-Shop in Limehouse* in the U.S.), and *Abduction: A Story of Limehouse* (1939). He also wrote more general sketches about London—*Out and About: A Notebook of London in War-Time* (1919), *The Outer Circle: Rambles in Remote London* (1921), *Whispering Windows: Tales of the Waterside* (1921), *The London Spy: A Book of Town Travels* (1922)—as well as such chronicles of his own life as *The Wind and the Rain: A Book of Confessions* (1924). Many of his Limehouse stories are narrated by a Chinese figure, Quong Lee, whom many critics have assumed to have been a real individual; but in fact he was an entirely imaginary figure drawn from the work of Ernest Braman, whose sketches of China—beginning with *The Wallet of Kai Lung* (1900)—were a significant influence on Burke.

During World War I Burke worked for the American branch of the Ministry of Information. In early 1918 he met Winifred Clara Wells, herself an aspiring writer who went on to write books under the pseudonym Clare Cameron. They married on September 19, 1918, and remained united for the rest of Burke's life. But their marriage was troubled: Burke's single-minded focus on writing led Winifred to feel neglected, and she carried on several affairs over the years. In 1929 the couple moved to 33, Tavistock Square, in Bloomsbury. Burke would later commemorate this period in his life in the memoir *Living in Bloomsbury* (1939). He remained as productive as ever, generating book after book, sometimes several in a single year. But all this work was not necessarily remunerative, and in 1936 the couple moved to a rural enclave, Gipsy Hill, in South London. In 1939 Burke made a desperate plea with the occult writer Dennis Wheatley, asking his help in getting a Civil List pension for himself. The pension was rejected, but his finances seemed to improve somewhat. In part this was due to an offer by the publisher B. T. Batsford to write a series of books about London. Burke complied by quickly generating *The Streets of London* (1940), *English Night-Life* (1941), and *Travel in England* (1942), as well as volumes of a roughly similar sort for other publishers.

All this work allowed Burke and his wife to move back to central London, where they lived at 66, Queensway in Bayswater. It was, however, here that Burke endured the bombing of London during the early years of World War II. In 1945 he was admitted to a hospital for pneumonia. His wife advised homeopathic treatment, but it failed, and Burke died on September 22, 1945, after an operation for peritonitis. His final memoir, appropriately titled *Son of London,* appeared in 1948.

John Gawsworth noted that the authors with whom Thomas Burke "might have liked to be placed" were W. W. Jacobs, F. Marion Crawford, Oliver Onions, O. Henry, and Ambrose Bierce.[5] It is no accident that all these writers either were exclusively devoted to the weird (at least in their short stories) or dabbled in it from time to time. What strikes us about Burke's weird tales is the degree to which—from as early as *Limehouse Nights* to the tales in *Night-Pieces* and beyond—the author runs the gamut of weird motifs, from psychological terror to pure supernaturalism to an engaging mix of fantasy and terror.

It would be unreasonable to expect the *Limehouse Nights* stories to feature any heavy dose of weirdness, as their prime focus is precisely the realism of both their settings and their characters, albeit with a liberal infusion of romance and exoticism. A single story in *Limehouse Nights,* "The Bird," can qualify as a weird tale, although it is in fact a grisly tale of the pseudo-supernatural in which a Chinese man, having murdered the captain of a sailing ship who had brutalised him, believes—to his own detriment—that the captain's ghost is speaking to him.

Burke continues the fusion of the Limehouse atmosphere and weirdness in "The Tablets of the House of Li," a poignant tale of benign supernaturalism. Two of Burke's most powerful stories, "The Bloomsbury Wonder" and "The Hands of Mr. Ottermole," demon-

---

5. Gawsworth, 8–9.

strate his most skilful merging of the mystery story with the strange. The former, published separately in 1929 before being gathered in the late volume *Dark Nights* (1944), seems on the surface nothing more than the account of a particularly savage serial killer (or gang of killers) who has murdered an entire family, leaving only one survivor; but as the narrative continues, we develop a chilling sense of the psychological aberration—bordering, indeed, upon psychic possession by the force of pure evil—that led the killer to his act. "The Hands of Mr. Ottermole," one of several weird tales in *The Pleasantries of Old Quong* (1931), is exquisitely balanced on the very borderland between psychological suspense and supernaturalism, and the final sentence may take us over the edge into the latter. And yet, this tale—adapted for radio in 1949 for *Suspense* (re-broadcast in 1950), and then for television in 1957 for *Alfred Hitchcock Presents*—was in 1950 voted by a panel assembled by Ellery Queen as the greatest mystery story of all time.[6]

Other stories in *Pleasantries* continue the pattern. The focus of "Desirable Villa" is a crime—but one set in the future. "The Yellow Imps," again set in Chinatown, tells the story of a man who kills another man after a strange encounter and then believes he is being followed by yellow imps. Is all this the result of a magic spell? Is it all in his mind? It is impossible to tell.

The stories in *Night-Pieces* are of such a wide range in mood, theme, and implication that they justify the celebrity that the volume has engendered. It is true that the book contains some stories that are purely of crime and suspense; but even these are gripping and effective. In "One Hundred Pounds" a young man who has ingratiated himself into the good graces of his grandfather seems disinclined to wait until that elderly gentleman's death to inherit the sum cited in the title. "The Watcher" tells of a burglar who kills a man who he believes has been a witness to his crime—but the truth proves to be quite different. On the threshold between mystery and psychological suspense is "The Black Courtyard," which vividly evokes echoes of Poe's "The Tell-Tale Heart" in its account of the protagonist's sense of dread after killing an old man. The pseudo-supernatural is featured in "The Horrible God,"

---

6. Witchard, "Thomas Burke," 176–77.

where an idol believed to have supernatural powers is shown to be something else entirely. And what do we make of "Funspot," where a man envisions a murder that proves to be his own? Somewhat related to this tale is "Events at Wayless-Wagail," where a man who has had a vision of an apparent murder in the future seeks desperately to avert or negate it—but finds that that is not so easy to do.

Two delicate stories underscore Burke's skill at employing benign supernaturalism. "Yesterday Street" displays an almost Bradburyesque sense of nostalgia as a man returns to the place where he grew up and appears to see his childhood friends, still young and innocent. "The Gracious Ghosts" features the novelty of ghosts of the *living*—a couple that had a falling out but are subsequently reunited. Much more malign are two other tales of witchcraft and precognition. In "Miracle in Suburbia" a man is given supernatural "protection" of some kind by a sorcerer—but what happens upon the sorcerer's death is unspeakably horrific. "Uncle Ezekiel's Long Sight" is the half-humorous narrative of a man who seems capable of making uncanny predictions—and he uses this skill cleverly in gaining revenge on an old enemy.

Without question, the most distinctive story in *Night-Pieces* is "Johnson Looked Back," one of the most brilliant tales of *second-person narration* ever written. What begins as the seemingly non-supernatural tale of a man pursued by some implacable enemy proves to be something quite different; and again echoes of Poe—this time "William Wilson"—are clearly evident. But this story is in some senses surpassed, at least in hideousness, by "The Hollow Man," an unforgettably loathsome tale of a man raised from the dead who haunts his killer. This seemingly trite premise devolves into something far more disturbing, especially as the dead man inexorably decays while stolidly haunting his murderer.

Other tales in *Night-Pieces* are perhaps less successful. "The Man Who Lost His Head" is the somewhat unsatisfactory story of a man who wants to make a new start in life but one day wakes up and finds that he has the face of a suspected killer. How this has happened is never clarified, although there appears to be some connexion with a person the man had met in a bar, who may or may not be acquainted with Satan. "Murder under the Crooked Spire" is a lacklustre crime narrative, while "The lonely Inn" is a routine ghost story set in a ghostly tavern. And *Night-Pieces* also contains three largely mainstream stories—"Father and Son," "Two Gentlemen," and "Jack Wopping"—that are included here chiefly to preserve the integrity of the story collection. And yet, they are fine stories in their own right and vividly display Burke's keen eye for telling traits of character and his profound understanding of class distinctions.

It is fitting that "The Golden Gong"—the one weird tale Burke wrote after publishing *Night-Pieces,* as John Gawsworth commissioned him to write it for the anthology *Thrills* (1936)—is his final contribution to the genre. It is a splendid summation of all the variegated strands of weirdness that he had utilised for the previous two decades: the exquisitely rendered Limehouse atmosphere; the subtle and ambiguous use of the supernatural (is the gong of the title, whose ringing by a small boy appears to summon a lovely and kind Chinese lady, a magical device?), the fusion of terror and heart-rending pathos, and a smooth-flowing, crisply muscular prose style that instantly evokes a sense of wonder in both setting and character.

Thomas Burke is one of many writers of his period who freely engaged in weirdness and terror while generating volume after volume of a very different sort. Because the weird tale at this time was not a concretised genre rigidly distinct from other genres or from mainstream fiction, authors could draw upon it whenever the mood struck them—or, more significantly, whenever they came upon a theme or motif that could be most pungently vivified by the manipulation of the strange. Amidst a mass of sound work Burke has written a few tales of exemplary power that deserve a high place in the canon of weird fiction. Whatever his ultimate rank may be, the sheer pleasure derived from reading such a gifted and fluent author is reward enough in itself.

—S. T. JOSHI

Johnson Looked Back
The Collected Weird Stories
of Thomas Burke

The Bird

It is a tale that they tell softly in Pennyfields, when the curtains are drawn and the shapes of the night shut out. . . .

Those who held that Captain Chudder, *S. S. Peacock,* owners, Peter Dubbin & Co., had a devil in him, were justified. But they were nearer the truth who held that his devil was not within him, but at his side, perching at his elbow, dropping sardonic utterance in his ear; moving with him day and night and prompting him—so it was held—to frightful excesses. His devil wore the shape of a white parrot, a bird of lusty wings and the cruelest of beaks. There were those who whispered that the old man had not always been the man that his crew knew him to be: that he had been a normal, kindly fellow until he acquired his strange companion from a native dealer in the malevolent Solomons. Certainly his maniac moods dated from its purchase; and there was truth in the dark hints of his men that there was something wrong with that damned bird . . . a kind of . . . something you sort of felt when it looked at you or answered you back. For one thing, it had a diabolical knack of mimicry, and many a chap would cry: "Yes, George!" or "Right, sir!" in answer to a commanding voice which chuckled with glee as he came smartly to order. They invariably referred to it as "that bloody bird," though actually it had done nothing to merit such opprobrium.

When they thought it over calmly, they could think of no harm that it had done to them: nothing to arouse such loathing as every man on the boat felt towards it. It was not spiteful; it was not bad-tempered. Mostly it was in cheery mood and would chuckle deep in the throat, like the Captain, and echo or answer, quite pleasantly, such remarks, usually rude, as were addressed to it.

And yet . . . Somehow . . .

There it was. It was always there—everywhere; and in its speech they seemed to find a sinister tone which left them guessing at the meaning of its words. On one occasion, the cook, in the seclusion of the fo'c'sle, had remarked that he would like to wring its neck if he could get hold of it; but old grizzled Snorter had replied that that bird couldn't be killed. There was a something about that bird that . . . well, he betted no one wouldn't touch that bird without trouble. And a moment of panic stabbed the crowd as a voice leapt from the sombre shadows of the corner:

"That's the style, me old brown son. Don't try to come it with me—what?" and ceased on a spasmodic flutter of wicked white wings.

That night, as the cook was ascending the companion, he was caught by a huge sea, which swept across the boat from nowhere and dashed him, head-on, below. For a week he was sick with a broken head, and throughout that week the bird would thrust its beak to the berth where he lay, and chortle to him:

"Yep, me old brown son. Wring his bleeding neck—what? Waltz me around again, Willie, round and round and round!"

That is the seamen's story and, as the air of Limehouse is thick with seamen's stories, it is not always good to believe them. But it is a widely known fact that on his last voyage the Captain did have a devil with him, the foulest of all devils that possess mortal men: not the devil of slaughter, but the devil of cruelty. They were from Swatow to London, and it was noted that he was drinking heavily ashore, and he continued the game throughout the voyage. He came aboard from Swatow, drunk, bringing with him a Chinese boy, also drunk. The greaser, being a big man, kicked him below; otherwise, the boat in his charge would have gone there; and so he sat or sprawled in his cabin, with a rum bottle before him and, on the corner of his chair, the white parrot, which conversed with him and sometimes fluttered on deck to shout orders in the frightful voice of his master and chuckle to see them momentarily obeyed.

"Yes," repeated old man Snorter, sententiously, "I'd run a hundred miles 'fore I'd try to monkey with the old man or his bloody bird. There's something about that bird. . . . I said so before. I 'eard a story once about a bird. Out in T'aip'ing I 'eard it. It'll make yeh sick if I tell it. . . ."

Now while the Captain remained drunk in his cabin, he kept with him for company the miserable, half-starved Chinky boy whom he had brought aboard. And it would make others sick if the full dark tale were told here of what the master of the *Peacock* did to that boy. You may read of monstrosities in police reports of cruelty cases; you may read old records of the Middle Ages; but the bestialities of Captain Chudder could not be told in words.

His orgy of drink and delicious torture lasted till they were berthed in the Thames; and the details remain sharp and clear in the memories of those who witnessed it. At all the ceremonial horrors which were wrought in that wretched cabin, the parrot was present. It jabbered to the old man; the old man jabbered back, and gave it an occasional sip of rum from his glass; and the parrot would mimic the Chink's entreaties, and wag a grave claw at him as he writhed under the ritual of punishment; and when that day's ceremony was finished it would flutter from bow to stern of the boat, its cadaverous figure stinging the shadows with shapes of fear for all aboard; perching here, perching there, simpering and whining in tune with the Chink's placid moaning.

Placid; yes, outwardly. But the old man's wickedness had lighted a flame beneath that yellow skin which nothing could quench: nothing but the floods of vengeance. Had the old man been a little more cute and a little less drunk, he might have remembered that a Chinaman does not forget. He would have read danger in the face that was so submissive under his devilries. Perhaps he did see it, but, because of the rum that was in him, felt himself secure from the hate of any outcast Chink; knew that his victim would never once get the chance to repay him, Captain Chudder, master of the *Peacock,* and one of the very smartest. The Chink was alone and weaponless, and dare not come aft without orders. He was master of the boat; he had a crew to help him, and knives and guns, and he had his faithful white bird to warn him. Too, as soon as they docked at Limehouse, he would sling him off or arrange quick transfer to an outward boat, since he had no further use for him.

But it happened that he made no attempt to transfer. He had forgotten that idea. He just sat below, finished his last two bottles, paid off his men, and then, after a sleep, went ashore to report. Having done that, he forgot all trivial affairs, such as business, and set himself seriously to search for amusement. He climbed St. George's, planning a real good old booze-up, and the prospect that spread itself before his mind was so compelling that he did not notice a lurking yellow phantom that hung on his shadow. He visited the Baltic on the chance of finding an old pal or so, and, meeting none, he called at a shipping office at Fenchurch Street, where he picked up an acquaintance, and they two returned eastward to Poplar, and the phantom feet *sup-supped* after them. Through the maze and clamour of the London streets and traffic the shadow slid; it dodged and danced about the Captain's little cottage in Gill Street; and when he, and others, came out and strolled to a bar, and, later, to a music-hall, it flitted, mothlike, around them.

Surely, since there is no step in the world that has just the obvious stealth of the Chinaman's, he must have heard those whispering feet? Surely his path was darkened by that shadow? But no. After the music-hall he drifted to a water-side wineshop, and then, with a bunch of the others, went wandering.

It was late. Eleven notes straggled across the waters from many grey towers. Sirens were screeching their derisive song; and names of various Scotch whiskies spelt themselves in letters of yellow flame along the night. Far in the darkness a voice was giving the chanty:

"What shall we do with a drunken sailor?"

The Captain braced himself up and promised himself a real glittering night of good-fellowship, and from gin-warmed bar to gin-warmed bar he roved, meeting the lurid girls of the places and taking one of them upstairs. At the last bar his friends, too, went upstairs with their ladies, and, it being then one o'clock in the morning, he brought a pleasant evening to a close at a certain house in Poplar High Street, where he took an hour's amusement by flinging half-crowns over the fan-tan table.

But always the yellow moth was near, and when, at half-past two, he came, with uncertain step, into the sad street, now darkened and loud only with the drunken, who found unfamiliar turnings in familiar streets, and old landmarks many yards away from their rightful places, the moth buzzed closer and closer.

The Captain talked as he went. He talked of the night he had had, and the girls his hands had touched. His hard face was cracked to a meaningless smile, and he spat words at obstructive lamp-posts and curb-stones, and swears dropped like toads from his lips. But at last he found his haven in Gill Street, and his hefty brother, with whom he lived when ashore, shoved him upstairs to his bedroom. He fell across the bed, and the sleep of the swinish held him fast.

The grey towers were tolling three o'clock, and the thick darkness of the water-side covered the night like a blanket. The lamps were pale and few. The waters slucked miserably at the staples of the wharves. One heard the measured beat of a constable's boot; the rattle of chains and blocks; mournful hooters; shudders of noise as engines butted lines of trucks at the shunting station.

Captain Chudder slept, breathing stertorously, mouth open, limbs heavy and nerveless. His room was deeply dark, and so little light shone on the back reaches of the Gill Street cottages that the soft raising of the window made no visible aperture. Into this blank space something rose from below, and soon it took the shape of a flat, yellow face which hung motionless, peering into the room. Then a yellow hand came through; the aperture was widened; and swiftly and silently a lithe, yellow body hauled itself up and slipped over the sill.

It glided, with outstretched hand, from the window, and, the moment it touched the bed, its feeling fingers went here and there, and it stood still, gazing upon the sleep of drunkenness. Calmly and methodically a yellow hand moved to its waist and withdrew a kreese. The same hand raised the kreese and held it poised. It was long, keen and beautifully curved, but not a ray of light was in the room to fall upon it, and the yellow hand had to feel its bright blade to find whether the curve ran from or towards it.

Then, with terrific force and speed, it came down: one—two—three. The last breath rushed from the open lips. Captain Chudder was out.

The strong yellow hand withdrew the kreese for the last time, wiped it on the coverlet of the bed, and replaced it in its home. The figure turned, like a wraith, for the window; turned for the window and found, in a moment of panic, that it knew not which way to turn. It hesitated a moment. It thought it heard a sound at the bed. It touched the coverlet and the boots of the Captain; all was still. Stretching a hand to the wall, Sung Dee began to creep and to feel his way along. Dark as the room was, he had found his way in, without matches or illuminant. Why could he not find his way out? Why was he afraid of something?

Blank wall was all he found at first. Then his hand touched what seemed to be a picture frame. It swung and clicked and the noise seemed to echo through the still house. He moved farther, and a sharp rattle told him that he had struck the loose handle of the door. But that was of little help. He could not use the door; he knew not what perils lay behind it. It was the window he wanted—the window.

Again he heard that sound from the bed. He stepped boldly forward and judged that he was standing in the middle of the room. Momentarily a sharp shock surged over him. He prayed for matches, and something in his throat was almost crying: "The window! The window!" He seemed like an island in a sea of darkness; one man surrounded by legions of immortal, intangible enemies. His cold Chinese heart went hot with fear.

The middle of the room, he judged, and took another step forward, a step which landed his chin sharply against the jutting edge of the mantelshelf over the fireplace. He jumped like a cat and his limbs shook; for now he had lost the door and the bed, as well as the window, and had made terrible noises which might bring disaster. All sense of direction was gone. He knew not whether to go forward or backward, to right or left. He heard the tinkle of the shunting trains, and he heard a rich voice crying something in his own tongue. But he was lapped around by darkness and terror, and a cruel fancy came to him that he was imprisoned here for ever and for ever, and that he would never escape from this enveloping, suffocating room. He began to think that—

And then a hot iron of agony rushed down his back as, sharp and clear at his elbow, came the Captain's voice:

"Get forrard, you damn lousy Chink—get forrard. Lively there! Get out of my room!"

He sprang madly aside from the voice that had been the terror of his life for so many weeks, and collided with the door; realised that he had made further fearful noises; dashed away from it and crashed into the bed; fell across it and across the warm, wet body that lay there. Every nerve in every limb of him was seared with horror at the contact, and he leapt off, kicking, biting, writhing. He leapt off, and fell against a table, which tottered, and at last fell with a stupendous crash into the fender.

"Lively, you damn Chink!" said the Captain. "Lively, I tell yeh. Dance, d'yeh hear? I'll have yeh for this. I'll learn you something. I'll give you something with a sharp knife and a bit of hot iron, my cocky. I'll make yer yellow skin crackle, yeh damn lousy chopstick. I'll have yeh in a minute. And when I get yeh, orf with yeh clothes. I'll cut yeh to pieces, I will."

Sung Dee shrieked. He ran round and round, beating the wall with his hands, laughing, crying, jumping, while all manner of shapes arose in his path, lit by the grey light of fear. He realised that it was all up now. He cared not how much noise he made. He hadn't killed the old man; only wounded him. And now all he desired was to find the door and any human creatures who might save him from the Captain. He met the bed again, suddenly, and the tormentor who lay there. He met the up-turned table and fell upon it, and he met the fireplace and the blank wall; but never, never the window or the door. They had vanished. There was no way out. He was caught in that dark room, and the Cap-tain would do as he liked with him. . . . He heard footsteps in the pas-sage and sounds of menace and alarm below. But to him they were friendly sounds, and he screamed loudly towards them.

He cried to the Captain, in his pidgin, for mercy.

"Oh, Captain—no burn me to-day, Captain. Sung Dee be heap good sailor, heap good servant, all same slave. Sung Dee heap plenty solly hurt Captain. Sung Dee be good boy. No do feller bad lings no feller more. Oh, Captain. Let Sung Dee go lis time. Let Sung Dee go. Oh, Captain!"

But "Oh, my Gawd!" answered the Captain. "Bless your yellow heart. Wait till I get you trussed up. Wait till I get you below. I'll learn yeh."

And now those below came upstairs, and they listened in the pas-sage, and for the space of a minute they were hesitant. For they heard all manner of terrible noises, and by the noises there might have been half-a-dozen fellows in the Captain's room. But very soon the screaming and the pattering feet were still, and they heard nothing but low moans; and at last the bravest of them, the Captain's brother, swung the door open and flashed a large lantern.

And those who were with him fell back in dumb horror, while the brother cried harshly:

"Oh! . . . my . . . God!" For the lantern shone on a Chinaman seated on the edge of the bed. Across his knees lay the dead body of the Captain, and the Chink was fondling his damp, dead face, talking baby talk to him, dancing him on his knee, and now and then making idiot moans. But what sent the crowd back in horror was that a great death-white Thing was flapping about the yellow face of the Chink, cackling: "I'll learn yeh! I'll learn yeh!" and dragging strips of flesh away with every movement of the beak.

The Tablets of the House of Li

When the sergeant of the dock police, years ago, stopped a mob of street-corner louts from tormenting a slightly intoxicated Chinese youth and robbing him of his family tablets, he didn't know that he was making a friend for life. He did not know that this man would save him in the hour of his deepest grief. He did not know that he was giving hostages to the secret powers that live in the highest air of the mountains of the unknown confines of Cathay. He only knew that outside the little marine store at the corner of Gill Street and West India Dock Road, he kicked three boys and cuffed another half-dozen; and having done this he went on his way and forgot it.

But Li Foo did not forget. He was, for the sergeant's comfort, a little too persistent in memory. He would cross the road to thank Sergeant Pidding. He would run after Sergeant Pidding and turn in front of him and bow and smile. He would point out Sergeant Pidding to others, and recite his courage and nobility, until the sergeant damned him for a fool and a nuisance. Certainly he was a fool and looked a fool—the type that boys intuitively pick out for comment and horse-play. He went about asking for it. His downcast face; his long, loping stride from the knees, as though treading down jungle grass; his sidelong, self-effacing looks, and his habit of hugging the walls of the byways, expectant of assault, all gave news of a victim who would afford good entertainment.

His folly was most clearly shown in his attitude to the sergeant's casual interference. He had thanked the sergeant at the time, and to English ideas that was sufficient. By no standards need he have repaid this trivial service by total self-annihilation. But he did, as I will show you. He borrowed a farthing and paid back a million.

He made himself debtor not only to the sergeant but to the sergeant's house, the sergeant's wife and the sergeant's child. He could not even pass the six-roomed cottage in King Street without a *kao-tao;* and

25

neither the sergeant's wife nor his small daughter was safe from the embarrassment of smiles and preposterous presents and promises of every
courtesy and service named in the Book of Rites and the Book of the
Mean. He bought unwholesome sweets for the child, and for Mrs. Pidding foolish flowers of which the remorseful hawker said that it was a
shame to take the money. And when the sergeant, with mild irritation,
cried, "For the Lord's sake get outa the way and forget it, yeh silly pie-
can!" he only smiled at the fashions b'long white man, and continued
his pious observances.

Even when away on his boat he continued to burn prayer papers for
the sergeant and his house; and in the same hour that his boat came up
the river he would show himself in King Street with some trophy of
travel for the child and fresh benedictions. So that at last he wore them
out, and they had to accept his friendship and his interest; and came,
after a year, to look for his visits and to return his interest in them by interest in him and his fortunes.

Four times a year he reappeared in Limehouse; and having made
offerings to Mrs. Pidding and the child, Anne, he would carry the sergeant to Charley Brown's or the "Blue Posts" or the Commercial, like
any dutiful son home from the sea.

They gathered from him the story of his insignificant family and saw
how he cherished the family tablets, and how the memory of his mean
ancestors was to him as sacred as the honour of the Cecils or the Percys.
If, by some timely act, the sergeant had saved the honour of the house
of Howard, he would have understood what he had done, and might
have suffered some glow of conscious virtue. But his social surroundings
did not allow him to see an old English family and an obscure family of
Cantonese workers from the same angle. The one was serious and august; the other was a rather pathetic joke. But there it was, brought into
his own house, and he had to accept it and smile; and a year later he accepted it anew. But it was not funny then.

The family tablets of Li Foo were to him as his life itself, for in them
dwelt the spirits of his fathers. They were his passport to the happy
fields and palaces behind the moon, the reward that would surely be his
for loving attention and duty towards the departed. Never were they out
of his keeping, for he was the sole survivor of his line; and, knowing that

the eyes of his fathers were upon him, looking to him to uphold the line, he was wandering the seas in the hope of gathering sufficient money whereby he might take a virtuous wife and thrust the house of Li into the honourable recognition of future ages. In the lodging in Oriental Street to which he came on each return to Limehouse, the tablets were suitably displayed beneath the joss, and sweet observance was made to them. He would sit piously before them and seek from them inspiration and guidance, which in trivial matters was sometimes given and in serious matters never.

He had none of your Western education, and so had no friends among the enlightened sojourners from his own country. By some pleasing miracle the corrupting influence of those advertising agents, the missionaries, had never fallen upon him; and he knew nothing of the convenient casuistry of Western religion or of the grave beauty of Western civilisation. His benighted mind had not yet overtaken the new ideas that Western business men were thrusting through his provinces. He knew nothing but the duty his father had taught him towards the Three Constant Virtues; and being, as I said, a fool, he was content to respect his father and adopt his ideas, untinged by progress, as sufficient to himself.

Oriental Street is a little backwater near the junction of King Street and Pennyfields—a backwater within that London backwater where the coloured roamers of the sea have found a resting-place. They come; they settle for a space; they go on; and wherever they go they carry their country and build it about them with banners of silk and bitter music and their joss and their tablets and the light of spent suns.

Into the silence of Li Foo's room, steeped in the tart odour of punk-sticks, floated the noises of the streets. There was the call of the London milkman. There were murmurs of electric tramcars, the rattle of a lorry, the howl of a factory hooter, the challenge of a fish-hawker; and through these noises came, faintly but persistently, the nasal note of a pipe, the footsteps of shuffling figures and a voice from the Yellow Sea crying "Ow-ah-bah-yow!" The London noises he did not hear; in that lost alley he was at home and wanted nothing of the barbarism of the streets beyond.

One other spot alone in the foreign city had meaning for him—a little house in King Street which he could see from his tiny window. In that house lay a solemn debt. To that house he must respond when called, for that house was virtually the keeper of his life; it had shown him the unrepayable service.

The time came when he must meet it, and he did not fail.

When the *Hilderic* was berthed in West India Dock, and the fires damped, stokers and crew were free for the shore. Black men came down the gangway, some with lean faces and straight hair, some with round faces and curly hair. Brown men came, too, and white men; the white men in neat serge and natty collars, the brown men in blue dungaree. A few Chinese came in ready-made lounge suits and coloured ties and yellow shoes, alarmingly Western. The last to step ashore was Li Foo, in canvas suiting with a blue scarf at his throat. He carried two or three small parcels.

He came through the dock gates in the hour of a December afternoon when the violet of the air was fretted by the yellow of the lamps; and made a straight way to King Street. He knocked at the door, his slow smile already making his face a moon; and the sergeant answered him. But there was no simultaneous wink and nod and grin to welcome him, and he did not enter. The sergeant's face was drawn, and it seemed that his eyes had not known sleep for some nights. He lifted a hand.

"Not to-night, ole son. No can. The kid—Anne . . ."

"How?"

"Ill. Very much ill." He was not looking at Li Foo but beyond him and across the street. Anne to him was as the tablets to Li Foo. "Very much ill. Much pain. All time. You understand?"

Li Foo nodded. His English was limited, but he knew the simple words of daily life, of grief and joy and hunger and trouble and fortune. "Uh-huh. I rest three weeks. I come, yess, to-morrow?"

"Ah. Do. To-morrow. Doctor here now."

Li Foo went away sorely troubled by the trouble that had fallen upon his friend and helper. He carried his packages to Oriental Street and engaged his room; and there he arranged his tablets and his joss, and sat before them and burned many prayer-papers and recited the story of the sergeant's intervention on behalf of the house of Li, and wrote it laboriously in fair written characters; and arose hopefully.

But his fathers were sleeping or engaged in business in distant fields, and next morning the news was worse. Urged by desire to do something, he bought chrysanthemums and fruit and guava jelly and water-lily flour at Lee Tack's store, and carried them to King Street; and they were accepted quietly and sadly as offerings that recalled happier times and for which there was now no occasion. He went back to his room, and called loudly upon his fathers to help one who had helped them. But there was no response. News came that Anne was worse . . . and again worse and weaker. And on the fourth day the sergeant came out and walked with him up and down the narrow street, and told him that no skill could save her. It was finished. Another night and . . . There was no man of medicine in the great city who could perform the miracle.

Li Foo said nothing. He folded his hands and went away, and all that morning he sat in the Public Gardens where the live scent of English flowers protests against the dead perfume of Chinatown's spices. He sat in thought, and at last his slow mind began to work and faint light came into it. His friend was bowed and broken. There was agony in his face and in his voice, so that Li Foo desired deeply that miraculous power might be his to salve and heal it; and as he pondered and remembered that drawn face, there came to him one terrible idea.

This man had saved for him his most precious possession; could he stand still while the man's most precious possession was in danger, when he might . . . Might? He could. Of that he was sure. He had lived long in the hills, and he knew much and believed much that the more enlightened had put aside. He knew that he could do this thing. It was put upon him to discharge his debt; this was the moment given to him to prove himself, even to the point of destruction. He had called upon his fathers whom he had so faithfully served, and they had not heard or would not hear. The debt must be paid, without thought of equity or cost. He must call again upon the powers.

Late that afternoon, a small figure, with head bowed to chest, slipped from Oriental Street into Pennyfields and across to King Street. The canvas coat was buttoned tight, and bulged, and the arms were laid across it as though holding a precious burden. The face held that dirty grey tinge that in the coloured man is the pallor of fear. A few figures were floating or shuffling about the street, and there was a sound of music from the "White Horse," and the usual evening noise of newsboys and homing workers. Nobody noticed the grey figure; nobody guessed what dreadful things were about to be done in King Street. In great cities spots of misery and terror are strictly localised; and anyway the seven millions have their own affairs.

At the sergeant's house he knocked, and the sergeant, opening to him, made dumbly to wave him away. But he was insistent. "You lis-sen. I come in. I make well. Yess. Oh, yess! Can do. You let. I speak you I help you when you want. I come help now."

Whether the sergeant understood or not, one cannot say, but he held the door back and let him enter. In the parlour Li Foo, holding his arms close, repeated his story. "I make well. You let."

The sergeant blew a great breath of exhaustion and sat down. What was the fool talking about? Nothing was of any use now. The doctor had gone; there was but one thing to wait for. What was the fool babbling about?

"I go up. Yess. I make well."

The sergeant's mind was not working. It held but one idea, and that idea filled it and clogged it. He got up. "All right. You want to see her. No harm in that."

They went up-stairs and went softly into the top room, from which came a soft moaning. The sergeant's wife was sitting on the bed, staring down at the pillow. Li Foo looked once at the bed; then round the room. Still clutching his coat, he spoke to the sergeant and nodded towards the bed.

"You speak her go 'way one time. Me alone. I make well."

"What?" The word was used as though the sergeant were not certain of its meaning.

"You go 'way one time. Me alone. I make well."

The sergeant looked about him as though asking for guidance or explanation. He put a hand on his wife's shoulder. "Just a minute, old girl. Down-stairs a minute. I'll—"

"Down-stairs? What for?"

"I don't know. He says— He says . . . I don't know. But come down-stairs."

"But what—"

"He wants to . . . it's no good. It doesn't matter. But he says he can . . . I don't know. Come down-stairs a minute."

They did not know why they left that room with Li Foo and the child in it, but they did leave. They went down-stairs. Li Foo softly closed the door and went to the bedside. The child was half-conscious and moaning. Her head was moving from side to side. Her arms were flung over the sheet. He bent over the bed, and with scissors cut one lock of hair from her head. Then he unbuttoned his coat and began his preparations.

Down-stairs the sergeant and his wife waited. They did not know what they were waiting for. They did not know what they were doing. They did not know how long they had been waiting, or how long they had been conscious of certain noises before actually noting them. But suddenly Mrs. Pidding said, "What's that?" and then both knew that they had been listening for some time to something that was not a moan.

It was a series of noises that were not the noises of a London house. Alien noises, as though something—they could not tell what—had got into the house. Each said, "What is it?" and sat with lifted face. But they did not move. The sergeant said, "There's something funny—something . . ." and his wife said "Yes—something . . ." and then in the midst of her grief said, "D'you think he's—he's—I mean . . ."

"What?"

"Well . . . Oh, I know it doesn't matter! Couldn't be any worse. But—these coloured people. You never know. They're not like us. He might have turned against us."

"Sit down, old girl; sit down. No—they're not like us. That's why—do sit down, girl. You can't do nothing. He's all right. He had an idea he could do something. Course, it's no good. But I thought there's no harm in—"

"But you don't know. He might . . ."

He waved her away. "I don't know, girl, I don't know. I told you so. That's the truth. What's it matter, anyway? He can't do any harm, and he might—"

"Might what?"

"I don't *know*. But—listen!"

From up-stairs came faint noises that had the sound of distant howls, and something like a low chant. There was a smell of burning, and it was not the smell of prayer-papers or punk sticks. There was a noise of things being moved about; and then silence. Complete silence; not even a moan. And after some seconds of silence, a series of little bangs, and then a sudden crash, followed by a long wail. Again silence, and then a soft padding overhead as of an animal moving round and round its cage.

"Whatever— I mean, what's he up to? Oh, go up! Go up and—"

"No. Sit down. I don't know. I can't tell. He thinks he's helping us. Sit down."

"But you must see what he's up to. These coloured men—oh!"

From up-stairs came a long howl—a howl that had no note of the animal or the human; a howl that filled every corner of the house.

"Ted—if you won't go up, I'll—"

"All right. I'll go and see."

He went slowly up-stairs, and blankly, without conjecture of what he was going to see. As he reached the door he saw that his wife was behind him. He put out a hand to stay her. Little gurgling noises came from the other side of the door. Holding his wife aside, he opened the door, looked in, and drew sharply back. "Go away. Go away. Go down. For God's sake go down!"

"What is it?"

"Go down. It's all right, but—go down." His tone compelled her to go down two steps, but she went no farther. He entered the room. As he did so, he stumbled over a little brass object, and stood still and said "Oh! Oh!" slowly. "Now what's been doing here? Now what . . ."

He looked round the room, and his wife, coming behind him, looked over his shoulder. She did not see the room; she looked straight at the bed, and suddenly, pushing her husband aside, went to it and stood still. Both stood still; and into their plain London minds came darkly a belief in strange doings. They did not question; they did not examine; they accepted what they saw.

The washing-stand was draped with a white cloth covered with red devices. On it stood two lacquered ornaments of twisted shape and foul significance. About the floor, arranged in a pentacle, lay the broken fragments of the tablets of the house of Li. In a small brass tray something was smouldering; and before it, on his knees, crouched a figure that had been Li Foo. He crouched gibbering, with hands folded about his breast; and, seeing him, they drew back from the unclean thing, and the sergeant cried:

"Foo Foo! What've you done? Oh, what you done to yourself?"

And then his wife cried "Look!" and they went to the bed.

The child was lying with eyes open and a little smile. She said: "The pain's gone now. I'm hungry. 'N then I'd like to go to sleep."

They looked from her to the figure at the wash-stand—no more the respectable Li Foo but a creature of the swamps. He turned towards them, and as he turned they again moved instinctively backward and stood there, while with smirched face and dripping lips he crawled out to hide his misery forever under the arches of the river. He had paid his debt; and the next day he was dead. He was found in great pain on one of the wharves, but as he had lain all night under a drenching storm there was nothing extraordinary in that or in his death.

THE BLOOMSBURY WONDER

As that September morning came to birth in trembling silver and took life in the hue of dusty gold, Mendel swore.

He had risen somewhat early, and was standing at the bathroom window of his Bloomsbury flat, and was shaving. He first said something like *Ouch* and then something more intense. The cause of those ejaculations was that he had given himself the peculiarly nasty kind of cut possible with some kinds of safety-razor, and the cause of the cut was a sudden movement of the right elbow, and the cause of that was something he had seen from the window.

Through that gracious gold, which seemed almost like a living presence blessing the field of London, moved a man he knew. But a man he knew transformed into a man he did not know. He was not hurrying, which was his usual gait. He wasn't even walking. He was sailing. There was rapture in the lift of the head, and the step was a schoolgirl step. His whole being expressed the emotion that overwhelms the soul in the moment when time stands still and life and the world are isolated and crystallised in well-being.

He seemed to be the one creature of purpose and understanding in a swarm of futile organisms; and this was so alien to the man, so sharply out of character, that it gave Mendel's right arm a shock. For really, as he had always known that sailing figure, he was so much a thing of cobweb and quiver that he belonged to twilight rather than break of day. To see him walking so, in the morning sun, was like seeing one's old boots turn into dancing shoes.

He was tall anyway, and was so thin, and his clothes fitted so tightly, that he seemed of abnormal height. He wore a black double-breasted overcoat, buttoned at the neck, black trousers and a nondescript hat. He held his arms behind him, the right hand clasping the elbow of the left arm. His slender trunk was upright, and his head thrown back and lifted. In the dusty sunlight he made a silhouette. Mendel saw him in the flat only, and he realised then that he always had seen him in the flat; never all round him. The figure he cut in that sunlight made Mendel want to see round him, though what he would find he did not know and could not guess. And to this day he doesn't know and can't guess.

In conventional society he would have been labelled a queer creature, that Stephen Trink; but the inner quarters of London hold so many queer creatures, and Mendel had so wide an acquaintance among them, that Trink was just one of his crowd. He could never remember how he came to know him, but for some five years they had been seeing each other about twice a week. Mendel liked him almost at once, and the liking grew. Though he was always aware, in Trink's company, of a slight unease, he took every opportunity of meeting him. Trink charmed him. The charm was not the open, easy charm of one's intimate friend; they never reached that full contact. It was more spell than charm; the attraction of opposites, perhaps. Mendel never could analyse his unease. Beyond a hint of knowing things that others couldn't know, there was nothing really queer about Trink. If he was at all odd, it was no more than the conventional oddity of Bloomsbury. His only marked characteristic was a deep melancholy, and when, later, Mendel tried to recall him he found that that was the one clear thing he could recall. He was one of those men whom nobody ever really knows, and who do not mean to be known. In talk, he appeared to open his heart, but Mendel knew very well that he didn't. There were always covered corners, and nobody could say surely that Trink was this kind of man or that kind.

Without being at all mysterious, he was a mystery. Indeed, it was his very "ordinariness" that made him so baffling. With the man of sudden twists and complexities, or the man of bizarre habits, people know where they are. The foibles, the secrecies, the explosions are sign-posts to character. But with the ordinary man—a scarce type—there is a desert; and when this ordinary man does extraordinary things, it is a desert of an unmapped country. Trink would have been passed over in almost any company, and usually was. Only when Mendel directed his friends' attention towards him, did they recollect having met him and examine their recollection; and then they were baffled. He had once asked five friends in turn what they thought of him, and was given pictures of five totally different men, none of whom he had himself seen in Trink. Each of them, he noted, had to hesitate on the question, and stroke his hair, and say: "Mmm . . . Trink. Well, he's just an ordinary sort of chap—I mean—he's a sort of—" Then, though he had been present ten minutes ago, they would go on to draw a picture as from some hazy memory. They seemed to be describing a man whom they weren't sure they had seen. Their very detail was the fumbling detail of men who are uncertain what they did see, and try to assure themselves by elaboration that they did at any rate see *something*. It was as though he had stood before the camera for his photograph, and the developed plate had come out blank.

In appearance he was insubstantial, and, with his lean, questing face and frail body, would have passed anywhere as an insipid clerk. He stressed his insipidity by certain physical habits. He had a trick of standing in childish attitudes—hands behind back, one foot crooked round the other—and of apparently going to sleep if you looked suddenly at him; and, when speaking to you, of looking at you as though you were his confessor. He had, too, a smile that, though it sounds odd when used of a man, was often described as winsome. The mouth was sharp-cut, rather than firm, and drooped at the corners. His hair was honey-coloured and in short curls. His voice was thin, touched with the east wind; and it was strange to hear him saying the warm, generous things he did say about people in the sleety tone that goes with spite. To everything he said, that tone seemed to add the words—Isn't it disgusting? If he said of any work of Mendel's that it was quite a good thing, the tone implied that it was disgusting of Mendel to do good things. If he said that it was a glorious morning, one felt that it was disgusting of mornings to be glorious. His eyes, behind spectacles, were mild and pale blue. Only when the spectacles were removed did one perceive character; then one could see that the eyes held curious experience and pain.

Wherever he might be, he never seemed to be wholly *there*. He had an air of seeming to be listening to some noise outside the room. He would sit about in attitudes that, since Rodin's Penseur, we have come to accept as attitudes of thought; but if at those times Mendel looked at his face he saw it was empty. He was not thinking. He was brooding. Though indoors he was languid and lounge-y, and his movements were the movements of the sleep-walker, in the street his walk was agitated and precipitous. He seemed to be flying from pursuit. One other notable point about him was that, quiet, insignificant, withdrawn as he was, he could be a most disturbing presence. Even when relaxed in an arm-chair he somehow sent spears and waves of discomfort through the air, sucking and drying the spirit of a room and giving those about him an edge of unease.

What his trouble was—if his melancholy arose from a trouble—he never told Mendel. Often, when Mendel urged him, flippantly, to Cheer Up, he spoke of This Awful Burden, which Mendel dismissed as the usual expression of that intellectual weariness of living which is called "modern," though, like most modern attitudes, it dates from centuries back. He had private means by which he could have lived in something more than comfort, but he seemed contented with three rooms in the forlorn quarter where Bloomsbury meets Marylebone—well-furnished rooms that one entered with surprise from the dinge of Fitzroy Square. He was a member of two of the more serious clubs, but used them scarcely twice a year. His time he employed in the Bloomsbury and Marylebone fashion—as an aimless intellectual. It is a common type; the elder Oxford or Cambridge that has never grown out of its second year. In the course of a lifetime they write one novel or one volume of poems or essays, and for the rest they write appreciations of obscure writers in obscure papers that don't pay their writers. They are to be recognised by their somewhat pathetic air of superiority and distinction. They have the outward appearance that the popular imagination gives to the creative artists, only no creative artist is ever half so distinguished in appearance as most of these translators and reviewers and art critics. Trink had not written a novel, but he did write metallic studies for all sorts of metallic Reviews; and all the time he was doing it he affected to despise himself for doing it and to despise the breed with whom he mixed. He attended all their clique and coterie gatherings—teas, dinners, Bloomsbury parties, private views—and took part in all the frugal follies of the Chelsea Bohemia. He was seen, as they say, everywhere. Yet at all those affairs, though he looked younger than most of the crowd, he had always the attitude of the amused grown-up overlooking the antics of the nursery.

Though not physically strong he had immense vitality, which he exhibited in long night walks through London. This was a habit which

Mendel shared with him and which, begun in childhood, gave him his peculiar and comprehensive knowledge of the body and soul of London. It was on one of those night-wanderings that they had first met, and later, knowing that Mendel was an early riser, he would sometimes, at the end of one of those rambles, call in for breakfast, and then go to sleep on his chesterfield.

Another of their points in common was a wide range of friendships. Most men find their friends and acquaintance among their own "sort" or their own "set," and never adventure beyond people of like education, like tastes and like social circumstances. Mendel had never been able to restrict himself in that way, nor had Trink. They made their friends wherever they found them, and they found them in queer places. An assembly of all their friends at one meeting would have surprised, and perhaps, dismayed, those of them who knew the two men only as writers in such-and-such circumstances. Mendel's specially intimate friend was an elderly man who worked as accountant in some obscure commercial office in Southwark. Trink's closest friend was a shopkeeper; a man who kept what was called a "general" shop at the northern end of Talleyrand Street.

Mendel, despite his own assorted friendships, could never quite understand *that* friendship. The shopkeeper had no oddities, no character, no corner where he even grazed the amused observation of Trink. It may have been, of course—and this fact explains many ill-assorted friendships—that they liked the same kind of funny story, or walked at the same pace in the streets, or liked the same kind of food and drink. Friendships *are* bound by slender things like that. Or it may have been that they were bound by love. There must have been more in it than mere liking, or Trink, being what he was, could have found no pleasure in the pale copybook talk of Timothy Reece. Mendel had seen them together, and had thought he could perceive on either side something almost of devotion. He had noted their content in long silence, when they merely sat and smoked, and their quick voiceless greeting when they met. Trink seemed to be happier with that mindless shopkeeper than with anybody.

Talleyrand Street makes part of a district of long, meaningless streets and disinherited houses. Once, those houses were the homes of the prosperous; now they cherish faded memories, and at night their faces are mournful and evocative. Fashion and prosperity have turned their backs upon them, and their walls enclose no stronger urge than furtive and shabby commerce. They lie, those streets and houses, in an uneasy coma, oppressed by a miasma of the second-hand and the out-moded—second-hand shops, second-hand goods, second-hand lodgings filled with second-hand furniture, and used by second-hand people breathing second-hand denatured air. They have not the cheerful acqui-escence of the poor who have always been poor but the craven chill of the "come-down."

Talleyrand Street is just one of those streets, and when Reece set up his shop he blunderingly chose the apt setting for himself and his family. They belonged there. They were typical of a thousand decent, hard-working, but ineffectual families of our cities. For four generations the family had not changed its social level. A faint desire to improve they may have had, but improving means adventure, and they feared adven-ture. On the wife's side and the husband's side the strain was the same—lukewarm and lackadaisical. There they had stood these many years, like rootless twigs in the waste patch between the stones and the pas-tures; and there, since the only alternative was risk and struggle, they were content to stand. Reece himself had the instincts of the aristocrat hidden in the habits of the peasant. One of life's misfits. He had the fine feature and clear eye of that type, but though he looked like what is called a gentleman, nobody would have taken him for one. His refine-ment of feature and manner came really, not from the breeding of pure strains, but from under nourishment in childhood.

His wife was largely of his sort. Her life had been a life of pain and trial, and it had taught her nothing. Her large, soft face was expression-less. The thousand experiences of life had left not even a finger-print there, and she still received the disappointments and blows of fortune with indignation and querulous collapse.

There were two boys and a girl. The girl had something of her fa-ther's physical refinement. Her head and face were beautiful; so beauti-ful that people turned to glance at her as she passed. Her manners and voice were—well, dreadful. She would often respond to those admiring glances by putting out her tongue. She was wholly unconscious of her beauty, not because she was less vain than her sex, but because her beauty was not to her own taste. She admired and envied girls of florid complexion and large blue eyes and masses of hair—chocolate-box beauties—and her own beauty was a glorious gift thrown to the dogs. To see that grave dark head and those deep Madonna eyes set against those sprawling manners and graceless talk gave one a shudder. It was like seeing a Sung vase set in the middle of a Woolworth store.

The two boys were two clods. They lived their lives in a kind of co-ma of eating, working and sleeping. They asked no more of the world than one long hebetude. One might say that they saw life as nothing but a programme of getting up, going to work, working, eating, going to bed. Only it wouldn't be true. They saw life no more than a three-months-old baby sees life. They were like millions of their fellow-organisms—deaf, dumb, torpid and myopic.

Those were the people Trink had chosen as special friends, and by all of them he was, not adored, for they were incapable of that, but liked to the fullest extent of their liking. He was their honoured guest, and on his side he gave to all of them affection and respect. As citizens they were entitled to respect, and they received it not only from him but from their neighbours. They had the agreeably-willing shop manners that customers like, and they maintained a constant goodwill. The two boys worked in a boot and shoe factory, and the shop was run by the Reeces and the girl, Olive. Olive knew enough about the business to do her bit without any mental strain, and she had a flow of smiles and emp-ty chatter that in such a shop was useful.

Those shops called "general" shops, often spoken of as Little Gold-Mines, are usually set, like that shop, in side-streets. It is by their isolat-ed setting that they flourish. The main streets are not their territory. Their right place is a situation as far from the competition of the multi-ple stores as possible, and in the centre of a thicket. In that situation they win prosperity from the housewife's slips of memory.

So the Reeces were doing well. Indeed, they were very comfortable and could have been more than comfortable; but they were so inept, and knew so little of the art of useful spending, that their profits showed little effect in the home. If they could not be given the positive descrip-tion of a happy family, at least they lived in that sluggish sympathy which characters only faintly aware of themselves give each other; and that was the feeling of the home—lymphatic and never *quite.* The wireless set worked, but it was never in perfect tone. The sitting-room fire would light, but only after it had been coaxed by those who knew its "ways." The hot-water in the bathroom was never more than very warm. The flowers in the garden were never completely and unmistakably blossoms. The shop door would shut, but only after three sharp pressures—the third a bad-tempered one. They bought expensive and warranted clocks, and the clocks took the note of the family and were never "right." New and better pieces of furniture were frequently added, and the rooms never succeeded in looking furnished. The colours did not harmonise nor did they scream. They made a grievous wail. Going one step beyond a good workman's dwelling, their home stopped short of even the poorest suburban villa.

Hardly a family, one would think, marked out for tragedy, or even disaster; yet it was upon those lustreless, half-living people that a fury of annihilation rushed from nowhere and fell, whirling them from obscurity and fixing their names and habits in the scarlet immortality of The Talleyrand Street Shop Murder.

It was about the time when those gangs called The Boys were getting too cocksure of their invulnerability, and were extending their attentions from rival gangs to the general public, that the catastrophe came by which Stephen Trink lost his one close friend. Beginning with small post offices, the gangs passed to little isolated shops. From all parts of London came reports of raids on those shops. The approach was almost a formula. "Give us a fiver. Come on. Gonna 'and over or d'ye want yer place smashed up?" Given that alternative the little shopkeeper could do nothing but pay. He might have refused, and have had his place smashed up, and he might have been able to get the police along in time to catch two or three of the gang and get them six or twelve months each. But that wouldn't have hurt them, since their brutal and perilous ways of life make them fearless; and he would still be left with a smashed shop, pounds' worth of damaged and unsaleable goods, the loss of three or four days' custom during repairs, and no hope of compensation. So, as a matter of common-sense, he paid up; and serious citizens wrote to the papers and asked if this was the so-called twentieth century, and how long would the public tolerate, etc.

Then, on top of those raids, came the murder of the Reeces.

Marvellous and impenetrable is the potency of words. By the measure and tone of certain syllables people are moved this way and that, they know not how; nor can those orators or poets who work upon them through these rhythms analyse the power by which they work. As numbers of illustrious men could not have lived the histories they did live, had they borne other names than those we know them by, so certain ideas press more profoundly upon our minds by the weight of the words in which man has clothed them.

There is a harmony between these words and their master-ideas, as between men's lives and their names; a poetic justice. You have the faint spirit-echo of Shelley; the cool Englishness of Shakespeare; the home-spun strength of Bunyan; the massy crags of Ludwig van Beethoven. Speak the word Mozart and the word Wagner, and you perceive the personal essence of either man's work. Hector Berlioz could not have pursued his high-fevered career under the name of Georges Jourdain. Nathaniel Hawthorne could not have written the spectral prose he did write had his name been Harry Robinson. Frederic Chopin could not have written his Preludes under the name of Jules Burgomaster. Oliver Cromwell, Napoleon Buonaparte, Charlemagne, Chateaubriand—the syllables of those names are steeped in a distillation of essential hues by which the characters and complexions of their bearers were fore-ordained. And so with ideas; and so, particularly, with that idea for which our sign and sound is *Murder.*

It could not have been more aptly named. It carries a shade and tone not wholly due to our association of it with the fact for which it is the graph. It could not represent an act of courtesy, or a dinner-dish or a Spring flower. There is dread and profundity in its very cadence. You may cry aloud "Jones has killed John Brown!" and the message carries nothing of that echo from the dark corridors of the soul that arises against our inner ears with the utterance of the word Murder.

By long association, murder is linked in our minds with midnight, or at least with dark; and those two conceptions of the cloaked side of nature combine in dreadfulness to make deeper dread. But harmonious combinations of dreadfulness, though they intensify each other, are dreadfulness only, and are therefore less potent to pluck at the heart than dreadfulness in discord with its setting; for *there* comes in the monstrous. Murder at midnight, though it will shock as it has shocked through centuries of civilisation, is a shock in its apt setting. But murder in sunlight is a thought that freezes and appals. It bares our souls to the satanic shudder of blood on primroses.

One can catch then the bitter savour of a certain moment of a sunny afternoon in Talleyrand Street. It was just after three o'clock of a September afternoon; a September of unusual heat. The heat made a blanket over the city, and in the side-streets life was in arrest, bound in slumber and steam and dust. In Talleyrand Street carts and cars stood outside shops and houses as though they would never move again. Even the shops had half-closed their eyes. Errand boys and workless labourers lounged or lay near the shops, sharing jealously every yard of the shade afforded by the shop-blinds. The faded Regency houses stewed and threw up a frowst. Through the dun length of the street the heat played in a fetid shimmer and shrouded either end in an illusion of infinity. The gritty odours of vegetable stalls, mixed with the acrid fumes of the cast-off clothes shops, were drawn up in the sun's path to float in the air and fret the noses of the loungers. The ice-cream cart, zoned with the Italian colours, made a cool centre for the idle young. A woman was offering chrysanthemums from a barrow piled high with that flower. Her barrow and her apron made a patch of living gold against the parched brown of the street.

Then, into this purring hour, came a figure and a voice. From the upper end of the street it came, crying one word; and the blunt syllables of that word went through the heat and dust, and struck the ears of those within hearing with the impact of cold iron. The street did not stir into life. It exploded.

Those nearest scrambled up, crying—not saying; such is the power of that word that it will always be answered with a cry—crying "Where? Where?" "In there—three-ninety-two." And the man ran on to Mirabeau Street, still crying; and those who had heard the word ran in a trail to number 392.

The shop, with its battling odours of bacon, cheese, paraffin, spice, bread, pickles, was empty. The runners looked beyond it. A small door led from the shop to the back parlour. The upper half of the door was glass, and this half was veiled by a soiled lace curtain. Its purpose was to screen the folk in the parlour—where they sat at intervals between trade rushes—from the eyes of customers, while those in the parlour could, by the greater light of the shop, see all comers. But since the curtain served a purely workaday room—the real private sitting-room was upstairs—it had been allowed to over-serve its time, and frequent washings had left it with so many holes that its purpose was defeated. People in the shop could, by those holes, see straight and clearly into the parlour; could see the little desk with account-books and bills, and could often see the cash-box and safe, and hear the rattle of accountancy. It was proved by later experiment that a man on the threshold of the shop could, without peering, see what was going on in the shop-parlour.

The leaders of the crowd looked hastily about the shop and behind the two small counters; then, through those holes, they had the first glimpse of what they had come to see.

The sun was at the back. It shone through the garden window and made a blurred shaft of dancing motes across the worn carpet and across the body of Timothy Reece. He lay beside his desk. The back of his head was cleanly broken. By the door leading to the inner passage lay the body of Mrs. Reece. She lay with hands up, as though praying. Her head was flung violently back, disjointed. Of the two boys, who had been spending the last day of their holidays at home, the younger, Harold, lay in a corner by the window, almost in a sitting posture. His head hung sideways, showing a dark suffusion under the left ear. The leaders looked and saw. Then someone said—"The girl!"

They pulled open the door leading to passage and kitchen. In the sun-flushed passage lay the twisted body of Olive Reece. Her head, too, was thrown back in contortion. One glance at the excoriations on her neck told them how she had met her death. Three glances told them of the dreadful group that must have made entrance there; one to kill with a knife, one with a blow, and one to strangle with the hands.

For some seconds those inside could not speak; but as the crowd from the street pushed into the shop, and those in the shop were pushed into the parlour, those inside turned to push them back; and one of them, finding voice, cried uselessly, as is the way in dark moments, "Why? Why all this—these nice people—just for a pound or two. It's—it's—*too silly!*"

He was right, and this was felt more strongly when it was found that this thing had not been done for a pound or two. The desk was locked, and the cash-box and the two tills in the shop were intact. Clearly this was not haphazard killing for robbery. There was a grotesquerie about the scene that hinted at more than killing; an afterthought of the devilish. Those people, who had led their ignoble but decent lives in ignoble streets, were made still more ignoble in death. The battered head of Reece, the crumpled bulk of Mrs. Reece, the macabre distortion of the symmetry of youth, were more than death. The peace that touches the most ugly and malign to dignity, the one moment of majesty that is granted at last to us all, was denied them.

So they lay in the floating sunshine of that afternoon, and so the crowd stood and stared down at them until he police came. Who had done this thing? Where were they? How did they do it in an open shop? How did they get away? Why was it done?

Then someone who knew the family cried, "Where's Percy?" And some went upstairs and some went into the little garden. But all that they found was an open bedroom window and signs of a flight. No Percy.

It was between three and four o'clock of the day when Mendel had given himself that razor cut that Trink made one of his "drop-in" calls. Mendel was accustomed to those calls. Trink would come in, potter about, turn over any new books and periodicals, make a few remarks about nothing, disturb the atmosphere generally, and then slide away. But that afternoon, Mendel noticed, he didn't disturb the atmosphere. He seemed lighter and brighter than usual. Something of the morning mood in which Mendel had seen him seemed still to be with him. Tired and pale he certainly was—perhaps the result of a night walk—but Mendel noted a serenity that was both new and pleasing, and seeking a phrase could only find the crude phrase, "more human."

He stayed but a short time; not fidgeting but sitting restfully on the chesterfield as men do after long physical exercise. Mendel remarked on this; told him that he had seen him that morning sailing through the square; and told him that the sailing and his present mood proved that plenty of exercise was what he needed, and that he would no doubt find, as George Borrow found, that it was a potent agent for the conquest of accidie—or liver. He smiled; dismissed the diagnosis of his trouble, and soon afterwards faded away, so that when Mendel resumed work he was barely certain that Trink had been there at all. He never saw him again.

But about an hour later he was aware that he was disturbed, and when, half-consciously and still at work, he tried to analyse the disturbance, he located it as something coming from the street; a sound that came at first from below the afternoon din, then rose to its level and spilled over it. It was the cry of newspaper boys. The ear of the born Londoner is so adjusted that it can isolate street sounds from each other and perceive any dislocation or fine distinction from the normal; and though Mendel was still concentrated on his work, and could not hear a word the boys were crying, his ear told him of a dire intonation that did not belong to Winners and S.P. Before he even listened to the cry, he knew that they were crying news of some disaster, and became curious about it. So he went to the telephone, and rang a friend on the *Evening Mercury,* and asked what was the big story. The friend gave it so far as it had then come in.

His immediate thought on hearing the story was of what it would mean to Trink. He had known Reece only slightly, through Trink, and terrible as the fate of the family was, they meant nothing to him, and he could feel for them only the detached and fleeting pity that we feel at any reported disaster with which we are not concerned. But for Trink, their friend, it would be a blow, and a keener blow since it came with such precision on top of his happy swinging mood of that day. He had just, it seemed, found some respite from his customary gloom, only to be brutally flung back into it, and deeper. Mendel thought at first of going round to him, and then thought not. He would want no intruders. It is the instinct of those in pain, physical or mental, to hide, since pain is as great a social offence as poverty, and the cruellest insult we can make to the suffering is to recognise their sufferings and offer them sympathy. He decided to wait until Trink chose to come in.

During the next hour or so the papers were publishing rush extras, and as the news had withdrawn him from work, and he could not return to it, he went out, bought all three evening papers and sat in a tea-shop reading them. There was no doubt that the affair, following the large publicity and discussion given to the shop-raids, had stirred the Press and alarmed the public. He saw it on the faces of the home-going crowd and heard it reflected in the casual remarks of stranger to stranger in the tea-shop and around the bus-stops. All that evening and night the word Murder beat and fluttered about the streets and suburban avenues, and wherever it brushed it left a smear of disquiet.

Accustomed as great cities are to murder, and lightly, even flippantly, as they take all disturbances, the details of this one moved them. Clearly it was no ordinary murder of anger or revenge, or for the removal of inconvenient people for gain. How could those little people have offended? Who would want them out of the way? If it was the work of The Boys, it might be anybody's turn next. If it wasn't the work of The Boys, and The Boys had never been known to go to such extremes, then, said the Press, it must have been the work of wandering lunatics of gorilla's strength and ferocity. And if they were loose, nobody would be safe. Private houses and people in the streets would be wholly at the mercy of such fearless and furious creatures as these appeared to be. In the meantime, they were loose; even now, perhaps, prowling about and contemplating another stroke; sitting by your side in train or bus, or marking your shop or home for their next visit. They *were* loose, and while they were loose they spread their dreadful essence as no artist or prophet can hope to spread *his.* Scores of mothers from the streets about Talleyrand Street, hearing the news and seizing on the Press conjecture of lunatics, ran to schools in the district to meet their children.

Through all the thousand little streets of the near and far suburbs went the howl of the newsboy, and its virulent accents went tingling through the nerves of happy households. To people sitting late in their gardens, veiled from the world, came at twilight a sudden trembling and sweeping of the veil as the wandering Chorus stained the summer night with that word. It broke into the bedrooms of wakeful children, and into the study of the scholar, and into the sick-room and across quiet supper-tables; and wherever it fell it left a wound. The Press, having given the wound, went on to probe and exacerbate it with the minutiae of horror;

ending with the disturbing advice to householders to see to their bolt and fastenings that night. It was the Splash story of the day, and each paper had a narrative from neighbours and from those who were near the shop at the time of the crime's discovery. At late evening the story was this.

Percy Reece had been found and interviewed. He explained his absence by the regrettable fact that he had run away. The information he could give was of no help to those engaged on the case. As that day was the last day of his holidays he had, he said, been taking things easy, and after the midday dinner he had gone upstairs to lie down. He left his brother in the garden. His father and sister were in the shop parlour, and his mother was in the shop. From two o'clock to five o'clock was a slack time with them. Most of the business came before twelve, or from five o'clock to closing time; the afternoon brought mere straggles of custom.

He remembered lying down on his bed, with coat and waistcoat off, and remembered nothing more until he suddenly awoke and found himself, in his phrase, all of a sweat. His head and hands were wet. He jumped up from the bed and stood uncertainly for a few moments, thinking he was going to be ill. And well he might have been ill, seeing what foul force was then sweeping through the air of that little house. Out of the sunlight something from the dark corners had come creeping upon it, to charge its rooms with poison and to fire it with the black lightning of sudden death.

At the moment he awoke this creeping corruption must then have been in the house, and in its presence not even so thick and wooden an organism as his could have slept. By some old sense of forest forefathers we are made aware of such presences. We can perceive evil in our neighbourhood through every channel of perception; can even see it through the skin. The potency of its vapours, then, must have worked upon the skin and senses of this lad, as the potency of the unseen reptile works upon the nerves of birds, and he awoke because a protecting presence had called him to awake. It must have been that, and not a cry or a blow, that awoke him because he said that, during the few seconds when he stood half-awake and sweating, he heard his mother's voice in a conversational murmur.

It was some seconds after that that the sweat froze on his face at the sound of his father's voice in three plodding syllables—"Oh . . . My . . .

God!"—and then of a noise such as a coalman makes when he drops an empty sack on the pavement. And then, almost simultaneously with the sack sound, he heard a little squeak that ended in a gurgle; and overriding the gurgle one "Oh!" of horror—his mother's voice—and another soft thud; and before the thud an "Oh!" of surprise from his brother, and soft, choking noises of terror. And then silence. And then he heard two sharp clicks, as of opening and shutting a door; and then a moment's pause; and then swift feet on the stairs.

Had he had the courage to go down on his father's first cry, his courage, one may guess, would have been wasted. Hands would have been waiting for him, and he too would have ended on a gurgle. But if he had had the courage to wait before he fled until the figure or figures on the stairs had come high enough to give him one glimpse, he might have had a clue to one of the men that would have helped to the others. But he didn't wait. He bolted. He offered the reporters no feeble excuse of going to raise the alarm or get help. He said that those sounds and the sort of feeling in the house so affected him with their hint of some irresistible horror that he didn't think of anybody or anything—only of getting out.

Peering from his door, he said, just as the sound of the feet came, he could see part of the staircase, and the sunlight through the glazed door between shop-passage and garden threw a shadow, or it might have been two shadows, half-way up the stairs. He could hear heavy panting. In the moment of his looking, the shadow began to swell and to move. He saw no more. In awkward phrases (so one of the reports said) he tried to say that he felt in that shadow something more than assault ending in killing, he felt something for which he couldn't find a word. So, driven by he knew not what, and made, for the first time in his life, to hurry, he turned from that house of dusty sunshine and death to the open world of sky and shops and people. He bolted through the upper window, into the garden, and over the wall, and didn't stop or call for help till he was four or five streets away; at which point the increasing cry led to a pursuit and capture of him.

He made his confession sadly but without shame. He *knew,* he said, that it was all over; that he could be of no use; that they were all dead. But when they pressed him *how* he knew, he relapsed from that moment of assertion into his customary beef-like stupor, and they could get no more from him than a mechanical "I dunno. I just knew." He was detained for questioning, and it appeared later that the questioning had been severe. But though at first there was an edge of official and public suspicion of him, he was able to satisfy everybody that he knew nothing, and was allowed to go home to some friend of the family.

No weapons were found, no finger-prints, no useful footprints. Nor had any suspicious characters been seen hanging about; at least, none markedly suspicious to the district, in whose misty byways queer characters of a sort were a regular feature, and whose houses were accustomed to receiving at all hours travelling strangers. Taking it at first sight as gang work, the authorities, it was said, were pursuing enquiries in that direction; which meant that for the next few days all known members of all gangs were rounded up and questioned or kept under observation. Already, at that early hour, reports had come in of the detention of unpleasant characters at points on the roads out of London—Highgate, Ealing, Tooting. Communication had been made with all lunatic asylums in and near London, but none could report any escapes.

There, that evening, it was left. Next morning there were further details, but nothing pointing towards an arrest. From some of the details it was clear that the affair, if planned at all, had been most cunningly planned and timed, and swiftly done, since the people were seen alive five minutes before that cry had shocked the still street. The more likely conjecture, though, was that it was the impulsive act of a wandering gang. A woman volunteered that she had visited the shop just after three, and had been served by Mrs. Reece. Nobody else was in the shop. She left the shop and went a little way down the street to leave a message with a friend, and having left the message she re-passed Reece's shop, and saw a man whom she did not closely notice standing at the counter rattling some coins and calling "Shop!" Her own home was twelve doors from the shop. She had scarcely got indoors, and taken off her hat when she heard that cry. In the immediate instant of silence following it she heard a church clock strike the quarter-past. Another statement came from a man whose house backed on to the Reeces'. He was on a night-shift, and went on at four o'clock. By daily use he knew exactly how to time himself to reach his work punctually from his home, and he left home regularly at ten minutes past three. He was just finishing dressing, he said, when, happening to glance through the window he saw Mr. and Mrs. Reece in their shop-parlour fiddling with account-books. That was at nine minutes past three.

Of the people who were in the street at the time the alarm was given, none could say anything useful. Indeed, the result was only more confusion. Fifteen people who had been near the spot were asked—Who was the man who rushed from the shop giving that cry? None of them knew him. They were then asked—What was he like? Not one could make a clear answer. Eleven were so surprised that they didn't look at him. The other four—who, if they had looked at him, hadn't seen him but wouldn't admit it—gave four different descriptions. One saw a tall firmly-built man with red face. One saw a short man in a mackintosh. One saw a man in shirt and trousers only—obviously a confusion with the flying Percy. One saw a stout man in a grey suit and bowler hat.

It seemed fairly certain, though, that the man who gave that cry could not have been concerned in the affair, since two witnesses had seen members of the family alive within less than two minutes of the alarm; and it was held that wholesale slaughter could not have been accomplished in that time. The man who ran out must have been the man who had been seen by the woman standing there and shouting "Shop!" He had not come forward, but there might be many innocent explanations of that. He might have been a man of nervous type who had received such a shock from what he had seen that he wished to wipe out all association with the affair. Or he might have been a quiet, shy fellow who would hate to be mixed up in any sensational public affair. Having given the alarm, and having no useful information to offer beyond what the crowd saw for themselves, he might consider that he had done his duty.

Generally it was felt that it must have been the work of a gang—either a gang of thieves who were disturbed by the alarm before they could get at the cash, or, as some paper suggested, a drunken or drugged gang; and the gang must have entered by the back or somebody in the street would have seen them. People in the neighbourhood, getting hypnotised by the affair, began to remember certain happenings centring on the Reeces which they considered strange and significant in the light of what had happened. Queer visitors, letters by every post, sudden outgoings, late homecomings—all the scores of everyday family happenings which, when isolated and focused by tragedy and publicity, assume an air of the sinister and portentous. If Mrs. Reece had gone out the day before in a new hat, they would have seen that as a possible clue.

Day by day the story mounted, and all fact that was thin was fortified by flagrant conjecture, and by "sidelights" and comparison with similar crimes. All of it led nowhere. A clue was being followed at Leicester. A broken and stained bicycle pump had been found behind the bath in the bathroom. Watch was being kept at the ports. Newspapers offered rewards to possible "splits" but none came forward to give their friends away. The Sunday papers carried a story hinting that certain news might be expected from Birmingham. The Monday papers ran Birmingham. But after two days all of them were proudly silent on Birmingham.

Thereafter public and Press interest declined. From being a Splash story it came to an ordinary column; then, from the main page, it passed to the secondary news page; then it fell to half a column, and at the end of three weeks it breathed its last in a paragraph.

In all that time Mendel had seen and heard nothing of Stephen Trink. He knew what he must be feeling about it, since he himself, though quite unwarrantably, had been moved by it. It meant little more to him than a news story; yet he passed those days in positive disquiet. Beyond the fact of having once or twice met the people, as friends of Trink, he had no interest in them. Yet whenever he thought about the affair, he suffered a chill, as though they did mean something to him; an entirely unreasonable chill which he could not shake off because common sense could not reach it.

Then, about a month after the affair had faded, he found among his post a letter from Trink. It was dated from Paris, and was an unusually long letter from one who scarcely ever wrote more than a post card. And a queer letter, though since it was from Trink that in itself was not queer. He read it at breakfast, and for some long time, an hour or more, he could not bring himself to put it down and face the day. When at last he did, he found work impossible. All that day and night he was haunted by a spectre of forbidden knowledge, and he went about his occasions perfunctorily, with a creeping of the flesh, as when one discovers a baby playing with a boiling kettle, or touches something furry in the dark. He knew then what it was that the boy Percy was trying to say. This was the letter:

"Dear Mendel,

"As we haven't met for some time I thought you might like a word from me. I've been here for a week or so, seeking a little change for jangled nerves. You understand. It was a dreadful business, and I didn't want to see anybody, especially friends. I'm here doing nothing and seeing nothing—just breathing. I suppose they've got no farther with it. Strange that people are so astonishingly clever in abstruse cases, and so often beaten by a simple case. But you know how often, in art, a subtle piece of work which the public imagines to have been achieved by laborious and delicate process, was in fact done with perfect ease. They all seem to have been misled by that matter of time. They assumed that that little time, for such a business, must imply a gang. No sound reason why it should, though. As William Nevison established an alibi by accomplishing the believed impossible in the seventeenth century—committing a crime at Gad's Hill in Kent one morning, and being seen at York at seven o'clock the same evening—so this man deceived public opinion. Four murders by different means had been accomplished in about two minutes. Therefore, said the public, it must have been a gang. But public opinion is always saying It Can't Be Done, and is always eating its words. What any one man can conceive, some other man can do. I'm satisfied that this was the work of one man, and I'll show you how he could have done it and how he could have got away. As to that, of course he got away by running away. If you say that a running man at such a moment would attract attention, well, that is what he did. He was clever enough to know that in successfully running away, it depends how you run. He covered his appearance and his haste by drawing the whole street's attention to himself. He knew enough about things to know that his cry would blind everybody. They might be looking, but they wouldn't be seeing—as we know they weren't. All their senses would gather to reinforce the sense of hearing. As soon as he was round a corner he could slip his hat in his pocket and put on a cap. Nothing makes a sharper edge on the memory, or more effectually changes a man's appearance, than the hat. Then he could take of his coat, throw it over his arm, and go back and join the crowd. It was no planned affair and no gang affair. It was the work of a man momentarily careless of results. Being careless, he made no mistakes.

"As to *how*—really very simple. It's just this—he was a man of extraordinary swiftness of act and motion. People don't seem to realise on what a slender thread human life hangs—until they fall down two steps, or receive a cricket ball in the neck, or slip on the soap in the bath. A man can be killed with less trouble than a rabbit or a hen. A pressure on a certain spot, or a sharp flick on a point at the back of the neck, and it's done. It could be done on the top of a bus, at Lord's, or at the theatre, or in your own home. That man, as I say, was swifter than most of us. He strolled into the shop. Calling 'Shop!' he went to the parlour door. There he met Reece. One movement. Mrs. Reece would turn. Another movement. The girl was coming through the door leading to the passage. Two steps and another movement. The boy comes through the garden to the shop. A fourth movement. And it was done. A movement overhead. The other boy stirring. He waits for him to come down. The boy doesn't come. He hears the noise of his flight. Then he makes his own by running full tilt into the faces of a score of people and crying his crime.

"As to why a man not a natural criminal or lunatic should have created this horror of destruction—that is not so easy. Before I can present what looks to me like a reasonable explanation, I must ask you to empty your mind of *your* reason and of that knowledge of human nature on which people base their judgment of human motive and human behaviour. It should never be said that people don't *do* these things because at some time or other some person does do those things. You must see it as clearly as one sees a new scientific idea—without reference to past knowledge or belief. This man *had* a motive for his wanton slaughter, but not a motive that would pass with common understanding. Neither hate nor lust nor the morbid vanity that sometimes leads stupid people to the committal of enormous crimes. Nothing of that sort. And he wasn't a madman without responsibility for his actions. He knew what he was doing. He committed more than a crime. He committed a sin. And meant to. Most men think that sin is the ultimate depth to which man can sink, but this man didn't sink. He rose, by active sin, out of something darker than sin. That something is the spirit of unexpressed, *potential* evil; something that corrodes not only the soul of the man in whom it dwells, but the beautiful world about him. This evil doesn't always, indeed, seldom does, live in what we call wicked people. It lives almost always in the good, and in comparison with them the positive wicked are almost healthy. For these good people are germ-carriers and are more dangerous than criminals or sinners. They can penetrate everywhere. We have no armour against their miasma. They do no evil, but they are hives of evil. They lead stainless lives. Their talk is pure. Yet wherever they go they leave a trail that pollutes the nobility and honesty of others. They diffuse evil as some lonely country places, themselves beautiful, diffuse evil. Happy for them, poor creatures, if they can discover and prove themselves before death for what they are. Some do. They are lucky. There's something in these people. Some awful karma from the world's beginning. Some possession that can only be cast out in one way—a dreadful way. Where it began one cannot say. Perhaps some nightmare sins, projected in the hearts of creatures centuries-dead, projected but never given substance, take on a ghost-essence and wander through the hearts of men as cells of evil. And wander from heart to heart, poisoning as they go until at last they come to life in a positive sin, and, having lived, can die. Nobody knows. But that's my explanation of those people. They're possessed. An incubus sits upon them, and they can only be rid of it by some active sin. They must express and release that clotted evil, and they cannot be cleansed of it before it's expressed, as a man cannot be cleansed of a fever before it's reached its climacteric. Once expressed, it can be met and punished. But abstract evil can't be met.

"Let's suppose that this man was one of these, consciously possessed of this intangible essence of evil, conscious of it as a blight upon him and those around him; tortured by it like a man with a snake in his bosom, and fighting its desire for expression and release until the fight became intolerable. There's only one way of escape for him—to sin and to sin deeply. Always he fights the temptation, and so, continuing to shelter the evil, he gives it time to grow and to make his own emanations stronger. But his only real hope of killing it lies in giving it life.

"And then at last he yields. There comes, one day, the eruptive, whirlwind moment of temptation, stronger than any he has known. All his powers of resistance go down in an avalanche. With a sigh of relief he yields. And then, with the disappearance of resistance, and with the resolve to sin, he would find, I think, the serenity of resignation filling his whole being. And when the thing was done, the sin committed, the most dreadful sin he could conceive, in that Satanic moment he frees himself for ever from his incubus, not by binding it but by releasing it. Like a long-embalmed body exposed to the air, it has one minute of life, and the next it crumbles into dust and he is free.

"By that sin he can now, as a fulfilled and erring soul, work out his penance and his redemption. That's all."

THE HANDS OF MR. OTTERMOLE

Murder (said old Quong)—oblige me by passing my pipe—murder is one of the simplest things in the world to do. Killing a man is a much simpler matter than killing a duck. Not always so safe, perhaps, but simpler. But to certain gifted people it is both simple and entirely safe. Many minds of finer complexion than my own have discoloured themselves in seeking to name the identity of the author of those whole-sale murders which took place last year. Who that man or woman really was, I know no more than you do, but I have a theory of the person it could have been; and if you are not pressed for time I will elaborate that theory into a little tale.

As I had the rest of that evening and the whole of the next day for dalliance in my ivory tower, I desired that he would tell me the story; and, having reckoned up his cash register and closed the ivory gate, he told me—between then and the dawn—his story of the Mallon End murders. Paraphrased and condensed, it came out something like this.

At six o'clock of a January evening Mr. Whybrow was walking home through the cob-web alleys of London's East End. He had left the golden clamour of the great High Street to which the tram had brought him from the river and his daily work, and was now in the chess-board of byways that is called Mallon End. None of the rush and gleam of the High Street trickled into these byways. A few paces south—a flood-tide of life, foaming and beating. Here—only slow, shuffling figures and muf-fled pulses. He was in the sink of London, the last refuge of European vagrants.

As though in tune with the street's spirit, he too walked slowly, with head down. It seemed that he was pondering some pressing trouble, but he was not. He had no trouble. He was walking slowly because he had been on his feet all day, and he was bent in abstraction because he was wondering whether the Missis would have herrings for his tea, or haddock; and he was trying to decide which would be the more tasty on a night like this. A wretched night it was, of damp and mist, and the mist wandered into his throat and his eyes, and the damp had settled on pavement and roadway, and where the sparse lamplight fell it sent up a greasy sparkle that chilled one to look at. By contrast it made his speculations more agreeable, and made him ready for that tea—whether herring or haddock. His eye turned from the glum bricks that made his horizon, and went forward half a mile. He saw a gas-lit kitchen, a flamy fire and a spread tea-table. There was toast in the hearth and a singing kettle on the side and a piquant effusion of herrings, or maybe of haddock, or perhaps sausages. The vision gave his aching feet a throb of energy. He shook imperceptible damp from his shoulders, and hastened towards its reality.

But Mr. Whybrow wasn't going to get any tea that evening—or any other evening. Mr. Whybrow was going to die. Somewhere within a hundred yards of him another man was walking: a man much like Mr. Whybrow and much like any other man, but without the only quality that enables mankind to live peaceably together and not as madmen in a jungle. A man with a dead heart eating into itself and bringing forth the foul organisms that arise from death and corruption. And that thing in man's shape, on a whim or a settled idea—one cannot know—had said within himself that Mr. Whybrow should never taste another herring. Not that Mr. Whybrow had injured him. Not that he had any dislike of Mr. Whybrow. Indeed, he knew nothing of him save as a familiar figure about the streets. But, moved by a force that had taken possession of his empty cells, he had picked on Mr. Whybrow with that blind choice that makes us pick one restaurant table that has nothing to mark it from four or five other tables, or one apple from a dish of half-a-dozen equal apples; or that drives Nature to send a cyclone upon one corner of this planet, and destroy five hundred lives in that corner, and leave another five hundred in the same corner unharmed. So this man had picked on Mr. Whybrow, as he might have picked on you or me, had we been within his daily observation; and even now he was creeping through the blue-toned streets, nursing his large white hands, moving ever closer to Mr. Whybrow's tea-table, and so closer to Mr. Whybrow himself.

He wasn't, this man, a bad man. Indeed, he had many of the social

and amiable qualities, and passed as a respectable man, as most successful criminals do. But the thought had come into his mouldering mind
that he would like to murder somebody, and, as he held no fear of God
or man, he was going to do it, and would then go home to *his* tea. I
don't say that flippantly, but as a statement of fact. Strange as it may
seem to the humane, murderers must and do sit down to meals after a
murder. There is no reason why they shouldn't, and many reasons why
they should. For one thing, they need to keep their physical and mental
vitality at full beat for the business of covering their crime. For another,
the strain of their effort makes them hungry, and satisfaction at the ac-
complishment of a desired thing brings a feeling of relaxation towards
human pleasures. It is accepted among non-murderers that the murderer is always overcome by fear for his safety and horror at his act; but this
type is rare. His own safety is, of course, his immediate concern, but
vanity is a marked quality of most murderers, and that, together with the
thrill of conquest, makes him confident that he can secure it, and when
he has restored his strength with food he goes about securing it as a
young hostess goes about the arranging of her first big dinner—a little
anxious, but no more. Criminologists and detectives tell us that *every*
murderer, however intelligent or cunning, always makes one slip in his
tactics—one little slip that brings the affair home to him. But that is only
half-true. It is true only of the murderers who are caught. Scores of
murderers are not caught: therefore scores of murderers do not make
any mistake at all. This man didn't.

As for horror or remorse, prison chaplains, doctors and lawyers
have told us that of murderers they have interviewed under condemna-
tion and the shadow of death, only one here and there has expressed
any contrition for his act, or shown any sign of mental misery. Most of
them display only exasperation at having been caught when so many
have gone undiscovered, or indignation at being condemned for a perfectly reasonable act. However normal and humane they may have been
before the murder, they are utterly without conscience after it. For what
is conscience? Simply a polite nickname for superstition, which is a polite nickname for fear. Those who associate remorse with murder are,
no doubt, basing their ideas on the world-legend of the remorse of Cain,
or are projecting their own frail minds into the mind of the murderer,

and getting false reactions. Peaceable folk cannot hope to make contact with this mind, for they are not merely different in mental type from the murderer: they are different in their personal chemistry and construction. Some men can and do kill, not one man, but two or three, and go calmly about their daily affairs. Other men could not, under the most agonising provocation, bring themselves even to wound. It is men of this sort who imagine the murderer in torments of remorse and fear of the law, whereas he is actually sitting down to his tea.

The man with the large white hands was as ready for his tea as Mr. Whybrow was, but he had something to do before he went to it. When he had done that something, and made no mistake about it, he would be even more ready for it, and would go to it as comfortably as he went to it the day before, when his hands were stainless.

Walk on, then, Mr. Whybrow, walk on; and as you walk, look your last upon the familiar features of your nightly journey. Follow your jack-o'-lantern tea-table. Look well upon its warmth and colour and kindness; feed your eyes with it, and tease your nose with its gentle domestic odours; for you will never sit down to it. Within ten minutes' pacing of you a pursuing phantom has spoken in his heart, and you are doomed. There you go—you and phantom—two nebulous dabs of mortality, moving through green air along pavements of powder-blue, the one to kill, the other to be killed. Walk on. Don't annoy your burning feet by hurrying, for the more slowly you walk, the longer you will breathe the green air of this January dusk, and see the dreamy lamplight and the little shops, and hear the agreeable commerce of the London crowd and the haunting pathos of the street-organ. These things are dear to you, Mr. Whybrow. You don't know it now, but in fifteen minutes you will have two seconds in which to realise how inexpressibly dear they are.

Walk on, then, across this crazy chess-board. You are in Lagos Street now, among the tents of the wanderers of Eastern Europe. A minute or so, and you are in Loyal Lane, among the lodging-houses that shelter the useless and the beaten of London's camp-followers. The lane holds the smell of them, and its soft darkness seems heavy with the wail of the futile. But you are not sensitive to impalpable things, and you plod through it, unseeing, as you do every evening, and come to Blean

Street, and plod through that. From basement to sky rise the tenements of an alien colony. Their windows slot the ebony of their walls with lemon. Behind those windows strange life is moving, dressed with forms that are not of London or of England, yet, in essence, the same agreeable life that you have been living, and to-night will live no more. From high above you comes a voice crooning *The Song of Katta.* Through a window you see a family keeping a religious rite. Through another you see a woman pouring out tea for her husband. You see a man mending a pair of boots; a mother bathing her baby. You have seen all these things before, and never noticed them. You do not notice them now, but if you knew that you were never going to see them again, you would notice them. You never *will* see them again, not because your life has run its natural course, but because a man whom you have often passed in the street has at his own solitary pleasure decided to usurp the awful authority of Nature, and destroy you. So perhaps it's as well that you don't notice them, for your part in them is ended. No more for you these pretty moments of our earthly travail: only one moment of terror, and then a plunging darkness.

Closer to you this shadow of massacre moves, and now he is twenty yards behind you. You can hear his footfall, but you do not turn your head. You are familiar with footfalls. You are in London, in the easy security of your daily territory and footfalls behind you, your instinct tells you, are no more than a message of human company.

But can't you hear something in those footfalls—something that goes with a widdershins beat? Something that says: *Look out, look out! Beware, beware! Can't you hear the very syllables of murd-er-er, murd-er-er?* No; there is nothing in footfalls. They are neutral. The foot of villainy falls with the same quiet note as the foot of honesty. But those footfalls, Mr. Whybrow, are bearing on to you a pair of hands, and there *is* something in hands. Behind you that pair of hands is even now stretching its muscles in preparation for your end. Every minute of your days you have been seeing human hands. Have you ever realised the sheer horror of hands—those appendages that are a symbol for our moments of trust and affection and salutation? Have you thought of the sickening potentialities that lie within the scope of that five-tentacled member? No, you never have; for all the human hands that you have seen have been stretched to you in kindness or fellowship. Yet, though the eyes can hate, and the lips can sting, it is only that dangling member than can gather the accumulated essence of evil, and electrify it into currents of destruction. Satan may enter into man by many doors, but in the hands alone can he find the servants of his will.

Another minute, Mr. Whybrow, and you will know all about the horror of human hands.

You are nearly home now. You have turned into your street—Caspar Street—and you are in the centre of the chess-board. You can see the front window of your little four-roomed house. The street is dark, and its three lamps give only a smut of light that is more confusing than darkness. It is dark—empty, too. Nobody about; no lights in the front parlours of the houses, for the families are at tea in their kitchens; and only a random glow in a few upper rooms occupied by lodgers. Nobody about but you and your following companion, and you don't notice him. You see him so often that he is never seen. Even if you turned your head and saw him, you would only say "Good-evening" to him, and walk on. A suggestion that he was a possible murderer would not even make you laugh. It would be too silly.

And now you are at your gate. And now you have found your door-key. And now you are in, and hanging up your hat and coat. The Missis has just called a greeting from the kitchen, whose smell is an echo of that greeting (herrings!) and you have answered it, when the door shakes under a sharp knock.

Go away, Mr. Whybrow. Go away from that door. Don't touch it. Get right away from it. Get out of the house. Run with the Missis to the back garden, and over the fence. Or call the neighbours. But don't touch that door. Don't, Mr. Whybrow, don't open . . . Mr. Whybrow opened the door.

That was the beginning of what became known as London's Strangling Horrors. Horrors they were called because they were something more than murders: they were motiveless, and there was an air of black magic about them. Each murder was committed at a time when the street where the bodies were found was empty of any perceptible or possible murderer. There would be an empty alley. There would be a policeman at its end. He would turn his back on the empty alley for less than a minute. Then he would look round and run into the night with news of another strangling. And in any direction he looked nobody to be seen and no report to be had of anybody being seen. Or he would be on duty in a long quiet street, and suddenly be called to a house of dead people whom a few seconds earlier he had seen alive. And, again, whichever way he looked nobody to be seen; and although police whistles put an immediate cordon around the area, and searched all houses, no possible murderer to be found.

The first news of the murder of Mr. and Mrs. Whybrow was brought by the station sergeant. He had been walking through Caspar Street on his way to the station for duty, when he noticed the open door of No. 98. Glancing in, he saw by the gaslight of the passage a motionless body on the floor. After a second look he blew his whistle, and when the constables answered him he took one to join him in a search of the house, and sent others to watch all neighbouring streets, and make inquiries at adjoining houses. But neither in the house nor in the streets was anything found to indicate the murderer. Neighbours on either side, and opposite, were questioned, but they had seen nobody about, and had heard nothing. One had heard Mr. Whybrow come home—the scrape of his latchkey in the door was so regular an evening sound, he said, that you could set your watch by it for half-past six—but he had heard nothing more than the sound of the opening door until the sergeant's whistle. Nobody had been seen to enter the house or leave it, by front or back, and the necks of the dead people carried no finger-prints or other traces. A nephew was called in to go over the house, but he could find nothing missing; and anyway his uncle possessed nothing worth stealing. The little money in the house was untouched, and there were no signs of any disturbance of the property, or even of struggle. No signs of anything but brutal and wanton murder.

Mr. Whybrow was known to neighbours and workmates as a quiet, likeable, home-loving man; such a man as could not have any enemies. But, then, murdered men seldom have. A relentless enemy who hates a man to the point of wanting to hurt him seldom wants to murder him, since to do that puts him beyond suffering. So the police were left with an impossible situation: no clue to the murderer and no motive for the murders; only the fact that they had been done.

The first news of the affair sent a tremor through London generally, and an electric thrill through all Mallon End. Here was a murder of two inoffensive people, not for gain and not for revenge; and the murderer, to whom, apparently, killing was a casual impulse, was at large. He had left no traces, and, provided he had no companions, there seemed no reason why he should not remain at large. Any clear-headed man who stands alone, and has no fear of God or man, can, if he chooses, hold a city, even a nation, in subjection; but your everyday criminal is seldom clear-headed, and dislikes being lonely. He needs, if not the support of confederates, at least somebody to talk to; his vanity needs the satisfaction of perceiving at first hand the effect of his work. For this he will frequent bars and coffee-shops and other public places. Then, sooner or later, in a glow of comradeship, he will utter the one word too much; and the nark, who is everywhere, has an easy job.

But though the doss-houses and saloons and other places were "combed" and set with watchers, and it was made known by whispers that good money and protection were assured to those with information, nothing attaching to the Whybrow case could be found. The murderer clearly had no friends and kept no company. Known men of this type were called up and questioned, but each was able to give a good account of himself; and in a few days the police were at a dead end. Against the constant public gibe that the thing had been done almost under their noses, they became restive, and for four days each man of the force was working his daily beat under a strain. On the fifth day they became still more restive.

It was the season of annual teas and entertainments for the children of the Sunday Schools, and on an evening of fog, when London was a world of groping phantoms, a small girl, in the bravery of best Sunday frock and shoes, shining face and new-washed hair, set out from Logan Passage for St. Michael's Parish Hall. She never got there. She was not actually dead until half-past six, but she was as good as dead from the moment she left her mother's door. Somebody like a man, pacing the street from which the Passage led, saw her come out; and from that moment she was dead. Through the fog somebody's large white hands reached after her, and in fifteen minutes they were about her.

At half-past six a whistle screamed trouble, and those answering it found the body of little Nellie Vrinoff in a warehouse entry in Minnow Street. The sergeant was first among them, and he posted his men to useful points, ordering them here and there in the tart tones of repressed rage, and berating the officer whose beat the street was. "I saw you, Magson, at the end of the lane. What were you up to there? You were there ten minutes before you turned." Magson began an explanation about keeping an eye on a suspicious-looking character at that end, but the sergeant cut him short: "Suspicious characters be damned! You don't want to look for suspicious characters. You want to look for *murderers.* Messing about . . . and then this happens right where you ought to be. Now think what they'll say."

With the speed of ill news came the crowd, pale and perturbed; and on the story that the unknown monster had appeared again, and this time to a child, their faces streaked the fog with spots of hate and horror. But then came the ambulance and more police, and swiftly they broke up the crowd; and as it broke the sergeant's thought was thickened into words, and from all sides came low murmurs of "Right under their noses." Later inquiries showed that four people of the district, above suspicion, had passed that entry at intervals of seconds before the murder, and seen nothing and heard nothing. None of them had passed the child alive or seen her dead. None of them had seen anybody in the street except themselves. Again the police were left with no motive and with no clue.

And now the district, as you will remember, was given over, not to panic, for the London public never yields to that, but to apprehension and dismay. If these things were happening in their familiar streets, then anything might happen. Wherever people met—in the streets, the markets and the shops—they debated the one topic. Women took to bolting their windows and doors at the first fall of dusk. They kept their children closely under their eye. They did their shopping before dark, and watched anxiously, while pretending they weren't watching, for the return of their husbands from work. Under the Cockney's semi-humorous resignation to disaster, they hid an hourly foreboding. By the whim of one man with a pair of hands the structure and tenour of their daily life were shaken, as they always can be shaken by any man contemptuous of humanity and fearless of its laws. They began to realise that the pillars that supported the peaceable society in which they lived were mere straws that anybody could snap; that laws were powerful only so long as they were obeyed; that the police were potent only so long as they were feared. By the power of his hands this one man had made a whole community do something new: he had made it think, and left it gasping at the obvious.

And then, while it was yet gasping under his first two strokes, he made his third. Conscious of the horror that his hands had created, and hungry as an actor who has once tasted the thrill of the multitude, he made fresh advertisement of his presence; and on Wednesday morning, three days after the murder of the child, the papers carried to the breakfast-tables of England the story of a still more shocking outrage.

At 9.32 on Tuesday night a constable was on duty in Jarnigan Road, and at that time spoke to a fellow-officer named Petersen at the top of Clemming Street. He had seen this officer walk down that street. He could swear that the street was empty at that time, except for a lame boot-black whom he knew by sight, and who passed him and entered a tenement on the side opposite that on which his fellow-officer was walking. He had the habit, as all constables had just then, of looking constantly behind him and around him, whichever way he was walking, and he was certain that the street was empty. He passed his sergeant at 9.33, saluted him, and answered his inquiry for anything seen. He reported that he had seen nothing, and passed on. His beat ended at a short distance from Clemming Street, and, having paced it, he turned and came again at 9.34 to the top of the street. He had scarcely reached it before he heard the hoarse voice of the sergeant: "Gregory! You there? Quick. Here's another. My God, it's Petersen! Garrotted. Quick, call 'em up!"

That was the third of the Strangling Horrors, of which there were to be a fourth and a fifth; and the five horrors were to pass into the unknown and unknowable. That is, unknown so far as authority and the public were concerned. The identity of the murderer *was* known, but to two men only. One was the murderer himself; the other was a young journalist.

This young man, who was covering the affairs for his paper, the *Daily Torch,* was no smarter than the other zealous newspaper men who were hanging about these byways in the hope of a sudden story. But he was patient, and he hung a little closer to the case than the other fellows, and by continually staring at it he at last raised the figure of the murderer like a genie from the stones on which he had stood to do his murders.

After the first few days the men had given up any attempt at exclusive stories, for there was none to be had. They met regularly at the police-station, and what little information there was they shared. The officials were agreeable to them, but no more. The sergeant discussed with them the details of each murder; suggested possible explanations of the man's methods; recalled from the past those cases that had some similarity; and on the matter of motive reminded them of the motiveless Neil Cream and the wanton John Williams, and hinted that work was being done which would soon bring the business to an end; but about that work he would not say a word. The Inspector, too, was gracefully garrulous on the thesis of Murder, but whenever one of the party edged the talk towards what was being done in this immediate matter, he glided past it. Whatever the officials knew, they were not giving it to newspaper men. The business had fallen heavily upon them, and only by a capture made by their own efforts could they rehabilitate themselves in official and public esteem. Scotland Yard, of course, was at work, and had all the station's material; but the station's hope was that they themselves would have the honour of settling the affair; and however useful the co-operation of the Press might be in other cases, they did not want to risk a defeat by a premature disclosure of their theories and plans.

So the sergeant talked at large, and propounded one interesting theory after another, all of which the newspaper men had thought of themselves.

The young man soon gave up these morning lectures on the Philosophy of Crime, and took to wandering about the streets and making bright stories out of the effect of the murders on the normal life of the people. A melancholy job made more melancholy by the district. The littered roadways, the crestfallen houses, the bleared windows—all held the acid misery that evokes no sympathy: the misery of the frustrated poet. The misery was the creation of the aliens, who were living in this

makeshift fashion because they had no settled homes, and would neither take the trouble to make a home where they *could* settle, nor get
on with their wandering.

There was little to be picked up. All he saw and heard were indignant faces, and wild conjectures of the murderer's identity and of the
secret of his trick of appearing and disappearing unseen. Since a policeman himself had fallen a victim, denunciations of the force had
ceased, and the unknown was now invested with a cloak of legend. Men
eyed other men, as though thinking: It might be *him.* It might be *him.*
They were no longer looking for a man who had the air of a Madame
Tussaud murderer; they were looking for a man, or perhaps some har-
ridan woman, who had done these particular murders. Their thoughts
ran mainly on the foreign set. Such ruffianism could scarcely belong to
England, nor could the bewildering cleverness of the thing. So they
turned to Roumanian gipsies and Turkish carpet-sellers. There, clearly,
would be found the "warm" spot. These Eastern fellows—they knew all
sorts of tricks, and they had no real religion—nothing to hold them within bounds. Sailors returning from those parts had told tales of conjurors
who made themselves invisible; and there were tales of Egyptian and
Arab potions that were used for abysmally queer purposes. Perhaps it
was possible to them; you never knew. They were so slick and cunning,
and they had such gliding movements; no Englishman could melt away
as they could. Almost certainly the murderer would be found to be one
of that sort—with some dark trick of his own—and just because they were
sure that he *was* a magician, they felt that it was useless to look for him.
He was a power, able to hold them in subjection and to hold himself
untouchable. Superstition, which so easily cracks the frail shell of reason, had got into them. He could do anything he chose: he would never
be discovered. These two points they settled, and they went about the
streets in a mood of resentful fatalism.

They talked of their ideas to the journalist in half-tones, looking
right and left, as though *HE* might overhear them and visit them. And
though all the district was thinking of him and ready to pounce upon
him, yet, so strongly had he worked upon them, that if any man in the
street—say, a small man of commonplace features and form—had cried
"*I* am the Monster!" would their stifled fury have broken into flood and

have borne him down and engulfed him? Or would they not suddenly have seen something unearthly in that everyday face and figure, something unearthly in his everyday boots, something unearthly about his hat, something that marked him as one whom none of their weapons could alarm or pierce? And would they not momentarily have fallen back from this devil, as the devil fell back from the Cross made by the sword of Faust, and so have given him time to escape? I do not know; but so fixed was their belief in his invincibility that it is at least likely that they would have made this hesitation, had such an occasion arisen. But it never did. To-day this commonplace fellow, his murder lust glutted, is still seen and observed among them, as he was seen and observed all the time; but because nobody then dreamt, or now dreams, that he was what he was, they observed him then, and observe him now, as people observe a lamp-post.

Almost was their belief in his invincibility justified; for, five days after the murder of the policeman Petersen, when the experience and inspiration of the whole detective force of London were turned towards his identification and capture, he made his fourth and fifth strokes.

At nine o'clock that evening, the young newspaper man, who hung about every night until his paper was away, was strolling along Richards Lane. Richards Lane is a narrow street, partly a stall-market, and partly residential. The young man was in the residential section, which carries on one side small working-class cottages, and on the other the wall of a railway goods-yard. The great wall hung a blanket of shadow over the lane, and the shadow and the cadaverous outline of the now deserted market stalls gave it the appearance of a living lane that had been turned to frost in the moment between breath and death. The very lamps, that elsewhere were nimbuses of gold, had here the rigidity of gems. The journalist, feeling this message of frozen eternity, was telling himself that he was tired of the whole thing, when in one stroke the frost was broken. In the moment between one pace and another silence and darkness were racked by a high scream and through the scream a voice: "Help! help! *He's here!*"

Before he could think what movement to make, the lane came to life. As though its invisible populace had been waiting on that cry, the door of every cottage was flung open, and from them and from the al-

leys poured shadowy figures bent in question-mark form. For a second
or so they stood as rigid as the lamps; then a police whistle gave them
direction, and the flock of shadows sloped up the street. The journalist
followed them, and others followed him. From the main street and
from surrounding streets they came, some risen from unfinished sup-
pers, some disturbed in their ease of slippers and shirt-sleeves, some
stumbling on infirm limbs, and some upright, and armed with pokers or
the tools of their trade. Here and there above the wavering cloud of
heads moved the bold helmets of policemen. In one dim mass they
surged upon a cottage whose doorway was marked by the sergeant and
two constables; and voices of those behind urged them on with "Get in!
Find him! Run round the back! Over the wall!" and those in front cried:
"Keep back! Keep back!"

And now the fury of a mob held in thrall by unknown peril broke
loose. He was here—on the spot. Surely this time he *could not* escape.
All minds were bent upon the cottage; all energies thrust towards its
doors and windows and roof; all thought was turned upon one unknown
man and his extermination. So that no one man saw any other man. No
man saw the narrow, packed lane and the mass of struggling shadows,
and all forgot to look among themselves for the monster who never lin-
gered upon his victims. All forgot, indeed, that they, by their mass cru-
sade of vengeance, were affording him the perfect hiding-place. They
saw only the house, and they heard only the rending of woodwork and
the smash of glass at back and front, and the police giving orders or crying with the chase; and they pressed on.

But they found no murderer. All they found was news of murder
and a glimpse of the ambulance, and for their fury there was no other
object than the police themselves, who fought against this hampering of
their work.

The journalist managed to struggle through to the cottage door, and
to get the story from the constable stationed there. The cottage was the
home of a pensioned sailor and his wife and daughter. They had been
at supper, and at first it appeared that some noxious gas had smitten all
three in mid-action. The daughter lay dead on the hearth-rug, with a
piece of bread-and-butter in her hand. The father had fallen sideways
from his chair, leaving on his plate a filled spoon of rice-pudding. The

mother lay half under the table, her lap filled with the pieces of a broken cup and splashes of cocoa. But in three seconds the idea of gas was dismissed. One glance at their necks showed that this was the Strangler again; and the police stood and looked at the room and momentarily shared the fatalism of the public. They were helpless.

This was his fourth visit, making seven murders in all. He was to do, as you know, one more—and to do it that night; and then he was to pass into history as the unknown London horror, and return to the decent life that he had always led, remembering little of what he had done, and worried not at all by the memory. Why did he stop? Impossible to say. Why did he begin? Impossible again. It just happened like that; and if he thinks at all of those days and nights, I surmise that he thinks of them as we think of foolish or dirty little sins that we committed in childhood. We say that they were not really sins, because we were not then consciously ourselves: we had not come to realisation; and we look back at that foolish little creature that we once were, and forgive him because he didn't know. So, I think, with this man.

There are plenty like him. Eugene Aram, after the murder of Daniel Clarke, lived a quiet, contented life for fourteen years unhaunted by his crime and unshaken in his self-esteem. Dr. Crippen murdered his wife, and then lived pleasantly with his mistress in the house under whose floor he had buried the wife. Constance Kent, found Not Guilty of the murder of her young brother, led a peaceful life for five years before she confessed. George Joseph Smith and William Palmer lived amiably among their fellows untroubled by fear or by remorse for their poisonings and drownings. Charles Peace, at the time he made his one unfortunate essay, had settled down into a respectable citizen with an interest in antiques. It happened that, after a lapse of time, these men were discovered, but more murderers than we guess are living decent lives to-day, and will die in decency, undiscovered and unsuspected. As this man will.

But he had a narrow escape, and it was perhaps this narrow escape that brought him to a stop. The escape was due to an error of judgment on the part of the journalist.

As soon as he had the full story of the affair, which took some time, he spent fifteen minutes on the telephone, sending the story through, and at the end of the fifteen minutes, when the stimulus of the business had left him, he felt physically tired and mentally dishevelled. He was not yet free to go home; the paper would not go away for another hour; so he turned into a bar for a drink and some sandwiches.

It was then, when he had dismissed the whole business from his mind, and was looking about the bar and admiring the landlord's taste in watch-chains and his air of domination, and was thinking that the landlord of a well-conducted tavern had a more comfortable life than a newspaper man, that his mind received from nowhere a spark of light. He was not thinking about the Strangling Horrors; his mind was on his sandwich. As a public-house sandwich, it was a curiosity. The bread had been thinly cut, it was buttered, and the ham was not two months stale; it was ham as it should be. His mind turned to the inventor of this refreshment, the Earl of Sandwich, and then to George the Fourth, and then to the Georges, and to the legend of that George who was worried to know how the apple got into the apple-dumpling. He wondered whether George would have been equally puzzled to know how the ham got into the ham sandwich, and how long it would have been before it occurred to him that the ham could not have got there unless somebody had put it there. He got up to order another sandwich, and in that moment a little active corner of his mind settled the affair. If there was ham in his sandwich, somebody must have put it there. If seven people had been murdered, somebody must have been there to murder them. There was no aeroplane or automobile that would go into a man's pocket; therefore that somebody must have escaped either by running away or standing still; and again therefore—

He was visualising the front-page story that his paper would carry if his theory were correct, and if—a matter of conjecture—his editor had the necessary nerve to make a bold stroke, when a cry of "Time, gentlemen, please! All out!" reminded him of the hour. He got up and went out into a world of mist, broken by the ragged discs of roadside puddles and the streaming lightning of motor-buses. He was certain that he had *the* story, but, even if it were proved, he was doubtful whether the policy of his paper would permit him to print it. It had one great fault. It was truth, but it was impossible truth. It rocked the foundations of everything that newspaper readers believed and that newspaper editors helped them to believe. They might believe that Turkish carpet-sellers had the gift of making themselves invisible. They would not believe this.

As it happened, they were not asked to, for the story was never written. As his paper had by now gone away, and as he was nourished by his refreshment and stimulated by his theory, he thought he might put in an extra half-hour by testing that theory. So he began to look about for the man he had in mind—a man with white hair, and large white hands; otherwise an everyday figure whom nobody would look twice at. He wanted to spring his idea on this man without warning, and he was going to place himself within reach of a man armoured in legends of dreadfulness and grue. This might appear to be an act of supreme courage—that one man, with no hope of immediate outside support, should place himself at the mercy of one who was holding a whole parish in terror. But it wasn't. He didn't think about the risk. He didn't think about his duty to his employers or loyalty to his paper. He was moved simply by an instinct to follow a story to its end.

He walked slowly from the tavern and crossed into Fingal Street, making for Deever Market, where he had hope of finding his man. But his journey was shortened. At the corner of Lotus Street he saw him—or a man who looked like him. This street was poorly lit, and he could see little of the man: but he *could* see white hands. For some twenty paces he stalked him; then drew level with him; and at a point where the arch of a railway crossed the street, he saw that this was his man. He approached him with the current conversational phrase of the district: "Well, seen anything of the murderer?" The man stopped to look sharply at him; then, satisfied that the journalist was not the murderer, said: "Eh? No, nor's anybody else, curse it. Doubt if they ever will."

"I don't know. I've been thinking about them, and I've got an idea."

"So?"

"Yes. Came to me all of a sudden. Quarter of an hour ago. And I'd felt that we'd all been blind. It's been staring us in the face."

The man turned again to look at him, and the look and the movement held suspicion of this man who seemed to know so much. "Oh? Has it? Well, if you're so sure, why not give us the benefit of it?"

"I'm going to." They walked level, and were nearly at the end of the little street where it meets Deever Market, when the journalist turned casually to the man. He put a finger on his arm. "Yes, it seems to me quite simple now. But there's still one point I don't understand. One little thing I'd like to clear up. I mean the motive. Now, as man to man, tell me, Sergeant Ottermole, just *why* did you kill all those inoffensive people?"

The sergeant stopped, and the journalist stopped. There was just enough light from the sky, which held the reflected light of the continent of London, to give him a sight of the sergeant's face, and the sergeant's face was turned to him with a wide smile of such urbanity and charm that the journalist's eyes were frozen as they met it. The smile stayed for some seconds. Then said the sergeant: "Well, to tell you the truth, Mister Newspaper Man, I don't know. I really don't know. In fact, I've been worried about it myself. But I've got an idea—just like you. Everybody knows that we can't control the workings of our minds. Don't they? Ideas come into our minds without asking. But everybody's supposed to be able to control his body. Why? Eh? We get our minds from lord-knows-where—from people who were dead hundreds of years before we were born. Mayn't we get our bodies in the same way? Our faces—our legs—our heads—they aren't completely ours. We don't make 'em. They come to us. And couldn't ideas come into our bodies like ideas come into our minds? Eh? Can't ideas live in nerve and muscle as well as in brain? Couldn't it be that parts of our bodies aren't really us, and couldn't ideas come into those parts all of a sudden, like ideas come into—into"—he shot his arms out, showing the great white-gloved hands and hairy wrists; shot them out so swiftly to the journalist's throat that his eyes never saw them—"into *my hands!*"

DESIRABLE VILLA

I do not for a moment (said old Quong) doubt it. You say the young lady claims to be psychic. She certainly is. She was filled all day, you tell me, with a sense of impending disaster and doom, of earthquakes and pestilence and the end of the world, and although you smile when you tell me that that very evening her lip-stick gave out at a critical moment of the dance, I see no cause for the smile. She had received her warning, and it was fulfilled. (With this pawn I now retrieve my queen.)

No; I have never doubted that coming events cast their shadows before, particularly those of an unpleasant nature. This is not entirely because these events take pleasure in obscuring our view of the sun, but because events, being static, are perceived by us before we reach them, and we perceive more particularly the unpleasant because in the dim light of the not-yet-reached the unpleasant looms far more heavily than the pleasant. But dim light is deceptive; it holds the essence of the event, but gives it vague or fanciful form; a first draft of what the thing is going to be—and we all know what poets do with their first drafts when they begin work upon them. In such a light twisted trees take the form of wounded soldiers, little hills take the form of fighting galleons; and, to the mental sight, exhausted lip-sticks take the form of earthquakes, and ill-made coffee takes the form of pestilence. That light is never to be trusted, because by the time we actually reach the event it is quite likely that the event will have changed its mind.

Take the case of that suburban villa, the story of which was related to me by a young schoolmaster of these parts. (Your move, I think.)

(I made my move, and the game of chess, which had been begun that afternoon, went on and on into the long night, like the Vanderbilt family or the Fulham Road. Between moves he told me the story of the desirable villa.)

All through one grey-skied afternoon of Autumn the young schoolmaster, whose name was Shafe, had been wandering round the northern rim of that cup which holds London, and he had come at twilight into the bleak and chilblain country of the north-east. He was then beyond Walthamstow and beyond that chain of reservoirs which makes the sudden bulge in the course of the River Lea. On what speck of the map he was he didn't know, but he was in a land that some dark corner of his soul told him was very much like hell. It was neither town nor country nor suburb, but something that blasphemed all three. There were bits of field and wood, and bits of paved street, and bits of marshy land. Here and there were some nakedly new shops, and a few houses that were occupied but were not yet blest with the gracious air that belongs to a house that is lived in. There were a hundred half-finished houses. The grass of the fields was sore with eruptions of brick and pole and tool-shed. The unweathered hue of the bricks made them red-hot to the eye. The unmade roads clutched at the feet like satanic hands.

At all points of the outer circle you may come upon these spots of horror. They are not of the stuff or the spirit of horror—merely a part of the necessary business of "developing" a residential estate; yet, though we all live in houses, the sight of this business of making houses affects most of us as an hour in a slaughterhouse would affect a lover of pork. This place, the young man could see, was to be the estate agent's realisation of The Ideal Home for people of small means—the unplaced people just above the self-sufficient dignity of the labouring class. There would be rows and rows of uniform six-roomed houses, with scullery, bathroom and electric light. Newly-married couples of that unplaced class would furnish their first little homes there. They would found their obscure families, and make pretty gardens, and live out their ignobly decent days in unwondering content. It stood for all that is simple and domestic and petty. His reason and observation told him this. But as that cadaverous light fell upon its litter, his reason was, he says, frozen, and his spirits were pressed into vapour. He could not see it as Kettering Park, N.E. He could only see it as a grouping of horror waiting upon horror.

And then, he says, as though his mind had launched horror into it, horror was born in it and took shape and substance to his eyes.

The workmen were just knocking off when he arrived, dropping their tool-bags in the night-watchman's shed, and slouching in twos and threes towards the station. But the little caravan "office" of the estate was still open, and potential tenants of the houses were still moving about the estate, and asking questions of the two clerks who were there to answer them. They went in and out of the shells of houses, peering and probing, and Shafe watched them with sympathy.

A small river bordered one side of the estate, and to get to the main road leading back to London he had to cross this river by a stone bridge some two hundred yards north of the estate. He crossed it, and turned southward again, on an uphill road, and had a clear view of the houses on the far side. It was then that he noticed—not because they were noticeable, but because they were there—a man and a woman coming towards a house on the limits of the property. They came awkwardly through the wet clay, and their trim town clothes and urban deportment made a queer vibration against the welter of country mire and the shrill newness of the houses. The man carried an umbrella, tightly rolled, and a newspaper. He had small features and a yellow moustache out of proportion to them. His overcoat, trousers and bowler hat were neither fresh nor shabby; just adequate. A clerk or accountant, Shafe thought, who had succeeded no farther than the point of making ends meet. The woman's face, what he could see of it, was the face of a woman of forty, and the droop of her mouth and her movements in walking suggested that this was a woman who felt that life owed her something. There are thousands of her in her rank of life.

Eminently respectable, both of them; eminently typical of the future residents of the estate; eminently negative.

The steep ascent of his path compelled him to walk slowly, and he had them in view until they entered the half-finished house at the end of the road-that-was-to-be. At this point his path turned inward to the river, and brought him closer to the house by sight, though the distance he had walked from the bridge had put it—because of the river—so much the farther from him. He could see into it, but he could not reach it.

He was at the nearest possible line to it when he heard the man's voice. It called: "Where are you?" The woman answered: "Upstairs. Back room." He could hear the man's boots on the uncovered stairs—

he says he can hear quite sharply that gritty clumping now—and then, through the unglazed windows of the upper back room, he saw them together. At that moment his throat surprised him by making a queer noise. It was an unsuccessful cry; unsuccessful because it came from the physical without direction from the mental. It was a muscular explosion, and the detonator was the simple fact that this eminently negative couple had become in that moment eminently positive.

The woman was standing near the window. The man was approaching her from behind. It all happened swiftly, in a group of seconds, but it was in the fraction of the second in which Shafe realised the man's intention and the woman's danger that he delivered that abortive cry. Before that second had passed into time the man's hands were around her throat, and he was dragging her backwards from the window and downwards. Shafe cried then, he says, with intent and clearly, but if the man heard him he did not let the cry disturb the business. From his point on the crest of the hill Shafe had to see the completed dreadfulness of the affair. He was an eyewitness and a possible saviour, and he was as useful as if he had been at Tilbury. It was not a matter of distance, but of time, and between him and them was the time needed to flounder through six yards of running river. He saw him drag her back and down. He could see the knuckles tightening. Her hat fell off, and her hands made aimless pawings at the air. The man's hands pressed into her throat, and forced the neck back, and worried it from side to side. He was like a dog with a rat, and the great yellow moustache gave him an air of insipid geniality that was as dreadful as the business he was doing. The thing was accomplished in silence. The woman made no cry, and the man's movements were small and tense. A few more wrenches to right and left, and then the body jerked three times and was still. The man got up. He smoothed his clothes and eased his collar. His attitude and expression were as casual as if he really had killed nothing more than a rat. He looked down at the floor and around the bare room as one looks before locking up for a holiday. Then he picked up his newspaper and umbrella from the floor, made a movement of dusting his hands, and turned to go.

By these commonplace gestures Shafe's tension was so suddenly eased that he let out a series of large directed cries towards the office of the estate, and began to run back to the bridge. He hoped to get to the office in time to stop the man from getting off the property, but, though he cried as he ran, his cries created no answer nor movement anywhere. Once or twice in his run he looked back to note the path the man was taking, but he could see nothing of him. He guessed that he was making a sly course through the scattered houses and trying to reach the road by some other way than the main entrance to the estate; and he made a spurt for it. He tore across the bridge, and reached it in a time that surprised himself. He caught one of the clerks, but his want of practice in running found him breathless, and some moments were wasted before he could get the story out. His first effort was almost a coded telegram: "That end house. Down there. Something happened. Send some one—stop man—brown overcoat."

The clerk looked at him with a sort of alert stupidity. Shafe saw that he understood nothing. "Something happened? Where? *What's* happened?"

"Comansee. But send some one stop brown overcoat."

The clerk walked a pace or two with him, a little moved by his vigour, but still withholding attention. When Shafe had achieved coherence he was still without interest. "A man and a woman went into that end house. About three minutes ago. A man in a bowler hat and brown overcoat. Carrying a rolled umbrella and a newspaper. About five foot nine. Woman about the same height wearing a grey coat. He attacked her in there. Didn't you hear me yell?"

The clerk stopped and looked at him with what used to be called a quiz. "Look here—what's all this? I don't know what you're talking about at all. Nobody's been down to that house. I been here all the time. There *was* a man and woman like you say went to look at it, but they went out past my office half an hour ago. At five."

"Then they must have come back another way. Because I *saw* them. Saw them and heard them in the house. I saw him do it. Anyway, come and see. But do something about the man first."

The clerk was clearly annoyed, and Shafe could see that he had eight or nine different and confused ideas about his visitor. But he called to his fellow, who stood by one of the brick dumps, and went over to him, and muttered and jerked his head backward to Shafe. They grinned. Then the other went perfunctorily through scaffold poles and granite kerbs towards the path that the man might have taken, and Shafe's young man came back to him. He came strolling, hands in trousers pockets, whistling. "Which house you say—the end one? I'll just come and have a look at it. But you can take it from me those parties left here at five o'clock. And they couldn't a-come back without my seeing 'em."

"Well, they did come back. You'll see when you get there. He brought her back and murdered her."

"Eh?" The clerk looked at him sideways and even more insolently. He was either a lunatic or drunk—a nuisance in any case, and possibly a dangerous nuisance. He called across to his fellow. "Don't go too far, Morton." Shafe could see Morton from where they stood, and he had had the house in full view while telling his story. Despite the quivering approach of the dusk, the light was still sharp and cold, and he was certain that nobody had come from the house since he reached the bridge, and it was certain that nobody had passed Morton. They went to it without secrecy, and walked straight to the front entrance. "Listen, now. If he hasn't got right away he's probably still in the house. So be careful."

Inside the house the light was not so good, but as the rooms were bare, only a glance here and there was necessary. He was not on the ground floor. "Now, then. Upstairs. It was the back room. You'll see something *there;* and you may see him in one of the others. Carefully." They went up, and Shafe looked first into the front rooms and the bathroom. Nothing there. Then he pointed to the back room. Despite the horror and pathos of the occasion, he says that he was aware of a detached interest in the prospect of seeing his cocksure clerk jump. He was guilty of the what-did-I-tell-you posture. "Now look in there." The clerk went in. Shafe gave him a few seconds to himself; then followed him. He looked round at Shafe with "Well?"

The room was empty.

If you have ever pulled a fire-alarm, and then found that the "fire" was a private bonfire, or tried to save a drowning man and found that he was a professor of swimming, giving an exhibition, you will understand how Shafe felt. The room was empty. All the rooms were empty. There was no corpse and no murderer. The clerk looked at him without any concealment of his grin. "Haven't made a mistake in the house, I suppose? Perhaps we'd better look over all of 'em."

"Perhaps you had. He might have carried it away while I was running. But this was the house. I was standing there—on the road just across the river. *I saw it in this house.*"

"Well, well, well! All I can say is, I've had a clear view of this house all the afternoon. Nobody's been in it except the two people you mentioned. And they went at five o'clock. And nothing's been near that house or come out of it in the last half-hour. Nothing *could* have come out without me seeing it—not out of any point of it—'cos it's in a corner. Certainly not a man carrying a bundle. No, sir. If you'll excuse me, I've got some things to clear up at the office." He turned towards the office with an air of conducting Shafe off the estate; and as there seemed nothing else to do Shafe went with him. On the way he made three firm attempts at stating that he had definitely seen the thing: then his voice refused to back him, and he gave it up. He made apologies for putting the clerk to purposeless trouble, and walked away, he says, with what air of normal behaviour he could summon. As he moved away he heard a grinning mutter, "Up the loop, I reckon."

He came away disgusted and distressed. Disgusted with himself for exposing himself to the clerk's gibes; distressed because if that thing hadn't happened, then nothing was happening. He wasn't walking, and the night wasn't coming on, and there wasn't any estate or any bridge. He had a foreboding of a nervous breakdown. He was certain that he was wearing boots and trousers, and he was equally certain that that thing had happened. But there was the fact that it hadn't happened, and if it hadn't happened, then he wasn't wearing trousers, and the world was skidding sideways from him. He thought of the usual explanation of ghosts, but it couldn't, he thought, have been a ghostly haunting, because ghosts don't haunt a house before it has been fully built and lived in, and they don't wear the fashions of to-day. He went home puzzled, disgusted, irritated and a little apprehensive; and it was three or four weeks, he says, before he shook off the damp memory of that afternoon.

Eight months later he came out of his school at midday and saw the contents bill of a special edition of one of the evening papers: "North London Murder." He saw it and noted it, but only as he noted other things that didn't interest him, such as "Test Match Result" and "Latest from Gatwick." The bill gave it no excited epithet, and he assumed that it had nothing to distinguish it from any other murder—it would be just one of those sordid affairs that happen in London four or five times a year. But while he was having his meal in a small eating-house near the school, he picked up a copy of the paper left by a previous customer, and found that most of its front page was given to the murder—a murder at Kettering Park, a suburb of North London. As you will guess, the combination of the words "murder" and "Kettering Park" started a mnemonic shuttle in his mind, and he began to read. Besides full details, the paper carried pictures of the victim and of the prisoner, who had been arrested and charged early that morning; and of course the pictures were what you are expecting them to be. He would have recognised anywhere the severe droop of the woman's mouth, or the fluffy moustache that was too big for the face. They were as familiar to him as the face of his dog or of the head master of his school, and he turned to the story with a feeling almost of relief.

That goblin memory, which at odd times of day and night had perched upon his brain, was now pulverised. The thing had happened; the idea had washed itself out in fact and was done with for ever. What he had seen had indeed been a haunting, but with a difference. It had been, not, as usually, a re-visitation of the event, but a ghostly approach to it. He had not been suffering from nerves; he had simply seen something before it happened; and when he understood that that was the solution of his afternoon at Kettering Park he felt easy, and knew what the story would be.

It was all there. The very villa of Kettering Park, bordering the river, which the couple had occupied for about six months; the newspaper; the umbrella; the hour (half-past five) it was all there, just as in the—

And then, he says, he dropped the paper. For, though all the details were there, the key-point of the thing was not. He picked up the paper and studied it again, and, as he read, that one missing thing brought the goblin back, and he felt again the damp and insubstantial sense of living in a world behind the moon. He felt as he had felt when the clerk called from the back room.

The body had been found in the upper back room of the villa. (Right.) An umbrella and a newspaper were lying beside it. (Right.) The hat was off and the coat was torn open. (Right.) Death was by strangulation. (Right.) A neighbour had heard the man come home, and had heard him call: "Where are you?" and had heard the answer: "Upstairs. Back room." (Right.) And then the thing went all wrong. The picture of the victim was the picture of the man. The picture of the arrested murderer was the picture of the woman.

But that (said Old Quong) is quite understandable. You see that something had happened in the interval between the approach to the event and the arrival at it, and, given all the circumstances of the first enactment of the affair, you can see what that something was. Intentions, good or bad, should be put into practice. Otherwise, they may float in the air and . . . Your move, I think.

THE SECRET OF FRANCESCO SHEDD

The story in to-night's paper (said old Quong, as we sat on tea chests opposite each other)—the story of the young inventor who claimed to have crossed the North Sea in his new collapsible coat-pocket boat, and was suspected of having crossed by liner, and then was convicted of having swum the entire distance in heroic time—that is an interesting story. We are so used to financiers masquerading as states-men, confidence tricksters masquerading as philanthropists, clerks mas-querading as Counts, that when we find that one whom we have admired as a rogue is really more honest than he has ever claimed to be, we naturally turn from him with contempt. He has dragged the human comedy down to the level of everyday.

Have I ever told you the story of Francesco Shedd? No? I wonder why I haven't. It reflects upon so many aspects of English religious, po-litical and social life, and has such a pointed moral, that I ought to have told it to you when you were quite young. Let me repair the omission. But first let us make some more tea.

Well, the young Francesco Shedd was a London warehouse clerk in the West India Dock, and not a very good warehouse clerk. Not only was he without interest in his job, but he was often guilty of completely with-drawing himself from it. He would be sitting at his desk, apparently at work, but when his superiors asked him a question, they had to ask it four times, and the fourth time they had to shout it, and reinforce the shout with a punch. "Hey! Wake up, there, you!" Mr. Shedd would then wake up with a jerk and a blink, and look at the questioner as though he had not before seen him. "What's the idea, Shedd—sitting there mooning like that?" "I wasn't mooning. I was watching something." "What can you watch on a bare wall?" "Lots of things." "Well, watch that

ledger for a change. And stop throwing pens about when I speak to you."
"I didn't throw a pen about." "You did. There it is on the floor."

Whether Mr. Shedd did throw pens at his superior I do not know; but I do know that he often wanted to. Warehouse-clerking affected him like that. He found it monotonous and irksome, and demonstrably inadequate as a stepping-stone to the pleasures of life. And he yearned for the pleasures of life. He wanted good clothes, and good food and drink, and bright surroundings and company—of which at present he had none. He wanted to move about from place to place instead of moving as shuttles move. Also he wanted to be admired.

Determined at last to escape from the warehouse, he looked about for some career that should fulfil his requirements. He thought at first of the career of commercial traveller, but this he abruptly dismissed. It fulfilled the desire to move about, but he doubted gravely the possibility of its fulfilling his other desires. His second thought showed him the way. The career that he was visualising was, of course, though he had not consciously known it, the stage. It was his visits to the theatre that had stirred him to unrest and desire. It was the people of the theatre whom he envied and admired for the colour and movement of their lives, the glitter of their society, and the interest of their society, and the interest of their work. It was one of them that he wanted to be; and now that he knew what it was he wanted he set about getting it.

He debated for some time the particular phase of stage work to which he should dedicate himself, and found great difficulty in bringing his conflicting selves into unanimity. When he attended a polite society comedy he felt that the polite society comedian was most to be envied. When he attended a romantic drama he felt that the romantic actor stood far above the drawing-room comedian. When he attended a knock-about farce he felt that the clown was surely the most popular of all types of entertainer. When he attended a musical comedy he felt that the singing and dancing hero was the figure he would most like to be.

However, as matters turned out, he became none of these. His indecision was settled for him by a friend. The friend took him one night to a music-hall, and there they saw the gorgeous and astounding entertainment of a Chinese conjuror. It chanced that the friend knew this Chinese conjuror, whose name, I regret to say, was Joe Clacton, and the friend took Mr. Shedd round to the conjuror's dressing-room. This actual meeting with a popular performer—the first performer Mr. Shedd had ever been privileged to meet—coming on top of the astounding entertainment, settled all Mr. Shedd's doubts. He would be a conjuror. It was the stage; it was moving about; it was admiration; it was fascinating labour; it was intelligent labour; and it was highly-paid. He could see no other form of labour that even merited comparison, and without delay he began to train himself as a conjuror.

The way, I need not tell you, was hard. It is hard for all conjurors, but it is notably and blasphemously hard for those who are not conjurors.

I will leave you to imagine Mr. Shedd's struggles and sufferings during the next two years. At the end of a year he could palm coins and could perform the less elaborate card-tricks. At the end of eighteen months he could cause flowers and the flags of all nations to disappear up his sleeve, and was just able to produce bowls of goldfish out of gentlemen's hats. But when he presented himself to music-hall managers, and they commanded him to do his stuff—which I believe is their customary way of granting an audition—they viewed his performance with a cold eye. They told him that when he had some tricks of a more provocative kind than those used by court jesters of the Middle Ages for the entertainment of unsophisticated kings, they might be willing to look at him, but at present . . .

Well, Mr. Shedd went home from each of these interviews hot and sad, but none the less determined to succeed. For weeks after each interview he would practise and practise, but, no matter how he practised, the nice professional touch always eluded him. With the assistance of his landlady's daughter he tried to perform Mr. Clacton's trick of the vanishing lady, and had to seek fresh lodgings. At his new lodgings he tried Mr. Clacton's trick of sitting, strapped hand and foot, in a chair, and setting fire to pieces of wood which had been selected by members of the audience and placed ten feet away from him; and again he had to find other lodgings.

At last, at the end of two years, he was frankly downcast and despairing; and it was while he was sitting one night in a back-room of Shoreditch, with his head bowed to the table, that he decided he would try no more. His dream was hopeless. He could not invent tricks, and he could not even master the tricks that were already in use. He would give up and go back to clerking.

And then, while he was sitting in that bowed position, brooding up-on his futility, something happened. When that something happened Mr. Shedd jumped up and gave a loud cry; then sat down again.

More things now began to happen, one upon the other—things that at first astonished and unnerved him, and then delighted him. Without warning, it had in that moment been revealed to him that he was a mas-ter, and those below heard him cry, "I can! I can! I can beat 'em all!" He, the man who bungled even the bowl-of-goldfish trick, was suddenly become proficient at far more difficult tricks—tricks that no other con-juror had thought of—tricks, he was honest enough to admit, that he himself had not thought of. They came to him, as it were, ready-made in perfection, without the slightest effort from himself.

He was in the middle of one of them when his landlady, disturbed by the queer bumps and bangs that were coming from his room, opened the door to investigate. She jumped back with a squeal—just in time to allow a cane chair to shoot past her head and down the stairs.

"God-a-mercy, Mr. Shedd! Whatever you up to? Throwing chairs at people. Might a-killed me. Gone off your head, I should think."

"I—I—I didn't throw it. I was just—just—"

"I know. Practising your silly old conjuring again. Why don't you give it up and get some work? Else you really will go off your head."

"That's all right, Mrs. Grammon. I shan't need to practise much more. I can do it now." Mr. Shedd had some difficulty in breathing, and he looked pale; but he found enough breath to add, "You wait a week or two. You'll see then. Don't you worry."

Well, in a week or two she did see. So did we all. We have all, I suppose, seen Francesco Shedd, and marvelled at him. We have all seen him sitting bowed and tense and pale in the centre of the stage, and, without moving from his chair or manipulating any properties, do-ing those tricks which placed him at the top of the bill and spread con-sternation and dismay among all other conjurors. We have all seen his Indian rope-trick, which not only set his rivals thinking that it was time for them to buy themselves annuities, but was the cause of intense political feeling in our Indian Empire. We have all seen his trick of bringing to view a woman whom the stage-hands could swear had never entered the theatre, and then making her disappear without any help from screens, veils, boxes, or trap-doors. We have all heard his orchestra of visible instruments played by invisible musicians.

But only a few people know the secret of his success, and those few had to wrest it from him under duress. I know it because he told me freely, but he was deeply sensitive about it, and if I tell it now it is because he is no longer with us, and cannot be harmed by its disclosure.

It is the custom, as you may know, for all conjurors and illusionists to meet together every month or so, and discuss their craft and exhibit their new mysteries and the mechanism of them. Immediately, then, following his first sensational appearance, which took place soon after his decision to abandon all hope—most of the best efforts are made in that mood—Francesco Shedd was cordially invited to become a member of this guild. To the surprise and extreme resentment of the group, he politely but firmly declined. Their resentment cooled, however, when the secretary pointed out that Mr. Shedd's reply was possibly based on a misunderstanding, and that he would write again. He therefore wrote again to Mr. Shedd, suggesting that Mr. Shedd had not fully understood the purpose of their meetings, and insisting that Mr. Shedd would be perfectly safe in revealing the secret of his marvellous tricks, since it was a point of honour among them that no member should make use of another member's tricks. None the less, Mr. Shedd made the same reply; he would not join them, and he would not reveal the secrets of his tricks to anyone.

And now they were really and justly resentful. Mr. Shedd's majestic attitude of refusing to associate with them was nothing short of an insult, and certain of the younger men spoke of reprisals. This was frowned upon; if Mr. Shedd wanted to wear the high hat, let him. Public entertainers did not retain their hold upon the public for ever, and there would probably come a time when Mr. Shedd, without engagements and without money, would be deeply sorry that he had refused the friendly hand held out to him. This was roughly agreed to, but two of the younger members agreed with unspoken reservations. Mr. Shedd had insulted the craft, and as Mr. Shedd was at the moment the most popular and successful and—of course—highly-paid illusionist in the

Western world, it was not to be borne. If Mr. Shedd would not reveal his secrets to his fellow-workers, he should be made to do so.

Mr. Shedd was then appearing at a West End hall, where half the bill was given up to his entertainment. He was playing to full houses, and was sending each audience away deeply mystified. Nothing so perfect and technically clean in the way of illusion had been seen before, and although sceptics could be found here and there—most of them in seats at the greatest distance from the stage—who told their fellows that they could see the wires, the majority of the audience were satisfied that they had witnessed sheer illusion. They were satisfied that they had seen the boy climb the rope, and that they had seen the boy's arms and the boy's legs and the boy's trunk fall down separately on the stage, and then meet, and get up and walk away. Trickery, of course, but marvellous trickery; no mere matter of wires.

Well, upon a Saturday night Mr. Shedd left the stage-door and climbed into his car. Without looking at the chauffeur, he spoke the one word "Home"; then leaned back and gave a deep sigh. He was thinking of his warehouse days, and of his old desire for a life of colour and movement. His mind turned agreeably upon the more than adequate fulfilment of his desire, and upon that moment when he had been bowed over the table. "There is a tide in the affairs—" he mused, but he was not permitted to finish the quotation; for at that moment, out of the darkness of the car, came a thick woollen scarf, which was pressed against his face, and two strong arms which flung him to the floor. For some seconds he struggled, but the sweetness of the scarf was overpowering, and after a few movements he went to sleep and was once again a warehouse clerk.

When he awoke he found himself in a bare room, lighted by two lamps. He was lying on the floor, and standing over him were two young men. His ankles were strapped, and his arms were bound behind him. He was aware of a slight headache, but his mind was clear enough to perceive his situation. One of the young men said: "Ah—he's all right now. Now we can get on with it." To which Mr. Shedd responded: "Get on with what? What is this—common theft, or blackmail, or what?"

"God forbid," said the young man piously, "that either of us should fall to anything criminal. We are the sons of good mothers, and we ask nothing more than that you should answer a few questions."

"There are other ways," said Mr. Shedd, "of asking questions, without attacking a man, drugging him and binding him. You could take him to lunch. You could take him out for a drink. You could call at his house."

"Quite," said one of the young men. "But we knew very well that you would not answer questions in the ordinary conditions of polite intercourse. We, too, are conjurors, Mr. Shedd, and we just want to know, purely as a matter of professional interest, what you have consistently refused to tell us—how you do your tricks."

"I shall not answer."

"I expected that. Pray suit yourself. Only, if you do not answer, I fear that Francesco Shedd will commit the grave professional offence of breaking his engagements. You are billed for next week all over Birmingham. If you do not answer you will not appear at Birmingham, and your value will drop. The week after that, I believe, you are at Glasgow."

"Do you threaten me?" asked Mr. Shedd.

"Oh, certainly," said the young man. "By all means. Nothing would induce either my friend or me to do anything criminal, but there is nothing criminal in entertaining a non-paying guest on an island off the South Essex coast. It is regrettable that after we get there we shall have no boat, nor any other means of communicating with the mainland, but remembering the life that we public entertainers have to lead such solitude has its attractions. What do you say, Mr. Shedd? If I were you, I would not break your engagements. It does one such damage with the public. And I can assure you that anything you may now say will never be used against you. We respect each other's secrets. We only want to know."

"It appears to me," said Mr. Shedd, "that you have me at a disadvantage. The cards are in your hands. I cannot judge, from this unwarranted assault upon me, what value can be placed upon your assurances, but it seems to me that I have no alternative but to trust you. If I speak, do you swear that you will not give my humbug away?"

The young men raised their right hands. "We swear!"

"Then I will tell all, and trust to your youthful decency. The truth is, young men, I could not give your society the secrets of my tricks, for the simple reason that I do not know how I do them."

"You don't *know?* Come, sir—you trifle with us."

"It is the truth. I do not know. I never could learn conjuring, and I myself am not a conjuror."

"Not a conjuror!"

"No," said Mr. Shedd sadly. "No. If by my trickery I have brought discredit upon an honourable and serious profession, I crave your forgiveness. But . . . I had somehow to earn my living, and I have but one gift—a gift which cannot be used for mercenary purposes in its proper sphere. I therefore used it in another sphere. Gentlemen—I trust my secret to your keeping—I am not one of you. I am an impostor. I am nothing more than an extraordinarily gifted spiritualistic medium."

THE YELLOW IMPS

I have heard many times (said old Quong) that conscience makes cowards of us all, but I have never had an authenticated case brought to my knowledge. What is undoubtedly true, and each of us can prove it from his own observation, is that conscience can and does make fools of us all. As it did in the tale of the yellow imps, which I have not, I believe, told you before. Indeed, I am sure I have not, because I only thought of it this morning; so I need not employ that disarming stroke of the polite English entertainer and request you to stop me if you have heard it.

(I had never at any time been under the necessity of stopping old Quong. My chief trouble was in starting him and keeping him in progress. The tale of the yellow imps seemed to work itself out like this.)

There was a high wind in London one October evening, and among others who struggled under it was a man in a blue macintosh. It made hats fly and frocks dance. It set the lamplight fluttering as a bird flutters when an alien hand approaches its cage. The pavements were glistening with recent rain, and it made them shiver. The roadways were lakes of ebony, and it set broken pieces of the lamplight skating upon them. It whipped columns of chimney smoke into one maelstrom. Only the houses stood rigid before it; they acknowledged it as a man acknowledges a buzzing fly.

But to man himself it was no mere fly: it was unloosed power; and to the man in the blue macintosh, with whom we are concerned, it was destiny. Dead bricks it could not move, but the man in the blue macintosh, symbol of the immortal, was its toy; and it was now driving him, against half his will, to commit the sin that the other half wanted to commit. It first pestered his face, and stung his eyes, and chilled his hands, and filled his heart with its own rage: then it drove him out of his path into Bayswater.

He was faintly aware that he was grateful to the wind. By assuming the function of destiny it made his half-purpose a purpose. He hadn't really meant to turn into that road; he believed that he had meant to go past it; but while he stood at the corner, thinking the thing over, a sudden gust caught him under his macintosh and sent him running some paces down it. When the gust eased he found that he was actually in Leinster Gardens, and that to get out of it he would have to turn and battle again with the wind; and he was tired of battling. Here, clearly, was the hand-push of destiny. Useless to resist that. Being in Leinster Gardens, he felt that he was meant to go on. The affair had been decided for him by the wind. His infirmity of purpose now became upright, and he allowed that wind, which could not move the houses, to whirl him to disaster.

In the lavender dusk the interlocked squares and terraces of Bayswater made a map of the land of nightmare. The lines of tall dark houses looming upward and stretching forward to infinity; the lines of lamps that waited like a frozen guard for a procession that never came; the deep hush; the sudden enclosed spaces of whispering trees, and the insane repetition of terrace upon terrace—all this made this bourgeois quarter the apt setting for a tale of horror. Horror seldom grows among horror; almost always it springs up in the incongruous air of pastoral beauty or urban decorum; but if ever horror should outstrip itself in London, Bayswater should be its setting.

Now that he had got into Leinster Gardens, he began to walk up and down, and for half-an-hour he went up and down, pad-pad-pad, eye and mind directed to one house. By the disposition of the street lights he was sometimes energy and sometimes reverie. Now, as he crossed the amber radius of the lamplight, he lived as a man; now, as he passed into the interspaces of purple, he was an impalpable organism. That flickering march was a miniature of his life. Pad-pad-pad he went, fixed like a shuttle in a groove of two hundred yards, while all around him beat the life of this city of glittering distances.

At six o'clock he was in the house. He was standing behind a velvet hanging that draped the connecting door of the smoking-room and the study. He was on the study side, and was peering through the opening of the hanging into its dusky depths. He saw a large room strewn with rugs of Daghestan and Kerman and Coulas, and set with appointments that confirmed the rugs. Clearly the study of a rich man of over-opulent tastes. There were deep divan chairs in glowing yellow hide. The dark yellow walls were dressed with Oriental banners and curved weapons. On brackets and tables stood Buddhas and Sivas, large and small. On the mantel-shelf and on other shelves were idols with movable heads; with the passing of heavy traffic, their shaven crowns nodded in various rhythms, as at some secret thought. These figures nodding out of the shadows fascinated the man: he had the feeling of being spied upon. Elsewhere were great vases of the Sung and Ming period, and carvings in coral and rock-crystal; and on the desk in the centre of the room, scattered among ink-stand and cigar-box and lamp-standard, were a number of small figures and netsukes in old ivory. The dominant note of the room, struck by the rugs and taken up by the wallpaper, the vases, the idols, the chairs and the ivory, was gold; and this note expressed its owner.

At the moment when the man behind the curtain, no longer beaten by the wind, was relaxing in his purpose under the hush and warmth of the room, it received three bursts of light from its electric lamps, and his victim stood within his reach. Gold, or hues verging upon gold, was about his person as well as about his room. There was the hard bronze face, the amber-coloured waistcoat, the amber cigar-holder, the watch-chain, and the russet tie; and as he stood for a second or two by one of the rugs he had the appearance of a golden god in a setting of gold receiving the homage of his nodding priests. That was his last appearance in magnificence, and it was an appearance of four seconds only, for at the fifth second he was on his back across the desk, and the floor was littered with cigars and the little ivory figures.

With one spring the man in the macintosh fell upon him. With fingers at throat, he forced the head back and back. But it was an uncalculated spring; it was taken in the moment when resolution was weakening; and there was no certainty behind it. Even with his fingers at that throat he couldn't be sure that he was going to do it. Even in the next few ticks of the clock, when he had in his hand a gold dagger snatched from the desk—even then he wasn't sure that he was going to do it. He could still, if he wished, drop the dagger and take his fingers from the throat, and try to laugh it away as an insane joke, or a rough-

and-tumble assault. But he didn't know whether he *did* wish to do that; he didn't know what he wished to do; the room had softened and bewildered him; and he was trying to make a firm decision this way or that when the gold man made it for him.

The gold man wrenched his neck aside, and through closed jaws spluttered one word. On that word down came the dagger into the neck, and down it came again into the side just below the arm. As it was drawn back for a third stroke, and the pressure on the throat a little loosened, the gold man made a death-heave and broke away. They fell, and on the floor, among the litter of ivories, they struggled softly. The vibration set the solemn idols nodding to each other—Look, look, look! There were slow gasps and hot panting. They spluttered. The gold man could make no words, but the blue macintosh was crisp. "There—that's shut *your* mouth. *You* won't talk much more. How's *that?*"

A third time the dagger came down, this time full into the throat. There was a gurgle, a sigh, and then peace. The blue macintosh got up. It was done. After months of approaching it and retreating from it, of nursing it and dismissing it, it was done. He had tried to frighten himself out of it by visualising himself as a murderer in the dock and in the condemned cell and on the scaffold. He had tried to laugh himself out of it by imagining himself doing it—a ludicrous picture. He had tried to kill the idea by observing it from the outside as the silly antics of a fool. And now he had done it. Well, he must see about fixing things.

He stood over the body and bent himself to a question-mark, listening. But the great house was silent and still. Nobody had seen him enter; nobody, it seemed, had heard their struggle, and, by familiarity with the man's habits, he knew that nobody would come to the study until the dinner-gong was sounded. He looked down at the body and the blood-stained carpet and ivories, and then at his own clothes. No marks or stains that he could see. The dagger was still in the body, and could stay there; by his precaution of wearing gloves the haft could hold no clue. To assure himself that he had missed no danger-points he made a quick glance round the room, and in the moment of that glance his forehead froze. At every point of the room was something that grinned and nodded at him. Then he remembered the idols and laughed. But the moment was useful; it showed that he hadn't yet come to himself. He must wake up and be wary. One must be specially wary in matters like this—much more wary than in his ordinary business. He found himself shaking a little, and his thoughts had a tendency to stray from the immediate business. That wouldn't do. His eye caught the glint of a series of decanters and glasses. Perhaps they would help. He never touched anything like that when on his regular business; but this was different. It was a new crisis for him, and a little slowing-down of his nerves might be useful.

He stepped through the litter of ivories and cigars, and opened the first decanter and poured himself a drunkard's draught. It was brandy. He drank it in quick sips, neat, keeping his ears tightened for the tiniest sound. When it was done he found that he was still trembling, still unable to fix his mind on the best way of meeting the situation. He turned to the next decanter and took a liberal one from that—whisky. In a few seconds he felt more at ease. A goods van went past the house, and the idols, which had recovered from the vibrations of the struggle, were set nodding again. With ferocious geniality he nodded back at them. One more peg—then he would be ready for a clean exit. He took it, this time in one gulp; then went across to the switches and turned off the light.

And here came another spot of panic. The sudden plunge of darkness gave him the shock of an unexpected plunge downstairs. He could have screamed. It was so complete a darkness that it came with a burning pain upon his hot eyes, and in the sudden void of black he staggered and almost fell. Staring into it, seeking his way to the window, he could see the projected aureole of his own eyes just beyond the temples; and as he looked past that glow into the pit of darkness he saw it filled not with bloody faces or nodding idols, but with amorphous bodies of fear. The corners of the black room were breeding grey shadows, and the grey shadows bred purple shadows, and the purple shadows bred other shadows blacker even than the blackness of the room. Each shadow was a growth of new and stronger fear.

Never before had he been afraid, and he did not know how to handle himself. The knowledge that he was afraid surprised him. He made a gesture of bewilderment. Putting his hands to his face, he found that they were damp with sweat, and that his heart was a dynamo. The hostile mixture of brandy and whisky was working, and as the realisation of that went slowly into his brain and showed him his danger, instead of

sobering him, it made him laugh. He told himself that he was too old a
hand to be flustered by accidents. He was drunk. That's what it was—
drunk. Just that. Those shadows were whisky and brandy shadows.
They weren't there at all. Funny one should feel afraid of nothing just
because one had killed a brute.

Still, it would be wise to get away, and to get away as tactfully as he
had come. He went to the window, swaying across the rug and turning his
ankle on the scattered ivories. In the middle of the room he stopped and
listened, wondering whether his drunken self might not have made some
noise that his other self had not heard. But the whole house seemed as
stark and dumb as the corpse on the floor. Only the ticking of the clock,
for sound, and the nodding of the idols, for motion. Nothing else.

He put his gloved fingers to the window, raised it without noise, and
looked out. He waited for a lorry to pass; then slid to the sill. He pulled
the window down behind him. He reached forward from a kneeling position, and with one hand grasped a gutter-pipe that ran down the front
of the house to the area. With the animal grace of a dancer he swung
himself clear of the kitchen windows and landed on his toes by the en-
trance-porch of the next house. Some half-minute he stood there with the
air of one waiting for the bell to be answered. This was his method of
proving whether an exit had been "clean." It seemed that it was. He heard
no stir anywhere, and met no curious eyes. With a glance of apparent disappointment he went down the steps and walked casually away. The wind
was behind him, as it had been behind him at half-past five.

Once out and free, he was conscious of the wild air, and discovered
that in the last half-hour he had not taken one full breath. Breathing was
a momentary luxury, and he breathed deep. He filled his lungs with the
rushing air, breathing in time with his long steps. He was making for the
canal, where he had planned to sink his macintosh and soft hat, and he
was almost upon it when his long breathing defeated him. He was feeling once again master of himself and of the occasion when, without
warning, earth and sky were twisted into one, and the moon came reel-
ing and crashing through the wind into a chaos of nausea and vomit.

When, some minutes later, he came up from this collapse, he found
himself clinging to the railings of Porchester Square. His legs were weak

and his ears were buzzing and his eyes were blocked by a picture of the gold man's face as he last saw it when they lay wrestling on the floor. A popular dance-melody came into his head. He tried to drive it away by thinking of other melodies and of conversational phrases, but it came back and danced upon his brain. He began to be afraid that he would sing it or whistle it. That would never do. Mustn't attract attention. Must be careful. With a jerk he pulled himself up, loosened his collar and prepared to walk on.

It was at this moment of moving away that he first became clearly aware of a noise that had been troubling his ear under the dance-melody: a little clittering as of fairy castanets. He looked about him, into the square, along the railings, and then at the pavement, and as he saw how the noise was being made a frozen wire went down his spine. He was nearly a mile from the house in Leinster Gardens, but there they were. They had trotted after him, and they were now trotting round him—the little golden blood-stained netsukes. His brain was still slumbering under the drink, but at this sight it came to a kind of cloudy awakening that deceived him into thinking it was a true awakening. There they were, clearly enough, running round his feet, jumping, curvetting in the frightful contortions of Oriental carpets. They were making arabesques all round him.

He did not attempt to imagine how the thing had happened. It *had* happened; and he was sensible enough to see the danger of the situation. If people passed and saw him like this, they might come and ask awkward questions. Certainly they would remember having seen him with these things all round him; and they would make a guess that he had stolen them and dropped them in running; and they might speak to the next policeman. He must pick them up and hide them. He bent towards them, toppled, and fell on his hands. In that position he groped for them and snatched at them; but in his nervous haste he was clumsy, and they were too quick for him. They dodged and doubled, and danced under and over his hand. Not one could he hold, and meantime they pestered him and leapt about him, and vexed his eyes with their dartings. He felt one of them warm and wet against his cheek.

Well, if he couldn't pick them up he must get away. He had forgotten now about the canal and his macintosh. The important matter was to get away from these blood-stained things, and he clambered up and turned his back on them, and went with a quick lurch through the square. He kept as much out of the light as he could. To deceive them he made two or three crossings and recrossings of the road. In Gloucester Terrace he could see nothing of them, and was applauding himself at having shaken them off, when in Cleveland Square his ear told him that his stratagem had failed. Close behind him came the sound of castanets. Soon they caught up with him and encircled him. He broke through them, and they again encircled him. He kicked at them, but still they made their undisciplined ballet between his feet. Some of them leapt at him in lilliput anger. The faces of these held the features of the dead man on the floor. He tried to turn back towards the stir and glare of Harrow Road, where he might lose them, but they buzzed and twisted about his knees with the infuriating pester of mosquitoes. For peace he was compelled to go forward.

He went at a half-running pace, and all the time they were with him. They kept about him, before and behind, in a sort of open order. When he ran, they ran; when he trotted, they trotted; and when he kicked at them he kicked only the air. He was sobbing now, striking with arms and legs. As he stumbled on through the lamplit dusk of Craven Road he was aware that the few people who passed looked curiously at him. No wonder. A man being chased by little golden men.

But he was not now concerned with the figure he cut. He was mainly concerned with dodging these damnable things. They filled him with the crawling horror of necromancy. He felt that they had Satanic powers drawn from all the objects of that room, and from their owner. Whichever way he turned they were with him, sometimes driving him, sometimes impeding him. Some of them settled on his trousers. With inward gasps, he struck them off. Some of them jumped high in the air and pattered elfin clog-dances on the crown of his hat. They played about him with the intimate devilry of efreets. As they pattered and buzzed, it seemed to him that they called on other little golden things to join them. Coming into a half-lit square, he was met by a new host. He turned right and left, but only when he went straight on did they suspend their pestering. Even at those dark corners where he could not see them he could still hear them and feel them.

He went forward at a shamble, and as he went he thought again of the canal. If he could get there he might elude them. If he could get into the water they couldn't follow him there. He could swim across or stay in the water; they surely couldn't walk on water.

He turned for the canal, but as he turned they made a cloud about him, and he lost his direction. He could only go blindly forward.

Then, as he came out of the square into a side-street, they seemed to turn aside to his right, the whole host of them. He was fighting them with both arms when he saw that there was a clear space on his left, and that they had dropped behind him. Before him he saw an open door and a lighted hall. If he could get in there.

He got in. In the hall a man met him. He addressed the man in whimpering indignation. "I say—look here—all these things following me. Can't get along the street for them. Perfect pest."

"Oh? What's the trouble? What things?"

"Those things out there. Little golden men. Followed me from Leinster Gardens. Worse'n mosquitoes. All round one's face."

"Followed you from Leinster Gardens? Let's have a look at 'em. Here—hold up."

He swayed, and supported himself with an arm on the wall. "Ah—all the way from Leinster Gardens."

"I see. You better sit down a bit. Little golden men, eh? Leinster Gardens? Come and sit down."

The Inspector led him to a farther room, and spoke to two men in the room. "Just look after this man. He's a bit faint." The two men got up, and as one of them caught the Inspector's eye, he closed the door and stood against it. The Inspector went to the telephone at the desk in the hall, and the October gale continued to rush down the street and fill the hall with companies of yellow leaves.

MIRACLE IN SUBURBIA

In a back room of one of the many old houses still left along London's southern riverside, an elderly man and a youth sat at a table
and looked at each other. The man had a bird profile and a probing
eye, and the hands that were clasped on the table were large and thin
and white. The youth had no profile, and his hands were neither thin
nor white, but large and red. They appeared to worry him. Once or
twice he put them on the table, in imitation of the man's easy pose.
Then he seemed to see them in comparison with the man's, and hid
them. From time to time, as though they were forgetful of their unseem-
liness, they came again to the table, clasping and unclasping.

The room, too, seemed to worry him. It was an odd room; out of
character with that stretch of the riverside; such a room as the youth had
never seen there or elsewhere. He had seen museums and their contents. This room contained none of the things he had seen in museums,
but it was filled with things that were not everyday furniture—queer
things; and it had the feeling of a museum. He could not give names to
the things; he knew only that he had never seen them in the British Museum or in South Kensington. Weird-looking things. Queer-shaped jars.
Wooden sticks. Circular things. Triangular things. Yellow papers with
all sorts of squiggles on them. He didn't like the look of them, but his
eyes continued to rove about the room and return to them.

The man noted his uneasiness. "Have a drink?" He went to a sideboard, and began to get out some bottles.

The youth said hastily: "No-thanks. No-thanks. I—I'm not thirsty."
He was not averse from a drink. He liked a drink with his friends. But
he did not want a drink in this room with this man. Under his reason,
under even his sense, he was aware that he was being warned not to
have a drink here, not to stay here. The table warned him. The things
hanging on the wall warned him. The window-curtains warned him. The

very nostrils of the man talking to him warned him. The room seemed
to be murmuring with distant drums. All the objects in it were throwing
off something that went to the secret corners of his being, and said,
"Have nothing to do with this place. Get out while you can."

But he couldn't be so silly as to make a sudden bolt; neither the
man nor the room had so far afforded any reason for that. He would
obey the feeling so far as to refuse a drink—you never knew with drinks;
so easy to put something in 'em—but that urge to get out was probably
just nerves. The man seemed quite a nice chap, and he couldn't *see* anything wrong with the room. There was no danger anywhere; nobody
was threatening him. If the man tried to attack him, that would be different. That'd be a reason for getting out. But a mere "feeling" was silly,
and the feeling that he had about this room was probably due to his not
having seen a room like it before. He must fight it down. The man had
said he had a proposal to make which might be profitable to the youth,
and the youth could do with a proposal or two of that sort. He mustn't
allow "feelings" to interfere with business.

"Well, if you won't have a drink," the man was saying, "let's get on
with our talk. I spoke to you in the coffee-shop just now because you
looked a likely lad for the work I want done. A simple piece of work,
and I'd pay well. H'm."

"I could do with a job. Been out nearly a year now. Tramping about
every day looking for something. Can't find anything, though."

"No? I thought that was the case. Well, now, I just want a little bit of
work done, and I'll pay for it what you'd probably have to work half a
year for in the ordinary way. For this piece of work, which you can do in
an hour or two, I'll pay you—fifty pounds."

"Fifty pounds?"

"Fifty pounds."

The youth seemed to try to visualise fifty pounds—fifty pounds all at
once. The picture, and the effort to produce it, made him frown. He
became suspicious. "Fifty pounds. . . . Must be something queer if you'd
pay all that. Fifty pounds. . . . Must be something not right."

The man smiled. "I like your recoil. I appreciate it. But you need
have no hesitation on that score. The answer to your remark is, in a
sense, yes and no. That is, a little technical point of what is called wrong-

doing is involved. But not the kind of technical point that could get you into trouble. Just a matter of"—he laughed—"taking something from somebody. But listen!" He held up a hand to stop the youth's protest. "Taking something from somebody who stole it. A perfectly honourable proceeding. An act that a dozen men of spotless respectability would be willing to perform, if they were young enough and agile enough. And I'm willing to pay fifty pounds—sums of money convey little to me, though I realise that they mean something to others—because I need a young man whom I can trust. A young man to whom fifty pounds would be a symbol of a vow of silence. That was why I picked on you. It's like this."

He leaned back in his chair and held the youth with his eyes. The youth frowned again in the effort of concentrating on what might be a complicated story. "A very valuable relic has been taken from a museum with which I'm connected. If we make the loss public we're likely to lose it. It will go abroad. We want no publicity; no scandal. We want simply to get it back. We know who has it and where it is. And a smart young man could get it without any trouble. And would do a service to society. And—further—without any danger to himself whatever."

"Oh . . ." The youth pondered. It sounded all right, but coming from this particular man it didn't seem quite as right as it sounded. He was an honest youth, and never would have eased his troubles even by the lightest of crimes. Yet this man's eyes and voice swayed him. It seemed that he was asked to perform a straightforward, but not quite proper, service, and was to be handsomely paid for it and protected from all risk. Well, if it *was* all right, fifty pounds was fifty pounds. Without that handsome reward he would have said no to the proposal, even if the act was a service to society. He was not a hero, and saw no reason for implicating himself in other people's troubles. On the other hand, if it was not all right, a reward of a thousand pounds and complete immunity would not have tempted him to common theft. He couldn't quite "get" this man. His chief feeling was that it wasn't all right, but under this man's eyes he couldn't feel that it was wrong. It seemed to be a private row about public property, and if that was so his moral sense told him that he would be justified in accepting the job and restoring the thing, whatever it was, to its owners. Still, there were one or two funny points about it.

"But if it's all right and above board, and as easy as you say, why are you paying all that money for the job?"

"I've told you. Fifty pounds probably seems a lot of money to you, but it's nothing to the historic value of this relic. Anyway, I should not be paying that money for the mere job. I should be paying it, as I said, for a man's honesty and for his keeping quiet. This matter must not be talked about to anybody. It's a delicate matter. Might lead to trouble with other countries. You understand? That's why I need somebody who knows nothing of the circumstances surrounding the affair, and somebody who will forget it after he has performed his service. Somebody who will never mention that service—nor what the object of the service was. Particularly that. No mention of the nature of the relic."

"I'm not much of a talker at any time."

"I've observed that on my visits to the coffee-shop."

"But what's this about no trouble and no danger? How can that be? If I'm taking something from another chap, he naturally wouldn't let me. Or what about a copper seeing me do it?"

"Even if you were seen taking it, nobody could harm you. You will be protected. You will approach that man freely and you will come away freely. I have power to protect you, and my power will accompany you all the time."

"Power? You mean some of your people—some of those interested in the thing?"

The man smiled. "I see you don't understand. And perhaps it's as well you don't. You will be more efficient for the work. But there are powers other than the powers of the hands and limbs. There are powers other than the powers of the brain. There is a power of the spirit. That is the power that will protect you."

"Mmm. . . . Sounds all right. So do lots o' things. But if you got all this—what you call power, I should think you could get it back easy enough yourself. Just say, 'Presto, come over here,' like the conjurers." He giggled. Was this old chap drunk—him and his talk about taking things from people and being protected by power?

"I see you don't understand. And don't believe. We who have this power may not use it ourselves. We may use it only through an instrument. *Then* it is effective. And no harm can come to our instrument. We can place our protective power around him."

"How d'you make that out? S'posing the chap that's got this thing goes for me, and—"

"If he does, no harm can come to you. You do not believe, and it is not really necessary that you should. But perhaps I may convince you. Look, I am putting my power around you now. I am calling up the power within you. Now!"

He pushed back his chair and stood erect, looking down at the youth. For some seconds they stared at each other. In the moment of his rising the man's body seemed to fill the room and to be bursting from it. The lamp on the mantelshelf threw its shadows enormously on the wall, and the shadows copied their movements and became a secondary couple engaged in silent, sinister business. The youth was faintly sensible of some disturbance of the air; then of some change in himself—a feeling of confidence and strength.

The first instinct was that the man was putting something over on him. He resented this, and wasn't going to have it. He was glad he hadn't had that drink. But with the feeling of confidence his resentment passed. This was good. This wasn't the hypnotism he had heard about. He wasn't this man's dumb servant; he was his equal. He felt that all the things he had often seen himself doing, he could do; that he had abilities which he hadn't even guessed at but which this man perceived. He felt as though up to now he had been tied up; an inarticulate, ineffectual youth; and that this man had released him. He stretched both hands on the table, no longer ashamed of them, leaned back, and stared at the man.

"You feel something? ... Ah. ... That is my power meeting your power—blending with it and clothing you. You doubted what I said. It is natural that you should. These things are known to few. But now you are doubting your own doubts. My power is over you. And you are aware of it. Now I will convince you utterly that if you serve me in this matter you will be protected from every kind of harm. See!"

In one rhythmic movement the man swung to the wall, tore down from it a naked Turkish sword, whirled it above his head with a long arm, and brought its edge, full swing, down upon the youth's right wrist.

The youth said "Oo, I say!"

"Hurt you?"

"No. Give me a start, like. Wasn't expecting you to do that."

"Ha! Look at that blade's edge. Feel it."

"Jee! Blooming razor." Then he seemed to realise that something odd had happened. His voice rose to a squeak. "Here—but—but you slashed that across my wrist with all your might. You—you— A thing like that'd cut through a table. And you—"

"I did. Look at your wrist."

The youth examined the wrist. "Can't see anything. Not a mark even."

"Of course not. Didn't I tell you that my power was protecting you? Give me one of those logs from that box by the fire."

The youth took up an oak log-wedge of twelve-inch thickness—and placed it on the table. "Now see. My power is not protecting that log, and so—" He made a second swing of the sword and brought it down on the log. The log fell in two pieces.

The youth stared. "Jee!"

"That sword, as you say, would cut through a table. But it cannot cut through you. Nothing could. Nothing can in any way harm you. Between danger and you stands my power. And so you can do this little business for me—er—and my colleagues with no more risk than you would face in walking from here to your home. Does this evidence convince you?"

The youth's face was blank. His sense and brain were in effervescence. "Well, if blooming miracles is evidence . . ."

"It was not a miracle—in your sense. It was a fact. What is commonly called a miracle is only a fact of applied knowledge. Now, will you do a little bit of work for us?"

"Well, if it's absolutely straight—yes. But I don't want to be mixed up in any funny stuff."

"It *is* absolutely straight. The circumstances of the affair prevent my giving you proof of that. You must take my word for it. That you will be guaranteed against all danger I have already proved. Nobody need be ashamed of performing such a service as this—the recovery of a valuable relic for its owners. . . ."

"Well, what do you want me to do? And what is this thing?"

"The thing"—the man lowered his voice, and for a moment seemed to lose the suggestion of bulk—"the thing is a porcelain goblet."

"Porce—*what?*"

"A por—a china jar. A simple china jar. But very old. And of great historic value. You will simply take it from the man and bring it here."

"Simply take it. . . . And what'll he do?"

"He may make some resistance, but no matter what he does he cannot harm you. I thought I had made that clear."

"Yes . . . yes . . . er . . . I see. You mean there might be a schemozzle but me being like I am now, his stuff won't come off. Like the sword? That's it, eh?"

"That's it exactly."

"Don't hardly seem able to believe it. More like a dream."

"Well, you have had proof with the sword. And you will have further proof. Now follow your instructions. . . . At half-past eleven to-night a man will come from a house in Sloane Street and walk along Sloane Square. A short man in spectacles, wearing a fawn overcoat and bowler hat. He will be carrying an attaché case. If he is not carrying a case the—er—jar will be in his overcoat pocket. He will go through that narrow street by the District station—he will be making for Pimlico Road. When he is in that narrow street, you will approach him and snatch the case, or take the jar from his pocket, and bring it here to me."

The youth, stirred by this picture of daring doings, giggled. "Sounds easy."

The man folded his arms and looked at him with cold eyes. "It *will* be easy."

The youth got up. "Y'know, I believe it will. You could make a chap believe anything in this room. I don't understand it, but after that sword . . ."

"Good. I see that you believe, and that you know you can do what I want. Here—" He put a hand inside his coat and brought out a bundle of treasury notes. "Fifty, if you count them, I think."

The youth stared. "Caw! This is a rum joint. Paying me before I've earned it. Before I've done the job."

"You will earn it. I am passing this over as proof of *my* good faith. Your good faith will be proved by your performance."

"But s'pose I was to bunk with the bag?"

"You will not bunk with the bag. For one thing, you are not that kind of young man. I know you. Anyway, the bag would not be worth five shillings, and the—the china jar has no commercial value. You could not sell it. But I—" For a moment he forgot the youth, and again he seemed to fill the room. "I, with that goblet, am lord of all beauty. With the Bool Museum goblet, I am lord of all—"

"You're how much?"

He recovered himself. "Er—I said claiming that goblet is a laudable duty."

"But s'pose I was copped by a motor-bus and smashed up?"

He made a *tch* of irritation. "How many times am I to tell you that so far as this matter is concerned, you are under protection. Now and always. You cannot be harmed by anything arising from this matter—neither now nor at any time. I am protecting you. Now are you ready?"

The youth made but a momentary hesitation. Then—"Yes, I'll do it."

"Good. It is now half-past ten. You have plenty of time for the journey to Sloane Square. You have your instructions. Make no mistake in them. I shall expect you back soon after twelve." He opened the door and led the way into the passage, and so to the front door.

The youth walked out with light step and swinging shoulders. His gaze was direct and his movements sharp. Within the last hour he had developed a profile. He was not aware of this himself; he was aware only that he was "feeling fine." Whether this was due to the fifty pounds in his pocket, to the thing he had witnessed in that room, or to something else, he did not know. He was content to feel fine and to go upon his errand.

As he went, he chuckled in self-communion. "Jee! Talk about the age of miracles. If anybody'd told me I'd a-seen a thing like that in these streets . . . He's a Dr. Caligari, he is. Almost frightens you, seeing a thing like that. And yet it don't. I don't feel that way at all. Going to do a hold-up and get away with it. Still, he says it's all right. Only taking something from a thief for them it belongs to. Wonder if it does belong to 'em? Still, he seems all right. And I made it clear I wouldn't touch it if it wasn't straight. I got a clear conscience on that. And I got me fifty pounds anyway. Better drop that at home on me way. Case there's anything sticky about the business, and it goes wrong. Then at least they'll have that to help 'em. But I reckon it'll be all right. He *makes* you feel everything's all right."

At half-past eleven he was waiting in the shadow by the Sloane Square District station. He had been there for fifteen minutes, waiting for the half-hour with no more trepidation than if he were waiting for a bus. He was wondering no more about the business; he seemed to be outside it, half-asleep. His mind would not be interested in it; even when the man appeared his pulse remained unchanged.

The man appeared at three minutes past the half-hour. He came into the Square from Sloane Street—a small man in spectacles, wearing a fawn overcoat and bowler hat, and carrying an attaché case. He walked softly, his eyes primly fixed on the pavement. He passed the youth without raising his eyes, and turned into the side-street. The youth followed, as casually as though he were merely walking that way, too.

Then, in the middle of the street, where the light was dim, he moved more quickly. A few paces brought him right behind the man. One hand, with a clean flash, grabbed the man's wrist; the other snatched the case.

That was easy. What would happen next he did not know, but he turned to make swiftly, without running, for Sloane Square. But this was not to be so easy. Before he had taken three paces the man was upon him. Two iron arms, unexpected from so slight a man, went round him. He staggered on his heels. One of the arms slid down his arm to reach the case. He closed his fingers over its handle, and gave a violent backward kick. It met a shin, and with its impact, there was a moment's easing of the arms. The youth took that moment to slip through the arms downward to the ground.

With his free arm he caught the man behind the knees, and they came down together. Silent, save for their gasping, they rolled on each other across the pavement. The man did not strike him, but fought for the hand that held the case. The youth held to it fiercely, struggling to rise. Then, with a sudden movement from the man, he found himself underneath, lying on his back with his neck against the curb. He made a few sharp struggles to reverse the positions, but within a second or so he saw that they were useless, and his throat went dry.

The dim light had shown him the man's hand shooting to his coat. Next moment he saw the hand lifted, and alongside the hand the dim light was caught by the blade of an open razor.

The youth's left hand still clutched the case. With his right he made a feeble effort to hold the man away, but the man, with his strong left, bent the arm back. The youth saw the razor sweeping down. Instinctively he shut his eyes. He felt the razor slash across his neck. He felt it go deep into each side. He gurgled and was aware of floating away.

It was a mere muscular movement that caused him to open his eyes, and it was then that he remembered what he had momentarily forgotten—that he was under protection. He opened his eyes to see that the man, half-squatting, had drawn back from him and was staring at him—at his neck—with eyes in which was a light of horror. With another instinctive movement the youth put his hand to his neck. His neck was whole. No wound. No pain. The man still held the open razor and looked stupidly at it. It was spotless.

Gripping the case, the youth rolled over and got to his feet. The man scrambled up with him and held out a hand. "Here—my case—my case." It was a plea more than a demand. The youth ignored it. He moved away, and the man with the strong arms put out a weak hand to detain him. "My case—my case."

Round the corner came a constable. He looked at their dusty clothes and torn collars. "What's all this? What's this?"

The youth answered him. "It's all right. Just a private dust-up. We're moving on now."

"Do it then."

The man tried to say something. "He—he—he—" and seemed unable to find further words.

"Well, what did he do?"

"He—he—he—"

"Now come on. Pack up and get home. And take more water with it."

The youth said, "All right," and went easily towards Sloane Square with the case. Behind him he heard the little man saying, "No, but he—he—he—" and the constable saying, "Come on now—take a walk." He saw the constable wave the little man towards Pimlico Road, and he saw the little man tamely go.

On the platform of the District station he waited for an east-bound train. Four times while waiting he said, "Jee!" Not in a mood of chuckling but in a mood of awe. He felt a little sick—not because he had been wounded but because he hadn't been wounded.

Half an hour later he delivered the case to the old man and went home. He got into bed with a blunt prayer—Jee!

For the next week life was good to him. Out of his vast store of fifty pounds, he used half-crowns and five-shillings at a time, presenting them to his mother as wages he had received for odd jobs. He took in delicacies for her tea. He bought his young sister a needed pair of boots. He saw prosperity ahead. Before it was exhausted he would certainly get a job; one bit of luck always led to another. Or with that capital he might start a little business. Or with ten or fifteen pounds of it he might go into partnership with a stall-holder.

Anyway, he was on his feet again, and all through meeting that—he almost thought of him as That Old Bonehead—a name which he and his friend, Fred, had used when discussing the old man in the coffee-shop. But after what had happened he couldn't use that term. He was a little afraid; it would be like mocking thunder and lightning. Something more respectful was needed, but he couldn't think of any word that would fit such an overwhelming man. The only events he knew comparable with what had happened were those he had learned of in religious lessons in school—making the sun stand still and those chaps that walked in the furnace. And you couldn't quite put a man who lived three streets away from you in an everyday suburb, in that class. That was Holy, and this man wasn't Holy. On the other hand, he must certainly be the most wonderful man in the world. He compromised by thinking of him as The Wonderful Old Man.

Once or twice during the week he felt a little twinge in his neck. But when he examined it in the mirror there was nothing to be seen; just a clean white neck, as usual. He concluded that the little man must have gripped his neck before he struck, and given a slight sprain to a small bone. You got that kind of thing sometimes at football on Saturdays, and often didn't feel it till the middle of the next week. After the second twinge, he ignored it, and went cheerfully about his plans for laying out his money.

Nine days after his little adventure he had his seven-o'clock tea, with two kippers, and then went into the parlour of their little four-room home, to read the evening paper and a book he had borrowed from the Free Library—a book which he found hard to read but which he wanted to read: a book on the Magic of the Ancients.

Half an hour later his friend Fred called. The youth's mother opened the door to him. "Hullo, Fred."

"Hullo, Mrs. Brown. Joe in?"

"Yes. He's in the parlour, reading, I think."

"Got a bit of news for him. He ever tell you about an old man we've met in Harry's coffee-shop?"

"No. Not that I remember."

"Ah. You hear a bang just now?"

"Might have. Yes, I believe I did. But there's all sorts of bangs around here. Lorries back-firing and that. You don't notice 'em."

"Well, the old man's blown himself up."

"Blown himself up?"

"Yes. Making some experiment, I suppose, and blown the house and himself all to bits. The whole front of the house. Blown clean out. I just come from it. There's crowds staring at it. Thousands. I thought Joe might like to come and have a look."

"Ah. Well, you'll find him in there. I must get on with me washing."

Fred opened the parlour door and stepped in, beginning his story with "I say, Joe, there's a—" And then Mrs. Brown heard a scream. She bustled into the passage. "What's the matter, Fred? Whatever's the matter?"

Fred stepped back into the passage with white face and open jaws. He put out an arm. "Don't go in. Don't go. Keep out."

"Why—why? What—what is it?"

But Fred could only say "Don't—don't go in. His throat! His throat!"

YESTERDAY STREET

Dominic left the taxi at the foot of the High Street, and settled himself to look up the length of the street from the station to the Park. Its features met his eye so familiarly that, though forty years had passed since he last walked along it, he felt that he had left it but a month ago. There had been little rebuilding. He saw motors and taxis in place of carriages and cabs, and motor-buses and electric trams in place of the old horse-vehicles, and a movie-theatre where the Gospel Hall had been.

But there, unchanged, was the draper's whose Christmas windows had been his delight. There, too, were the little side-streets, changed only in the direction of creeping shabbiness; and there was the very sweet-stuff shop which had once had his halfpennies and pennies, its window arranged precisely as in the past. There was the Diamond Jubilee Clock Tower. There was the Italian restaurant. And there was the confectioner's, whose window, occupied each December by a Christmas cake of twelve huge tiers, had been one of the Christmas sights of North London.

Noting these points, he thought, as all men think on Going Back—Had he really been away forty years? Or did he only fancy it? Had all those things—what he called his Life—really happened to him, or had he only invented them as something he would like to happen? Had he really lived in a dozen countries, and was he really rich and living in a suite at the Palermo? Funny thing, growth.

Often, in the past, he had thought of the place, and of the boy who used to live in it, but the thought had been merely abstract and perfunctory; he hadn't been interested. Now, with his feet on its stones, he found how easily he could recapture it all, and how thickly long-buried memories perked up. The confectioner's, bearing the same name and the same fascia front as in his day, reminded him that he used to buy there, from a table in the doorway, assortments of yesterday's cakes—two

117

or three for a penny. And with that came memory of a crime, when once, in buying a pennyworth, he had, by sleight of hand, gone off with five instead of three. He looked away from the shop; he had an idea that the back of his neck was blushing. Two shops into which he could see had, in his day, been kept by erect, slightly-grey men, with beards. It had been the custom, he remembered, to slip into the doorways of those shops and shout "Kruger!" and run. They were now kept, he noted, by bald, withered men; but in the movements of those men he recognised the terrifying seniors of his own day. He felt that if they looked at him he would run.

He turned and went slowly up the street, noting on right and left many a familiar name. He tried to discover the effect upon him of see-ing again a crude kind of life with which for years he had had nothing to do, and at first he could not locate or name it, definite though it was. Then, as he went farther into the street, he found that he felt, of all things, just a little frightened. Yes; it *was* a little frightening to re-cross the threshold of the past, and to see again so much of the furniture of his early life in the position in which he had left it. There it stood, as though in a locked room, just as when he had said farewell to it (as he thought, for ever) and had left his boyhood there, and entered youth and manhood elsewhere. Walking among it now, unlocking it, as it were, he caught all the stored odours of that boyhood, and half-wished that the street had been pulled down and rebuilt. For of these buildings almost every one had known him and had received something of him. Through forty years he had been moving, changing, widening his inter-ests, seeing and hearing new things, and living six different kinds of life. While here, static and scarcely touched by the forty years which had given him forty outlooks and a million emotions, here were the relics and fix-tures of the beginning of it all—a beginning he had until now forgotten.

Strolling up to the Clock Tower, the thought came to him that with the High Street almost as it was, the little fountain still there, the Park just as it was, and those two old men still there, it was possible that his own street was still there—Levant Street, wasn't it? And just possible that his very home was still there—the little cottage with the tiny front garden. And even possible that the garden had the same flowers—London Pride, he thought they were. In coming here he had had no thought of seeking out his home; he had assumed that it would long ago have been swept away. He had come merely to look at the old suburb, though he couldn't have said why he wanted to look at it; why the fancy, or rather imperative desire, should suddenly have possessed him on this particular morning to go and look at it. For the past ten years he had made extended visits to London three times a year, and never once had he even thought of coming here. Yet this morning the fancy to see the place had been so strong that he had meekly followed it. Now that he was here, and so little change had happened, he decided to look for Levant Street. With all the other old stuff and old people still here, it was quite likely that the street and the old cottage were still here. Where forty years had left no mark, anything was possible. Everything about the place, he thought, was so set and solid, that it even wouldn't surprise him to find the boys still there—just as he had left them—Jimmy Gregory, his special friend, and—who was it?—yes, Victor Jones—and—ah, yes—Jenny Wrenn. The High Street and the shops hadn't grown up, so perhaps . . .

He shook his shoulders. Stop it. You're getting morbid. You're a bit depressed at Coming Back, and finding it all as it was. One ought to be able to look at it coldly—as a cast-off skin. But one can't. Funny. . . . Street looks bright enough, and yet it's all—somehow—melancholy. Aching. As though there were a shadow behind it, pressing on me. Pulling me and claiming me.

He stopped by the brown granite pillars of the familiar grocery store, and here his mind began to waver between the man he was, with his affairs centred in a suite at the Palermo, and the boy he had been. For a while he could not fix himself in either. Then, staring about the street, he found that his visual memory had called up the faces of those boys and their clothes, and his ear had called up their voices, not vaguely, as in reverie, but vividly. And Jenny Wrenn. Little Jenny Wrenn, the fourth party of the quartet. It was the thought of her, on this spot, and the clear image of her, that for a space blurred the fact of his Palermo life, and took him right back. The forty years, the travel, the experience, and the money now slid out of his mind and left it empty, save for three boys and a girl in these streets.

Memories fell upon him as sharply and as separately as raindrops. How many times he had come with her, or she with him, to this very store, each pretending to assist the other in "errands" for their mothers? And how many times they had gone laggingly home in the winter twilight, hand in hand, and silent. Jenny Wrenn in her blue-and-white pinafore and darned stockings and red tam o' shanter. Jenny Wrenn with the brown hair and the solemn eyes and the trick of standing on one leg and nursing the ankle of the other in her hand. How often they had stood together at dark corners, thrilling to the music of a street-organ. How often she had brought him buttonholes of marigolds from her front garden. How often they had waited for each other after school and gone on forbidden walks in the Park. How often they had "joined" things—the Band of Hope, the Sunday School—so that they might be more together.

He was letting these memories come to him on the pavement outside the store, when, in one special moment, there came with the memories the odour and flavour of strawberries and cream—and so potently that the dish might have been in his hands. He recalled then that their last meeting had been over a feast of strawberries and cream provided for them by the childless and "comfortable" widow, Mrs. Johnson, in honour of his leaving school and going away.

Following this came a sharp memory of a long-distant summer. Had the memory come when he had left his taxi, it would have been of something from a remote world and of another creature; but outside this store it came to him as intimately as last week. It was a summer when he and Jenny Wrenn had been sent together for a fortnight at a farm in Surrey. He recalled fourteen days and evenings of bliss. Of climbing trees, and lying in the sapphire dusk of the wood, and knocking each other about, and getting bad-tempered, and calling each other nasty names, and "making it up." He recalled the afternoon when he had buried her too deeply in the hay, and she had struggled out and fought him with real hatred. And he recalled those quiet half-hours in the coppice before bed-time, when they had sat on a low branch of a tree and stared at the country, and held hands, and didn't know why.

Fourteen days and evenings of bliss; two hundred and twenty-four hours of active being, every ten minutes of which had been *lived.* Since those days he had given much of his leisure to poetry, and had even played at the practice of it. But though to-day his mind was stored with it, and though as a boy he had known nothing about it, he realised now that he had known something better. He had known poetry itself, and had lived it. He wondered again whether he had ever really had any life than that; and then he was irritated with himself for wondering such nonsense. He moved away from the store and jerked himself back to his everyday, and wished he hadn't come to this dilapidated suburb.

He decided that he wouldn't stay long. He had a lunch appointment at the Palermo with some friends who had never seen this London suburb, and could not have said where it was; friends who had never played marbles in a side-street. He would just go along and see if Levant Street was still there, and then he would find a taxi and get out of this place which, much against his expectation, was so depressing and disarranging him. He had thought to look at it with superior eyes—success kindly glancing at its early beginning; but it wasn't following the rules. It was gripping him and reclaiming him. If he had guessed that it would be doing this to him he wouldn't have obeyed that sudden wish and wasted a morning on it. However, now he was here, he would just take a look at the old street, if it was still there, and then get back to civilisation.

He strolled along the High Street to the point where he remembered his street had stood, and with not much surprise he found it still there. Where, in his day, the corner shops had been a cheap greengrocer's and a cheap butcher's, they were now a tobacconist's and a cheap draper's; but generally the silhouette of the street was the same. At the top end was a new row of flats, but beyond them still stood the school and the little houses with their tiny front gardens.

He stood for a moment looking into it, and again the Palermo and the rest of his life was swept out of his mind, and again, as he entered the street, a troop of things-past entered and took possession of him, and changed him from the serious figure known to many serious people into just Don, a boy of thirteen. He entered it with timid, hesitating steps, and the "frightened" feeling was a little stronger here than it had been in the High Street. From the school downward, the rest of its length held all the points it had held forty years ago. The little front gardens, some trim, some neglected; the Chapel; the little shops; the tiny public-house; and the one house which belonged to a century ago, set back behind a carriage-sweep, empty in his day and empty now.

Before each of these points he paused, his mind dazzled by a confetti of memories which the sight of each showered upon him. Then, very slowly, he moved on to look for number 64, and point by point—each clearly remembered—he came to it. There it was—almost as he had left it. Number 64, the little house which had been his first home. And sure enough, its garden was still bright with London Pride. He crossed the street and stood before it. Smaller, of course, than when he was a boy. He had expected that. Windows which look large to children, and knockers which only an effort can lift, become minute when seen again through the eyes of manhood. But, though smaller, it was still itself. The wooden palings, the fanlight, and the cobblestone edging to the bed of London Pride were just as he had left them. In imagination he looked beyond its door and saw the little rooms which had known him so intimately; which had known his first breath and his first dreams, and which held, as it were, the spiritual fingerprints of the creature he had been and now was not, and yet was. In that little house were preserved, as in acid or in amber, all the little moments, the particles of himself, which he had given it.

And as he stood before it, it seemed to him that all those particles came rushing out to greet him, bringing with them excitement, amusement, sadness, and here and there a touch of shame. Here, even more clearly than in the High Street, he could see himself; and it was disconcerting thus to see himself. Between the two, that self and this self, he was aware of reproach, regret, disappointment, weariness.

He did not look long. He stayed only for an aching minute; then turned away. But in turning away he sent a glance down the street towards other of the little houses where he had been a guest of schoolfriends.

And then, with head half-turned, he stumbled off the kerb, and was only half-aware that he had stumbled. He did not step back to the kerb. He stood where he was and kept his glance where it was. His glance was held by the little house numbered 82, and he gave it even more attention than he had given to his own house. His mind spoke the number, "Eighty-two." Yes; that was right. That had been her house.

He stepped back to the pavement and continued to gaze at number 82. He could not take his eyes from number 82, because, outside number 82, leaning against the wooden gate of the little garden, filled, as in the past, with marigolds, was a slim figure in red tammy and blue-and-white pinafore, standing on one leg.

Manhood had taught him to control all outward expression of emotion, and the two people who were then passing saw only a middle-aged man stepping on to the pavement and looking idly at the houses opposite. They saw no staring eyes or pursed lips or rutted frown, but his mental state was that which some people express in this way. His face and eyes were calm; it was the spasm that went across his chest and down his spine which was the private equivalent of staring eyes and pursed lips. The resemblance of the scene to the scenes of forty years ago was so acute that for a few moments he could only pace up and down. The very house—and outside it a child matching in every detail, so far as he could see, the Jenny Wrenn who had lived there and had been his sweetheart. It was so striking a likeness that in default of any other explanation he wondered whether his Jenny Wrenn could still be there and this child her grand-daughter. If she were there, he wondered whether he could face her, and decided that he couldn't, and again wished he hadn't come.

But, being here, he wanted to know; so, under pretence of examining the numbers of the houses, he began to cross the street. He did not wish to embarrass or scare the child by looking closely at her, but he wanted a nearer view. He proposed to pass her, and pause, and ask if she knew a Mrs.—he would invent a name. But he had scarcely reached the middle of the road when he stopped. From that point he could see something which made the likeness frighteningly exact. There, on the brown stocking of the left leg, was the self-same darn in black wool which, he remembered, had so distressed his Jenny's sense of fitness. At sight of that, the "frightened" feeling which this Coming Back had inspired reached its crisis and became panic. He felt that he must get out of that street—and quickly.

But he was not allowed to get out. Even as he turned she removed any scruple he had had of embarrassing or scaring her, and offered him every chance of looking closely at her. She came forward from the gate, and stepped into the road, and stood in front of him. Then as she stood there, swinging one leg backward and forward in the familiar way, a hotter spasm went across his chest. Jenny Wrenn looked at him and smiled and said: "Hullo, Don. Where you been? Jimmy Gregory's looking for you."

Standing in the middle of the road, he stared deep into the young face; stared for some seconds. Then, forgetting his panic, forgetting himself and all rule and all law, he said, without thinking and very softly: "O-oh. . . . It's really *you.* You're still here?" The screwed-up black eyes gave him a mischievous smile. Through the smile she said: "Why, of course. Look—Jimmy Gregory wants you."

He turned; and there, in the school play-ground, was Jimmy Gregory, waving to him and running. And down the street he saw Victor Jones coming towards them with his usual weary slouch. And, as both boys approached them, Jenny sidled up to him and leaned upon him, as she always did; and in that moment he was no more depressed or frightened or amazed. The common air of that little street became in that moment a great and gentle wave of peace and well-being which poured upon him and through him. Lacing the air was the faint odour of strawberries and cream.

One little spot of everyday remained with him to tell him that the oddest thing about all this was that none of them seemed to recognise that he was grown-up, or to pay any attention to his gold-headed cane and his slim, brilliant boots. They treated him as they always had treated him. He looked up the street to the point where it entered the High Street, and he saw that everything of the High Street was as it was five minutes ago—taxis, motor-buses, electric trams—and that the little houses among which they stood were showing wireless aerials. Yet there they were, the four of them, making a casual cluster in the roadway, as usual, giggling and talking of this and of that—of what their teacher had said or done that morning; of the magic-lantern show at the Chapel last night; of the coming Band of Hope Treat. They were all going that evening—all four of them—to get their tickets for the Treat, and he found himself telling them that he had heard that part of the Treat would be a nigger entertainment. From somewhere unseen came the pathetic music of a street-organ. It was playing a popular song of their time—a song he had once thought "lovely"—*Little Dolly Daydream.* Jenny began twinkling her feet to its time.

The last remnants of his to-day self slipped from him. He found it impossible to think, and, having tried, found that he didn't want to. He was caught in some silver-silken net, and he was content to be caught. He couldn't bother to make out what had gone wrong (or perhaps right) with Space and Time; he accepted as a fact that the modern world was all about him, and that here he was with his gold-headed cane and the children he had known long ago. And they were real; visible and touchable. He tested this by giving a gentle tug at one of Jenny's curls, as he had often done. She replied by jerking her head and butting his arm—hard enough to hurt. After that, he was conscious of nothing save that he was Don among his old friends, with a faint memory of having been other things.

Jimmy Gregory nudged him. "Got your marbles?" He said: "No. Left 'em indoors." "All right—lend you some of mine. You can pay what you lose after dinner."

Then he and Jimmy Gregory were crouched in the roadway playing marbles, and Jenny was stooping over them, with brown curls hanging, bubbling rude remarks about his bad play; and he was very happy. He found, while playing, that his gold cane *had* been noticed, and that, most oddly, they did not question it or appear to regard it as unusual. Jenny took it from him—"I'll hold that stick while you're playing—or trying to."

At the end of the game he had lost heavily. He had borrowed ten of Jimmy Gregory's marbles, and, despite a few fluking wins, which at one time gave him sixteen, had lost the lot. "That's ten," Jimmy said; and Dominic said: "That's right. I'll bring 'em out after dinner. See you before class." "That's all right."

Jenny wanted to know what he was going to have for dinner, but he had no information. He never had known until he got home. Jenny reported that she had seen her mother preparing a large steak pie. Gregory and Jones looked wistful. Then, with the sudden transitions of boys, Jones caught him by the shoulder. "Look here, Don—know why you're always losing?"

"No." He listened with respect to Jones. Jones always knew things—except the kind of things you learn in school, which he never could learn.

"Well, you haven't got the knack. You put your thumb too far back on the finger. Look here—this is how."

They stooped over the little hole in the roadway, and Jones took Dominic's large hand in his small hand, without appearing to notice its size, and bent the large thumb to the right position on the large finger. "Now try." He tried, and found that the marble had better direction. "I see. I see, Vic. Thanks for the tip."

For some few more minutes they stood talking, arms on each other's shoulders. Then, abruptly as they had met, they parted; and the episode was ended. Jenny was just asking what they should do now, and Gregory and Jones were suggesting a game of egg-cap, when a factory-hooter sent out its melancholy howl. In chorus they said "Hooter. One o'clock," and turned to break up. Dominic too turned; he knew that one o'clock was dinner-time in their homes and his. Gregory and Jones sauntered down the street, looking back to cry "See you after." Jenny slipped into her garden and pulled a marigold, and came to him and stuck it in his coat, with gurgles of laughter. Under the laughing, with her face close to his, she whispered "After school?" He nodded. "Go over the Park—round the Fern Pond?" He nodded and she nodded. They parted in a ballet of conspiratory nods. He saw her slip into her house, and saw the door close on her waving hand. Then, save for three commonplace women, he was alone in that little by-street. Alone, but with dusty trouser-knees, and with a marigold in his coat.

He did not remember getting out of the street. The next thing he knew was that he had reached the High Street, and was moving a little unsteadily, and blinking at the speeding traffic. The glowing peace that had enveloped him and filled him while with the children was gone, and he was now aware, not of his earlier depression and fright, but of disturbance; a shake-up of his inner being and of his relations with daily life. He knew that he had in his nature a dark streak of the dreamer, and was sometimes apt to let imagination and fancy play a little wantonly. But he also knew that what had happened had been no prank of imagination or fancy; no trance or dream-state. What had happened had happened as definitely and as really as the passing of those motor-buses and taxis. The children had been there, and they had been real; and they were there now. He could see them, he was sure, again. Though perhaps nobody else could.

He realised that he had been visited by an Experience; something that had never before visited his sober life. But that was all he did know. Neither imagination nor fancy could suggest why he should have had this particular Experience just now. He had met none of the other people he had known in those days—not his mother, or Jenny's mother, or Mrs. Johnson, or the school-teachers. Only those three. But he had had the Experience. There was the marigold in his coat, and he could still feel the bump on the arm which Jenny's head had given him.

They had all gone in to their dinner, but he did not go to his dinner, or to his lunch. He forgot the Palermo appointment; forgot everything save his mental chaos. He was just able to retain enough control to recognise that it was chaos.

He lifted his stick to an empty taxi, and ordered the driver to Westminster. At a Westminster garage he hired a car. "Drive into the country. What? Oh, anywhere you like, so long as it's the country."

Once out of London, with the car open, and trees and fields and hills and sky about him, his mind cooled. He did not try to think out his adventure; he lay back in the car and brooded upon it. Underneath the disturbance he was aware of a little thrill of delight. The figure of Jenny, and her chatter, remained close to him and held an aroma of—of what? Violets? Daffodils? Hawthorn? The image of London, and of the Palermo and its dining-room and grill-room, and of the solid, adult people who lived there or lunched there, came to him distastefully. Thrusting themselves into his mind, also distastefully, came the people he would have to see to-morrow—City people, who took him seriously as a business-man. He half-wished that they could have seen him playing marbles.

Brooding upon Jenny and the boys, he began to see that the ache of which for many years he had been conscious, and of which many middle-aged men are conscious, was simply an unappeased desire to return to the point where the thread of childhood's other-world had been snapped. By some grace he had been allowed, just for an hour, to return.

He did not notice where the car was going or in what county they were. He noticed only green-hedged lanes and high downs and skies and rushing air, and it was not until he realised that these things had been around him for some long time that he looked at his watch. Five o'clock. By force of habit, the sight of five o'clock on his watch told him that he needed tea, and he took up the speaking-tube and directed the chauffeur to stop at the next decent-looking inn.

After passing two or three at which the chauffeur shook his head, they stopped at a trim little place on a river-bank. "You'll find this all right, sir." He entered the inn's little lounge, gave an order to the land-lord for tea, and for the chauffeur's tea, and sat down by the window. The landlord bustled out and within a few seconds bustled back.

"Seen to-day's paper, sir?"

"No. . . . Thanks very much." It was not true. He had, in fact, seen six papers but had scarcely looked at them. He had seen them in bed, with his early tea, and had glanced at the political article and the foreign page of one of them, and had then decided on his visit to his old sub-urb, and had tossed the rest aside. He took the paper from the landlord listlessly, and went on staring through the window. But the view from the window was not attractive, and he began idly to look through the paper. It was necessary, before to-morrow, that he should re-adjust him-self to the man he was. It was for this reason that he had taken the car trip. The paper might be an additional help.

Drinking his tea, he ran his eye down column after column. The paper was one of the popular sort, with all the popular features. With-out absorbing what he was reading he read the facetious column; read the Social Gossip column; read the Special Article; and wondered whether anybody else ever read these things. He turned to the second-ary news page and the provincial reports. For a few seconds he glanced at this as he had glanced at the other pages, and was about to drop the paper when his glancing changed to positive attention. His eye, as though under guidance, fell upon three paragraphs in different columns of the page. It ignored all the rest of the page and went one—two—three—to the different points. They brought him from his slack, loung-ing attitude, and made him sit upright. His casual interest became eager. His tea became cold.

He read them one by one, and when he had read them he sat back again and stared at the flowered wallpaper. He stared motionless for some twenty minutes, and at the end of that time his disturbance had gone, and he was himself.

He got up, put the paper gently aside, and strolled out to the passage to settle his bill. The landlord, in taking his money, noted his quiet smile, and spoke about it in the kitchen. It was the smile of a man who appeared to like the place and to find it good. The chauffeur, too, noted it, and returned it.

"Back to the shadows now."

"Beg pardon, sir?"

"Back to the old Palermo."

"Very good, sir."

The paragraphs which had caught his attention were three small news items. There had been a motor smash in Devon, in which two people were killed. One of them was a James Gregory, director of a chemical works. There had been a fatal fire-damp disaster at a northern colliery. The chief engineer, Victor Jones, in attempting a rescue, had himself perished. There had been a climbing disaster in the Alps, which had resulted in the death of three tourists; among them an Englishwoman, a Miss Jane Wrenn, school-teacher, of London.

Funspot

Once a month Morton passed that street. The business of the firm for which he worked as a collector took him once a month to an office just beyond the limits of the recent spread of the City; an office which called itself City, but was, indeed, North-East.

To reach that office from the Tube station he had to pass that street, and after passing it once a month for two years he found that it had grown upon him and become part of his imaginative life. Every time he passed it, its name, in conjunction with its dark, dishevelled aspect, struck him as bizarre.

After a while, he was wanting to do something about it. Write a song about it or a paragraph about it, or somehow get it into the news. He wished he knew some newspaper man who could make it known. He wanted to see it in headlines; he thought it would look well—"Funspot Street." It seemed to him to cry for dramatisation, and he wished it were possible for him to give it celebrity and immortality.

Funspot Street: he saw it on newspaper bills and he heard the radio announcer mentioning it in news-bulletins, and heard the giggles which the name would arouse in a million homes.

He wondered sometimes why it never had been in the news. It was surely made for it. By the look of it it was the sort of street whose people would be fairly regular guests of the police courts, and whose name, when they gave it as an address, would give great chances to the men who write those facetious stories about other people's troubles, which have taken the place of serious police court reporting.

Constantly thinking about it, and seeing it in many connections, comic and dramatic, he decided finally that it would look most apt in type as:—

THE FUNSPOT STREET MURDER

He could see the sub-heads and cross-heads. Shocking Murder in Funspot Street. . . . Early this morning the police were called to a house in Funspot Street. . . . Detectives working on the Funspot Street tragedy are in possession of an important clue which is likely. . . . Funspot Tragedy Arrest. . . . No Reprieve for Funspot Murderer. . . . And so on.

No; comedy wouldn't do. It called for tragedy, and the more squalid and grotesque the tragedy the more fitting. Something out of the inkwell of Baudelaire or Poe, or De Nerval. He could half-see the kind of thing that would fit, and on each monthly visit to that district the fascination of the name and of fitting it with the right story provided him with entertainment for several evenings. He would add extra details to the half-formed idea in his mind, discarding those of last week in favour of some with a keener edge of the bizarre.

He wasn't a writer, and found it difficult to write two paragraphs in sequence, but the name of that street became almost a muse to him; a spur to do what he couldn't do, and write it into prominence.

He never did write it; but after long brooding there came a time when Funspot Street and its Horrible Tragedy were so clear in his mind that in abstracted moments he could hardly believe that it hadn't happened.

He could locate the house, the room, the time (it would be midnight, of course), and he could visualise the act itself as though he had been an eye-witness. He could see the room and its flimsy, shabby furniture. He could smell the stale, unopened reek of it. He could see the gas-bracket and its incandescent mantle, which would be broken and the flame spluttering.

He could see the violently flowered wallpaper, discoloured in places, and elsewhere peeling off. He could see the strip of cheap carpet, with holes at the points where feet had constantly rested. And he could see the man who had somehow, by some aberration, got into this squalid hole, away from his regular, decent surroundings.

A slim, neatly-dressed fellow, something like himself. And he could see the blowsy woman, the fitting chatelaine of such a house. He could hear the violent noises, and he could see the man turning in fury and disgust and striking the woman and rushing from the room.

And then the mid-day papers, with Funspot Street front-paged. And then the daily and hourly hunt for this decent young chap, just as it might be himself, who, for all his previous decency and integrity, would leave his name in certain records, and be exhibited at Madame Tussaud's as "The Funspot Street Murderer." Not even complete tragedy to mark his sudden fall, but tragedy streaked with the ridiculous. . . . Funspot Street.

In building the story he attributed to the man, at the moment of walking to the scaffold, a burning grievance. Not at his fate, not at the irresponsible moment which had led him to his fate, nor at his capture, when many men who have committed that act have escaped capture. But at the fact that it didn't happen in some other street—in Cavendish Street or Jermyn Street or Kingsway. Over-riding remorse and resignation and the natural horror of the situation would stand this crowning indignity to a man's *finis*—Funspot Street. He felt that it was a good story, if only he could write it.

The salary which his firm considered an adequate balance to the services he rendered did not permit him much evening entertainment; a theatre or music-hall once a month, perhaps, and the movies once a week. Other evenings he spent in wandering about London, getting for nothing an entertainment superior to anything for which one pays money.

On these walks, while observing the pageant, he let his mind play round his Funspot Street Tragedy, going over it again and again, detail for detail. He wished, whimsically, that somebody would put it into action; that there really would be a murder in Funspot Street, just like that, and that the evening paper contents bills would flash it at him. But they never did.

It was on one of these walks, when he was wandering round the strange, lost byways of Islington, and playing with the trial in the Funspot Street Tragedy, and the duel between prisoner and counsel, that something thick touched him softly on the forehead. For one moment he was aware that he was looking closely at a puddle in the road, and that above his head was the number-plate of a taxi and the wheels of a motor-bus. He was aware also of disturbed voices, and then of a babble; and then, through the babble, a firm voice which said: "All right . . . we know him . . . we'll look after him."

That was all he heard in that moment. Next moment, it seemed, he heard a voice saying, in a low growl: "See if he's got the day's collection on him." And then another voice saying: "'M. Here it is."

His eyelids seemed of iron, but he managed to open them. They gave his eyes a sight of a strip of cheap carpet, with holes here and there. Above him he saw a gas-bracket, with the flame spluttering. Then he saw a violently flowered wallpaper, and places where it was peeling off.

Over him stood a large, heavy man. Just behind the man stood a blowsy woman wearing a flashy, stained frock which he thought he had seen before. In the woman's hands was a bundle of Treasury notes secured with a rubber band.

At the sight of them, and the memory of the words he had heard, his brain began to move. He realised that he had been robbed. The other details passed back into dream, but the fact that he had been robbed remained as a fact. Somehow or other he managed to scramble to his feet and to make a fierce lunge at the woman.

The mid-day papers of next afternoon had Funspot Street well on their bills and on their front pages. But Morton never saw them. The last thing he saw was a poker in the hand of the blowsy woman.

UNCLE EZEKIEL'S LONG SIGHT

Uncle Ezekiel was one of those domestic pests which may be found in thousands of the humbler English homes. The well-to-do have means of parking their Uncle Ezekiels elsewhere; poorer people have to suffer them. These pests sit most of the day and all the evening by the fire. They smoke; they eat; they doze; they grumble; and they monopolise the armchair. They have their little "ways" which they expect everybody to humour, and they make irritating old-man noises. They are seldom beautiful and generally useless; but they are profuse in their criticism of those about them, particularly the young.

This Uncle Ezekiel, pest of a little home in a little South London street, matched all other Uncle Ezekiels save in one minor detail. He was useful. Not until the last year of his life did anybody discover that he was useful, but when it was discovered, this bent and snappy old figure changed the lives of many people of whom he had never heard.

The discovery was made by the lodger of the house, who sometimes came down and talked to the old man, not because he liked him but because he liked talking. Uncle Ezekiel's name for him was "that — broadcaster," but he only merited the contempt of that term because he was a young man of some crude power which just then expressed itself in talk. After discovering Uncle Ezekiel's usefulness he expressed his power in other directions.

One Friday evening, while making bright conversation, he remarked that the home team were playing at Bemmerton, where they'd never been lucky. Uncle Ezekiel, whose nose was in his beard, and whose eyes were closed, said, "Ar. But they will be this time. They'll have a big win—5–1."

"Five-One? But they haven't got an earthly. Ford's outa the team, Harper's got a bad knee, and there's a new man being tried out, and—"

"Don't contradict me! I'm old enough to be ya grandfather. But I'm glad I'm not. Tell ya, they'll win 5–1. And Harper'll get four o' the goals. You young chaps think ya know everything."

"But how could they win against the team the others are putting up? And how could Harper—"

Uncle Ezekiel woke up then. "Eh?"

"How could Harper get those goals?"

"Who's Harper?"

"Why—Harper. What we're talking about."

"What *were* we talking about?"

"About the match to-morrer."

"Were we? Where's me terbakker? Someone's always hiding me terbakker."

"Here it is, Uncle. But about the match—"

"Oh—the match. Can't ya talk about anything but football?"

Freddie Pantrome tactfully changed the subject and forgot the old man's ridiculous forecast. But at five o'clock the next afternoon he recalled it. From the evening paper he learned that their team had won 5–1, and that four of the goals had been scored by Harper.

At first he only realised that the old man had been right; it was not until he pondered the matter that he saw its full significance. Since he had been right once, in such detail, was it possible that he might be right again? If so, this threw open a wide door to Mr. Pantrome. Old men— and old women, too—were queer. They were less cluttered with the things of this world. It did happen sometimes that they could see things. He resolved to test it. There was an important re-play on Monday afternoon, and it looked a fairly even match; nothing to choose between the teams.

On Sunday evening, when Uncle Ezekiel was dozing in the best chair and the best corner, he brought up the matter. "Big match to-morrow, Uncle. Starlings playing Nightingales. What hopes!"

Uncle Ezekiel growled, "Starlings'll win. Four-None."

"Four-None? Starlings couldn't do that against—"

"Tell ya Starlings'll win. Don't contradict. Nasty habit you've got—"

Next day Freddie had a busy dinner-hour. He left the engineering yard where he worked, and ran to the Post Office to draw two pounds from his savings. It was a big risk, but Freddie knew that big men only got through by taking big risks. With the two pounds he sought out five or six of the bookmakers' runners, and laid out five shillings here, five shillings there, five shillings with another, and ten shillings with the most important.

At half-past four that afternoon he tried to tell himself that it was just a bit of fun, and that really there was nothing to it. But the greater part of himself was listening for the newsboy, and when he heard that voice he shot out to the gate, and grabbed a paper from the boy. "Football Results—Starlings *v.* Nightingales (re-play), Starlings 4, Nightingales 0." He had grabbed the paper before handing the penny. Having read the result, he passed sixpence to the boy and waved him on. The boy stared; turned the sixpence over twice; bit it; then graciously permitted himself to be waved on.

That evening Freddie owned seven pounds more than he had owned in the morning. And he began to ponder the enigma of Uncle Ezekiel even more deeply. He wondered whether his powers centred solely on football, or whether they could be applied to other things. He resolved on another test. Newmarket was opening on Wednesday. Racing had never much interested him, but next day he bought all the sporting papers, and studied, not form, but prices.

Having noted the runners, notably those of long price, he went downstairs and kindly entertained Uncle Ezekiel by reading to him about the building strike. He went on reading until Uncle Ezekiel dozed off, which was achieved in two paragraphs. Freddie's voice, in a confined space, was grey grit, but full of lights and inflexions in yards and other open spaces. Then he said, "Wonder what'll win the Big Race to-morrow, Uncle. What do *you* think?"

"Think?" Uncle growled from his beard. "I don't think. I *know.* Ice Cream Cornet."

"Ice Cre— Why, it's thirty-three to one to-night."

"I can't help that. It's goin' to win. Don't take up everything I say, like that. I know more'n you."

"I admit that, Uncle. You certainly do. I wonder what'll do the four o'clock."

"The four o'clock. That'll be the one carrying the little feller with the moustache. Can't think of his name."

"That'll be Trollope. Riding Ampersand. Sixty-six to one. And if you say it'll win, Uncle, of course it will. What a nice surprise for some of 'em."

Freddie was still not accepting Uncle in full faith, but he decided to play with five pounds of his seven, and if it went he would still have two pounds more than he had last week. Next day he did not consult the runners. He went to the offices of the local bookmakers. He laid a pound with two of them on Ice Cream Cornet. With a third (and larger) establishment he laid a pound on Ice Cream Cornet; all winnings on Ampersand. With a fourth he laid two pounds on Ampersand.

On the following Monday he collected four figures. His first dealings with his wealth were to buy Uncle Ezekiel a case of whisky and a hundred cigars. Uncle Ezekiel looked at the whisky and smelt the cigars, and said, "What's this for?"

Freddie said, "It's for you."

"Why? You come into money, or something?"

"In a way, yes. You gave me the winners of two races, Tuesday of last week. And I backed 'em."

"Winners of two races? Did I?"

"Course you did. Don't you remember?"

"I don't. You was talking about the building strike last Toosday. Lot o' rot you was talking, too. Still, if you say I did, I s'pose I did. I always take people's word. *I* never contradict. S'pose you make ye'self useful fer once, an' open one o' those bottles."

That was the beginning of the founding of the fortune of Mr. Frederic Pantrome. His natural kindness in talking to a lonely and craggy-tempered old man, though it derived from his equally natural love of hearing his own voice, brought results which these things seldom bring. He cast his bread upon the waters and it came back spread with caviare.

In Uncle Ezekiel he had found the gate to an Eldorado, and the Open Sesame for this gate was as simple a business as lighting a cigarette. When he wanted advance information, all he had to do was to read to the old man until he got him dozing, and then shoot the question. The answer came automatically—and always correctly.

Two months after that first football match, Freddie had an office of his own and rooms on the other side of the bridges in Southampton Row. He was no fool. Easy money did not mean to him easy living and fatuous luxury. It meant an opening to interesting work and a variety of operations in the world of mechanical invention. He continued to be a visitor, twice a week, to the little house in the side-street, and he continued to talk and read to Uncle Ezekiel. On the Cesarewitch and Cambridgeshire he became, by Uncle Ezekiel's unaware help, independent for life. With twelve different bookmakers he placed bets varying from fifty pounds to a hundred pounds on the double, and had only to wait until the second race was run. The first was won by a favourite; the second by an outsider.

With a few more ventures of this kind, and two Stock Exchange speculations, on which Uncle's advice was totally against the market, his money grew and grew—as money will grow, once you have enough of it. Towards the end of the year he had so much that it ceased to interest him, and he no longer needed Uncle's help for himself. He used it for the benefit of his friends, and for discovering which inventions were worth backing.

The odd thing was that nobody else could get anything out of Uncle Ezekiel. Freddie did not, of course, disclose the source of what his friends called his infernal luck, and his enemies, of whom he had made a few, grudgingly called his remarkable judgment of the course of affairs. He never mentioned Uncle Ezekiel or any other uncle. But neither Uncle Ezekiel's niece, nor her husband, could get anything out of him. They had seen the results in Freddie's case, and received benefit from it, but they couldn't do it themselves. They couldn't get him dozing. It was only Freddie's flat, arid tones that could produce the right kind of doze. Not that they needed to do it, for Freddie had recognised that his fortune had come from that little house, and he was handing back to them as much as they wanted of it.

During the last year of his life Uncle Ezekiel could have wallowed in luxury, had he been the wallowing kind. But the critical attitude suited him better than the acceptant, and Freddie and Freddie's visits were still received with something short of approval.

"Well, what y'inventing now? Something to make life more difficult, I s'pose. What's that you brought? Oysters? Grrr. . . . Now you got up in this fancy world you got all these fancy notions. I 'ate shell-fish. Ain't you 'eard me say dozens o' times that what I like is a good steak-and-kidney pudden? Not the kind that fool of a niece o' mine makes, but a real one. And then you bring me oysters. And last time it was pheasant. Don't I deserve any consideration? You keep saying it was my advice what made you. And well it might be. If more young people'd listen to their elders what've 'ad more experience of life. But if it was, why don't ya do something about it? These 'ere cigars. You say they run to half a crown apiece. More fool you. Most of 'em I gave away. What I like is a good *smoking* terbakker. Try and remember that. But I never can get what I want. This dam-fool chair you bought me. All these dam-fool tricks fer raising it and shifting the back. Why couldn't ya get me a sensible chair?"

"All right, Uncle Ezekiel. I'll have it taken away and get you a really—"

"Who said I wonnid it taken away? I like it. To look at. You can send me summan else to sit in."

"You do love complaining, don't you, Uncle?"

"What if I do? I bin complained at by other people most o' me life. Time I did a bit fer meself."

"All right. . . . By the way, d'you know what happened last week?"

"Course I do. I read the papers, don't I?"

"I mean to me. Two things. I was interviewed by the Press about that new aero engine I'm backing—for a 'plane that'll fit round a man's body. And I met the most wonderful girl in the world."

"You would. Any young feller with as much money as you got couldn't 'elp meeting 'er. Or being met by 'er. I thought you was the one sensible young feller there was. My mistake."

Freddie ignored this remark. Uncle Ezekiel was awake, and was speaking from his own restricted mind. He was valuable only when he was half-asleep. Freddie went on talking about his engine. ". . . What it means is that if you want to go from London to Paris, you just go. You just take off from your own front door. If we can get it right, people in this street could have 'em. Just take off from here and go anywhere they wanted to go. Margate, Egypt, Persia—anywhere. And the whole contraption no bigger than a suitcase. The big feature about the thing—a bit of blind genius in the chap whose idea it is—is the elimination of—"

Uncle Ezekiel's nose was sinking deeper into his beard. Freddie noted this and ran on from "elimination" to "Olive." "Olive's frightfully keen on it. She's the daughter of a big man I've been dealing with. Clever girl. She understands things. We get on jolly well together. She wanted to make the first experimental flight in the thing, but I won't let her. Too risky."

Uncle Ezekiel growled from his beard. "No risk. It'll be all right."

"Will it?"

"Ar. Safe as anything else. You'll make a Do with that thing."

"I hope so. Because Olive's so keen on it. She's a wonderful girl. I wonder if she really cares for me."

"Course she does. And just the girl fer you, too. This time next year you'll know that."

"How shall I know it?"

"'Cos you'll be married to 'er, o' course."

Freddie smacked the table and said "Ha!" Uncle Ezekiel woke up with the smack. "Wodya making all the noise fer? You always was noisy, Freddie, when you was living 'ere. Banging about, just when I was 'aving forty winks. You know 'ow bad I sleep. And that reminds me. Don't go giving that fool of a niece of mine any more money. Nor Joe. You already given 'em more'n they know what to do with. There's 'er getting Lord-knows-what kind o' dresses. And now talking about moving to a larger 'ouse. And about buying me a cottage t'meself and a woman to look after me. Nice upset that'd be fer me, wouldn't it? 'Ave a bit o' consideration."

"But I must give them something. I got my fortune from this house—from you—and everybody ought to share it."

"That's all right and proper. But don't give 'em money. People oughtn't t'ave money till they're old. Then they're sensible enough to realise it ain't worth 'aving."

Nearly a year after that first football bet, Freddie sat with Olive in a restaurant in Jermyn Street—one of the four quiet and band-less restaurants remaining in London. They were celebrating the successful trial of the new Everybody's 'Plane.

Freddie, who now had a flat in Pall Mall, was almost unrecognisable from the crude young man who had made those football bets. It was not that his outward appearance had changed so much as his whole bearing. It was not that he was wearing fine clothes, but the way he was wearing them. He did not carry his prosperity with any show of swagger, or any awkwardness. To his native force he had added poise, and he carried his success as something he had always known and taken for granted. He treated money as though he had always had it, and he stepped into this new mode of life as an exile returning to his true home. His voice had lost its flat tone; it was not so easy for him, as it had been, to send Uncle Ezekiel into a doze.

During dinner, the subject of Uncle Ezekiel came up; not by name but by reference. "By the way," Olive said, "you've told me once or twice about a queer old friend you've got. Some labouring man living in South London who advises you. Who gets knowledge of what's going to happen. Those winners you gave young Jack—I think you said *they* came from him."

"They did. And everything else I've got."

"Sounds hardly believable, but if you say so, it must be so. I've heard you say you put complete faith in anything he says."

"I do. He's always right."

"'M. . . . He'd be useful to a government if there was any trouble breaking in Europe, and they wanted to know which group to back. But I suppose they wouldn't pay any attention to him."

"I've thought of that. He *would* be useful. And I'm giving him every attention he can need to keep him with us. In case of anything like that. And if they laughed at the idea, I think I could soon convince them with a few immediate things—like to-morrow's winners, and what they'd win by; and what price any given stock would be at four o'clock any afternoon."

"Well, I wonder if he could do something for me."

"Anything you like. What is it?"

"I know it sounds silly, but . . . It's about Dad. You know he's sailing for America on Wednesday. On the new boat. Its maiden voyage.

Well, I've got a feeling about that boat. Not because they started work on it on the thirteenth, and it's sailing for the first time on Friday, but . . . some other feeling. I wonder if you could find out from him if it's all right."

"Sure. Let's see. It's Friday. I'll see him on Sunday evening, and give you a ring."

On Sunday evening Freddie found it difficult to get Uncle Ezekiel off. He wanted to talk about his niece's objectionable behaviour with money. He wanted to talk about the boy next door who was learning the clarinet. But by a determined insistence on the state of affairs in the Near East, and frequent references to "sanctions" and "plebiscites," Freddie finally got him off. It was hard going, but he stuck to it.

"Well, what's the best news *you* got?"

"The best news? I'm not sure. But the most interesting, I think, is the situation in the Near East."

"Near East me big toe. Don't y'ever 'ear any new risky stories? Mixing wi' the best people, as you do, y'ought tuv picked up a few by now."

"I'm afraid I've been too busy."

"Ar. You'll learn better one o' these days. You'll learn that yer own fireside's more important than any Near East or any other bit o' the compass."

"But you'd find it really interesting if you'd let me explain. You see, it's like this. The territory set aside by the treaty—"

Uncle Ezekiel turned his back. Freddie droned on. He droned until he saw that Uncle was nodding. Then he broke a sentence to ask, "What about the *Panwangler,* Uncle? Making its maiden voyage on Wednesday. Friend of mine's sailing on it. My future father-in-law, I hope. Olive's father, Mr. Dreamersdew."

"Eh?" Momentarily he came out of his doze.

"The *Panwangler.* Making its maiden voyage on Wednesday. Mr. Dreamersdew's sailing on it."

"Oodya say?"

"Mr. Dreamersdew. I was wondering if it'd have a good voyage."

"Mr. Dreamersdew. 'M . . . Dreamersdew . . . *Panwangler* . . ." For some seconds he seemed completely asleep. Freddie had to recall him.

"Well, Uncle, what about the *Panwangler?*"

"*Panwangler*'s all right. Good ship."

"Will Mr. Dreamersdew do any good business in New York?"

"Mr. Dreamersdew'll do a lot in New York."

"I'm glad to hear that. He was hesitating about going."

Uncle Ezekiel jerked his head, opened his eyes, and puffed. "Wassat? Talking about going? Well, yer 'at's on the sideboard. Nothing stopping ya that I know of."

Four evenings later Freddie stood in front of Uncle Ezekiel, holding a newspaper to him. Or perhaps, so threatening was the manner, *at* him. "Look at that. Look at it." He was cold and stern. He knew that he had no right to be angry with Uncle Ezekiel, but he *was* angry. "Olive's father. They trusted me. I trusted you. I told them it was safe for him to go. And now look at that."

"That" was a report of the sinking of the *Panwangler*. The list of sixteen survivors did not carry the name Dreamersdew. "Olive'll never forgive me." He looked down at Uncle Ezekiel who was blinking at the page of the newspaper. "What was the matter with you Sunday night? How did it happen? You've never been wrong before about anything. How did you come to be wrong about this?"

Uncle Ezekiel mumbled and chewed his pipe-stem. "I dunno. P'r'aps it was because I was thinking. I can always do it better if I don't think."

Freddie dropped the paper and gave a large sigh. He stared at the wall of the little kitchen, and moved his feet nervously. "Why did I ask you? Why didn't I leave it alone? Olive couldn't have blamed me then. She'll feel now . . ." He took the two paces which was all the tiny room allowed for a walk, and stared at a grocer's almanack.

He was still staring at it when he was aware of a queer noise in the room. He looked round to locate it; first on the floor; then at the fire. Then he found its true source. Uncle Ezekiel was laughing. He turned on him with: "Dammit, man, what on earth are you laughing about? Haven't you got any feelings? A think like this—and you laugh. . . ."

Uncle Ezekiel coughed and choked. "Sorry. I was laughing at me being wrong. All through thinking. I got it right about the *Panwangler* when you first mentioned it. I saw it. And then I woke up and got thinking. Thinking of Dreamersdew. When I was caretaker at 'is place. Thinking of the time when the missus was on her dying bed. And wanting things. And 'e turned me off 'cos I answered back when 'e called me a Useless Ole Slacker."

Late that night Uncle Ezekiel died in his chair. The family were surprised; they had thought he was looking so well lately. They didn't know that it was the necessary and inevitable full-stop to one who had misused a great gift for selfish revenge.

The Horrible God

Mr. Rainwater wasn't easily scared, but for the last three or four days he had had a strong feeling that he was being followed, and it was upsetting him. He knew that the feeling of being followed is often a symptom of a neurotic or morbid state, but that wasn't his state. He was quite healthy, and free of melodramatic or nervous imaginings. He was being followed. He could feel it through his skin. He could feel it in the air the moment he left his home. He could feel pursuit and the prickings of danger.

Towards midnight that evening his suspicion became certainty. He was walking down Shaftesbury Avenue towards Piccadilly and was in the thick of the crowd coming from the theatres when, clearly and with electrical urgency, a voice reached his ear. It was a keen mutter, and it said: "I speak as a friend. The vengeance of the god Imbrolu is a terrible vengeance. He seeks his own place."

Rainwater turned swiftly. He collided with two girls just behind him who were giggling and talking of Ronald Colman. On one side of him a policeman was striding. On the other side was a wall. Two paces ahead was a newsboy, and walking away from him were a couple of nondescript youths who had evidently been drinking.

As the crowd swirled round him he looked here and there for the possible speaker, but could see nobody to whom that queer mutter could have belonged. It was not an English mutter.

On the opposite side of the street was a large negro in a brilliant blue suit; in a bus coming from Piccadilly Circus sat a man of muddy colour and Oriental features; and outside the Monico, some 30 yards away, was an Algerian rug-seller. But the distance of these men from him made it impossible for any of them to have spoken those words in his ear two seconds ago.

He stood and considered. It was odd; very odd. The voice had been

147

so sharp and so close that it must have been addressing him. It had come right into his ear, as though the mouth had been touching his shoulder. Yet nobody to whom he could trace it. He knew, of course, the trick of self-effacement; that sleek movement by which a cat will pass round you before your eyes without your seeing it, and which certain people can achieve by a cessation of mental action. He attributed the vanishing of the speaker to that, and he had reason for believing that the speaker was not English. The message, he was sure, was meant for him, and no other person in the crowd; he was sure that it connected with his feeling of being followed, and that everything connected with that horrible idol.

The idol had been worrying Rainwater for some time—even before the following had begun. It was an idol of a kind he had never before seen; an idol which gave him the shudders every time he looked at it. As a collector of native bric-à-brac, he was accustomed, even hardened, to the many variations upon certain themes of which the black mind, in its more exalted fervours, is capable.

But this . . . The most cloistered nun, knowing nothing of the images by which men express the baseness of man, would have known at a glance that this thing was in form and spirit horrible. The most experienced Madame of a Buenos Aires sailors' hotel would not have confused it with the realistic emblems of native religions which her customers brought from their voyages and with which they improved her knowledge of anthropology. It was just a masterpiece of unrelated horror.

The artist who made it had withdrawn from the unfenced fields of religious ardour and had immured himself within the narrow dogmas of art—just to show, apparently, that art, with all its fetters of form and technique, could outsoar anything achieved under the licence and tolerance by which the darker religions distinguish themselves from art.

Certainly he had succeeded. Never had Rainwater, under that cloak of respectability which hides so many anomalies, even imagined anything like it. Nor had anybody else whom he knew. Of all his acquaintances among curators of museums, not one could put a name to it or even conjecture the country or island of its origin. When he showed it to them they stared and whistled.

And that was all he could get from them. They could tell him that it wasn't Egypt, that it wasn't Java, that it wasn't Easter Island, or Haiti, or

Liberia; but they couldn't tell him what it *was.* They could only tell him that he'd better put it away or throw it away.

He put it away at the bottom of one of his curio cabinets. He couldn't give it away, because nobody he knew would have accepted it. All his friends were married. And as a collector he couldn't bring himself to throw it away. Yet, in keeping it in his rooms, he felt a distinct unease, as though in possessing it he were partly responsible for its horror and had had a share in making it.

He *wanted* to throw it away, or burn it, or drop it over one of the bridges, but whenever he reached the point of setting out to do it, the collecting instinct mastered him. If the thing had been emitting an evil smell into his room he still wouldn't have been able to screw himself up to throwing it away. So he kept it locked up, and only took it out now and then, which made him feel more guilty.

If a friend was announced he would hurriedly hide it. If he heard his housekeeper's step outside the door he would throw a newspaper over it. When he had had it for three weeks his demeanour had become almost furtive.

And then began that feeling of being followed and its climax of that muttered message. He wished he had never seen the wretched thing, or, having seen it, had resisted the temptation to buy it. The thing itself was a horror and now it was leading to this uncanny following and this uncanny message delivered in a crowded street. He didn't know what to do about it.

It wasn't the threat that disturbed him so much as the stealthy following and the manner in which the threat had been delivered. If it was the ju-ju of some tribe or creed with representatives in London why couldn't they come to him openly? Why the following about, which had begun apparently from the moment he bought it, when he had been followed to his home? And how could he put the little hideous god back in his own place when nobody, not even scholars, knew whence it came?

He walked on in some disturbance. Every now and then he looked back or stopped by a shop whose side-window reflected the path behind him, but he saw nobody who might be the follower, and did not expect to. Whoever had been following him the last few days was an experienced shadower; clever enough to convey the horrid sense of his neighbourhood and clever enough to remain unperceived.

Mr. Rainwater was beginning to realise that there is something in being followed which is more shocking than a revolver at the head or a knife at the throat. There is nothing to grasp; nothing to combat; only a persistent nagging at the nerves, which in time can wear you down.

And Rainwater was being worn down. If they wanted their god they could have it, so far as he was concerned. He couldn't throw an artistic treasure away, but if it meant something more to people than it did to him they were welcome to it, if only they would come and ask for it. They must know his address or they wouldn't be able to follow him as they did. Why, then, this menacing and muttering of vengeance?

On reaching home he learned that they did know his address. His housekeeper met him in the hall. She held a grubby piece of pink paper. "I don't know what this is, sir, or how it came. I found it on the mat under the evening paper. Would it be anything you know about?" She passed it to him. It bore six words in an ungainly scrawl: "Imbrolu waits. You have been warned."

Mr. Rainwater made a noise of irritation.

He passed it back to her. "No, I don't know anything about it. Some odd bit of waste paper that blew in, I should think." But he went upstairs feeling a little sick. When he got to his room he went first to the little cabinet in which he kept the horrible thing.

The room was filled with the results of his collecting mania. They hung on the walls, they stood on tables and they decorated half a dozen glass cabinets; tribal work mainly, all of it bizarre. The horrible thing was not resting in one of the glass cabinets. It was in an old lacquer cabinet—a nest of drawers three times concealed within other drawers. He had just opened it and had reached the drawer containing the thing when, without conscious impulse, he went to the window and moved the curtain aside. He moved it aside casually; he dropped it swiftly.

On the opposite pavement under the overhanging trees of a front garden, was a motionless figure. The figure was dressed in a raincoat, and its soft hat had the brim turned down. To see the face was impossible, but something about the pose of the figure conveyed to Mr. Rainwater the sense of alien ideas. He turned from the window, shut all the drawers and doors of the cabinet, without looking to see if his treasure was there, and dropped into a chair by the fire.

He had scarcely dropped when he got up again; found a glass; mixed himself a drink. He went back to the chair with it, and dropped again. He wasn't a coward and he wasn't a man of stout nerve. He was like most of us, in between, and ready to admit when he was shaken. He was a mild and amiable man, but could, as mild and amiable people can, be capable of ferocity when really roused and when there was some concrete object of his ferocity.

Such as a man who insisted on having the window of a railway carriage closed on a warm day.

But against intangible hostility, or against anything unfamiliar, he was a reed. His heart didn't give way, but his nerves did. None of the incidents of the last four days had made him afraid, but they had brought him to the edge of a breakdown. He needed a drink.

Sitting there in the midnight silence he began to hear, or to think he could hear, odd noises from the street. Little soft noises, of the kind that make people ask each other in whispers—"What's that?" Once or twice, without knowing why, he looked over at the lacquer cabinet, and found himself relieved to see that it was still there and still a lacquer cabinet.

He wanted to go to the window again, but couldn't. He wanted to know if the figure had gone, but there was the possibility that he would see it standing in the same position; and he didn't want to see it. There was nothing in the figure itself, or in its attitude, to disturb anyone: it was just a solitary and motionless man. Yet its mere presence conveyed a stream of menace and portent and alarm which was the more potent for being obscure.

It created that shrinking of the skin which man always knows before the nameless peril. In its immobility it was horrid, and Mr. Rainwater didn't want to see it. Also, he had a feeling that, horrid as it was in stillness, it would fill him with more horror if it moved.

He wanted to go to bed, but couldn't. He had half an idea of taking the horrible idol from the cabinet, opening the window, and flinging it out to the watcher. But if it fell in the roadway it might smash, and that might mean more of this furtive persecution. And he felt that he couldn't stand much more of it. He was accustomed to a peaceful life, and he could not adjust himself to this invasion of his peace.

Somehow or other he must get rid of the thing. He couldn't give it to a museum, because that might bring persecution on the museum's curator, and if he burnt it or dropped it in the river, he still wouldn't be free of their attentions. And he couldn't hand it over to them because they never came near enough to him. If he took it out now, and went downstairs to give it to the solitary watcher, he was certain that the solitary watcher would have vanished.

But about three o'clock in the morning, after his third drink, which had done his nerves three times no-good, an idea came to him. A simple idea which should have come to him when the persecution began. He would pass it to the people most able to deal with the situation. He would resell it to the shop where he bought it, at any price they cared to give. It was a dim little shop, kept by two swarthy old men who looked as though they could understand and answer any roundabout messages.

On that resolution he went to bed, not caring whether the house was surrounded, or whether he was to be burgled or assassinated, or not. He was beyond caring. His nerves had jittered so much under the persecution, and had developed such a side-jittering from the three heavy drinks, that they were now exhausted. Anything could happen, but Mr. Rainwater was going to bed.

Nothing did happen; and after a miniature breakfast he took the horrible god from the private drawer of the cabinet, packed it carefully in tissue-paper, put it into his overcoat pocket, and set out for the shop, followed, he was sure, all the way.

He did not get rid of it so easily as he had hoped. The partners were not in a buying mood. When he offered it, saying that he was tired of it, and that it was not in keeping with the rest of his collection, they hesitated. They answered as curio-dealers always do; they did not want it. Those things, they said, were not easy to sell. When they could sell that kind of thing they got a good price, but they might have to keep it in stock for a year, two years, five years, before finding a customer. They had had it in stock for three years before Mr. Rainwater bought it.

Mr. Rainwater asked: would they make an offer? They replied that they would hardly dare. The offer would be too ridiculous. They really did not want it; the small demand for such things made it impossible to offer a price at all relative to the artistic value of the thing.

Mr. Rainwater said sternly: "Name a price."

Under compulsion they named, with confusion and apology, ten shillings.

"I'll take it." He pushed the horrible god across the counter. They tendered, across the counter, sadly and with deprecation, a ten-shilling note. He took it; said "Good morning"; and walked out into the morning sun.

Outside, he took a deep breath, said, "That's that, thank God," and walked away as though liberated from clanking chains. He walked all the way to his club, and did not once have the feeling of being followed. This restoration of his normal life filled him with the holiday spirit, and he spent the ten shillings, and more, in a super-excellent lunch.

That evening, in the little shop the partners smiled at each other. "Yes," said one, "we have done well with this thing which the English sailor carved for us. Eight times we have sold it; and eight times we have frightened the buyer into bringing it back." In a mocking sing-song he recited: "The vengeance of the god Imbrolu is a terrible vengeance. He seeks his own place. . . . These superstitious English!"

FATHER AND SON

Sam was hard-up; and when Sam was hard-up the very few scruples that composed the trifle which served him as conscience got out of the way. He wasn't hard-up as you and I are hard-up; he wanted only a few shillings. But relatively his situation was as acute as yours or mine, and he had none of the instincts and training which enable us to put up with it and wait till things change. He couldn't put up with anything that interfered with his wants.

He wasn't a rogue. He wasn't the kind of lad who, needing a few shillings, would go out with the smash-and-grab or hold-up boys. He was a jellied eel. His face at a passing glance in the street was a normal face, but if you took a long look at it you began to think of something out of the Wiertz Museum. He had no zest for goodness and no guts for evil. All he could be was mean and milky. Mean and milky in his good tendencies and mean and milky in his rebellions.

He was rebelling against circumstance that afternoon, but there was nothing of the Cromwell or Garibaldi in his rebellion. His rebellion took the form, not of knocking things over but of slinking round them. He was looking, as he always did, not for a fight with circumstance, but for an easy way out. He leaned against a lamp-post at the corner, interfering with the sunshine and doing his bit of rebellion. He needed a few shillings, and that trifle told him that he mustn't even think of taking them. That was dangerous. He must justify and protect himself in getting them. He must earn them. He was not delicate as to the manner in which he earned them, but he barred all other ways of getting them, except possibly cadging them, and there was nobody from whom to cadge. So he leaned against the post, blinking and considering how he might earn them.

He wouldn't have had to do any considering if his father had continued to do his duty in the matter of petty cash. But lately his father had Turned Nasty. After being a constant and easy source of supply he had begun to be reluctant in handing out shillings. He had begun to nag. He had told his son what he himself was doing at eighteen. From the tone in which he related this, it appeared that he was dissatisfied with his son. It appeared, too, that he himself had been the exemplar upon which numbers of men who wore honours and owned large balances had modelled their lives. It appeared that Samuel Smiles would have added another chapter to his book had he lived long enough to hear about Sam's father. It appeared, most certainly, that it would be useless to ask the old man for those shillings.

No doubt the old man's friends were responsible for this change of attitude. They had never quite approved of Sam, and when he had made complaints to them concerning the old man and pocket-money, he had won none of their sympathy. They had talked of Regular Work, and of Spongers and Pieces of Wet String. They had spoken of the old man's usual attitude to his son as unduly generous, while admitting that other people would have called it dam-foolish. They had trespassed beyond the bounds of courtesy by foreshadowing his probable fate had he been *their* son. They had left him feeling bad about things.

It was while he was brooding upon their words and upon his problem that he remembered the talk there had lately been about the large amount of tobacco which was going round the neighbourhood. It was going round, too, at such a price that, considering the current duty, only a philanthropist, willing to lose money for the benefit of others, could have sold it at the price. Authority, he knew, was much concerned about this business, and wanted to interview the philanthropist. But it couldn't locate his address, and it was hampered in the search for it by being unable to quote his name.

Sam knew both. And Sam had read stories about men who did the hazardous work of detecting crime without official help, and who served their country quietly and without any desire for limelight. So, when the bars opened, he left his lamp-post, and went in and deliberated the matter over a lonely half-pint. It looked safe and it looked virtuous. It ought to be done. And it ought to be worth something when done. And it might lead to other things. Small beginnings . . . as his father was always saying.

When he saw the bottom of his glass he came to a decision. He would earn private gratitude, and anything else that might be going, by a virtuous piece of work. He put the glass on the counter, straightened his tie by the mirror, and set out to do it. There would be a girl at the corner to-morrow night. That was the source of his need of shillings. A man must have a few shillings in his pocket when he meets a girl. And he must do his duty as a citizen.

So he went and did it. The man he went to see received him somewhat coldly. But he listened to what Sam had to say, and when various questions brought some long-wanted details, he thawed. He admitted at the end of the interview that Sam had been useful, and he returned the service. Sam went out to the twilit street with the clear mind which comes with a problem solved.

He was waiting at the corner next evening, in full ease of mind, for the encounter with the girl, when a young, alert man came to him.

"You're wanted at the station."

"Who—me?"

"Yes, you. Won't take you a minute. Just an identification."

So he went with the young man, and in the hall of the station he saw one or two officers; two civilians, looking somewhat awkward; and a third civilian sitting meekly on a bench. The third civilian looked up at his son with eyes that registered nothing in particular and little flicks of a dozen different emotions.

One of the officers whispered to Sam: "D'you see here the man you say is doing this tobacco game?"

"'Mm. Sitting on the bench there."

"Ah. What name d'you know him by?"

"Joe Swot."

"Oh. . . . Same name as yours, eh? Any relation?"

"My father."

"Your—" The officer's eyes registered something very particular. "Oh. . . . Really. . . . That's interesting." He looked Sam over. Then he looked at the old man, sitting with drooped hands. Then he looked back at Sam, with an expression which suggested that something in the air had gone sour. "All right. You can go." He put an emphasis on the word "go."

Sam hesitated. He hadn't seen it like this. He didn't like the officer's manner, and he didn't like the hard eyes of the two civilians, and he didn't like the stares of the other officers. This didn't seem a fitting reception to one who was doing his duty. They were all looking at him in a thoroughly offensive manner, as though there were something unpleasant about him. He wanted to ask them about their looks, but as they were still staring at him, and the stares were becoming almost hypnotic, he restrained himself. He turned and slouched out. He slouched so definitely, to show his nonchalance, that he didn't notice the little threshold against which the doors fitted. He caught his foot in it; stumbled; and went headlong down the steps.

Those inside turned to look, and in that moment the old man made a dash for the door. There were cries of "Stop. . . . Hold him. . . . Quick." Two officers sprang after him, but they over-ran themselves. The old man had stopped abruptly in the doorway. He stood there bent, peering down into the half-darkness.

"Hurt yehself, son? Did y'urt yehself?"

Johnson Looked Back

Don't look behind you, Johnson. There's a man following you, but don't look behind. Go on just as you are going, down that brown-foggy street where the lamps make diffuse and feeble splashes on the brown. Go straight on and don't look behind, or you might be sorry. You might see something that you'll wish you hadn't seen.

He's a blind man, Johnson, but that makes little difference to him, and is of no use to you. You can't hear the tapping of his stick because he hasn't got a stick. He can't carry a stick. He hasn't any hands. But he's been blind so long that he can walk the streets of this district without a stick. He can smell his way about, and he can feel traffic and other dangers through his skin.

You can turn and twist as you like, and use your mortal eyes as much as you like, but that man without eyes will be close on your trail. He's faster than you. He's not impeded by perception of the objects that reach you through the eyes. You are not used to the uncertain cloud of fog and blears of light; you have to pick your steps. He can march boldly, for he marches always in clear, certain darkness. If you use cunning he can meet all your cunning. Without seeing you, or hearing you, he will know just where you go, and he will be close behind you. He will know what you are going to do the moment you have decided to do it; and he will be at your heels.

No; it won't help you at all to look behind you. It will only sicken you. It's not a pleasant spectacle—this man, blind and without hands, silently and steadfastly dogging you through the curling vapour. It's much better for you not to know that you are being pursued by this creature. The result will be the same anyway; you won't escape him, and it may save you a few minutes of misery not to know what is coming.

But why is he pursuing you? Why did he wait so long at the entrance to that dim street, whose very lamps seem to be ghosts of its darkness, to pick out your step from many others, and to follow you with this wolf-stride? You will not know that until you see him face to face. You have forgotten so many things; things that the strongest effort of memory will not recall, but your pursuer hasn't. He remembers; and all these years he has been seeking you, smelling about the streets of London, knowing that some day he is certain to strike the forbidding street down which you went when you first shook him off, and that he will find you there. And to-night he has found it and has smelt your presence there, and is with you once again.

Purpose is pursuing impulse. You are idle and at ease. He is in ferment. You are going to visit that abandoned house because it occurred to you to visit that abandoned house. He is following you because he has been waiting for nothing else. So there you go—he patient and intent; you, with free mind, picking your steps through the fog-smeared street. You have nothing to worry about. You walk through the fog with care, but with that sense of security which even the darkest streets of London cannot shake in Londoners familiar with them and with their people. You don't know what is catching up with you, and so long as you go straight ahead and don't look—

Oh, you fool! Johnson—you fool! I said—"*Don't* look behind you."

And now you've looked. And now you've seen. And now you know.

If you hadn't looked behind you would have escaped all the years of pain that are now coming upon you. It would have been all over in a few seconds. Now you've made it more dreadful. You've filled your mind with knowledge of it, and you're going to increase your torment by trying to get away. And above those two pains will come the pain of a struggle.

You won't get away. You have no chance at all. The man behind you is blind, and has no hands; but he has arms and he has feet, and he can use them. Don't think you can escape by dodging down that alley. . . . That was a silly thing to do. Alleys hold fear more firmly than open streets. Fear gets clotted in their recesses and hangs there like cobwebs. You thought you were doing something clever which would perplex him, but you won't perplex him. He is driving you where he wants you. You thought that if you could get into the alleys, and twist and turn and double along the deserted wharves, you could shake him off. But you can't. It's just in the alleys that he wants to have you, and you went there under his direction.

Already you're helping him because you're feeling the clotted fear which has been hanging in these alleys through the centuries. You're getting muddled. You've lost count of the turns you've taken, and you're not sure whether you're going away from him or fleeing breast to breast upon him. You saw him in all his maimed ugliness, and you see him now in every moving heap of fog that loiters at the mouth of each new alley. Long before he is upon you, he has got you.

If you hadn't looked back, doom would have fallen upon you out of nothing. But you looked back, and now you know the source of that doom.

You might as well give up padding through the alleys. Their universe of yellow-spotted blackness is only deluding you with hope of refuge. No corner is dark enough to hide you from eyes that live in darkness. No doors can cover you from senses as keen as air. No turn that you take will carry you farther from him; you are taking the turns he wants you to take.

There! You've turned into a little square which has no opening save that by which you entered. You're done. You can't hear him coming because he's wearing thin list slippers; but he's very near you. He's very near that entry. You've no hope of getting out. When he seizes you it would be better to yield everything, cat-like, and go with his desire and his attack. Better that than to fight. Only fools fight the invincible. But of course you *will* fight.

Hush—he's here. He's at the entry. He's in the square. You know that he's moving towards you; you know it as certainly as steel knows magnet. And then, though the fog-filled square gives you no more sight than your enemy, you know that he has halted; and you feel the silence dripping about your ears, spot by spot.

And now he has made his spring. He is upon you, and your fists fly against him. But you cannot beat him back. His blows fall upon you, and they wound and sting. You cannot fight him as you would fight another man. Your blood is cold but your brain is hot, and your nerves and muscles receive confused commands. They begin to act by themselves, automatically and without force. Your brain is preoccupied by this man.

It's no good, Johnson. Better to give in. You're only prolonging it. Your fists are useless against handless arms, or against feet. The fight is unequal. You have fists to fight with. He has none. And this lack of his puts all the advantage on his side. For a blow with the fist is painful and damaging; on the right point it may be fatal. But a blow with a stump, while equally painful and damaging, is something more. You're realising that. It stains honest combat with something anomalous. Its impact on the face is not only a blow: it is an innuendo. It makes you think when you ought to be fighting.

And with the blows from those handless arms there are the blows from what seems to be an open hand. They tear along your face and about your neck, and each blow brings nausea. Not because it's a blow from an open hand, but because you know that this man has no hands, and because the feel of it is too long for a hand. And then you know what it is. The man with no hands is fighting you with his feet. You could put up with that if he were using feet as men do use them; if he were kicking you. What sucks the strength from your knees is that his feet are behaving like hands. You feel as a dreamer feels when fighting the dead. You are already beaten, not by superior strength, but by blows from handless arms and from feet behaving as hands. And you know that it was your work that robbed him of his hands and left him to use his feet as hands.

And now you're down. And now one of those feet, more flexible and more full of life than any common hand, is on your neck. And the fog in this little derelict square deepens from brown to black. The foot presses and presses, very softly and very heavily; and your eyes become black fog and your mind becomes black fog. Black upon black, increasingly, until with the last rush of breath you are swallowed into a black void and a black silence and a black cessation of being.

And so, Johnson, you destroyed yourself, and because you looked back you had the full bitterness of knowing that you destroyed yourself. For this blind and maimed and ferocious creature of the velvet steps was, of course, yourself. This creature without sight and without hands was your other self, your innermost guide, whom you so constantly thwarted and denied and broke. It was you who blinded him that he might not see your deeds, and it was the things you did with *your* hands which corrupted his, until he was left with none, and at last turned upon you. And then you looked back, and you saw yourself stalking yourself to destruction; and in the last blackness of terror you understood.

Happier for you if you had not looked back, and had not understood. For then, after a sojourn in the still dusk of Devachan, you would have returned to amend a wasted life by another pilgrimage. You would have returned blind and maimed to a life of struggle and frustration, poverty and contumely and pain. And you would have called it, with a shrug, what most men call it—Luck.

But you looked back. You are one of the few who die with full knowledge of their pursuer. So, with the blindness and mutilation, and the poverty and the pain, you will carry yet another tribulation. You will carry the tribulation of remembering *why* you are suffering.

TWO GENTLEMEN

This tale comes out of the lavender-blue distance of years and years ago, when street-bands were playing Sousa's new marches and when London had a Chinatown.

In that period, which to us is faintly aromatic, Young Fred was busy about the down-stream waterside earning his living. He did not earn his living by dealing in this or that commodity, or by manufacturing useful or useless things, or by working for other people's profit. He earned his living by the study of human nature. Novelists study human nature, and if they are good novelists they enrich the subject of their study. But almost every subject of Young Fred's study was a little poorer after Young Fred had studied him. As a golddigger he could have given profitable lessons to the ladies of Broadway and the Riviera.

On the evening of a day that had been as dull as a wet day empty of business or friends can be, he sat in his back bedroom and stared at wet roofs and red chimney-pots. Things in his world were not going well. Money was running short; and worse—the supply of Mugs, the source of money, was also running short. He was faced with the problem of making bricks without clay, straw, old newspapers, or whatever bricks are made of. Black rain falling on grimy roofs is not a notable fount of inspiration, but Young Fred continued to stare through the window, and burn Woodbines, until he reached that state of semi-trance which is the only invitation the Muses recognise.

It was when he was well sunk in this mooning and all-forlorn state that the Muse came. It came not *via* the black rain but *via* a band which was playing—or would have said it was playing—at the corner of his street. It had just finished transmuting a Sousa march into a dirge, and was beginning an air from a new musical play called "The Geisha"—a song about "Ching-chang, Chinaman . . ." when the Muse descended and slipped an Idea into a corner of his mind. At the moment of its arrival it had no shape. It was a mere homunculus of an idea. But within a few seconds it began to grow and to take an agreeable form. As it grew in his active mind, there emerged, from the corner where memory lives, two images which seemed fit companions for it. The images were Mr. Wo and Mr. Wum.

Young Fred had not made any close and deliberate study of Mr. Wo and Mr. Wum, but in his normal passings to and fro they had come under his unsleeping observation. He had noted them and their characteristics, and had filed them in his mental cabinet for possible future reference. They appeared to him now as the perfect vehicles for the materialisation of the Idea.

They were close friends. Their friendship was not the casual, intimate, all-confessing friendship of common Englishmen. It was a friendship of dignities and reserves. A stranger, even if he could have eavesdropped on their private talk, would never have guessed they were deeply attached to each other. Neither knew much about the other, or sought to know; did not know even whether the other was rich or poor. Theirs was a philosophical friendship. There was no warmth in their expressions; no Chinese equivalents of "Dear old chap" or "Man, you talk like a dam-fool." They went for slow walks together, talking little. They took meals at each other's homes, gravely and ceremonially; and though they had done this twice a week for some years, they still did it as though it were happening for the first time and they were the guest of a new acquaintance. When they did talk their speech was aloof and scrupulous in courtesy; mostly impersonal. But the bond between them, though imperceptible, was strong, and each knew that at any crisis he could call upon the other and be served.

Outside themselves, nobody knew, or had evidence for judging, that they were friends. Nobody, that is, save the exceptionally gifted Young Fred; and you could no more hide things from him than you can from children at Christmas-time. It was in their peculiar friendship that he saw his opportunity, and the morning after the arrival of the Idea he set to work to put it into action.

His first visit was to a Post Office, where he bought a bill-stamp. On this bill-stamp he put some writing centring upon the figure of fifty pounds. He then went along the streets with that air of sober citizenship which is worn by all business-men when they are engaged upon some notably slimy bit of work. He maintained this air through most of that morning. At the suitable hour of eleven o'clock he called at the home of Mr. Wo, and desired a few minutes' private conversation.

In a little room at the back he explained to the courteous Mr. Wo that he was in business as a commercial and financial agent (which sounded as though it meant something, but gave no hint of its meaning) and that he had been approached, in the ordinary way of business, by Mr. Wum. Mr. Wum, it appeared, needed, until the end of the month, a small loan; a mere matter of fifty pounds. At this Mr. Wo exclaimed that of course he would readily lend his friend that sum, or two and three times that sum. To which Young Fred hastily interposed a quick No. No; that was not Mr. Wum's way. He had no desire to incommode his friends by introducing wretched commercial details between them. He preferred to keep business and friendship apart. That was why he had approached the obliging Young Fred. Young Fred, on his side, was wholly willing to make the advance, and had no doubts at all of Mr. Wum's personal integrity. Still, business was business and commercial risks were commercial risks. So, as he knew that Mr. Wo was a friend of Mr. Wum, it occurred to him that Mr. Wo would have no objection to guaranteeing the bill. Mr. Wo assured him that his surmise was sound, and that he would have pleasure in doing as requested. Whereupon Young Fred produced the bill, and Mr. Wo brought out his writing-brushes and endorsed it as blackly and solidly as ever a bill was endorsed.

Young Fred then thanked him, while assuring him, with true business courtesy, that it was, of course, a mere formality; and politely took his leave. The next two days he spent in unavoidable idleness, merely hanging about the streets to observe Mr. Wo and Mr. Wum on their walks, to note their demeanour to each other, and to let them see him. If his plan were miscarrying, Mr. Wo would surely challenge him during those two days. But though Mr. Wo distinctly saw him on three occasions, he made no sign; by which Young Fred guessed that he had calculated correctly.

On the third day he made another visit to the Post Office, and bought another bill-stamp, which also he covered with writing concerning the sum of fifty pounds. With this in his pocket he went gravely to the home of Mr. Wum, which was some distance from the home of Mr. Wo. To Mr. Wum he represented himself as a commercial and financial agent who had been approached, in the ordinary way of business, by Mr. Wo. Mr. Wo, it appeared, needed, until the end of the month, a small loan; a mere matter of fifty pounds. At this Mr. Wum exclaimed that, though it was somewhat inconvenient, and he was never well furnished with pounds, he would readily make every effort he could to provide his friend with that sum. To which Young Fred hastily interposed a quick No. No; that was not Mr. Wo's way. He had no desire to incommode his friends by introducing wretched commercial details between them. He preferred to keep friendship and business apart. That was why he had approached the obliging Fred. Fred, on his side, was wholly willing to make the advance, and had no doubts at all of Mr. Wo's personal integrity. Still, business was business, and . . . (see the foregoing).

When Young Fred left the shop he left it with the second bill-stamp blackly and solidly endorsed and backed by Mr. Wum.

For the next fifteen days he had nothing to do but wait for the end of the month. He spent the time in laying plans of another kind for some future business, and in observing Mr. Wo and Mr. Wum about the streets, and in letting them observe him. Neither made any sign of having seen him, save perhaps the faintest shade of embarrassment when he passed. To Mr. Wo his presence was a distressing reminder that his good friend Mr. Wum was in some difficulty, and was for the time being under an obligation to Mr. Wo for having backed his bill. To the sensitive Mr. Wo obligations on either side were pieces of grit whose existence a gentleman could not even mention. To Mr. Wum also the presence of Young Fred was a distressing reminder that his good friend Mr. Wo was in some difficulty, and was for the time being under an obligation to Mr. Wum for having backed his bill; and to the sensitive Mr. Wum obligations were what they were to Mr. Wo.

When, therefore, three days after the turn of the month, Young Fred called upon Mr. Wo and stated, with more than usual business gravity, that he regretted the necessity of his visit, he felt, not that it was a shame to take the money, but that he hadn't really earned it. It was too soft.

Mr. Wo heard with marked distress that his friend Mr. Wum had been so entangled by misfortune as to be unable to meet the bill. And when Young Fred explained that it was thus forced upon him (Young Fred), by ordinary commercial procedure, to ask Mr. Wo to honour his guarantee, Mr. Wo at once honoured it. In passing over the money, he set Young Fred's brain galloping by an assurance that he would willingly do as much again for his unfortunate friend.

At the home of Mr. Wum the report of Mr. Wo's default in the matter of the bill, owing to delay in expected remittances, caused similar and even stronger distress. To the distress caused by the thought of his friend's misfortune was added the distress of finding the fifty pounds.

But a visit to a compatriot, who was actually in business of the kind which Young Fred claimed as his, produced it. And Young Fred took a bus to the west, and spent the evening and a bit of the hundred pounds in the heavy English equivalent of Provençal song and sunburnt mirth.

The beautiful thing about the affair—apart from Young Fred's handling of it—is that while many a friendship has been wrecked by the backing of a bill, this friendship was thereby strengthened. Each was so gratified at having been, as he thought, of service to his friend, that he soon forgot the gritty fact that his friend was under an obligation to him; and they became still more drawn to each other.

Such delicacy between friends has its merits. It enriches the texture of the friendship itself, and it enables the Young Freds of this world to live in comfort. Still, so far as the pocket is concerned, the moral is that friends should be as open and blunt about mutual service as City men are. Between whom, as you know, the Young Freds get no chance.

THE BLACK COURTYARD

Nobody saw him. In the late evening of that winter day he came creeping from that riverside courtyard—a courtyard thick with darkness, and alive only with silence and the eyes of blind houses; and nobody saw him. He was slim, and his body in movement was elastic. He walked with a rhythmic padding step. He presented himself to the eye as a heavy overcoat, a soft hat, and a muffler.

That evening, in all parts of London, was an evening of intense darkness; starless and heavy with rain. But in the east the already dark streets were put to confusion by a river-mist. In this mist the lamps were dabs of phosphorescence. The shop-lights blessed only a foot of the pavement, and even the torches of the stalls could achieve no more than a luminosity which was no light at all.

Belated shoppers moved in and out of the little shops in the form of floating faces. The narrow thoroughfare was populous with the creatures of all nations, but amid the shifting veils of mist one could not know white man from Cingalese, nor yellow man from negro, nor honest man from skulker. They were no more than spectral shapes of Man.

Perrace, the muffled figure coming from the courtyard, was one of them.

Nowhere was the darkness more intense than there. So intense was it that it seemed to have a quality of life. It menaced the eyes and pressed upon the face. Its silence seemed to whisper upon the ears. It was an organism of blackness whose tendrils almost throttled the breath. But to Perrace and his purposes this profusion of darkness was kind.

As he came from the courtyard the river sent to land the howl of a foghorn, and from distant byways came the cries of roysterers. A banjo could be heard; a gramophone; an over-tuned radio. Thick, rough life, and the rumour of unseen life, surged all about him; but Perrace, padding his solitary way, was concerned with death.

He padded along the High Street. He padded up Love Lane. He padded along Cable Street and along Brook Street, and as he passed from one street to another the tempo of his padding increased, and gave him the air of one in flight.

He *was* in flight. He was fleeing not from fear of arrest, but from fear of a courtyard thick with darkness, deaf to noise, and alive only with the eyes of blind houses. Those houses had seen nothing; in that darkness they could not, even unshuttered, have seen; yet their very blindness had shot him with a deeper fear than the fear of capture. They and the courtyard in which they stood were before him now. They were like figures threatening. They seemed to say "We didn't see, but we *know.* And we're going to make you pay." In the effort to shake them from his eyes he padded faster and faster. He turned into Stepney Causeway, and loped along it, and did not fall to his customary rhythm until he came out to the misty glitter and clamour of Commercial Road.

There he paused, uncertain of his next action. But his mind told him that action was imperative: he must not linger; he must not be seen here. He debated by which way he should return home, but so many ways came to his mind that he could not decide upon one for thought of the others. Then, when he had hesitated some two minutes, a string of westward buses, lumbering out of the mist, settled the matter for him. Their presence brought him out of his paralysis; with automatic movements he boarded the first of them and climbed to the top. He sat down with a heavy sigh.

Life on a sudden seemed unaccountably strange. He was still alive, breathing through his nose, seeing with his eyes. Yet his state of being was not the state of being of a few hours ago. He was sitting on a bus; a bus like other buses; but charged to his mind with some intense and un-bus-like essence. Like that courtyard and that darkness and those houses, it seemed alive. This was Perrace sitting on the bus—Perrace, himself yet not himself. The same hair, the same eyes, the same hands, the same flow of conscious memory. Yet a Perrace who was a stranger to him.

At the bottom of his mind was a faint feeling, or perhaps a faint hope, that soon he would wake up and find himself warm and comfortable in his bed at Kingsland Road. The top of his mind knew that he wouldn't.

He looked down at his overcoat. It was his overcoat, his quite ordinary overcoat. Since the day he bought it he had never really seen it. Now he saw it, and the coat, too, seemed to come to life. He had put it on that afternoon as casually as he always put it on. But that was before the Idea had come to him. He knew that he would not take it off casually. It was now an experienced overcoat; a dramatic overcoat; it had been in that courtyard. It might even become a famous overcoat.

At that thought he shivered, and felt sick. Events of the last two hours recurred to him. They had the complexion of that truth which is insistently truth but incomprehensible by human reason. That accursed courtyard had created them.

He recalled the courtyard, and he recalled the dark room, and he recalled the bent, questioning figure of the old man. And he recalled the old man lying still and pulseless on the floor. And he recalled the escape by the window. He recalled how often he had haunted that courtyard, and how often the courtyard had haunted *him*. He recalled how it had set things in his mind. How it had lived there, peacefully malignant, suggesting sin, but never the price of sin. How it had beckoned him to give it the story for which it was made. He recalled the many times when he had looked into it and looked at a certain house, and had thought of the hundreds of notes which the stupid feeble old man was known to hoard; notes which meant so much to one who was out of a job. He recalled how he had planned the affair over drinks in the—what was the name of the place? He recalled how he had first brushed the idea aside—its mere presence had given him a fit of tremors—and how, later, he had gibed at himself for a coward, and screwed himself up to it. He recalled how clear it had been in his mind during the long evening.

It was when he had come to set it to action that it had gone blurred and feverish. Coming out of the courtyard had been like a waking-up. He could not recall entering the house; he could only dimly recall being there. He could not recall what he had started to do; he could recall only what had been done. He could not recall what desk or cupboard or safe he had opened. He could not even recall the contents of the room. He could recall only its darkness and its shape. He could not recall finding the money, nor, if he found it, what he had done with it. He knew only that he had brought none of it away. He could not recall the entrance of the miser to the room; he could recall only the patch on the dark floor.

The two really vivid memories were of going into the courtyard, and of coming out of it. Once or twice he had a feeling that it had never happened, but in the moment of the feeling a dim glow of memory told him that the feeling was merely a reflection of his agonised wish. He was suffering and making forlorn efforts to escape the suffering.

Above the imps of thought that were dancing on his brain hovered the word *MURDER.* It seemed ludicrous, insane almost, that this word could be fastened to the name Perrace. This Perrace was known to his few acquaintances as a fellow like other fellows. A fellow who had no life beyond the life which society allows to a poor man—the life of a steady worker, a respectable nine-o'clock-to-six-o'clock employee who held no opinions to attract remark, who did nothing to-day that would be remembered tomorrow, and to whom nothing outside routine ever happened. And now he had broken the bounds of routine and opened its quiet to the claws of peril and dread.

Never again would he sleep securely. Never again would he walk the streets carelessly. Life and death had broken in upon his coma, and he, who had hitherto faced only the shadow of them, must now, through the memory of a black courtyard, face the reality. And he was not ready to face it. He had acted before he had reached the mood for action. He was un-prepared. He hadn't *meant* to do it. Yet they would brand him, and if they seized him they would talk about him as though he were an animal, and not Perrace, the ordinary, likeable fellow. And then they would kill him.

He had always been assured, as most of us are, that while other men might commit murder, he, Perrace, never could. He had read in news-papers of men who committed murder, but he had read of them as monsters, remote creatures of another plane and another state; not as fellow-creatures of the world he lived in. They were not men who rode in buses and worked in offices and were sometimes out of a job, and sat in tea-shops and went to whist-drives and did a bit of gardening on Sat-urday afternoons. They were Murderers; something apart.

Yet this night he had been presented in that courtyard with himself in that shape, a self which he knew was his but which he could not rec-ognise; a self from which he revolted. Perrace, the ordinary likeable fel-low, turned within an hour into a creature who belonged in that affrighting gallery in the basement of Tussaud's.

It was ludicrous. It was like a tale of a millionaire forging a cheque for five pounds. But a persistent spot in his brain said: "Yes—but true." His quiescent mind said: "It isn't. It isn't. I didn't do it. I didn't." His active mind drowned it with "You did. You did. You may not have meant to, but you did."

Under these conflicting mental revolutions he suffered a loathing of his existence, and a bilious horror of the black courtyard. It was beginning to torment him. It danced in his mind, and his mind interpreted it to his sight and his body as clammy shadows touching the skin. In that long ride through Stepney, Aldgate and the City, he saw, wherever he looked, a courtyard thick with darkness, deaf to noise and alive only with the eyes of blind houses. A courtyard that might tempt a man and encourage him to all manner of enormities, and then turn upon him.

He left the bus at the Bank and caught a last bus for Shoreditch. He was aware that he moved rationally and spoke rationally, but this behaviour, he knew, came from the last automatic movements of his real self. That self, the self he had known these thirty years, was now lying numb and bemused. It seemed to be fading from him, his being was slowly passing into possession of a new stranger-self. He did not like this new self, and fought against surrendering to it. But there was no question of his surrendering. It was insistently taking possession of him—a nervous, feverish self that had crept out of a courtyard thick with darkness and deaf to noise. He wondered whether all murderers were possessed like this. From their behaviour in court he felt that they were not. Murder seemed to make them stronger instead of weaker, more callous instead of more sensitive.

In his room at Kingsland Road he took off his overcoat and hung it on a coat-hanger. From the other side of the room he turned to look at it. It seemed to look back at him. He took off his boots and looked at them, and they too seemed different from other boots. Mighty and terrible boots. At any moment, he foolishly felt, coat and boots might become articulate. The sight of them began to fret his already fretted mind. He gathered them up and stowed them into a cupboard. For the next half-hour he padded about the room. From time to time he brushed his arm across his eyes. Somewhere on his retina was the image of a black courtyard. He went to the mirror to see if he could find it. Then realised his own folly, and gave a weak laugh, and again felt sick.

Under this sickness he crept to the bed and fell on it, and, not expecting sleep, slept. But in the sleep he was aware that he was sleeping on the stones of a black courtyard.

He awoke as Perrace, to a few shreds of his own self not yet destroyed; but in a few seconds, when fully awake, he realised that he was no longer Perrace. He was a creature out of a black courtyard, and he existed only in relation to that courtyard. He was its prisoner. Overriding the memory of last night's affair was the more awful presence of this manifestation. He was in the world, but he was enclosed from it. He could see it only through the shadows of his courtyard.

He strove to shoulder it away by movement. He got up and exercised himself. He plunged his head and neck into cold water. He went over himself with a rough towel. He felt too sick to eat the breakfast his landlady had prepared, but he drank two cups of tea and nibbled some bread. At ten o'clock he went out and walked wherever the streets led him.

Throughout the day he loafed about the main streets of the poorer quarters. He wandered from Oxford Street to St. John's Wood, from there to Camden Town, then to Finsbury Park, to Highgate, to Islington, to Euston Road, to Charing Cross, Waterloo Road, to Kennington, Camberwell, Peckham.

After some hours of walking at his gentle padding pace, his mind cleared and things began to adjust themselves. In the light he regained something of his old self; a little of the everyday confidence he had known before yesterday. He began to feel that he had exaggerated the affair and his own fears. In the afternoon sun the black courtyard seemed far away in distance and in time and in conception. Neither the morning papers nor the evening papers carried a line about that courtyard. No doubt in a day or two it would fade from his mind as other incidents faded from the mind. Within a month he would perhaps have to make an effort to recall anything about that courtyard. It might be weeks yet before the secret was discovered, and there would be nothing by which they could connect it with him. In a momentary facetiousness the thought occurred to him that anyway it was his first offence.

But when night came upon the city he learned that the courtyard was only beginning its work upon him. He had not noted the approach of dusk, and he was walking along Rye Lane, Peckham, when the horror descended. The haunting took material shape.

He was certain that it was Rye Lane. He had seen its name on a plate at a corner. Yet, turning suddenly from a brilliant shop-window, he found that he was not in Rye Lane. Shops and lights had disappeared. He was in that black courtyard.

He could feel its darkness upon his face; he could hear its crowding silence; he could see the sightless eyes of its houses. A dry choking seized his throat. He turned in panic to get out of the place. He tore through the courtyard, and down the entrance alley. As he ran, he was aware of shouts and noises. Dimly he saw scared faces about him, and heard the grinding of brakes. He had a vision of a lorry striking his shoulder, of a bus-driver making a scowling face. But they were phantasmagoria floating across the fact of the black courtyard, and he gave them no attention. Every nerve of him was centred on getting out of the courtyard.

But he was not to get out of it. He was its prisoner. He thought he had got out of it, but, on crossing the road and taking the first turning, he found he was in it again. There it was, in Peckham, clear to the eye—a riverside courtyard thick with darkness. This time he fought his way out of it, and stood at its entrance gasping. Real people moving along Rye Lane passed him as shadows, and an elfin voice came out of the air—"How's a chap get like that so early in the evening? Quick work eh?"

The words, faint as an echo in a valley, suggested something to him, though for some time he could not locate the suggestion. Then it came to him in clear terms—a drink. A drink was what he wanted. He hadn't had any drink or any food all day. A drink might rid him of this horror. But the idea of a drink brought a crowded, noisy bar; and he could not face a crowded, noisy bar. He wondered whether he might find a quiet, side-street place near by.

A little bland-faced man was passing the mouth of the alley. He stopped him. "Er—could you tell me if there's a quiet little bar anywhere near here? Little place a respectable man can go to?" The bland-faced man looked at him. "Yes. But a respectable man can go anywhere, can't he? Still, if you want a quiet place, go up here and take the first on the left."

He thanked the bland-faced man, and went swiftly up the half-lit road. Projecting from the corner of the first turning on the left he saw a signboard—"The Anchor and Hope." He saw it as a portent. Reaching the first turning, he went to the left, anticipating the soothing effect of the drink. He went to the left, and walked into a courtyard thick with darkness and deaf to noise.

He came out of it cursing the bland-faced man, and sobbing. He fell into a loping run. He pressed his fingers to his eyes, and rubbed his face. He uttered automatic noises. His voice said "Damn—damn—damn," and many coarser words.

In a long blue-lit street his breathing made him pause. Looking about him, he saw that the street was a street and its lamps were lamps. He took off his hat and rubbed his hands round his head. Nerves, he told himself. Nerves; just nerves. That's what it was. That courtyard wasn't there. Couldn't be there. An attack of nerves. He was just *seeing* it. Well, he wouldn't see it. It wasn't there at all. It was just nerves. Nerves. Nerves.

But with that discovery he learned that he had admitted another enemy. He had admitted a word, and the word, once admitted, pattered on his brain until even the haunting of the courtyard seemed less horrible. It walked with his feet, and beat with his pulse, and floated before his eyes. Nerves. . . . Nerves. . . . Nerves. . . . Nerves. The shape of the word, as it spelt its letters before him, was of something spidery and ghastly. The sound of it became like a wail from an asylum. Nerves. . . . Nerves. . . . Nerves. . . . Or like the last rush of breath from a dying old man. Nerves. . . . Nerves. . . . Nerves. . . . Eugh. . . . Eugh. . . . Eugh.

"You better go home," he told himself. "You better go home. That's the best place."

He went home. Somehow he found his way back to Kingsland Road. He went by buses that glided through one black courtyard after another, and he walked through black courtyards. In a shop in one of these courtyards he bought a quart bottle of stout, and at last he came to his room in a black courtyard, and the room itself was a black courtyard.

He sat on the bed in that courtyard and said "Oh. . . . Oh. . . ." and "Oh, dear. . . . Oh, dear. . . ." He poured a glass of the stout, and drank it off. It soothed him, and within a few minutes the room began to resume the features of his old room. He drank another glass, and sat with hands limply hanging over knees. "I must be going mad. I must be going mad. Oh, if only . . ." He drank another glass; and soon the stout, working upon the exhaustion of the day's walk, brought sleepiness. It brought, too, the complete removal of the courtyard. As he sat on the bed, it faded from eye and mind, and all that he could see resolved itself into his own familiar room.

But in sleep it came back. It came back in all its detail. The courtyard itself, the shuttered house, the dark room, the bent old man. They danced and whirled about his consciousness. They were figures. They were colours. They were sounds and smells. They changed their form; they changed their character; they shifted from solid to vapour. But always, whatever their form or figuration, in their impact upon the brain they were black courtyard, shuttered house, dark room, bent old man. It seemed that he had not finished with them. It seemed that they were beckoning him. At times their attitude penetrated to his consciousness as friendly and encouraging. It seemed that there was something they wanted of him. But when he awoke, he awoke with a moan and a gasp and a sensation of choking.

The day repeated the yesterday. In the thin winter sunlight he was safe, but once the night had come the courtyard fastened upon him and enclosed him. London was one black courtyard. Beyond it he could see gleaming tram-cars and buses, and blazing shops, and streets crowded with faces dull or bright. But he could reach none of them. He could not get out. He could only pad round and round his courtyard, moaning.

Late in the evening, an idea came to him. "See a doctor." Somewhere in the everlasting black courtyard, a few paces back, he had noted a brass plate. With some trouble he found it again, and fifteen minutes later he was sitting in a pleasant consulting-room. The atmosphere of the room, the furniture, the bright fire, the dog's-eared back-numbers of illustrated papers, restored him to a sense of everyday. Here were peace and warmth; nothing foolish, it seemed, could live here. It was a haven of sanity and sense to which the sailing courtyard could not penetrate.

By the time the doctor came in he was collected and calm. He gave a fictitious name and address as easily as though it were his own, and began to state his case.

"Know anything about nerves, doctor?"

"A good deal of the little we can know. What's the trouble?"

"Haunted."

"Mmmmm. I see. Being followed, eh?"

"Oh, no. No. Not that. But . . . wherever I go I see a dark court-yard. A dark courtyard. It seems to close me in, like. Even Regent Street becomes a dark courtyard. Black."

"Yes. Well, there's lots of dark courtyards in London. You *would* see a lot if you go about much. There's one or two off Regent Street."

"Yes, but . . . It's everywhere. Even at home. Though I feel all right here. This is the first place I've been free of it for two days. It don't seem able to get at me here. Perhaps it can't come where there's strong people. I was wondering if you could give me some—" His voice broke. His eyes were staring past the doctor. "Oh, God—look—it's there. It's there!"

He was half-way from his chair, his hand pointing, to something behind the doctor. "The window. I can see it outside the window." The doctor did not look towards the window. He kept his eyes on his patient. "What is it you're seeing?" "It's there—outside the window—the black courtyard. All dark. And little houses."

"Yes, yes. Of course. I know."

"What d'you mean—yes, yes? Look yourself. Look through that window. Tell me what's really there."

"A dark courtyard. With little houses."

"You—you— You playing with me? Humouring me? Or—"

"Of course not, man. If I look out of that window I can see a dark courtyard with little houses. Same as you can. And everybody else. I've been seeing it every night since I've been here—these twelve years."

"It's there, then?"

"Of course it's there. . . . Now then—sit down. Take it easy. Let's try the old reflexes."

There was a ten-minute examination. The doctor went to his desk and made some notes. He turned to the patient. "What you want is a change. Complete change and rest. You're just on the edge of a break-down. But before you can get anything out of change and rest you must get this thing off your mind. You've got a dark courtyard on your mind.

Something unpleasant must have happened to you in a dark courtyard. Well, the right thing to do is to go back to that courtyard, and—"

"Go *back!*"

"Yes. Don't look so scared, man. It's the cleanest way. Go back to that identical courtyard and those little houses. At night. And face whatever it's got. Go over it all again in the identical spot. Challenge it."

"You don't know what you're asking."

"Yes I do. I'm asking you to make a drastic effort. It's the only way. Nerves are like mad dogs. Run away, and they'll get you. Face 'em, and you're all right. You must go back to that place. At night, mind you. Face it out. And if you face it and go over whatever happened there, you'll probably find that the second experience will cancel the effect of the first. A mental medicine."

"I don't think I could. You don't understand. You wouldn't—"

"You can do it. If you make yourself. Anyway, try to. Get as far as you can. I can suggest nothing else. *I* can't rid you of this thing. Only yourself can do that. Nervous troubles can only be cured by the patient. The doctor can't cure 'em."

For five nights more he lived with his horror. Through the orchestration of his waking and sleeping life it recurred and persisted like a main theme gone wild. Life, once an affair of light beat and homely tune, had become a fugue upon a black courtyard. And it seemed that there was no stopping it. Nothing he could do would obliterate it. Memory operated upon nothing else. It carried it and dandled it and frisked it under his very eyes, until his surface and his core were a black courtyard at midnight.

It was not until his whole being had become a scream of "What can I do? What can I do?" that he saw the only thing to do. A perilous thing, certainly, but a thing that would lead at least to escape from *this.* He felt that he could live no longer with it. If, then, death was the only escape, he must take that way. But not by the river or the gas-fire. Those ways were certain and fixed. The doctor's way was almost equally certain of ending in disaster, but it was the "almost" that decided him to take it.

If the police were waiting for him; expecting him, as a bungling amateur, to follow the false popular tradition and return to the place—well, that way of ending, hideous as it was, could be no worse than this present horror. And it was possible . . . it might be that they were not waiting for him. He had searched each day the morning and evening papers, but never a line had he seen about any discovery in any riverside court. It might be that nothing had become known. It might be that the doctor's advice was not only sound but safe; that this one secret visit would indeed ease him of his burden. And that he might not only lose burden and danger of the law's penalty, but win the money he had forgotten to bring away. Suppose he risked it?

With that, resolution came to him. His spirits rose. His nerves ceased their jangling. He would risk it, and he would go that night. It seemed a propitious night—the exact week from *the* night—and it would at least mean action and a result of some sort.

So at ten o'clock that night he went. In Kingsland Road the air was clear, but by the river there was again a mist, and again he passed through its streets as no more than a heavy overcoat, a soft hat, and a muffler. He found himself strangely careless of what might be waiting for him, and he walked with his usual padding step. He felt in good health—confident and strong; and when he came to the little street from which the alley led, he went lightly along it. He turned swiftly into the alley, and thence came once more into a courtyard thick with darkness, deaf to noise, and alive only with the eyes of blind houses.

For some seconds he stood still. But he saw nothing to alarm him, and heard nothing, and with quick, quiet steps he moved to the house in the corner.

There he waited. He looked round the court—challenged it, dared it. It made no demonstration. It did not threaten him. It did not frighten him. It was a court only, like other courts. Now that he was there, it seemed well disposed towards him. He wondered how he could have been so foolish as to let it weigh upon him. He must have been out of sorts last week.

He turned again to the little house. Yes; this was where he had stood, just at this shutter, just above this grating that made a right-angle with the basement window. He bent to the grating and listened. No clear sound at all came to him—only a whispering wave of silence. He touched the grating, and found it as loose as he had left it last week. It would lift easily. He lifted it, and as he lifted it a shaft of memory lit his mind.

He stood with it in his hand, and remembered that this was exactly how he had stood a week ago when he had come over faint. Exactly—the same attitude, the same finger of the left hand supporting the grating, the same movement of the right arm towards the window, the same—

And then he found himself in action. He had not directed himself to this action, but he *was* in action. He was underneath the grating, crouching in the tiny aperture before the window. His knife was working on the catch of the window. The catch slid back. With delicate fingers he lowered the window, and within four seconds he was in the house.

He switched on his torch, and its darting light showed him a dirty unkempt kitchen. But here the shaft of memory blurred and faded. He could not recall this kitchen. He moved the torch and it showed him a door and a staircase. He could not recall that staircase; but even while trying to recall it he found himself ascending it with his rhythmic padding. He reached the top and saw a passage leading to the front door, and in the passage two other doors, and another staircase. This again was strange to him, but he found himself on those stairs, going softly up, and he found himself in another and tinier passage, also with two doors. He found himself trying the handle of one of them, and working upon its lock with a wire key. And then he found the door open and himself in the room.

He darted his torch about the room and saw a chest, and a bureau, and a copper box. He went first to the chest, worked upon its lock, and routed among its contents. He was blank of all thought and all feeling; blank of all memory of repeating last week; blank of all concern of the dead old man. He was just an organism of action. At the bottom of the chest his hand touched a packet that rustled. He brought it out, and his torch showed him what it was. He thrust it into his pocket, and dived again, and found another and another. Pound-notes in packets.

The chest yielded three more packets. When he felt that he had exhausted it, he turned to the bureau. A few twists of his wire key opened it, and he dived his hand into its drawers. His hand found more and more, and he filled his pockets with them.

It was just when he was turning from the bureau to the copper box that he heard a sound. Scarcely a noise; just that faint disturbance of the air which is made by the presence of a living creature. He turned his torch flat to the floor, and with an undirected movement reached to the fireplace. His hand found a fire-iron. As his fingers closed upon it, he moved swiftly and shot the beam of the torch at arm's length towards the door.

It showed, just inside the door, the bent figure of an old man.

At that sight he knew what he had to do. Something that he had not been ready to do before, but for which he was now ready.

The old man made a faint cluck and shuffled three paces towards him. Perrace took one pace, and met him. From behind his back the fire-iron came down on the bent head—one, two—the old man fell— three, four.

He dropped the fire-iron and stepped back. His breath came out in a long rush, and with it came all the weight of fear that had been his burden. In that moment some immaterial shuttles seemed to readjust themselves, and bring into being a Perrace that was himself, but stronger. He was conscious of elation. No courtyard now could hold any terrors for him. He had rounded upon his haunting and materialised it. The live idea he had killed, as he had killed the old man. It was now a dead fact.

He shot the light of the torch upon the old man to satisfy himself that the thing was fully done; then switched off the torch, buttoned his coat, and gently felt his way down the stairs.

He came out from the basement window into a courtyard thick with darkness, and alive only with silence and the eyes of blind houses. This time it said nothing to him. He scarcely noticed it. It was just a place where he had cleared up something that had puzzled him. He padded from it into the alley, and so into the misted side-streets, and melted into other narrow streets until he appeared in firm shape at Fenchurch Street station. There, mixing with the crowd coming from a late Tilbury train, he took a taxi to Soho, and from Soho another taxi to Euston. From Euston he took a bus to Dalston, and from there he walked home.

In his room he made a close examination of his clothes, and found that he had been lucky. He stowed his money away in a suitcase and two boxes, and softly whistled a little tune. He went to bed, and slept better than he had slept for many weeks.

He slept until ten o'clock, when his landlady woke him to tell him that two important-looking men wanted to see him.

THE GRACIOUS GHOSTS

There are some houses, grim, reticent houses, which should have a ghost and haven't. There are others, bright, airy, happy houses, which shouldn't have a ghost but have one. The bright little house overlooking Regent's Park, which Lyssom had just taken, was one of these. It had an overdose; it had two ghosts.

They were not disturbing ghosts, save in the sense that all ghosts are disturbing. There was nothing eerie about them. They made no effort to "get at" people. They did not cause doors to open, or knock china about, or make rustlings at midnight. They were, indeed, remarkably well-behaved, and as nice-looking a pair of ghosts as one could wish to have about the place. They were almost company for Lyssom, and, after the first shock of the realisation that they *were* ghosts, he found himself accepting them without even a raised eyebrow. He was a lonely, middle-aged fellow, stout and bald, and it was pleasant for him to have something bright and young to look at.

For these ghosts were boy and girl. They were not Elizabethan, nor even Victorian. The girl was about seventeen and the boy about twenty; and, judged by their style of dress, they belonged to the immediate post-war period—about 1919. They first appeared while Lyssom was at dinner a few evenings after he had moved in. It was September, and still daylight. He was reaching for the bottle of Moselle when his hand stopped and his eyes remained fixed on the French window which opened to his little garden. Mentally he said, "What the devil—" then opened his mouth to say, "I beg your pardon, but—" Then he closed his mouth and said nothing, for he realised that the pleasant young couple who had thus suddenly appeared in his dining-room weren't really there.

They were there to sight, clear enough, but they were standing against the frame of the French window, and just as he was about to speak he noted that though their bodies were directly against the frame he could still see the frame through the young man's shirt-front. He sat motionless, watching. Then he smiled. The boy and girl looked at each other; then looked away; then looked again at each other. Then the girl's hand moved about an inch towards the boy's. And the boy's hand moved and clasped it, and lifted it and kissed it. Next moment Lyssom was looking at a French window, and nothing else.

In the fortnight that followed he got the habit of waiting for his visitors to appear. Their presences appeared only three times a day. At breakfast-time in the hall, looking at each other with morning smiles; around dinner-time by the French window; and between eleven and midnight at the foot of the stairs—the girl half-way upstairs, the boy at the foot. For Lyssom it was rather like a story; he developed an interest in the young shadows and wanted to know what happened to them, and why.

He wondered why they always appeared in the same places, and why the thing stopped at smiles and that impulsive hand-kissing. He wondered whether a motor-smash, a sudden illness, or a fire had claimed both of them. Sometimes there were breaks in their appearance—three or four days when there was no sign of them; and then they would appear regularly again, three times a day. This gave him further matter for speculation, and as his time was his own he did a good deal of speculating on the problem. But he could devise no explanation that satisfied him. He could only live with these amiable shadows, and wonder.

Then one afternoon he spoke of the affair to an acquaintance at the club, a man with a taste for oddities. The acquaintance, after listening some time with merely polite attention, became alert and showed a more serious attention. He woke up when Lyssom was describing the young people, their faces and hair and dress. "Oh, really. . . . Ah. . . . 'M. . . . Interesting that. Let me see, where is this new place of yours?" Lyssom gave him the address. "Ah, yes; of course. I ought to have remembered. Yes—the Panberrys' old place. I know it. Been empty some years, hasn't it? Care to ask me to dinner one evening?"

"Why, yes, if you don't mind a bachelor dinner?"

"Don't mind? Bachelors' dinners are always the best, old man. They have time for dining. Dinner is an event with them, not a quick prelude to the drawing-room. What evening?"

Lyssom named an evening. "But I don't know whether you'll see them, if that's your idea. Maybe it's only me that can see them."

"I'll chance that. I'm fairly sensitive to things of that sort if they're about. And I know that house quite well, so I won't be an intruder or an alien influence."

On an evening of the next week Lyssom and the acquaintance, Carton, were at the dining-table in the Regent's Park house waiting for the soup. It was a round table, and Lyssom had placed his guest and himself so that both had a clear view of the window and the garden. Lyssom's man had just served the soup, and retired, when Lyssom looked quickly at Carton to see if he were "receiving" anything. He was. His hand holding his spoon was arrested in mid-air, and Lyssom saw that he was seeing just what he himself was seeing. He was staring at the French window, but he seemed rather more surprised than Lyssom had expected him to be. His face, indeed, registered blank astonishment. He had spoken as though he had seen ghosts before, yet now he was staring at the window with wide eyes and a puzzled mouth. Explosively he said "But—" and went on staring. For quite a minute he stared without moving—"struck silly," as Lyssom expressed it.

Then, at the moment when the hands of the young figures met each other, he set down his spoon. Still keeping his eyes on the window he lost his vacant look, and his face broke into an amused smile. Twice he nodded his head, as though something had been made clear to him; and in a little murmur he said, "I see. . . . I see." Then he turned to Lyssom. "If you want those ghosts laid I think I can lay them."

"I don't know. They don't disturb me. I find them rather company. Of course, they might upset some of my guests some time. People get so scared of the unusual. But how would you go about it?"

"Oh, there won't be any fuss. No chalk circles or pentacles or candles. Quite a simple matter. And I think it'd be better to lay them. For their own sake. It's a duty which the haunted owe to the haunters."

"But they don't look miserable. All the ghosts I've heard or read about are unhappy. Something on their minds, and they died before they settled it, and can't rest until it's settled. But these don't look like that. They look quite happy."

"None the less, they'll be happier when they're laid; and I think I can do it. They're a nice couple, and they deserve it."

"*Were* a nice couple, you mean."

"Yes, of course. *Were.* I forgot. They look so alive."

"When do you think you'd like to try the laying?"

"Oh, one night next week. I'll telephone you. I may need some help. There's a man who knows a lot more about these things than I do, and he could probably advise me. I'll let you know."

Late the next week Lyssom had a telephone call from Carton. Carton had got in touch with his friend, and wanted to bring him along to dinner. "Nice chap. Research chemist. And there's a woman I know I'd like to bring, too. Charming woman. You'll like her. Scots, and has something of the Scots' second-sight. So she might be useful in a case like this. She's coming down from Scotland to-morrow for a few days; so shall we say Wednesday?"

Lyssom said Wednesday; and that evening Carton arrived with his two friends, Philip Rode and Miss Maclaren. They were, as he had said, pleasant people, and they seemed immediately at home with their host and his place. Each of them had the slim face and grey eyes of the spiritual type, and Lyssom was aware of a strong, warm feeling in the room which suggested that things were about to happen. The preparatory atmosphere, he thought, for the ghost-laying. The dinner went agreeably, and they talked of this and that, but nothing was said about ghosts. Miss Maclaren appeared to be much interested in research chemistry, and asked many questions which the chemist expounded as fully as he could. Carton talked of recent doings in Whitehall, and the chemist, when he wasn't answering questions, listened to his host's talk of the latest French painters.

After dinner Lyssom showed his collection of modern French works, and when that was done, and it came to whisky-and-soda time, he began to look at Carton, wondering when he would start the business they had gathered for. But Carton was deep in the subject of Japanese expansion, and kept in it until 11 o'clock, when Miss Maclaren said she must go. The chemist asked if he might drive her home—he had his little two-seater outside—and could he drop Carton somewhere? Carton said he was staying awhile; he wanted to convert Lyssom on the question of sea and air power; and the two guests went off alone. Their phrase of thanks to Lyssom seemed genuine.

It was not until they had gone that Lyssom remembered something. "Rather odd, Carton—they've appeared every evening for the last fortnight, but to-night, when we wanted 'em, they didn't appear. I forgot about it at dinner. Forgot to look for 'em. Was it hostile presences, d'you think? Though those young people seemed quite the sympathetic sort."

"No; it wasn't that."

"'M. Well, did your friends give you any advice how to handle it? And when are you going to make a start?"

"No. I didn't ask 'em. No need."

"Really? You know how to manage it, then?"

"No. No need for it now. It's done."

"Done? When was it done?"

"Early this evening. Before we arrived. You won't see your young ghosts any more."

"How was it done?"

"Well, you noticed they didn't appear this evening at the French window. They couldn't. They were at the table."

"What—behind us?"

"No, with us."

"I didn't see 'em."

"You did. Philip Rode and Miss Maclaren. They were your ghosts. I was expecting you'd recognise 'em, though they are both fifteen years older than their ghosts."

"Rode and Miss Maclaren? Ghosts? But they're alive. Ghosts are of dead people."

"Not necessarily. Ghosts of living people can haunt a beloved spot as effectively as ghosts of the dead—if they're a strong spiritual type and if they have reason for thinking and thinking about a certain place. That's what was happening here. Those two spent a summer here when he was about twenty, with the Panberrys. I was a guest part of the time, and watched the start of their affair. Then there was a break of some sort; quarrel, perhaps. I don't know. But they lost sight of each other. You can see, though, what happened later. Always they were thinking of each other and projecting themselves, in memory, to this place where they spent those rapturous hours of first love. But with such unusual force that they became visible. I recognised 'em at once as soon as their ghosts appeared at the French window the other evening. And I knew they were both still living. So I laid your ghost by asking 'em separately to meet me in town, saying I'd like to see 'em again. Then, when I'd brought 'em together early this evening, I dragged 'em along to the place where their affair began. And they laid their ghosts by their physical presence."

JACK WAPPING

At half-past four of a January morning, young Jack Wapping was recalled from an unconsciousness free of dreams into a consciousness full of that morning and the prospect of the Daily Sweat. The thing that recalled him was a peremptory carillon played upon his half-crown alarm clock. This carillon was being played at the same time upon alarm clocks in a hundred curtained bedrooms of Spadgett Street. It was Industry's call to arms, and Jack Wapping obeyed it with as much concern as the soldier obeys *réveillé;* and for a stronger reason. The soldier's failure carries loss of liberty and increased servitude. Jack Wapping's failure would have meant freedom from servitude and increased liberty—liberty to walk the streets and to owe for his rent, and to seek State relief for himself and his young wife.

He obeyed it as he obeyed it upon three hundred mornings of the year; first by giving it an unspoken imprecation (he was not sufficiently awake to swear aloud); then by sitting up in bed and rubbing his head. His next movements were to reach out and switch off its icy tinkle; to fumble for matches and light a candle; to get out of bed and stretch and shiver; and to huddle on the elements of dress.

Half-clothed in vest and trousers, he took the candle and, with delicate blundering, so as not to wake young Mrs. Wapping, he left his two-room home (with use of kitchen) and descended to that kitchen. There he set a kettle on the gas-stove; then turned to the sink and put head and neck under the tap and got busy with strong-smelling soap. He did no Daily Dozen or Half-dozen. He had neither the time for them nor the need of them. His daily tasks gave him sufficient physical exercise to set up several sedentary workers. With a soft whistling of the theme song of the last talkie he had seen he dried himself on a rough roller towel. He did not shave; for him that point of toilet belonged to the evening when he returned from work and was his own man. But at a six-inch mirror he brushed and combed his hair with zeal, and appeared satisfied with what the mirror showed him.

It showed him a young man with brisk, thick hair, a firm jaw, a clean eye and a sardonic mouth. A young man of nippy movements, and with feet on the earth. A young man of fine muscle and good figure. A young man whose expression said he would disbelieve almost anything you told him, because experience and observation of his fellows have taught him that credulity exists only to be exploited. A young man of that age—twenty-three—when the less primitive are racked by introspection; and a young man who had been earning his living these seven years, and was now supporting a home and founding a family; and beholden to nobody but the givers of Work.

When the kettle had boiled he mixed himself a cup of cocoa, and carried it and the candle up to the sitting-room. He drank it while finishing his dressing. When he had put on an old flannel shirt, a stained and dilapidated suit, and a knotted scarf, he was ready for his working day. He had three suits—a working suit, a second-best, and a best; and his new suits passed through the three stages. A working suit did not cease to be a working suit until it fell to pieces.

He raised the blind and looked out, and *grrrrrr'd* at what he saw—darkness, dripping roofs and a floating brown mist.

Having well washed himself, his next step was to make himself dirty again by lighting the sitting-room fire for the missis. When this was well going, he took from the table his bag, containing tea-can and a stout packet of bread-and-butter and cake (his breakfast), reached to a peg for his cap, and set off. But before he left he paused at the bedroom door to do something silly. He thrust his head into the room, saw that Mrs. Wapping was still asleep, and blew her a flirtatious kiss on his fingers. This was part of his morning ritual.

Ten seconds later he was out in that lamplit darkness, part of a procession of Labour towards the District station and the first workman's train. Six o'clock is the hour when his hammer must be lifted to its daily business; an hour when the clerks and the directors and the secretary are still in bed. He was part of a procession of old men, old women, young men and young girls—all of them cold, some of them with coughs, some of them with rheumatism, some of them with other incipient sickness; but none of them daring to stop off from Work while they could get about. Jack Wapping overtook and passed most of them. He walked with an easy swing, and he had no cough or rheumatism or headache to slow his step. And he had no imagination, or that coughing procession through the darkness might have dismayed him.

At the station he packed himself into a carriage which was built to hold forty and was holding sixty. He greeted a few "sight" acquaintances with a bright nod, and personal acquaintances with a word or two: "Dirty morning." . . . "This cold enough for ye?" There was not much talk in the swaying train. Half-past five in the morning is not the social hour. He held his bag in one hand, and with the other he held a strap and his daily paper, folded at the sporting page. Fifty other men were engaged with papers in equally difficult conditions. The general atmosphere of the carriage was self-enclosure and Grump. An outside observer would have judged that all these people were very unhappy. They were not. They were cheerful people—even those with coughs and rheumatism—and the Grump was not theirs; it was January's and Half-past Five in the Morning's.

When the train reached his station Jack Wapping fought his way out and swung easily up the stairs. In the street he overtook an elderly workmate. "Better put some snap in it, mate. Two minutes to. Don't want to lose a quarter."

The mate was not stirred. "All right 'smorning. Beson's on the gate."

"Ah! Nice chap, Beson."

"All! Not like Mathews. Anyone'd think the Works was *his*. Anyone'd think *he* was losing money if we was five minutes late."

"That's right. Lickspittle, him. Thinks they'll take notice of him and give him promotion. As if they cared a damn who's doing the work and who's slacking. They don't know and they don't care as long as it's done. Been with the firm thirty-eight years and ain't learnt that yet. I believe in giving these people what I get, don't you? If they consider me, I'll consider them. If they only give what they're compelled to give, we can do the same, eh?"

They passed the gate-keeper thirty seconds after the hooter had ceased, when the gate should have been shut, and Jack went straight to his shop. There were greetings. "Morning, Joe. . . . Morning, Fred. . . . Morning, Jack." Coats came off, and the man at the furnace took his shirt off. Hammers began to swing. The little shed became noisy with a jazz of rings and taps. Across the noise they talked. "What you do last night, Jack?" "Dirt track. Me and the missis. She didn't half get worked up. Wants to go again. What you do?" "Missis thought she'd like to see a picture. So we went to the Palindrome. Jolly good, too. One o' these Gang films. You ought to go and see it." "What you do, Arthur?" "Did a job of work. Repainted the scullery. Two coats. My blasted landlord won't do a thing for ye, though he's supposed to. He knows if he puts y'off long enough you'll do it yourself. He's no fool." "What you do, Fred?" "Went to the Young Russia meeting. You chaps oughta been there, too. You'd 'a heard something. Remember what I said last week about the party leaders? Well, you should 'a heard this chap. It's just what I said. They're all the same once they're nobbled. They're out for—"

Five voices, including Jack's, shouted "Shuhr . . . up! Sick o' that stuff."

"But it's right. If you chaps'd only use yer brains and think a bit. You grouse about turning out at five in the morning, and rotten pay, and yet when people are trying to help you, you say Shut Up. Don't even go to the meetings. You're being exploited all round—by your own people as well as the bosses—and ye won't hear the truth. Look at the economic ramp. . . . Look at the bankers. . . . Look at the . . ."

Jack Wapping loosed his voice at full strength. "Oh, shuhr . . . up. We get this every bloody morning. Talk about something interesting."

"I am."

"Well, it don't interest me. I don't wanter get muddled up with that stuff. It may be true, but I got enough to do thinking about earning me living. I got meself and a wife and a kid coming. It's my job to look after 'em. All these *Ideas* may be very fine, but I got no time for 'em just yet. First I got to pay me way. And that takes me all me time, see?"

He was supported by a chorus of "That's right," and this and the eight-o'clock breakfast hooter stopped further oratory. Tools were dropped; bags were opened; seats were claimed. The communal tea-pot was handed round and cans were filled. The atmosphere became companionable. Jack studied his morning paper. "Well, boys, what are we doing to-day?"

The question bore no reference to the day's work. Its reference was to horses, and which horses Shop No. 4 should favour with its communal shillings. For four of the day's races they chose a horse, and one shilling (never more than that), subscribed by the six of them, went on each horse. Fred the Red was as ardent in this as any of them.

"There's a good thing for the two-thirty. I had a word about it from the chap next door. His boy's a stable-lad at Newmarket."

Jack Wapping was sceptical. "Yeah? And what'd a stable-lad at Newmarket know about a horse trained at Epsom? Form's the thing you got to look at. Form. Now for the two-thirty I should say—"

The discussion went into committee and was ended only by the hooter announcing the end of the twenty-minutes breakfast. The decision was the daily decision to await the half-past ten sporting editions.

When these arrived, the choice for each race was solemnly made, and Fred collected the twopences and went out to put the shillings on with the bookmaker's runner who waited outside the gates. Once this, the serious business of the day, was done, the shop became a cosmos of Work and a study for any painter who set human beauty above pretty beauty. It showed brown, sweaty muscles, animal breathing, brutal rhythms. It showed the curse of Adam in being. It showed fire and dirt, and the power and fine facility of human hands. The young men of the group, in their rough strength and symmetry, could have passed as the gods of old poems. The old men were patriarchs and carried unflagging old age in its own stern beauty. It made a little epic of energy and skill, gross and splendid.

But Jack Wapping knew nothing about this. He knew that he was at work, which was sufficient to justify him in his own eyes. He knew that he was alive, and that he had this daily job at the forge and earned his living by it, and that life on the whole was pretty good. He knew that there was some mystery about this matter of Life which nobody seemed able to get at, and he felt that it could be left to others to worry about. He was too much *in* it to bother about its mystery, and he wasn't capable of much thought. When he did think it didn't seem to lead anywhere; it only muddled you. There were things he approved and things he disapproved, and that was as far as he could go. He liked his meals and his home and his wife and his half-share of the back garden and his

Saturday afternoon football, though he would have liked all these to be a bit better than they were. He disliked all changes. He disliked having to work so hard for such slender pay, and he disliked the Trade Union which helped to keep his wages from going lower. He disliked strikes because they upset the even tenor of things, and because he felt a bit mean about holding out on people—even if they were holding out on him. His ideal life was a life of independence of others, a life of the work he would choose to do with no interference from other people; a life into which he could put the best work of which he was capable. His philosophy was expressed in two words with which he answered all enquiries about his affairs—"Mustn't grumble." And most of his time was spent in doing just that. Grumbling at the weather; grumbling at his pay; grumbling at the price of things; grumbling at the behaviour of other people; and suspicious that everybody and everything were not what they seemed. If you told him that Henry Ford was the ideal employer, he wouldn't believe it. If you told him that Russia was the only country where the worker was honourably treated, he wouldn't believe it. If you told him that the Labour Party was operating for the benefit of the workers, he wouldn't believe it. If you told him that God is in His heaven, and that life is continuous on different planes, he wouldn't believe it. They sound all right, but he knows there's a catch somewhere. There always is in anything that seems good.

But all this was on the surface. Within himself he knew that he Mustn't Grumble; that things might be a lot worse; that he was Rubbing Along pretty well with £2 18s. 6d. a week and a little home and a wife, within limits, as good as they make 'em. He knew that he wasn't a slacker and that he was getting as much money as the next man who did the same kind of work; and with that he was content. There was really very little to grumble about, but to *appear* happy went against his English grain. He used his grumbling as a mask to suggest a doughty manhood which would have nothing but the best.

At the twelve-o'clock dinner hooter his hammer fell from his hand and he reached for his coat, and made for the gate. Two of his mates followed him. They went across the road to a restaurant labelled "Old Joe's." Old Joe undertook, in his announcements, to supply "A Good

Workman's Dinner, 9d." and usually he did. But his success or his failure brought him the same return—ninepence and grumbles.

Over the dinner—Irish stew and liberal potatoes—they talked little. They did not go to dinner as to a gracious interlude in the day. They did not eat for the pleasure of a harmony of flavours, or for any gratification of the palate. They ate to satisfy a craving hunger, and they did not eat prettily. But when the Irish stew and the sultana roll were done, they talked. They discussed the prospects of Chelsea, and whether West Ham's star man would have recovered from his injury by Saturday. They discussed their gardens. They discussed the manager of their section of the Works. Fred the Red wanted to know why office-workers—even down to office-boys—got their pay during their annual holidays and Bank Holidays and Christmas, while they, who happened to work with their hands, and were the backbone of the Works, couldn't have a summer holiday without losing pay. Was it fair? What was the idea? Why was a clerk so much considered above a skilled ironworker? Was it—? Jack Wapping agreed that it wasn't fair, and went on to talk of the way his missis cooked tripe. A way which would open their eyes. Next time he found a real winner, at a man's size price, they must come round to his place and try it. What about Sunday? Not that there was any pleasure in going out on Sunday. He himself loathed Sundays. Summer wasn't so bad; you could muck about in the garden and do things. But winter . . . what was there to do? All these miserable religious people shutting everything up. Just the day when people got the time for entertainment and pleasure they shut everything up. Thought they could make you go to church by doing that. Well, it'd take more than that to get him inside a church. Why couldn't we have a Sunday like they had in other countries—all the amusements open? And them that was working could have a day off some other day of the week. The very day when millions of people who couldn't travel during the week, could travel to see their friends, was the day the railways cut down their services. Sunday was hell. He wished he could work Sundays and have Tuesday off when things were open. Fred the Red took up the challenge.

"Serves you right. Because you won't organise. You won't attend meetings, even. If you want a free Sunday you can get it. You only got to make a bit more noise than the religious crowd. But all you do is grouse. And when anybody tells you the way to shake off the shackles of—"

"Oh, for Gawd's sake don't start that muck all over again. This ain't Hyde Park. Listen—there's the hooter."

Back in the shop he swung into work. The process of digesting a quickly-eaten and ill-balanced meal robbed him of a little of his morning ardour, but the afternoon held a spot of interest which kept him going. It kept them all going—the speculation as to the fate of their communal shillings and individual twopences. Was that money going Down the Drain, or would it bring them extra packets of cigarettes, an extra something for tea; perhaps a visit to the Dogs? If they came through on two or three races at a long price it would mean a new something-or-other which they had long desired. Naturally this afforded them matter to occupy the mind, and though it was a daily event it came to them freshly each day. Success meant that pleasant prize which appeals to the rich, to the comfortable, and the poor; to those who need it and to those who don't. It meant Money for Nothing.

The afternoon's labour was broken by the news of each race. They had backed horses in four races, a shilling on each horse; which meant an outlay of eightpence per man. The result of the first race was given by the newsboy at the gate without purchase of a paper, a courtesy rewarded by occasional drinks. Their employers should have blessed this result; it sent a new spurt of energy through the shop. Their first horse had come home at 100–8. They were safe for the day and Money In; two shillings per man. The other three results gave them no trepidation. If all went down they were still Money In. They gave Fred the Red hearty smacks: the horse had been his choice.

On the second race they were losers, and on the last race they were losers; but the third race set them up for the week. A winner, an outsider, tipped by only one newspaper prophet; and the price 66–1. They congratulated each other on an outstanding day—fourpence out and twelve-and-six in, each of them. It was sunshine and wine to them, and the shop's hum of work had a cheerful note. Employers set upon getting the best out of their men often ignore human nature. They think of swimming-baths, light and airy workshops, gramophones; when, human nature being what it is, they could get the best every day if they would only find winners for their men.

At four o'clock Fred the Red made tea from the communal tea-caddy, and they switched on the lights, and for ten minutes they took a "mike." They returned to labour with zest, and at the five o'clock hooter they were still going strong. But at the first blast tools were flung down, and they stretched and looked for their coats and packed their bags. The firm had no rush of work so there was no question of overtime. Jack Wapping did not like overtime, but he missed no chance of it. He liked his rest and recreation, but overtime pay at the rate of time-and-a-half was worth the sacrifice. This overtime pay he always handed to the missis to put away for her own clothes.

They straggled out into the dark evening, some slowly, some alertly. Jack Wapping shouted an airy "Good night, boys," and "Don't be late in the morning," and "Hope we have another day like to-day," and a few seconds later was well up the street. Work was done. He was a free man and a citizen, soiled and grimy, but sure of himself. He was tired but he did not slouch; his youth wouldn't let him. He walked as sturdily and swiftly as in the morning. In his late 'teens he had been something of a sloucher, but that was because he had few interests—nothing to do in the evenings and only the dull old people to go home to, with their complaints that he should do this and shouldn't do that. Now he was his own man, with a home of his own and a wife to turn to. It made a difference to a chap.

He debated what they should do that evening; the pictures, the local music-hall perhaps, second house. Or there was a six-penny dance at St. Peter's Hall. Or he might put up those new shelves that the missis wanted at the side of the fireplace. Plenty to do. He debated subtle and amusing little ways of springing the great news about the day's horses—go in with a long face of ruin; or throw the money into the room before he entered; something like that.

But when he got home and went upstairs to his room, these things seemed silly; not the real Jack Wapping. He entered as he entered every evening; casually, the sober Englishman. "Hullo." "Hullo." "Been busy?" "Pretty fair." "What you have for dinner?" "Irish stew." "Good?" "Not so bad. Might 'a been a lot better before it was good. How you been?" "Oh, pretty fair." "'M. Like to do anything to-night?

We can, y'know." "Can we?" "Ha. Had a good day to-day. Two winners. One of 'em sixty-six-to-one. Twelve-and-six in to-day. So anything you want. . . ." "Well, suppose we save it. I don't quite feel like anything to-night." He became concerned. "Oh . . . er . . . is it?" "Oh, no, just usual." "I see. . . . Well, I'll go and have a wash. Then I'll be able to give y'a kiss—eh? See anybody to-day?" "Mother came in 'smorning to see how I was. And I had a cup of tea 'safternoon with Mrs. Rayne." "Good."

The scullery, common to the three families of the house, was empty. At the sink he stripped to the waist and splashed soap and water over head and shoulders. When he was dry he made a careful shave. Then he slipped his coat over his shoulders and ran upstairs to the bedroom.

Ten minutes later he came out—a new Jack Wapping. Shining face, blue collar and shirt, bright speckled tie, second-best grey suit. He entered their living-room with a hearty and long-drawn "Ha! Feel better after that. Now we'll have a kiss—eh?"

They had a kiss. Mrs. Wapping admired him. She felt that any woman could be proud of him when he was dressed for the evening. "I got herrings for your tea. They're good for you." "Right-o. I dessay I can manage 'em."

He managed three of them and seven slices of bread-and-butter. Over the tea he told her of the day's doings—the job of work they were on; how they had selected the horses; the latest outbursts of that pie-can Fred the Red; how old Arthur's kid had been knocked down by a motor-bike. . . . When he could eat no more he helped the missis clear away, and while she washed up he went to the "easy" chair with a cigarette. It was not a very easy chair; most of its springs were gone; but with a couple of cushions it wasn't so bad. Like the rest of the home, it was an oddment, battered and fourth or fifth hand. They had picked up their home in junk shops and in the street market, but it was *their* home. Nobody could take it away; it was all paid for. He had seen enough of young chaps furnishing with new furniture, and unable to keep up the payments, and having it taken away from them, and sleeping on the floor. That wasn't his idea of the way to start life. Battered stuff his, perhaps, but all paid for. The only new article in the room, which stood out in its newness, was the clock presented by his mates of Shop No. 4.

He sat with legs stretched out, relaxed, approving his home, his wife, his condition and life generally. This was the best part of the day. He thought if Fred the Red was set as *he* was set he'd probably have no time for his crackpot ideas.

After half an hour of this alert reverie, which was as near as he ever got to thinking, he shook himself. "This won't do." He got up and fished in a corner behind a cotton curtain for a tool-box. The rest of the evening he spent in making and fixing three small shelves for the little alcove on the other side of the fireplace, and chatting amiably with the missis while working. By half-past nine the job was done, and the missis agreed with him that he had made a Proper Job of it. They debated whether it should be stained green or brown, and decided on green as lighter. Jack would get the stuff and do it to-morrow evening. She went downstairs to get his regular supper—cocoa and cake.

He took his supper in the easy chair, drowsily. Twelve-and-six was on his mind. "Twelve-and-six," he said, with a wink. "Twelve-and-six in, old girl, eh? A few days like this every week, and we'd be on velvet, eh?"

"Time you went to bed, Jack. You're half-asleep now."

"You're right." He got up and made preparations for the morning, and Mrs. Wapping began to pack his breakfast. On all nights except Saturdays ten o'clock was his bedtime; and six hours' sleep was necessary to his energetic frame, and he could always have slept longer.

In bed in the darkness, with his young wife and coming child beside him, he thought over the day and over things generally. He was keeping his end up. When you have paid rent—eleven shillings for two unfurnished rooms—and Trade Union sub. and Health Insurance and Unemployment Insurance and Slate Club and Weekly Workman's Ticket, there isn't a lot left out of £2 18s. 6d. to meet the rest of life with. But though Friday afternoon (pay day) usually found them down to a penny or twopence, they were doing it. How they did it he didn't know, but they did it in defiance of all the scientific theories of the economists and of those amateur philanthropists who lay down schedules for working-class families. He was keeping his end up, and that was enough for him. The condition of England, the rigid laws of trade, the meaning of money—of these things he knew nothing. The looming object in his life was Work, and he had got Work. If God had asked him if there was anything he now wanted his only answer would have been—an easier job and better pay. As he sank into sleep there was nothing that troubled him but the missis. He wondered when her time would be coming. He hoped it would be all right. Accidents happened sometimes. An awkward business. It gave him a little tremor.

He was still thinking about it when an interval of drowsiness interrupted him; and the next thing he consciously knew was that the alarm clock, set for half-past four, was delivering its call to arms.

ONE HUNDRED POUNDS

Granpa Ben lived in a crowd, but he lived alone. He lived alone because he wasn't much liked and didn't try to be. He suffered—or said he did—from a number of complaints, and was eager to make them vocal. He sat every morning at his cottage door in one of those little rural patches which one finds here and there enclosed in London's labyrinth. It was a patch of scattered cottages with long gardens, and a couple of small fields bare of grass. All around it the metropolitan fever ran, but never penetrated to it. It was quiet, bedraggled, and forgotten. There, at his door, he would sit every morning delivering his *appassionata* to any who would listen. They were not many, and they did not listen long.

Scarcely anybody went into his cottage. His only regular visitors were the woman who cleaned it each morning, and one other. This was the one person who could put up with his old-man egotism, his old-man ways, and his old-man talk. His young grandson. It is rare for the young to tolerate the old, even when they are pleasant, but young Bertie not only tolerated Granpa, but appeared to like him.

Granpa Ben didn't think very highly of the human race, but whenever he let himself go on that topic—and he often did—it was understood that the human race didn't include Bertie. The human race didn't give up their Wednesday evenings to sitting with the old man and telling him the local gossip. The human race didn't come in and nurse him when he was sick. The human race didn't come in on Sunday afternoons and read the paper to him. For the human race he had only a grr-cha. For Bertie he had only benedictions.

Bertie was the one person he could trust. He didn't think much of his youngest daughter, whose son Bertie was. He didn't think much of his elder brother. And he didn't think much of his other daughter, or of any of her children. Bertie was the only one he cared for and the only one he wanted to see. Bertie was the only one who paid him any attention in a way that looked as though he liked paying him attention. The others, when they had done it, had done it perfunctorily. They were free, so far as Granpa Ben was concerned, to go and hang themselves; and he had told them so. They were a rough lot, and he didn't trust them.

Of course, when a distant and still older relative of Granpa's left him his life-savings, amounting to one hundred pounds, some of them came round to see him. He expected they would, and he had spent the afternoon in preparing for them various rounded, if not polished, phrases. They did not stay long. Before they had time to congratulate him he told them that none of it was for them and they needn't waste their time smelling round for any of it. They were a rough and stupid lot, and they hadn't done anything for it, and would only waste it. When he (Granpa) was gone, it was to be all for Bertie, and he would make a will that very night. Bertie was a nice, quiet lad who would handle it sensibly.

Their reception angered them, and the announcement, a sort of pendant to the reception, dropped pepper on the anger. They went away with a few of the best soldiers' farewells to Granpa, and with much bitterness towards Bertie. Among themselves they said things about Bertie; the kind of thing that disappointed legatees always say about the favoured one. Bertie, they said, had known what he was up to. Bertie was a sly one. Bertie must have guessed there'd be something to come into. Bertie and his Wednesday evenings and his reading the paper on Sundays. Urrch. . . . They expressed the hope that the old man would make a mess of his will so that it would be set aside. One or two expressed the hope that he would peg out that night before making the will. They expressed hopes about Bertie in terms which no modern novelist has yet found an excuse for printing.

When Granpa went up to the lawyer's office to collect his inheritance he demanded the company of Bertie. At the lawyer's office he demanded his money in cash. Cheques, he said, didn't look like money, and he didn't trust them. Bertie said that a cheque would be better, as he could pay it straight into a bank or into the Post Office. Granpa said he didn't want no banks and no Post Office; he could look after his own money. Bertie said it was dangerous to keep money in the house—as much money as that—particularly in the kind of place where they lived.

The lawyer, too, said it was dangerous, and advised cheque and bank as the safest and most usual. Granpa told them both to mind their own business. All his life he had kept his bit of money under his hand, and it was as easy to keep a hundred pounds as it was to keep a few shillings. If people wanted to rob you, they'd rob you for a few shillings as certainly as they'd rob you for a hundred pounds. The lawyer said that wasn't his experience. A hundred pounds was a concrete sum with potential uses. With that sum a person could get away, could go abroad out of danger, and still have some of it left for beginning a new life; whereas a few shillings meant nothing but a few petty purchases. The one was a definite temptation to any violence; the other wasn't. Granpa said the lawyer's experience was limited. Many robberies had been committed for the sake of a few beers and cigarettes, some of them with violence, and one or two with murder. But the lawyer needn't worry. Anybody who was going to get Granpa's hundred pounds would have to be a smarter man than Granpa; and anybody who was going to murder him to get it would have to be tougher. He doubted that such people existed.

So he carried his hundred pounds away with him in a little packet of notes, and, despite Bertie's exhortations all the way home, he said he was going to keep it in his cottage. Under his hand, so that he'd always know where it was. So Bertie, like most other people who argued with Granpa, had to let him have his own way. When they got home to the cottage, the old man took the packet from his inner pocket, and put it on the mantelshelf. "Well, there it is. And it's going to be yours, me boy. But it's not going to stay there for long. I'm going to find a home for it, what nobody else'll find till me will's read. . . . Yes, Bertie, that'll be all yours when I'm gone. Sit down, me boy. We've had a tiring day. I think we deserve a little drop o' something hot." So they had the something hot, which was cocoa for Bertie and rum with a slice of lemon for Granpa. Granpa kept looking at the mantelshelf, and nodding. "Yes, it'll be all yours, me boy, when I'm gone, and I hope you'll see that none o' them others get any of it. They're a low lot. Of course, you won't get it yet awhile, y'know. I'm not going out yet."

Bertie said, dutifully: "I certainly hope not, Granpa."

"No, me boy. But you'll be a bit older by the time I do go, and you'll appreciate it more. You'll be able to put it to better uses."

Bertie said, "Yes."

"I don't believe in people having money too young," the old man went on. "Not even when they're as steady as you. Later on, you'll thank me for minding it for you."

Bertie agreed, and said that later on he would know more about the business which interested him—the business of newspaper and tobacco shop—and would certainly be better able to use the money to better advantage. But he again urged his Granpa to put it into a bank. Granpa said no, he wouldn't. Bertie urged that, sleeping alone in the house, he was open to all sorts of attack. People would hear—indeed they already knew—that he had come into money, and might take a chance on his having it in the house. He ought to have somebody to sleep with him. Granpa said he didn't want nobody. Bertie said that with the rough lot around them, anything might happen. Granpa thanked Bertie for his concern, but said he could look after himself. Perhaps Bertie might keep a look-out on his way home, and if he saw anybody suspicious about, he might see what they were up to, and if necessary he could warn his Granpa. But apart from that, he needn't worry.

So Bertie went off, though with no sign of not worrying. Granpa locked the door after him, bolted it, and set the catch. Then he went back to his living-room, and sat down to his final night-cap.

For some time he sat in that pleasant state of mazy reverie which he would have described as "thinking things over." There was a certain gratification in being in possession of a hundred pounds. He didn't want it himself; his needs were few and were covered by his pension. The gratification arose from the fact that it annoyed so many people. To annoy people usually involved some tiresome activity; here he was annoying quite a number of people without doing anything. He was chuckling at the image of their annoyance when his ears half-caught a sound—a baby of a sound which he couldn't be sure was a sound. At first he thought it was such a sound as would be caused if somebody had touched ever so lightly the latch of the door. Then he thought it wasn't. It was probably the shredded sound of a cold cinder cracking, or of the fork slipping down the rim of his supper-plate.

Ten seconds later he had forgotten about it. He sat in drowsy comfort, wondering what he should have for dinner to-morrow. He thought of sausages and then he thought of roast lamb. Still wondering, he passed one or two stages towards the edge of sleep when he heard, and heard clearly this time, a little sound which wasn't the same as the first sound but was no more natural or friendly than that sound. It was the sound which is made when a boot touches gravel and sharply draws back. He sat up then. He reached to the lamp and turned the wick low. He sent his being into his ears, and became nothing but a listener. But after a second or so all he could hear was drumming silence. He heard it so long that finally he ceased to hear it because it was everything. A sudden movement of his hand as it scraped his trousers to still an itching on the knee had the effect of a buzz-saw.

Some seconds after the silence had recovered from the scrape of his hand and was again in possession of the room, his being passed from his ears to his eyes. Something beyond the doorway of his living-room had moved. He was so keenly listening at that moment that his eyes were not properly reporting to him. They reported only that they had something to report. He called them into action, and began to look. He looked over the back of his chair, and as he looked he located the movement. He looked into the little entry which came between his living-room and the door. It was in darkness; the dim light of his lamp did not reach it. But though it was in darkness it was not in such complete darkness as to make movement imperceptible.

The latch—the latch of his front door—was moving. It was moving without sound; a gentle up and down; once, twice, three times. Then it rested. It was as still as it always was, and for a moment he couldn't be sure that he had seen it move. But in the succeeding moments he knew that it had moved, and that he had heard those noises, and that the noises and the movements were connected. Also that the two details meant a burglar or burglars. Somebody, as Bertie had said, who had heard about his money and was working on the chance that he might have it in the house.

All right. If that was their game he would join it. He sat still, and watched. His eyes then received another movement; a much clearer movement this time because it had a white covering. It was the movement of the forepart of a hand coming through the little letter-slit and feeling for the middle bolt.

Confronted with this intelligence Granpa proceeded to action. He got up. Despite his age and those infirmities he was always talking about, he got up without a sound, and when he got up he had the poker in his hand. With old-man movements but young-cat stealth he crossed the room to the dark entry. He stood aside from the door, keeping his breathing as subdued as possible. He bent down and listened. Somebody, he was certain, was on the other side of the door, listening, too. For some seconds the man inside and the man outside crouched and listened and waited, only a wooden board with lock and bolt separating possible murderer from possible victim.

Then, when Granpa knew from the feel of his skin that somebody with no love in his heart was outside that door, he made two soft movements. He slipped lock and bolt, and opened the door. A crouching figure darted back but not swiftly enough to escape Granpa's third movement, which was a downward sweep of the poker. The figure went down with the poker. Granpa saw it down, and ran back to the parlour for his lamp.

In his haste he wasn't as quick as he wanted to be in turning up the wick. His hand was shaking. When he got to the door with the light the figure was still there, but it was not alone. It had been joined by another figure. A young girl was bending over it. He recognised her—Mary, Bertie's special friend. "Why—Mary—what's all this? What you doing here?"

"It's Bertie."

"Bertie? Good God, what've I done? I struck him down. Bertie? Good Lord; I thought it was the burglar, and I struck him down. He must 'a been coming to warn me, or chase 'em off. I asked him to keep a look-out going home. He kept telling me to be careful. He must 'a chased 'em off just as I come out. Why couldn't I 'a copped them instead of him? And now I've struck him down, and perhaps— Oh, God."

Mary snapped at him. "It's all right, it's all right." She had one hand on Bertie's wrist, feeling his pulse, and the other on his head. "He isn't dead. He's only stunned. Look—he's coming round." The old man dithered round her with "That's good, that's good." She waved him off. "Well, don't stand there doing nothing. Silly! Go and get some water.

And a cloth. He'll be all right in a minute. But get some cold water—quick."

She kept her hand on Bertie's wrist till the old man had gone inside. She was a nice girl, and she wanted to spare the old man the sight of the knuckle-duster and the bit of wire which had slipped out of Bertie's sleeve.

THE MAN WHO LOST HIS HEAD

The accident that befell Peter Smothe was no such accident as is met by compensation from our popular daily papers. Their catholic and imaginative lists stop short of that kind of accident.

It is said of many of us when, in times demanding the packed thought of an hour, we are unable to attain even a moment's reflection—that we have lost our heads. The term is one of those passionately tropical images which fall so glibly from the lips of accountants, stockbrokers, cricket-umpires and other repressed poets. But with Peter Smothe the thing happened. He did actually lose his head, and lived to know that he had lost it.

It began in that restiveness which comes to many a man at fifty. He came to see his life as flat and unprofitable. He looked about him and saw—or thought he saw—other men leading vivid-coloured lives; lives as full of zest and effulgence as a fire-opal; while his own had been safe, warm—and dull. He was fifty, and he had had none of that highly-charged life of which he read in the newspapers. He forgot, of course, that they were they, and he was he; and that a man cannot choose his way of life. He can be only what his chemistry and his karma allow him to be. He can be only himself. To seek to be something else is to throw the whole mechanism of his being out of gear.

But Peter Smothe was sick of being himself, and at fifty he decided to be something else; anything else. He felt it a sorry thing that a man's life should run on one set of rails. That a man should spend his little span in being but one kind of man—a soldier, an actor, a geologist, a scholar, a lawyer, a painter. Why couldn't he have a little of each? He realised that at fifty it was too late to try for a little of each, but at least he would have something different. He had had enough of his rails, and since most of his life was gone, this was the time, if ever, while he was yet able and healthy, to try something new; something utterly alien to his previous experience.

213

So, upon a fine morning, he packed a small bag, and left his Kensington flat without any word of his intention; and was never again seen in it.

He had no clear plan, other than escape into a new world. A passing delivery van gave him his first pointer. He saw the words "Pentonville Road," and he hailed a taxi, and said, "Pentonville Road." He stopped the taxi half-way up the long ascent of that road, and went down a side turning. There he took the first turning on the right. He walked down this littered street, studying its decrepit houses. One of them, not so decrepit as the rest, had a card in its window—"Lodgings for a Respectable Single Man." He knocked at its door, and when it was opened he crossed the threshold of that house and of his former life.

In that street he remained for four months. He was within a threepenny bus-ride of his own home, yet, after a week or two, as far from it as if he were in Iceland. He became one more of the annual hundreds of Mysterious Disappearances.

And he became a new man. He ate in squalid little eating-houses. He hung about the Islington streets and talked to all sorts and conditions. He consorted in bars with the less-favoured specimens. He learned to use their talk, and do their things, and soon to accept their thought. He told himself that he was having a high old time. He looked back on his staid bourgeois life with impatience and contempt. To think of the years he had wasted on it. He wondered how he had endured it so long. He wondered why he had looked with shivers on the kind of life he was now leading. He gave his old self a grimy laugh.

He felt that he was now leading the real Bohemian life; not the well-to-do imitation of it; and realised that it was the life he had always, secretly, wanted to lead. His friends, he thought, would call it *going to pieces*. He himself called it *branching out*. He thought of the anecdotage with which he could surprise them when the mood took him to return. He thought of the wisdom by which he could shock the innocence of two of them, who claimed to know things because they dabbled in social service. He did not know that he was not going back.

There came a night when he met, in an obscure tavern near King's Cross, a man from whom he would have shrunk a few months ago, but whom now he saw as an Interesting Man. The creature was dark-haired and untidy; his face and hands were so unclean that they gave dreadful hints about the rest of his body. He wore a tattered overcoat with the collar turned up. The collar was buttoned and the rest of the coat hung from him in a fork. He used the unclean hands to stress the key-word of every sentence in a way that suggested the Near East, He, too, was about fifty, but he had led a more tumbled life than Peter Smothe, and his face was lined and drawn. But the eyes were brighter and more alert than Peter Smothe's. They had been called to look upon strange and unexpected things in their fifty years, while Peter Smothe, until four months ago, had seen little that was strange and unexpected. He still had, in moments of repose, the calm eye of the club-man.

The stranger, having selected Peter Smothe for his audience, began to talk of things he had seen. He revealed not only alert eyes but a brain. It was not the kind of brain Peter Smothe knew in Kensington and in his clubs; but he would have been disappointed if it were. The man talked of really strange things, and talked of them as casually as men talk of a visit to the theatre. He talked of The Power. He talked of the *Petit Albert* as others talk of the latest novel. He talked of the sword and the cup, and of things he had seen done in Greece.

"Mind you, I don't talk in this way to these people here. It would be a waste. But you, sir, I perceived at once, are an educated man. You think. These people"—he waved the soiled hand and the funereal fin-gernails—"these people—cattle—dross for cemeteries. Impossible to talk to. But you, I see, think things out. You are not bemused by such child-ish nonsense as laws, and such artificially-created things as crime. Dope—don't you agree? All dope. When I see the way that tenth-rate little humbugs in power bemuse the mass of the people with their stale old tricks, I could—" He finished on a crescendo of profanity.

Peter Smothe hugged himself. "Most interesting man," he thought. "Lovely Type. Quite like one of these master-criminals." Aloud he said, "Won't you have a drink with me?"

"Don't mind. Make it a whisky and peppermint." When the drinks came he said, "Suppose we sit down. Could you pull that other chair over to this table?" Smothe went over and fetched the chair. The soiled hand shot into the pocket of the soiled overcoat. The soiled hands carried the glasses to the table. The hand that held the glass of Peter Smothe went back to the overcoat pocket. "Now we can talk. . . . My views perhaps may seem extreme to you, but often to reach the desirable middle it is necessary to exert ourselves towards the extreme. There was a man I knew in Greece. An extraordinary man. You'd have liked him. Satan we called him. I learned a lot from him. Oh, a lot. Not all I wanted to learn, or I wouldn't be in this place talking to you. But enough to be useful from time to time. *His* views I used to consider extreme, but I found he was only aiming further than he wished to reach. Which is what I always do. I remember once in Marseilles, when I was in some little trouble—"

Peter Smothe repeated to himself that This was Lovely. He was in touch with the real underworld of which he had read in novels. This man, talking a farrago of street profanity and sham education, good phrases and illiterate phrases, was a Find. He decided that he must cultivate him.

After a return of drinks they parted on Peter Smothe's suggestion that they meet the next evening. The stranger thought it likely that they would. He could not be sure; affairs might detain him; but he hoped to be there. If not, some other night. As they went out Smothe trod on a tiny empty capsule which lay by the stranger's feet. He did not notice that he had trod on anything.

He walked to his dingy room in a queer state of elation and fatigue. The man's appearance and talk had elated him, but something else about the man had exhausted him. It was as though he had sucked all vitality from the air about them, and left Smothe only the nitrogen. His head was light and his legs were heavy. It was a clear, dry night, and still early—just the night for one of those prowls in dim quarters which had become a habit with him. But he found that he wanted only to be in bed. The ten-minute climb from King's Cross to that bed called for an effort. It seemed unattainably distant. Every hundred yards seemed a mile. But after some hours of plodding he made it, and was surprised to see that his clock showed that he had left King's Cross twelve minutes ago.

❀

His first awareness of himself next morning was that he was a living Thirst. He could not realise arms or legs, or life itself. His whole being was Thirst, and his only sense-perception came through the throat. He got up to seek water, and drained three glasses. Within a few minutes his mind and body resumed the normal coursing of life, and he felt able to wash and dress.

Having washed and half-dressed, he prepared to shave, and it was here that the normal coursing of life was again arrested, and his being became one extreme sickness. He had just taken up the shaving-stick, and had tilted the mirror, when he dropped the shaving-stick and almost knocked the little mirror to the floor.

The face that looked back at him from the mirror wasn't his.

He had tilted the mirror in the casual faith that it would show him what it had shown him throughout every day of all his years—a chubby pink face, a little blond moustache, blue eyes and thin blond hair. What it did show him was black, lank hair, a lined and drawn face, dark, restless eyes, a black forecast of beard, and a general air of grubbiness.

Wondering whether it were nightmare, or if he were still suffering from last night, he rubbed his hand heavily across his face, and looked again. There was no doubt of it. He was awake; from the street came the cries of the morning; from below came the familiar sounds of that dingy house; from the window he saw the bedraggled figures he saw every morning. And in the mirror he saw a face that was not his.

Before he understood the full implication of what had happened, and the frightful dilemma in which it placed him, he was aware only of that sickness which comes to all men in presence of the unaccountable. Something had happened which *didn't* happen; something out of nature; something against the sun. We live by a peaceable faith in the course of nature; a faith which takes so much for granted that if the morning sun were to shine upon us from the west, and the stars appear in daylight, we should stand still in dismay. For the moment Peter Smothe stood still in dismay. Four times he went to the mirror, and four times he sat down and stared at the carpet. The impossible thing *had* happened. He had a new face. The rest of his body was the body he had known for fifty years. His hands and legs, which he examined slowly and in fear, were his. The face was not.

At the fourth examination of it, he felt that, strange and repellent as it was, he had seen it before. He spent some minutes in trying to re-member where he had seen it, and only after searching about all the queer faces he had seen in the last few months did he recall last night. The Interesting Man in the bar. And then he recalled the unusual effect of two glasses of light beer. The face he saw in the mirror was the face of the Interesting Man.

When, in the course of an hour, he came to consider his position in relation to everyday affairs, he realised that he could not face the woman of the house. He would be a stranger. He would be a stranger every-where. One thought came to him; the thought that comes to every man in every kind of disaster. Flight.

At eleven o'clock when, as he knew by custom, the woman was out, he fled. He took his bag and fled, and boarded the first bus that came along. He sat in the bus with the desolate feeling of being Nobody. His light pretence in leaving home and sinking his identity under an as-sumed name was now changed to dismal fact. He was not Peter Smothe, and he was not really the Interesting Man in the bar. He had achieved completely what he had thought he wanted: he had got away from himself.

He left the bus at the Strand, and took the bus behind it, which was labelled for Waterloo. He did not know why he should go to Waterloo, but he decided that he might as well go there as anywhere else. It was distant from Islington and from Kensington, and it was a quarter which, outside the platforms of its station, was known to nobody of his own sort.

In a dim street off Lower Marsh he found a room to let, and into it he took his misery. He hunched himself on the narrow bed, and tried to realise what had happened, and to follow out its implications. But the thing would not resolve itself into thought; he could only look at it and wonder. A wild hope came to him that as this mad thing had happened, so it might un-happen. It might last only for a while. Whatever madness was at work upon him might exhaust itself, and he would find himself again Peter Smothe. He thought of his Kensington flat, and prayed that the thing might pass, and that he might be again Peter Smothe, and abandon his foolish antics of the last few months. Every fifteen minutes he went to the mirror, but the mirror had nothing for him.

Towards late afternoon his feeling of sickness increased, and he realised that he had eaten nothing. With an effort he dragged himself out to seek some secluded eating-house. But he went no farther in his search than some twenty paces.

He had scarcely left the house when two men confronted him. They confronted him very solidly, one on either side of him. The stouter of the two said, "Just a moment. We are police-officers. What's your name?"

"Er—what—er—Peter—er—Arthur Exford."

The man studied him. "You answer to the description of a man wanted by the Southampton police. Known as Boris Gudlatch."

"That's not my name. And I've never in my life been in Southampton."

"I see." The officer looked at the poor street and the shabby creature, and seemed trying to reconcile the street and the shabbiness with the delicate voice. He made his decision on the street and the shabbiness, and took Peter Smothe by the arm. "You better come along to the station. If there's a mistake we can soon settle it." He turned to his companion and nodded towards the house. His companion went to the house, and Peter Smothe was taken to the station.

At first he was bewildered and incoherent, as all respectable men are when their arms are taken by policemen. He could not clearly grasp what was happening, or why, or what he should do. He could only utter feeble protests. At the station he was told that he must expect to wait awhile, as officers were coming from Southampton with witnesses. If a mistake had been made, he would no doubt understand that the interests of justice must be served even at inconvenience to innocent people. He continued to protest. "I don't know what it's all about. I've never been in Southampton in my life, and my name isn't the name you mentioned. I'll admit that it isn't the name I gave." Under this new trouble he forgot the trouble that had come upon him in the morning. There was no mirror in the station, and he talked to them as himself. "No. It isn't the name I gave. I had a private reason for giving that. Nothing to do with anything that would interest you. I've just been going about

London seeing life. Actually, my name is Peter Smothe. My address is Helsingfors Mansions, Kensington. You'll find me in the telephone book. And you can ring up and ask my man to come along."

"You were there yesterday?"

"Er—no. No, I wasn't there yesterday. I haven't been there for a month or so. I told you I've been wandering about London. But I left my man enough to go on with, and he'll probably be there."

"Well, we'll ring him up."

They rang up, and they told Peter Smothe that his man was coming along by taxi, and had expressed some anxiety concerning the disappearance of his employer. The officer, not certain whether he had an amiable eccentric, or a bluffing criminal, gave the benefit to courtesy, and assured him that if he were the man he claimed to be, everything would be all right, save for the inconvenience, which couldn't be avoided.

Within half an hour his man arrived, and he got up from his hard chair with a gasp of relief. "Hendrick!" Hendrick took no notice. He turned to the officer, "Where's Mr. Smothe?" The officer said, "There." Hendrick looked round the room. "No. That's not him." Peter Smothe became indignant. "What's the matter with you, Hendrick? I *am* here." Hendrick looked again at him. "Don't know what you're talking about. You're not *my* Mr. Smothe."

"But I *am*. Hendrick—my parrot—Mulvaney. You know the parrot, Mulvaney. And my collection of enamels. And the cabinet in the corner with the Bohemian glass. Hendrick!"

The officer looked at both of them. Hendrick looked at the officer and indicated Peter Smothe with a nod. "Seems to know a lot about Mr. Smothe's habits and his flat. But that ain't Mr. Smothe. I been with Mr. Smothe eleven years. I ought to know him. He went off sudden-like some months ago, and I haven't seen him since. But that ain't him. My Mr. Smothe was yellow-haired and pink. Chubby face, sort of. Blue eyes. Always very neat and what you might call spruce. *That's* no more him than I am."

"But, Hendrick—"

Hendrick was thanked for coming, and Peter Smothe was left alone. He was left alone for half an hour, which gave him time to realise his folly in sending for Hendrick. The impossibility of explaining to Hendrick that though he had lost his head he was still Peter Smothe. The impossibility of explaining to police-officers that a man could lose his head, and go about with a head that didn't belong to him. The impossibility of explaining anything.

And then his loneliness was broken. Four other men came into the room. They were ushered in by an officer and they sat down on chairs, gingerly and self-consciously. An odd lot. A man who looked like a clerk; a man who smelt of fish; a man who looked wicked enough to double-cross Satan; and a man who couldn't look anything because his eyes were everywhere and his face was constantly changing. The only point they had in common was shabby appearance.

They had had only the time to look round the room and grin or grimace at each other when a big man came in and presented a young girl to the company. She stood in the doorway and looked them over one by one. The big man said, "Well?" Without hesitation she pointed to Peter Smothe. "That one." "Sure?" "Absolutely. Wearing different clothes, but the face is unmistakable. I saw it quite clearly when he stood in the light before he started running." "Thank you." He called through the door: "Take Miss Jones to the next room. Don't let her see the young man. Then send the young man."

A young man came in. He, too, studied the company. The officer lifted his head in enquiry. The young man nodded. "Yes—over there by the window. That one." He pointed to Peter Smothe.

"Sure? He says he's never been in Southampton at any time."

"I'm certain that's the man I saw. Different clothes, but the face—I saw it quite clearly for some seconds. Don't see faces like that every day. Not in Southampton, anyway."

The young man was waved out, and when he was gone the four other men in the room were waved out. The officer turned to Smothe.

"Two witnesses have identified you as a man wanted by the Southampton police. I hold a warrant for the arrest of that man, known, among other names, as Boris Gudlatch, on a charge of murder."

"Mur—"

"It is my duty to detain you and take you to Southampton to answer a charge of robbery at a jeweller's shop in Humstrum Street, at five o'clock yesterday afternoon, and of murdering John Smith. It is my du—"

"But I tell you again I've never in my life been in Southampton. It's ridiculous. It's rubbish. These people are making a mistake. I—"

"You are at liberty to make a statement, or not; as you please. If you wish to make a statement, it is my duty to warn you that anything you may say may be used in—"

"I've not been out of London at all the last four months. I was in London all day yesterday. I was wandering about all the afternoon, and I can call witnesses who saw me at nine o'clock near King's Cross, and—"

The officer had held up his hand, but it wasn't the warning hand that made him break off. It was the realisation that he had spoken to nobody through the whole afternoon, and had stopped nowhere; and the realisation that a man could have been in Southampton at five o'clock, and yet have reached a King's Cross bar by nine o'clock.

"If you don't wish to make a statement," the officer said, "it would be better to say nothing for the present."

So Peter Smothe said nothing. He saw the utter futility of making a statement. He saw the impossibility of an alibi, and the idiocy of telling this man, or any man, that somebody took his head away last night and gave him his present head in exchange. He closed his mouth and dropped his hands, and suffered himself to be taken to Southampton and confronted with three more eye-witnesses.

Six weeks later he learnt his lesson. He learnt in exaggerated form what every man learns in some degree who commits his kind of folly. He learnt that when a man wilfully flies from his life; when he wilfully loses his true self—or his head—he has lost it for ever.

MURDER UNDER THE CROOKED SPIRE

The apt setting and circumstance for the successful murder are manifold. Some assassins, with unconscious fitness, choose violent settings for their deeds of violence. They take their "prospects" to riversides at midnight; to subterranean caverns; to unvisited hilltops; to forlorn cliff paths, or to the dreadful hollow behind the little wood. Others, not so violent, choose quiet settings for their quiet devilry. They take their "prospects" to unoccupied villas in demure suburbs; or they work in the peace of domesticity, and so respect that peace that they disturb it with no harsher weapon than a helping of weed-killer from the garden-shed. There is, indeed, no end to the settings which, by their fitness for purpose, connive at and collaborate with the evil that men do.

But none, I think, could be more apt than that chosen nearly a century ago by Mr. John Platts of Chesterfield, the city of the Crooked Spire, for his solitary excursion into evil. For Mr. Platts pursued his daily affairs in circumstances which were ideal for murder; circumstances which surely offered a constant temptation to murder. He was so placed that throughout his working hours he was surrounded by blood, and could appear in public at any time of a working day with blood on his hands or on his clothes without exciting the least tiresome conjecture among his fellows. Queer noises and the sound of blows could arise in his shop and no neighbour would attach sinister intent to them.

Mr. Platts was a butcher and kept a slaughter-house.

He was a young man of twenty-two, squat, bull-necked, and only five feet tall; and had been engaged for a year or so in this business before he saw its potentialities in the matter of settling old scores. When he did realise this, he put it to the test, and very nearly committed the successful murder. It was a murder that would have satisfied the Master, who, in his essay, laid down once and for all the requirements of a murder which could be considered as a contribution to this Fine Art. It would

223

also have satisfied the amateurs of his imaginary Club, and would have notably stirred that connoisseur nicknamed Toad-in-the-Hole. It did, in fact, for almost twelve months, rank as one of the many successful (*i.e.,* undiscovered and unsuspected) murders of England, and would have passed into the long but uncompiled catalogue of these disasters, but for the sanitary zeal of the owner of a courtyard in which was a pond used as a public shoot.

I say "zeal" because a hundred years ago, sanitary attention to public places was not given daily or even weekly; often not at all. The man who was responsible for discovering that there had been a murder stated that he had been frequently employed by the owner of the yard to empty that particular pond; "frequently," as it appeared in evidence, meaning once a year. Mr. Platts had doubtless counted on that pond remaining as undisturbed as other ponds on private property; and it was only the perverse and unpredictable factor of a landlord's annual concern for public health that brought him to the gallows.

The murder was discovered late in 1846, and Mr. Platts was tried and condemned in 1847. But the deed was done in 1845.

At that time Mr. Platts was running his butcher business at Chesterfield—it was situated in The Shambles—in partnership with a man named George Collis, destined to be his victim. Collis, a young man of twenty-six, apparently financed the business, and sometimes financed Mr. Platts; and the sole motive of the murder was that Platts owed his victim some two or three pounds, and the victim was pressing him for the money. A motive that may sound frivolous for an operation so profound and irrevocable, until we remember that in the past many a murder was committed for less than that sum.

At the beginning of December, 1845, Mr. Platts decided that he must find a way out of his three-pound trouble. Accordingly, on December 7th, which happened to be a Sunday (a sad slip on the part of Mr. Platts, since that choice of day fixed in people's minds certain things which, coming on any other day, they would have ignored): on December 7th Mr. Platts made an appointment with his partner that they should meet that evening at the shop of a mutual acquaintance, and he would settle. George Collis accepted, and in the half-lit murk of that December evening, while the godly were stepping to worship at church or chapel, he set out to keep the appointment, blessedly unaware that he was keeping an appointment with Death. At the same time Mr. Platts also set out and, to the accompaniment of church bells, made *his* way to the appointment, which, in his case, was an appointment with Murder.

This was no crime of impulse; it was planned and the mutual acquaintance at whose shop they were to meet—a man named Morley— was in the plan. He, too, owed money to Collis; and it was agreed that Platts and Morley should jointly dispose of Collis, and by this act evade payment of their debts, and benefit from whatever plunder the pockets of the victim might afford. And there was a shadowy third, unnamed in the report of the trial and indicated only by asterisks, who appears to have been brought in by the murderers in case their joint assaults were ineffectual. He played his part in the affair, and at one point of the proceedings was seen by several people but not recognised.

People saw, indeed, though obliquely, a great deal of this business. The odd thing about it, that marks it from most murders, is that it was a murder committed, so to speak, under everybody's nose. Nobody *saw* the murder, and nobody at any time saw a corpse; but many people *heard* it. Heard it distinctly; heard blows and a fall and heavy breathing. But they heard these sounds from a slaughter-house, and naturally none of them guessed what actually was happening. Only the fact that it was a Sunday caused them, as I say, to note certain goings-on in The Shambles, and to remember those goings-on some nine months later. But at the time of noting them they only chaffed Mr. Platts on his Sabbath activity, and murder was undreamt of. When at last it was discovered, not a spot of direct evidence could be brought against Mr. Platts. The evidence upon which he was arrested, tried, and ultimately condemned, was cumulative and damning enough, but it was purely circumstantial.

At about a quarter to seven of that Sunday evening of 1845, Mrs. Franks, of the "Angel" tavern, near The Shambles, had in her public parlour two regular customers—Mr. Collis and Mr. Platts. From their talk it appeared that they had on this occasion met by accident, and were on their way to another meeting-place. They chatted amiably and drank with each other, and at seven o'clock went out together. At a little after eight, Mrs. Franks again saw Mr. Platts, but this time he was alone. Mr. Collis never again visited her tavern.

At ten minutes past seven a young carpenter, named Heathcoat, was passing through The Shambles when he heard voices coming from a shop which he knew to be Morley's. The door was open and he looked in. He saw Morley, Platts, Collis and another man—the shadowy third—whom he did not know. From their tone and attitude they were disputing. It sounded interesting, and he stood aside to hear more of it. But he was disappointed. It seemed that one of them had heard footsteps outside, for, just as the dispute was reaching a point of excitement, the shop door was banged and barred. He went on his way and thought no more of the incident.

At half-past seven a young man named Slack, on his way to his usual Sunday evening drink and talk, saw two men supporting another, who appeared to be very drunk. His legs kept giving way. He recognised one of the men as Platts. He saw them arrive at Platts' shop, and saw them push the drunken man inside. He saw the man fall down, and he heard the door being bolted and saw a curtain fixed over the ventilation holes of the door. Judging the affair to be the end of a binge, he, too, went on his way, and thought no more of it.

A few minutes later, a man named Harvey, a friend of Platts, was passing the shop when he came to a sudden stop. The shop was in darkness, but he heard a sound of blows—blows delivered on something soft. "What's Jack Platts up to," he thought; "killing a calf on a Sunday?" He waited a few seconds, and was rewarded by hearing a human noise—long and loud breathing, as of one in pain. He was on his way to a house opposite, the house of some people named Bellamy, with whom Platts also was acquainted. Knocking at their door, he told them what he had heard and wondered whether Platts were ill. The two Bellamys and himself went to the shop and knocked, and stood in the dark street listening. Only a wooden door separated them from the terror within.

"Art tha ill, Platts?" they asked. "Art th' alone?"

To which Platts, whose voice they recognised, answered, "Ay. I had some rum at the 'Angel,' and it turned me queer. I'll be all right soon."

"Wouldn't tha like a light? Shall us bring some water?"

"No. I'll come over in a minute."

They went back to their house, and told a guest, a Mr. Kirk, about the business. Platts had for some time been "walking out" with Kirk's daughter, Hannah. Mr. Kirk appears to have been a lively and facetious fellow. He put his own interpretation upon the presence of Platts in his shop on a Sunday. He, too, went across to the shop and hammered on the door. "You, Platts—open the door, tha little beggar. Th' ast got my Hannah there." The answer was silence. Mr. Kirk then threatened to break down the door and get Hannah out, and upon that Platts opened the door and stepped out to the street. Kirk tried to push past him, but Platts pulled the door to. Kirk said, "I'm going to have her out." Platts said, "She isn't here, James. She's at church, and I'm going to meet her when church is over." Kirk then demanded what he was doing in his shop on a Sunday, and Platts explained that he had some meat left over from Saturday, and had come to let a little air into the shop.

They left the shop together, and went across to the Bellamys. Kirk noticed that Platts had a long scratch on his left hand which was bleeding. "How didsta get that?"

"Caught it on a meat-hook when I was opening ventilator. I'll get Mrs. Bellamy to dress it."

The Bellamys noticed that he was in a rather agitated mood, but put it down to his sickness. He went to the kitchen to wash his hand, and Mrs. Bellamy bandaged it for him, and Mr. Bellamy gave him a drink. They talked of this and that, paying little attention to what was said. When, in the course of talk, Platts said that he had heard of a raffle at Mansfield for a watch, and was going to put in for it, they forgot it a minute after it was said. But it came back to them nine months later.

After his drink and a rest, he got up and said he would go and meet Hannah coming from church. On the way he made his second call at the "Angel," where Mrs. Franks noticed his bandaged hand.

"Now what's tha been doing?"

"Caught it on a meat-hook."

"Ah, that's nasty. Tha'll have to be careful of that, case it festers."

The "Angel" was the house to which the bell-ringers of the near-by church repaired when service had begun, and Platts was accustomed to spend his Sunday evenings in their company. But this evening he did not stay long; he excused himself by saying that he had to meet Hannah, and he left them, and met Hannah and took her to her home.

While he was doing this, Mr. Holbrook, proprietor of an eating-house, was sitting in a tavern in another part of the town waiting, with his best patience, for his friend George Collis, who was already half an hour late. He had seen him at half-past six that evening, and they had appointed to meet at this tavern at nine o'clock. It was then half-past nine, but Mr. Holbrook waited; in small provincial towns appointments partake a little of Spanish appointments; they are seldom kept to the dot. He waited till ten o'clock; till half-past ten; till eleven; till midnight. Still no George Collis. At that he gave it up and walked home. His way took him through The Shambles, and past the shop of John Platts. He was surprised to notice a light in the shop and to hear sounds of things being moved about. He tried to look in but found that all apertures were covered. Like all the rest, he went on his way and for a long time thought no more about it.

It is a common notion that the chief characteristics of small-town life are curiosity about neighbours, and that unmathematical game called "putting two and two together." Curiosity the people of The Shambles did display, but it was momentary, and none of them bothered his head with doing sums. Each of them saw a little or heard a little that Sunday night, but none of them, save one, saw enough or heard enough on his own account, to lead him to suspect anything deeply wrong. And as the majority of them did not come into contact with each other, there was no opportunity of pooling notes. Not until the trial were all the isolated and unmentioned observations of some ten witnesses added up. When they were they made a most conclusive sum.

From that Sunday evening George Collis was no more seen or heard of. The young carpenter Heathcoat, who saw him in Morley's shop, was the last person to see him alive. He also saw what *had been* Collis, but remained ignorant of the nature of what he had seen. On the Monday evening he was waiting near The Shambles to meet his brother, who lived in a different part of Chesterfield, when he was attracted by the movements of three men. His brother came up just then, and he drew his attention to them. "Look—there's Jack Platts and Morley. Don't know who the other chap is. Wonder what they're doing." They saw three men creeping through the darkness with a bundle about five feet long. The bundle appeared to be heavy; at every few yards they rested. The brothers watched them carry their burden into a spot called Bunting's Yard, where the big pond was. "Wonder what they're doing," the first brother repeated. "They look a bit queer."

"Oh, nothing. Happen they're just clearing out some offal from their shops. Taking it down to field to bury it."

They turned away, and did not recall the little incident till nine months later, when it made one more point against Mr. Platts.

During the week Mr. Platts was noticed to be in possession of a pair of laced boots, different from those he usually wore; also he had a watch. He did not claim that this was the raffled watch. When it was remarked upon, he said he had bought it from a local character known as Lanky Bill. (But at the trial Lanky Bill, from whom the defence, for reasons of their own, forced an admission that he had been in prison and lived with two prostitutes, denied that he had sold anybody a watch. He had never had a watch to sell.) Mr. Morley was also noticed to be paying off some small debts which had been running some time. He appeared to have plenty of loose silver.

After a week or so, and towards Christmas, people who had missed George Collis from his usual resorts, and who knew that he was in partnership with Platts, asked Platts if he knew what was become of him. Mr. Harvey asked him, and Platts said he had probably gone to Manchester. He added that he would like to see him, as he (Collis) owed him five pounds. To another enquirer he said he had heard that Collis was in Macclesfield. To another he said he had seen him outside the town driving a chaise.

Still no suspicion rested upon hilt save in one mind—the mind of Mr. Harvey. Mr. Harvey was given to thinking, and he had his doubts about the goings-on of that Sunday evening, and did not refrain from uttering them. More than once he said to Platts: "Jack, I could have sworn you had somebody in the shop." On each challenge, Platts denied it; but Mr. Harvey was not satisfied. He even went so far as to utter more than doubt, and Mr. Platts came up against the utterance. A blacksmith with whom he did business spoke of it in the course of casual conversation. "Jack, there's strong suspicion that tha murdered somebody on Sunday."

"Who says so?" asked Mr. Plats, not at all perturbed.

"Tom Harvey."

"Arrr . . . Reason he suspects me is because I was in me shop on a Sunday letting air in, and fell over lantern and cut me finger."

As the months went on even Mr. Harvey seems to have shed his doubts, and soon George Collis was forgotten by all save his mother and his fiancée. In those days disappearances of young men from small towns were common. It was a time when people could move about freely, and did. Strangers came to a place from nowhere and natives disappeared into nowhere, and nobody asked questions. A man could travel unrestricted to any European country, and could take any job in any country for which he was fit; and Europeans could come freely to England. There were no passports; no barriers against "aliens." Also, it was a peak period of emigration. America and Australia were wide open; and many a young man, restless under his daily routine, walked out of his home without warning, to appear later in Australia and not to reappear in his home-town for perhaps twenty years, if ever. Families were used to this, and if one of the young sons disappeared it was assumed that he had "gone for a soldier," or shipped as a sailor, or gone to "foreign parts."

But in August, 1846, light was given to many people to see what they might all along have seen and what only Mr. Harvey had seen.

One morning, towards the end of that month, Mr. Valentine Wall was busy cleaning out the big pond in Bunting's Yard when he found his work obstructed. By the aid of pitchforks he and his assistant found that the obstruction was a number of bones and a saturated coat and trousers. This conveyed little to Mr. Wall; he assumed that the bones were cattle bones, thrown there by the butchers, and that the clothes were cast-off clothes carelessly got rid of at the most convenient spot. He put them in a truck, and told his assistant to shoot them into a dust-pit in a near-by field. But the assistant had another look. He noticed that two of the bones had coloured garters round them, and that the articles of clothing, when put together, made almost a complete outfit. Only the boots were missing. As a dutiful citizen, and to be on the safe side, he reported the matter to the police. The police came and saw and summoned a doctor. The doctor declared the bones to be human bones, of a man between twenty and thirty. He found on the front of the skull three deep fractures.

Enquiries were now set about, and when the story became known, Mr. Harvey, Mr. Bellamy, Mr. Kirk, Mr. Heathcoat, Mrs. Franks, Mr. Slack and some others recalled the mysterious vanishing of George Collis. They recalled that he had last been seen on a Sunday evening of December, and Sunday evening recalled to them a particular Sunday evening marked by curious goings-on. In the taverns round The Shambles they began to talk. When the bubble of talk had subsided a little and cleared itself, all the events of that rainy Sunday evening began to crystallise around a scratched hand out of business hours, and a pair of boots and a watch. Some of them went to the police. The police went to the mother of George Collis.

She told them that she had last seen her son on the afternoon of December 7th of the previous year. When he left her house he was wearing a black surtout, canary-coloured waistcoat, brown trousers and black neckerchief. The neckerchief bore his initials. He always wore laced boots and stockings, and with the stockings he used one white garter and one red garter. He had with him a canvas purse and a watch. All this, save boots, purse and watch, corresponded with the clothing found.

While the remains were being removed by the police, watched, of course, by all the inhabitants of Bunting's Yard, Mr. Platts passed by. One of the crowd, a woman, spoke to him. "They say it's the body of George Collis. Dosta think he did it himself?" To which Mr. Platts answered that he had last seen Collis on a Saturday of December, when Collis had two razors with him and "threatened to make away with himself." He forgot, apparently, that razors don't cause fractures of the skull, and that he had been seen with George Collis in the "Angel" on *Sunday* evening.

Next day an inquest was held upon the remains when some, but not all, of the evidence in police possession was given. In addition to the evidence of the "Sunday night" witnesses, the police also had evidence that Platts had on two occasions offered for sale, and later had pawned, the watch he had acquired soon after December 7th; a watch which had been recognised as once belonging to George Collis. The evidence offered at the inquest, meagre as it was, proved sufficient, however, to make one person very ill. On the day the inquest was closed the man Morley was taken with a fever. Two days later he died in delirium.

With the evidence, published and unpublished, in their possession, there was nothing for the police to do but to arrest John Platts. He was arrested early in September. He was tried in March of the following year. He was hanged outside Derby gaol on the morning of April the First.

It was a clear case from the beginning, but one little puzzle remains; the puzzle that gives the story its special interest. It is that shadowy third. Who was he? Why was he allowed to remain at liberty and anonymous? Why did Platts shield him and, in the confession he wrote in the condemned cell, represent him by asterisks?

THE LONELY INN

The tall man on the lawn outside the cottage gave the cottage a long look and nodded at it. "Seems to be a perfect week-end cottage. Just big enough for us and easy to run. Ought to have some good weekends here."

The man with him agreed. "Yes. Hasn't got everything but almost everything. Good view from the lawn. Stream over there. Woods on the left. Even the house-agent must have strained his Arabian vocabulary in listing it."

"Yes. Village quite interesting, too. People seem a bit surly, though."

"You must give country people time. We've only been here two hours, remember. Maybe the soil's got something to do with it. Certain soils make cheerful people; others make taciturn people, or hot-tempered people."

Their wives appeared at the cottage door. "Why don't you boys go and explore a bit? There's nothing to do in here. The maid's left everything. We've only got to heat the soup. Dinner'll be eightish."

The tall man said, "Right." And then to the other—"What about it, Mac? Shall we stroll and see if we can find the local?"

Mac nodded, and they went through the gate into the lane. To the right lay the village, a mile away. They had seen it an hour ago. They turned to the left. The lane here was little more than a grass-track. By its width it appeared to have been at one time a road, but now its surface was rough grass corrugated with wheel-tracks. The grass in the ditches on either side was of somewhat stronger hue.

It was a winding lane, and at no point did it disclose more than a hundred yards of itself. The hedges stood high, and afforded no view of the surrounding country. "Almost like a shrubbery," the tall man said. "Wonder where it leads to eventually, and whether we've got to come back the same way." They followed its bends for some minutes, and

233

then the tall man said "Ha!" explosively. And then: "The oasis. I see a sign. Let's hope it isn't a desert mirage. But I'm sure I saw a sign, just over the hedge-top." At the next turn he gave his friend a facetious pat. "There we are! Thought I wasn't mistaken. As we're in Derbyshire they ought to have some of the real Derbyshire ale. Step out, my lad."

The inn's exterior was somewhat weather-beaten; almost uninviting; but it was an inn. It had known no paint for some years, and its door and windows had a bedraggled aspect. The door and its stone front bore brown and black patches. It showed a faded sign of "The White Cockade."

The two men paused. The tall and talkative man said, "H'm. Hardly one of the picture-postcard inns. But that's no fair test. All its good points may be inside. I've found several like that. Anyway, it's the only one, so . . ."

They went in. They found the inside no compensation of the outside. They entered a dim and silent tap-room. It contained the usual fixtures of a wayside public-house—old wooden benches, old wooden trestle-tables, an old and wide fireplace with the ashes of the last fire of winter, and an old and strong smell. Nothing in the place was grey in colour; yet it offered a general feeling of greyness. The landlord, standing listlessly behind the stained bar, was a man of heavy features and sunless eyes. The very type of man who ought not to keep an inn. His physical appearance accounted for, if it did not explain, the air of lost-heart and letting-things-go which hung over everything. One light, a shaded lamp, lit a small pool about the bar. The rest of the room was a muslin of shadow which gave common objects an uncommon shape.

They ordered their drink, and the landlord served them without "Good Evening" or other word. The beer was good. They drank, and looked about them. It was then, when their eyes, fresh from the bright evening, had become adjusted to the half-light, that they noted a slight stir among the shadow. Looking more closely, they saw that the room, which they thought was empty, held company. Some half-dozen dim figures sat along the benches and on chairs. No two sat together. They sat at intervals, each self-enclosed. They were men of ordinary appearance, in soiled or ragged clothes of miscellaneous quality and style; but their silence and their attitudes made them extraordinary.

The horrific figures evoked by the lobster nightmare or the unchaining drug cannot so freeze the human mind as the sight of the ordinary creature in the extraordinary attitude or state. De Quincey's picture of the fat man of Keswick sitting alone on his lawn in shirt-sleeves on a bitter March midnight brings more of the authentic recoil than any of his laudanum visions.

And so these dumb and solitary figures affected the two visitors more than any scene of ugliness or violence. Something in their peculiar arrangement suggested that they were sitting like that with some reason. It was as though they had placed themselves like actors on a stage, awaiting the rise of the curtain. The silence of the place, whose silence was underlined by the intermittent drip-drip of the beer-tap, also had an effect, and when the talkative visitor wanted to say something he found himself muttering.

He touched his friend. "Queer place, Mac." The other nodded. "Must be a side-entrance somewhere, I guess."

"Why?"

"Well, I didn't see anybody come in, but a minute ago I'd have said there were four people in the far corner."

"So there were."

"Well, there's six now. And there were two just behind us."

"Yes."

"There's three now."

Mac looked about him, and found that his friend was right. He found, too, that the company, without moving, was exchanging signals. He saw a head nod, and then another head respond to it. He caught his friend's eye, and together they watched the invisible message pass visibly along the room in nods. It was as though a row of Victorian mantelpiece images had been set in motion. All these people, it seemed, knew each other; yet sat apart holding no communication beyond nods.

He brought his earthenware mug sharply to the counter. He expected it to make in that silence a startling report, and had made the motion deliberately in the hope of bringing a touch of life to the room. But somehow, possibly by the shape of the room, it made only a faint noise, and the company ignored it. His friend turned to him: "Wonder if there's a deaf-and-dumb institute near here. And if this is Founder's

Day." He looked at the landlord. "Customers not very talkative," he said. The landlord continued to stare at nothing. He looked at Mac, and they exchanged a smile.

It was while he was taking a cigarette from the packet held by Mac that he became aware that the silence was being very gently troubled. At first he thought it was the swishing of a curtain. Then he knew that it was a whisper. A whisper was passing along the benches and chairs, and once or twice he caught its burden. *That's him. That's him.* He saw that Mac had heard it, too, and as they turned and looked at the benches they found the dilapidated faces of the company fixed on them. It seemed to him, as he turned, that they were fixed on him, but with the next glance he saw that they were all looking beyond him, at Mac. The moment they saw that they were observed, the faces dropped, and each man resumed his former pose of looking at his knees.

Mac picked up his mug and finished it. "Fit?" His friend nodded. They stepped out of twilight into orange sunset and scented fields and limpid light. They took some six paces from the inn; then the tall one stopped and said, expressively: *"Gawd!"* He took three deep breaths. Then: "I'd like to show that place to some of those literary blokes who write about the old village inn, and the mellow company, and the rich rustic voices, and Uncle Tom Cobleigh and all."

Mac agreed. "Still, we can't have everything. The cottage is about perfect, so we shall have to put up with the local. But what a hole. And not merely dull and dingy. Something more than that about it. We must investigate again. A place like that in this gorgeous country must have a reason for being what it is. Some story behind it. And why were they so interested in me?"

"Lord knows. Don't look as though they could be interested in *any-thing*—let alone an everyday specimen like you. Perhaps they'd seen you in the village, though, and were thinking of giving you the village greeting—'arf a brick."

"Huh. . . . Well, I've found some queer pubs in my ups-and-downs of England, but that's the queerest so far."

❀

The next day, Saturday, they spent in a motor-run of exploration, and got back to the cottage between six and seven. After a little pottering, Mac said, "Coming down to the lousy local?"

"Not this evening, I think. I've got about four or five letters I want to answer, so's to have to-morrow free. You go."

"Right. I'd like to have another look at it. Something about it fascinates me. It had the feeling of something going to happen."

"Don't be long, though. I've got an appetite. Don't want to have to wait dinner."

"Needn't worry. I've got one, too. I'll be on time."

Mac stepped out of the door as the other settled himself at a table. As he passed the open window he heard his friend call, "What's the date?" He answered, "April thirty," and swung down the lane.

And dinner was late. They waited until twenty to nine, and then, as Mac had not returned, they waited no longer. "I suppose he's managed to get the deaf-and-dumb school talking, and can't tear himself away. He'll have to have what's left, and have it half-cold. Ethel can't go down and drag him out. Create a bad impression on our first week-end—wives pulling husbands out of pubs. 'Father, dear father, come home with me now.'"

Ethel was dealing with soup. "Oh, he'll turn up when it suits him. He's done it before. When he finds an interesting local, as he calls them, he forgets time."

But he did not turn up. They left the door unlocked until one o'clock; then, as he had not turned up, they went to bed. "If he turns up now he'll have to throw gravel at the window. Gone off on a binge, perhaps, with one of the deaf-and-dumbs, and staying the night. Probably turn up with a hang-over about church-time to-morrow."

But he did not turn up. He did not turn up at church-time or at any other time. The trio left at the cottage never saw their Mac again.

At about mid-day his friend went out to look about, and to enquire at the local and in the village. Just outside the gate he met the old man whom they had engaged to keep the garden tidy during the week.

"Morning. D'you happen to have seen anything of my friend?"

The man looked at him dully while the question sank in and wandered through his mind to pick up some association with "my friend."

"Your friend?"

"Yes; the man who came with me. You saw him yesterday."

"Ar—'im. What would he be like?"

"Stocky figure. Red hair. Horn-rimmed glasses."

"Oh . . . 'im. No. I ain' seen 'im. I remember 'im. Scotty, I says to meself."

"Yes. He is a Scot. Well, he went out yesterday evening—down to the inn here—and was coming back in an hour. But he didn't come back last night. Nor this morning. I wondered whether you'd seen him or heard anything of him."

"No-o. I ain' seed 'im."

"I was just going down to the inn to ask if he'd been there. Thought perhaps you might have been there last night and seen him." He went into the lane and turned to the left. The man stopped him.

"This way, sir."

"No. This way. The inn's down here. Down the lane."

"You mean up the lane."

"I mean down the lane."

"You mean up the lane. The 'Green Man,' just outside village."

"I don't. I mean down the lane." He pointed to the left.

The man stared at him. "Dinno of no public down there."

"No? I see you don't know your own country. Often happens that the stranger finds what the inhabitant misses." The man looked puzzled. He stroked the stubble of his chin. He seemed about to say something but didn't say it. He was dealing with a Londoner. Queer things, Londoners. Said what they didn't mean, and twisted words about, and called it wit. Played silly games called *pulling your leg.* Sometimes they weren't quite right in the head. Zanies, some of 'em. This seemed to be one of that sort.

"I dinno of no—"

"Ah, but I do. I'm just going along there to ask if my friend called in last night. If you care to come along I'll show it to you. And you can sample the brew."

"I'll come along with ye, but—"

They went along. They went down the twisting lane. The gardener held his puzzled expression, but made no remark. They went along until they came to the elm, through whose branches the sign had been visible.

"Just at the next bend," the tall man said; and they made the next bend. Having made it he looked about him. "Funny. Must have been the *next* bend." They went on and followed the next bend, and this bend marked the end of the lane and its junction with a main road. The tall man now did some staring. "Well . . ." He looked back up the lane. "Can't have *passed* it, can we?"

"No, sir, we din pass it."

"I remember it as just this side of that elm." He took a few strides up the lane. "Yes. This side of the elm. Just opposite that gap in the hedge. I could have sworn that— And I'm certain we never left the lane. But if so, what the devil—"

The gardener watched him with blank expression. He appeared to have no interest in the proceedings. He was humouring a Londoner. The tall man turned to him. "Well, if it wasn't in the lane where was it? How did we lose ourselves? You—" Then something in the man's blank face arrested him.

"There bent no public in this lane. Nor anywheres bout 'ere. Nothing bout 'ere for four miles. Not till ye come to the 'Golden Lion.' And that be along the road—four mile."

The tall man stared at him and then at the lane, and then shouted. "But man, we did come to a pub here. We did have drinks in it. In the lane. A dismal place."

The gardener looked sad and shook his head. With rustic civility, or polite contempt, he refrained from comment. He repeated only "Bent no public in this lane."

"But, man. I tell you—" He broke off. He realised that he could not insist on the fact of his pub, because nowhere in the lane was there any pub. There had been a pub, and now there wasn't a pub. He strode backwards and forwards. "What's happened here? What funny work's going on here? We can't both have been insane. We did come to a pub here, and we did have drinks. What do you make of it?"

The old man stared at the horizon. "If there'd been a public 'ere I'd 'a known it. I come down 'ere twice a week. Never no public 'ere in my time. Nor in me faather's time. But I do remember me granfer telling me that 'is granfer told 'im there were a public down 'ere."

"What!"

"There *were* a public down 'ere. I do remember me granfer telling me that 'is granfer told 'im it were burnt down. It were mixed up in sommin in 'istry. Nigh on two unnerd year ago. I dinno the rights of it, but 'e did say sommin' bout some kind of war. And a lot o' Scotties come 'ere. And one of 'em sold the others. And the people set fire to the place, and they was all burnt. 'Cept the one that sold 'em. And 'im they cursed with their dying breaths."

THE WATCHER

The dim little shop stood at the corner of two dim streets of a North London suburb, far away from the main road. It stood alone in a world of little houses, and its air was forlorn and dejected. It was closed now, and its blinds were down, but even when it was open it looked little less forlorn. It seemed to have no self-respect; to be only perfunctorily a shop, and the people who kept it clearly didn't care whether they kept a shop or not.

That sort of shop in bright and busy surroundings is dismal enough, but this shop, set alone at a corner of a street that was gritty, ill-lit, and empty of people, seemed at the last gasp of depression. It was so ordinary, so much a replica of thousands of other lonely corner shops in dim streets, that it spread a slow stain of foreboding on the evening.

It even sent a touch of this foreboding to the shabby man who was approaching it. He was approaching it on definite and urgent business, and was anxious to reach it and get the business done; yet, as he came nearer to it and saw its face, his step hesitated and he regarded it with dislike.

He was approaching it on a quest for money. It is odd how much money can be found in poor streets. Thieves go for big houses, where there is little but marked jewellery and plate, when, if they only knew, many a house in a dim back street is as valuable as any of the big houses. The stuff is more easily to be got at, and it is in negotiable and untraceable form—silver, gold and Treasury notes. Stories of people who mistrust banks and keep all their money in their homes often appear in the news, and each known story may be taken to represent fifty unknown. One might say that in every poor street there is at least one house with a good hoard.

This little corner shop had one, and the fact of it was not unknown. It was known to the shabby Mr. Roderick. He had known of it long ago, but until lately the knowledge had been knowledge only, with no personal meaning for him. The fact that they kept a large store of money in that place was merely an item of interest like learning that the Browns had another baby. But now it was more than that. Mr. Roderick's circumstances had changed, and with them Mr. Roderick himself had changed.

To the new Mr. Roderick that knowledge was an asset; it could be applied to his problems. The statement that knowledge is power is true, but only if you know how to apply one particular atom of your million atoms of knowledge to a particular occasion. Mr. Roderick had done so. In the thrall of a particular occasion he had suddenly netted out of the pool of his mind the particular atom of knowledge, which could lift the thrall. He wanted, urgently, to cross the sea, and it was while searching for the means of the journey that recollection came to him of the little shop he had known so many years, and its secret bank of which, by accident, he had become aware. He had not seen it for six months, but a quiet visit the day before had told him that it was still kept in the same haphazard way by the same haphazard people. And a little quiet watching this evening had assured him that they still followed their weekly custom of going out in a group every Wednesday evening.

He had watched them go, and had counted them. He knew their usual time for returning, and felt that he was safe in assuming that they would keep to it. It was a time that gave him leisure for the job in hand. He could go at it without a rush. He didn't feel like rushing it. It might be more difficult than he thought. He didn't like the look of the place, somehow; seemed to be something "wrong" with it, though he knew it was all right. He sent a glance up the dark street each way; then shook his shoulders, slipped out of the doorway that had sheltered him, and slipped over a wall to the back entrance.

And then he was there, working at a window. He worked swiftly; he was familiar with the windows of that district. He was also familiar with the back entrance, and many a time in the past he had stood at the back door and talked to members of the family. Within less than a minute the window was open, and he was slipping through it. All his movements suggested something slipping.

Once inside the house he stood stock still. He knew how to stand still, so still that all his nerves were at rest, his muscles motionless, and his breathing imperceptible to anybody within two feet of him. He stood like this while he counted up to a hundred. Then he began to move across the room to the door.

Had you been there, you would not have seen him move. You might have seen him at one spot of the room, and then at another spot; but you would not have seen him move. The darkness was no barrier; he knew this room; he went across it in three shots.

The stock-room, the little room behind the shop, was the room he was after. He slid across a section of the passage, and reached it. There was a door to open, but he dared not risk a light in the passage. He turned his head aside, and looked at nothing, and used his fingers on the handle. He put all his being into those fingers, and they turned the handle without the tiniest shred of sound. And they pushed the door quarter-inch by quarter-inch, until there was sufficient space for him to pass from one darkness to a deeper darkness.

He was in the stock-room. Here he switched on his electric torch; holding it close to the floor. He glanced round the room. It was much as when he had last seen it; piled with wooden crates, biscuit tins, cardboard boxes and packing-straw. He looked keenly at the disused fireplace and noted that none of the crates covered or obstructed it. He could get at it without risking the noise of moving anything. He crept across the floor and turned the torch into the chimney. He ran his fingers over the bricks of the right-hand recess. As they touched a certain brick his breath ran out softly. The hiding-place was still in use.

He turned the torch upon that brick and with delicate fingers began to edge it out. The movement produced no sound, and he had made no sound in entering the place; the empty house was enveloped in a cloth of silence. Yet when the brick was half-way out his hand dropped, he switched off the torch, his easy body stiffened like a cat's, and he shot round and faced the door.

He faced only blackness; yet, though his ear had heard nothing, his sense had warned him of something—a step, was it? Or a movement of human lips? Or the unclasping of a human hand? He stared into the blackness, listening with all his body; and the repulse that the shop had seemed to give him when he first came to it was repeated. It was like a presence.

But, keenly as he listened, through all the senses, there was no sound, no sound at all. It must have been a little flick of loose wallpaper, or the dropping of a speck of plaster, or the settling of a bundle of the packing-straw. The house was, as he had known it would be, empty. It must have been one of those things, or just his own nerves. He turned again to the stove.

But the house was not empty. There was another man in that house who had also thought it empty, but who was now doubting. He had heard nothing, but he, too, was aware of something, and was also listening with all his body. He did not move from where he was; he just listened. And Mr. Roderick, with his hand on the disused stove, only six yards away from the unseen listener, also listened. These two listened for each other, but while one listened and stood still, the other listened and went on with his work.

Softly the first brick came out, and softly the second. And then the third. Not a sound came to the unseen listener; yet he knew that somebody was there and at work.

When the fourth brick was out, Mr. Roderick flashed his torch into the cavity and saw his reward. Three flat tin boxes. His other hand entered the cavity, and the boxes went from the cavity to his pocket so softly that they seemed to fly in. A fat envelope completed the hoard, and that, too, flew in. Then, still with soft movements, he replaced the four bricks, and stood up.

It was as he stood up that he had again, and this time more powerfully, the sense of a presence. But he had done his business, and could not now bother about the possibility of there being somebody in the house. He had done his business undisturbed, and he must now bother about getting out. He turned to the door, holding the torch well downwards, and then shot back to the stove and lifted the torch.

The torch, shining on to the floor, had shown him a pair of slippers and the lower part of trousers. The torch, lifted, showed him an erect, old man standing against one of the crates and steadily gazing at him.

He knew then that the man had been there all the time; had seen all his actions; had seen the transfer of the hoard; would be able, since he'd worked by the torch, to describe him. For two, perhaps three, seconds they stared at each other. Then, as he realised his situation, Mr. Roderick's right hand went to his breast pocket, the torch went out, and a life-preserver crashed on to the man's head.

The man went down with a muffled bump. The crate went with him and its fall shook the floor. And at that Mr. Roderick lost control of things. The episode—the strain of the burglary itself, the sense of being watched, and then the discovery that he had been watched—had shaken him. He switched on the torch and rained blow after blow upon the body on the floor. He was still striking when he became aware, not merely of a presence, but of noise.

A noise of men in the passage. And then a noise of men at the door. And then a noise of men in the very room. And then they were on him, and two of them were defeating his struggles and had him down and helpless.

One of the men said, "My God! It's poor old Gregory." And another said: "Why? Now why kill the poor old chap?" And another said: "Look—he's been at the stove. I wonder what for?" And one of those holding Roderick and running through his pockets said: "That's what for—see?" And held up the fat envelope. The first man said: "Yes, but why murder?" And turned to Roderick, and repeated, "Why? Why on earth did you want to kill a poor, harmless old man? So unnecessary. Why?"

Roderick snarled at him. Then said: "Because he'd seen me, of course. I had to. Or I wouldn't have had a chance. He'd been watching me at it. I had the torch on, and he had a clear view of me. Could have described me and identified me. I *had* to quiet him."

The man gave him an odd glance. "You seem to know where they kept their money. Which is more than I do, though I live next door. But you haven't been here lately, I reckon. Have you?"

"Not for some time."

"Ah. I see. That explains. If you had, you'd 'a known that this poor old chap—their uncle—had come to live with them. And you'd 'a known that he's stone blind."

EVENTS AT WAYLESS-WAGTAIL

You might have thought he had taken a dislike to the green wallpaper of his book-room. In a casual moment he had raised his eyes from his desk to look at nothing. Having raised them he kept them fixed on the wall before him. He bent forward from his chair, elbows on desk. He was seeing something more than a green-papered wall. He was seeing a murder.

Visions came to him at day-time as easily as dreams come to ordinary people at night. Always they carried their own touch of the peculiar. They were never of the immediate present. All of them were set some little distance ahead. Usually they were pointless. He would be sitting alone, or walking in the garden or in the street, and between him and whatever he was looking at, there would flash a scene or an incident in living miniature. A country road, and a man, sharply defined, bending over a car. A crowded restaurant in a foreign city, and three particular people at the nearest table, quarrelling. Two lovers walking in a busy street. A man going up the steps of a club, and slipping on the top step. Things like that.

If the time were winter, his vision would usually be related to next spring. If it were spring he would see some moment of the following autumn. With each picture, which came vivid and clear as life itself, there was always some detail, such as state of the weather, flowers, a calendar, which gave him the period; often the very day and hour. He could seldom make anything of these glimpses of futurity, and paid little attention to them. Why, when they had no personal significance for him, they should thus visit him, he could not guess. He assumed, casually, that some shutter or perception which, with other people, remained sealed was, with him, loose, and so at moments would let in a random flash of the time-stream. He let it go at that, and usually forgot the visions in the moment of their fading.

247

But the present vision was something different. It was a vision to which he must attend, and upon which, perhaps, he might be able to act and be of service. There was murder being done, and it concerned recognisable people in recognisable circumstances. Both scene and figures were strange to him, but the detail was so exact that if ever he could see that place and those people in life, he would know them. That was why he was staring so intently, trying to fix the essential points on his visual memory.

The vision had opened with a view of a village; an English village straggling round a green. There was a duck-pond on the green, with white railings round it. The houses dotted along the green were cottages and villas. Some of the cottages had thatched roofs. Most of the villas had whitewashed fronts and green doors, and little covered balconies. Judged by the flowers in the gardens and the foliage of the trees, the period was early autumn, and the fall of the thin sunshine indicated mid-afternoon.

He saw it as clearly as though a model of the village had been designed and set in mid-air before him. But this model was alive. The boughs of the trees were waving, the bright clouds were moving, and the ducks were paddling round the pond. Even as he was absorbing the scene, human life came into it. A man of about thirty, in sporting tweeds, came from one of the larger houses, with "Avoca" painted on its gate, and moved along the green towards a house next to the church; a house bearing the name "Cranford." He carried a newspaper and looked into it as he walked.

Stern could see the paper and its headline. It was the *Morning Mercury,* and its date was September 3rd of that year; three months distant.

The man stopped outside "Cranford," opened the gate and went up a little garden path bordered by red stone. Along one side of the house was a lawn, a continuation of the lawn at the back, and as the first man entered, another man of about fifty—an energetic fifty—came from the house to the lawn. He was of large figure, erect and grey. He carried a serviceable hammer, and went towards a patch of broken fencing. This he began to nail up. He hammered the nails fiercely, and his actions and the set of his body implied that he would do everything fiercely. As the younger man approached, he appeared to hear his step, and he turned. The glance he gave his visitor was not too cordial. They did not shake hands. They stood for some moments on the lawn in talk, and Stern got the impression that their talk, though not quarrelsome, was on the edge of it. Then the elder man indicated the door and went into the house. The other followed him.

Stern next saw the hall of the house. It made a small square. At different points were golf-clubs, tennis rackets, thick boots—all the litter of the hall of a country cottage. The walls were decorated with old engravings. On a small table was a copy of that day's *Times*. It was dated September 3rd.

He saw the men stand in the hall some paces from each other. He saw their brows darkening and their lips thrusting. He saw the elder man point at the younger, and make a contemptuous movement with his hand. He saw the younger man's jaw shoot forward. He saw him take a quick step towards the other. As he moved, the elder man swung up his arm, still holding the hammer. The younger man came on, the other sidestepped, and brought the hammer down.

He saw the younger man crumple to the floor like a dropped pillow-case. He saw the other drop the hammer, and go down on one knee. He saw his face dark-red at one moment and at the next chalk-white. He saw him fumble over the body and raise the head. He saw him put his hand on the pulse and then on the breast. And he saw him get up with eyes that held pain and dismay.

And then the space between him and the green wall of his book-room was vacant. The vision was gone.

For some minutes after it was gone he sat staring and thinking. When he moved it was to reach for paper and pencil, and set down every detail of what he had seen, with a rough sketch from memory of the structure and appearance of the village and its houses. His next business was to consider some means of identifying the place and the people.

What he had seen was, he felt, not an inevitable event, but the event as it would happen *given those circumstances.* The two men had been alone with every opportunity for quarrel and attack. The event was set for that hour, and, given the propitious setting, it would happen. But had a third person been present it might have been frustrated; the fit circumstances would have been thrown out of harmony. With his fore-knowledge it should be possible for him to disarrange the circumstances, and so put the event out of that particular stream. If he could locate that village and those men, and contrive to make their acquaintance, it should be possible for him to find some excuse for being in their company on the afternoon of September 3rd. And if he were in their company it would be a simple matter to disturb the appointments of the occasion, to change the scene of their meeting, and to see that no hammer or other weapon was in the hand or within reach.

With so clear a picture of the place and people in his mind he felt that he would have little trouble in locating them, since there were yet twelve weeks to go before the foreshadowed event. He set about the business that evening. After casting about for the best method of approaching the task, he remembered a friend who wrote touring notes for a motoring paper. This friend, who spent his days and weeks cruising the highways and byways of England, might be able to provide some clue which would narrow the search; might be able to locate, from Stern's description, the district or the county where such a village might be found. With some such direction, Stern could then start hunting in that district, and he was certain that if he came within sight of the village of his vision he would know it not only by his eyes but by his skin and blood. It remained in his mind as part of an actual experience; as a village he had personally known and walked in; and if he could once get near it he knew that he would feel "warm" and easily find it.

It happened that he had no search for it. Calling his friend on the telephone, he said, "Listen, Jack. I want you to try to remember if you've ever seen on your wanderings a village like this. I'll describe it. I want to find out just where it is, and its name. It's got a green, and on the edge of the green there's a pond, and round the pond there's white railings. The road runs along one side of the green, and the village makes a rough half-circle on the other side. There's a church on one point—perpendicular—with elms round it."

"That describes four hundred villages."

"Shut up. There's a number of thatched cottages, standing separate here and there, and in between these there's a lot of two-storied houses of late-eighteenth- or early-nineteenth-century. White-fronted, and most of 'em have green doors and brass knockers. And they've got those iron verandahs with curved canopies, like you see at old-fashioned seaside places."

"Very lucid. The identical village leaps to the mind at once."

"Don't be silly. Listen. There's just two other points I've got, but they probably won't convey anything. I guess I'll have to see you and show you a sketch I made. Something in the sketch might give you a clue. The points are—that right next to the church there's a white house labelled 'Cranford.' And towards the other end there's a house labelled 'Avoca.' I didn't notice the names of any others, and probably—"

"What was the last one?"

"Avoca."

"Avoca, did you say? Same as Thomas Moore's Sweet Vale of Avoca?"

"Yes."

"And another one called Cranford?"

"Yes."

"Ha! I believe I can work that cross-word. Anything else you remember about it?"

"Well, the Cranford house seems to belong to a fellow about fifty. Biggish. Iron-grey. And I believe there's a fellow living at Avoca—fellow in the thirties. Sporty, plus-fours fellow. Reads the *Morning Mercury.*"

"Uh-huh. That'd be the doctor."

"What? You know him?"

"Sounds like the same chap. I've stayed with a plus-fours doctor in his thirties, who lives at a house called Avoca in a village. And he knows a man of the kind you describe who lives in a house next to the church."

"Marvellous. It was a lucky stroke that made me ring you first. Is the village as I describe it?"

"Pretty much. Just an ordinary village. The other details seem to fix it."

"And where is it?"

"It's Wayless-Wagtail. In the Thames valley. Why all this interest? Thinking of settling there?"

"No. But I'd be glad if you'd do something for me. Are you likely to be going there within the next week or so?"

"Probably. I see young Winterslow off and on, when it occurs to me."

"Will you take me next time you go and introduce me to him?"

"Well. . . . I could. But why? Don't know that you'd have much in common."

"Perhaps not. But that's one thing I want you to do for me. The other is, not to ask why."

"'M. . . . Sounds all very mysterious."

"You needn't worry. I just want to meet him. It won't do him any damage at all, and it might do him a bit of good. But don't ask why. Just introduce me casually, without any reason. And I'll answer all your questions in a month or so."

"All right. How about Sunday after next? We could drop in for lunch. I'll call for you about eleven."

Ten minutes after the car had left the Bath Road a few miles beyond Reading, it turned into a lane, and two minutes later Stern saw in reality the details of the village he had seen in vision on the wall of his book-room. Every detail matched. The green, the pond, the church, the balconied houses and the thatched cottages. By the church he saw "Cranford," with the strip of lawn at the side; and a hundred yards beyond it they came to "Avoca." As the car drew up, the younger man of his vision, Dr. Winterslow, came out to meet them. He was wearing just the sporting tweeds he had worn in the vision; the only difference was that they were fairly new, while in the vision they had clearly had a bit of wear.

During lunch, Stern exerted himself to make an agreeable impression on Winterslow, and felt that he had succeeded. They found a common ground in fishing talk, and it was easy for him to get the invitation to further meetings which he desired. Once an angler finds that a brother-angler doesn't know the local streams, it is seldom that he can resist urging him to come and try them. No streams afford such catches as an angler's own streams. He was pressed to come for a long week-end, and he foresaw that after that long week-end he would be able to make other visits. He would be able to invite himself for September 3rd, or to drop in casually on the afternoon of that day.

He found Winterslow a pleasant, easy-going fellow, but with something of a tongue. He was looking for some cause of a dispute between the doctor and the elderly man of "Cranford," and he guessed that he had found it in the doctor's tongue. In conversation, he hit off the peculiarities of the village residents in sentences that sounded bland until they were considered, when they revealed little spots of acid. They were remarks such as many people like to repeat to the subject of them, leaving the subject to turn them over and discover the sting. Had Winterslow made a few remarks of that sort about the man at "Cranford," it was certain that a man of his choleric type would resent them more fiercely than open criticism.

Bitterness finds richer ground for growth in villages than in cities. The leisurely days, the restricted social radius, and the lack of new air from the outside to blow away yesterday's echoes, make it easy for a chance remark to breed an enduring feud. Judging by the scene of his vision, and from what he had now learned of Winterslow's caustic turn of mind, something of the sort had happened here. He hoped that some reference to the fiery neighbour might be made during lunch, but though other residents were mentioned, he was left out. Towards the end of the meal Stern tried himself to introduce him.

"Pleasant house, that one next to the church. Regency period, I should say."

"Yes. They knew how to design houses and rooms in those days. And how to fit their design to the surroundings."

"Anybody interesting own it?"

"No-o. Just a type. Type you find in every village. Sun-dried sahib from India's coral strand. The Bombay Duck. A strip of dried fish. With as much individuality as all the other strips of dried fish. And speaking of fish, what about that week-end? Perhaps we could fix it now."

🐦

Having made the week-end visit, Stern found himself, as he had expected with so easy-going a fellow as Winterslow, invited to "drop in any time." To keep the acquaintance warm until September, he dropped in twice between June and the middle of August, and at about that time he invited himself for the second of September, with the suggestion of staying the night.

He arrived on the evening of the second, with the details of his vision still fresh in his mind. He had no clear plan of how he would handle the situation next day, if it arose—and he believed it would; he decided that he must await the event and take his cue from any chance that offered. The one point on which he was clear was that he must not let Winterslow out of his sight at any time of next afternoon.

The situation did arise. Winterslow himself took the first step towards the death foretold for him in the vision; the death that Stern was there to avert. Soon after lunch he asked Stern: "Care for a stroll? Don't think you've seen our church. Not much interested in ecclesiastical stuff myself, but they say there's some fine Norman work in it, and one specially good window. And a couple of fine marbles which I do think are worth seeing." For a moment Stern hesitated whether to suggest a stroll in some other direction, or to fall in with the idea and let Winterslow enter the situation and be saved from its climax by his own presence. If he took Winterslow in another direction, it might mean merely postponing the meeting of the two men, and the incident of the vision might work itself out on a later occasion. If it were met at its appointed time it might, *barring accidents,* be thwarted.

His hesitation was settled by Winterslow, who picked up from a chair that day's *Morning Mercury.* "Just take this along. Article in here that might interest the old Bombay Duck. We shall be passing his place."

As they went along the green, Stern noted that the scene was precisely the scene of his vision. The time was exact; the fall of the sunlight, the movement of cloud, the light breeze on the tree-tops—all were as he had seen them. Even the ducks on the pond were distributed as he remembered them, and when they were half-way towards the church the flight of a rook across the skyline made current fact of another point of the vision. When they neared the church—and "Cranford"—Stern found his pulse increasing. The event was now very close, but the lawn of "Cranford" was empty; and he wondered whether perhaps his presence had already thrown the thing out of adjustment. For a moment he felt as a child feels when it puts the penny in the slot of the mechanical-farmyard machine, and wonders whether it really will come to life, as promised.

Then the door of "Cranford" snapped open, and out came its florid, iron-grey owner, carrying nails and hammer. Stern caught his breath, and waited for the next move. Winterslow made it. As the man began work on the fence they reached his gate, and Winterslow pushed it open and entered. Stern followed close behind him. His eye and brain were set on every turn of the succeeding seconds.

The sound of their steps brought a glance from the man, but he went on hammering, until Winterslow was near him. "Seen to-day's *Mercury,* Colonel?" He stepped back from the fence then, still swinging the hammer, and faced them.

"No, sir. I read papers written by adults for adults."

"Aha." Winterslow was unabashed by his reception. "You like the old dignities, eh? The old English journalism. But we live in American times now. Everything young and swift. Still, you'll admit, I think, that Lord Simla's an adult where India's concerned. Interesting article by him on the situation in the *Mercury.* Thought you might like to see it."

"Thank you, sir; no. I don't care to have papers of that sort about my place." Stern, watching them closely, saw in the Colonel's eyes an expression which seemed to finish the sentence with "nor people of your sort about my place."

"All right, then. I just thought you might be interested."

"I'm not. And listen, Doctor Winterslow"—swinging the hammer—"I'd like a word with you."

"Sure."

The Colonel moved to the open door and into the hall. Winterslow followed. Stern followed, too. The Colonel stared—or rather, glared—at him. The glare said, "Impertinent intruder—get out." Stern accepted the glare and remained close by Winterslow. The Colonel then seemed to think that his "word" to Winterslow might be a little more, rather than a little less, effective if delivered in the presence of a third party. He turned from the third party with, "Look here, Winterslow, I want to know—" when the third party earned for himself a fiercer glare by interrupting him.

Stern took a pace towards him, and committed a graver impertinence. "What an unusual kind of hammer, sir."

"Unusual, sir? I don't see anything unusual about it."

"Is it Indian?"

"No, sir, it's not Indian. Nor Chinese. Nor Afghan. It's a hammer."

"But really, sir—excuse me—if I may—" Ignoring the boiling of the Colonel's face, he reached forward and took the hammer from the Colonel's hand. The Colonel, unaware that in that moment he was being saved from the brand of murderer, let it go, mainly because he was taken by surprise at the fellow's sheer audacity. Ten seconds later when he was prepared with protest, the fellow was babbling about hammers.

"No, it's not so unusual as I thought. It was just something in the form of the claw that I thought was different. I'm rather interested in tools. It's odd that the everyday tools of man have scarcely changed from their beginnings. Most of the hammers of to-day are of the same style as the earliest hammers you find in museums. Farm-carts, too. Practically the same as you see in the earliest English decorations. The hammer must be the primary tool of man, I fancy, though it offers a parallel to the problem of the chicken and the egg—which came first: the hammer or the nail? The hammer—" Stern had no idea what he was saying or what words he was finding; he was talking merely to cover his action in taking the hammer and to hold the situation. He finished lamely. "Forgive my blithering on like this. You wanted to give the doctor a message, I think."

"I did. And the message is—that I don't wish to put him to the trouble of making further calls on me. He's a nuisance to the village. A nuisance. As he says, I prefer the old dignities. I've no use for the young impudences."

Winterslow looked first surprised; then angry. "Really, Colonel. . . . Something's wrong with you this afternoon. I thought you were rather frigid when I came in."

"Frigid? I'm always frigid, sir, with Bounders."

"Are you talking to me?" Winterslow's shoulders came forward. "I know you're a hot-tempered old man, but—" He took a step towards the Colonel. The Colonel lifted his arm. Stern, holding the hammer, stepped between them. "Please . . . please. I don't know what the trouble is, but—"

"The trouble is, sir, that your friend, if he is your friend, is an impudent fellow. Gibing at his betters. A thorough nuisance." The Colonel's heat seemed to cool in shooting his sentences at a third party. "I don't know who you are, and I don't recall inviting you in. But since you're here you can do something for me. You can take your friend away."

Winterslow looked as though he had something blandly mordant to say, and was about to say it when Stern caught his eye, and made a furtive signal conveying weighty and mysterious business in the garden. Winterslow looked at him, and at the Colonel, and said, "Oh, all right; anything for a quiet life," and strolled out with Stern. The Colonel slammed the door on them.

"Nice chap," Winterslow said. "Nice chap, isn't he, the Bombay Duck? What's going on in the garden?"

"Nothing, that I know of."

"What were you making that wild signal for, then? I thought you meant there was something doing out here."

"No; I only wanted to get you out of that brawl."

"I see. Probably would have developed into that. If he'd said much more I really believe I'd have gone for him. Don't know what's got him this afternoon to set him on me. Looked quite murderous. But you never know, with these old boys. Synthetic products of chutney and curry and hell-fire foods. . . . I say, you've got the old boy's hammer. You'll lead him right into murder if he sees you."

Stern looked down and found he was still carrying the hammer. He went back a few paces and dropped it by the broken fence. When he rejoined Winterslow at the gate, the young man, in his easy-going habit, seemed to have forgotten the ugly scene. He began talking about the marbles in the church.

❀

Late in the following year, when Stern was sunk in his real work, and had wholly forgotten the human duty he had performed for a comparative stranger, he was called to the telephone. His touring friend was speaking.

"Oh, Stern—remember that place you wanted to know all about some time ago. Where you met the doctor chap and went fishing two or three times. Wayless-Wagtail. . . . Well, I was there this afternoon, and as you seemed fond of the place, and knew the people, I thought you might like to know."

"Know what?"

"Oh, there was a bit of a mess-up there this afternoon. And our friend, the doctor chap, was in it. Winterslow."

"Winter— Oh, yes—I remember. A mess-up, you say? How? What sort?"

"Oh, sudden death. Outside the church. They were having what we call Words. And he just went over and out."

"What—Winterslow? Who struck him? I suppose it was—"

"No. The old Colonel Johnny."

"The *Colonel,* did you say? Not Winterslow?"

"Of course not. He's healthy enough. No—the Colonel. Tried to swipe at Winterslow, and went down and out. Heart failure. Winterslow said he tried to do it the same day a year ago. When you were there."

THE HOLLOW MAN

He came up one of the narrow streets which lead from the docks, and turned into a road whose farther end was gay with the lights of London. At the end of this road he went deep into the lights of London, and sometimes into its shadows. Farther and farther he went from the river, and did not pause until he had reached a poor quarter near the centre.

He made a tall, spare figure, clothed in a black mackintosh. Below this could be seen brown dungaree trousers. A peaked cap hid most of his face; the little that was exposed was white and sharp. In the autumn mist that filled the lighted streets as well as the dark he seemed a wraith, and some of those who passed him looked again, not sure whether they had indeed seen a living man. One or two of them moved their shoulders, as though shrinking from something.

His legs were long, but he walked with the short, deliberate steps of a blind man, though he was not blind. His eyes were open, and he stared straight ahead; but he seemed to see nothing and hear nothing. Neither the mournful hooting of sirens across the black water of the river, nor the genial windows of the shops in the big streets near the centre drew his head to right or left. He walked as though he had no destination in mind, yet constantly, at this corner or that, he turned. It seemed that an unseen hand was guiding him to a given point of whose location he was himself ignorant.

He was searching for a friend of fifteen years ago, and the unseen hand, or some dog-instinct, had led him from Africa to London, and was now leading him, along the last mile of his search, to a certain little eating-house. He did not know that he was going to the eating-house of his friend Nameless, but he did know, from the time he left Africa, that he was journeying towards Nameless, and he now knew that he was very near to Nameless.

Nameless didn't know that his old friend was anywhere near *him,* though, had he observed conditions that evening, he might have wondered why he was sitting up an hour later than usual. He was seated in one of the pews of his prosperous Workmen's Dining-Rooms—a little gold-mine his wife's relations called it—and he was smoking and looking at nothing. He had added up the till and written the copies of the bill of fare for next day, and there was nothing to keep him out of bed after his fifteen hours' attention to business. Had he been asked why he was sitting up later than usual, he would first have answered that he didn't know that he was, and would then have explained, in default of any other explanation, that it was for the purpose of having a last pipe. He was quite unaware that he was sitting up and keeping the door unlatched because a long-parted friend from Africa was seeking him and slowly approaching him, and needed his services. He was quite unaware that he had left the door unlatched at that late hour—half-past eleven—to admit pain and woe.

But even as many bells sent dolefully across the night from their steeples their disagreement as to the point of half-past eleven, pain and woe were but two streets away from him. The mackintosh and dungarees and the sharp white face were coming nearer every moment.

There was silence in the house and in the streets; a heavy silence, broken, or sometimes stressed, by the occasional night-noises—motor horns, back-firing of lorries, shunting at a distant terminus. That silence seemed to envelop the house, but he did not notice it. He did not notice the bells, and he did not even notice the lagging step that approached his shop, and passed—and returned—and passed again—and halted. He was aware of nothing save that he was smoking a last pipe, and he was sitting in somnolence, deaf and blind to anything not in his immediate neighbourhood.

But when a hand was laid on the latch, and the latch was lifted, he did hear that, and he looked up. And he saw the door open, and got up and went to it. And there, just within the door, he came face to face with the thin figure of pain and woe.

⊛

To kill a fellow-creature is a frightful thing. At the time the act is committed the murderer may have sound and convincing reasons (to him) for his act. But time and reflection may bring regret; even remorse; and this may live with him for many years. Examined in wakeful hours of the night or early morning, the reasons for the act may shed their cold logic, and may cease to be reasons and become mere excuses. And these naked excuses may strip the murderer and show him to himself as he is. They may begin to hunt his soul, and to run into every little corner of his mind and every little nerve, in search of it.

And if to kill a fellow-creature and to suffer recurrent regret for an act of heated blood is a frightful thing, it is still more frightful to kill a fellow-creature and bury his body deep in an African jungle, and then, fifteen years later, at about midnight, to see the latch of your door lifted by the hand you had stilled and to see the man, looking much as he did fifteen years ago, walk into your home and claim your hospitality.

When the man in mackintosh and dungarees walked into the dining-rooms Nameless stood still; stared; staggered against a table; supported himself by a hand, and said, "Oh."

The other man said, "Nameless."

Then they looked at each other; Nameless with head thrust forward, mouth dropped, eyes wide; the visitor with a dull, glazed expression. If Nameless had not been the man he was—thick, bovine and costive—he would have flung up his arms and screamed. At that moment he felt the need of some such outlet, but did not know how to find it. The only dramatic expression he gave to the situation was to whisper instead of speak.

Twenty emotions came to life in his head and spine, and wrestled there. But they showed themselves only in his staring eyes and his whisper. His first thought, or rather, spasm, was Ghosts-Indigestion-Nervous-Breakdown. His second, when he saw that the figure was substantial and real, was Impersonation. But a slight movement on the part of the visitor dismissed that.

It was a little habitual movement which belonged only to that man; an unconscious twitching of the third finger of the left hand. He knew then that it was Gopak. Gopak, a little changed, but still, miraculously, thirty-two. Gopak, alive, breathing and real. No ghost. No phantom of the stomach. He was as certain of that as he was that fifteen years ago he had killed Gopak stone-dead and buried him.

The blackness of the moment was lightened by Gopak. In thin, flat tones he asked, "May I sit down? I'm tired." He sat down, and said: "So tired."

Nameless still held the table. He whispered: "Gopak. . . . Gopak. . . . But I—I *killed* you. I killed you in the jungle. You were dead. I know you were."

Gopak passed his hand across his face. He seemed about to cry. "I know you did. I know. That's all I can remember—about this earth. You killed me." The voice became thinner and flatter. "And then they came and—disturbed me. They woke me up. And brought me back." He sat with shoulders sagged, arms drooping, hands hanging between knees. After the first recognition he did not look at Nameless; he looked at the floor.

"Came and disturbed you?" Nameless leaned forward and whispered the words. "Woke you up? Who?"

"The Leopard Men."

"The what?"

"The Leopard Men." The watery voice said it as casually as if it were saying "the night watchman."

"The Leopard Men?" Nameless stared, and his fat face crinkled in an effort to take in the situation of a midnight visitation from a dead man, and the dead man talking nonsense. He felt his blood moving out of its course. He looked at his own hand to see if it was his own hand. He looked at the table to see if it was his table. The hand and the table were facts, and if the dead man was a fact—and he was—his story might be a fact. It seemed anyway as sensible as the dead man's presence. He gave a heavy sigh from the stomach. "A-ah. . . . The Leopard Men. . . . Yes, I heard about them out there. Tales."

Gopak slowly wagged his head. "Not tales. They're real. If they weren't real—I wouldn't be here. Would I?"

Nameless had to admit this. He had heard many tales "out there" about the Leopard Men, and had dismissed them as jungle yarns. But now, it seemed, jungle yarns had become commonplace fact in a little London shop. The watery voice went on. "They do it. I saw them. I came back in the middle of a circle of them. They killed a nigger to put his life into me. They wanted a white man—for their farm. So they brought me back. You may not believe it. You wouldn't *want* to believe it. You wouldn't want to—see or know anything like them. And I wouldn't want any man to. But it's true. That's how I'm here."

"But I left you absolutely dead. I made every test. It was three days before I buried you. And I buried you deep."

"I know. But that wouldn't make any difference to them. It was a long time after when they came and brought me back. And I'm still dead, you know. It's only my body they brought back." The voice trailed into a thread. "And I'm so tired."

Sitting in his prosperous eating-house Nameless was in the presence of an achieved miracle, but the everyday, solid appointments of the eating-house wouldn't let him fully comprehend it. Foolishly, as he realised when he had spoken, he asked Gopak to explain what had happened. Asked a man who couldn't really be alive to explain how he came to be alive. It was like asking Nothing to explain Everything.

Constantly, as he talked, he felt his grasp on his own mind slipping. The surprise of a sudden visitor at a late hour; the shock of the arrival of a long-dead man; and the realisation that this long-dead man was not a wraith, were too much for him.

During the next half-hour he found himself talking to Gopak as to the Gopak he had known seventeen years ago when they were partners. Then he would be halted by the freezing knowledge that he was talking to a dead man, and that a dead man was faintly answering him. He felt that the thing couldn't really have happened, but in the interchange of talk he kept forgetting the improbable side of it, and accepting it. With each recollection of the truth, his mind would clear and settle in one thought—"I've got to get rid of him. How am I going to get rid of him?"

"But how did you get here?"

"I escaped." The words came slowly and thinly, and out of the body rather than the mouth.

"How?"

"I don't—know. I don't remember anything—except our quarrel. And being at rest."

"But why come all the way here? Why didn't you stay on the coast?"

"I don't—know. But you're the only man I know. The only man I can remember."

"But how did you find me?"

"I don't know. But I had to—find you. You're the only man—who can help me."

"But how can I help you?"

The head turned weakly from side to side. "I don't—know. But nobody else—can."

Nameless stared through the window, looking on to the lamplit street and seeing nothing of it. The everyday being which had been his half an hour ago had been annihilated; the everyday beliefs and disbeliefs shattered and mixed together. But some shred of his old sense and his old standards remained. He must handle this situation. "Well—what you want to do? What you going to do? I don't see how I can help you. And you can't stay here, obviously." A demon of perversity sent a facetious notion into his head—introducing Gopak to his wife—"This is my dead friend."

But on his last spoken remark Gopak made the effort of raising his head and staring with the glazed eyes at Nameless. "But I *must* stay here. There's nowhere else I can stay. I must stay here. That's why I came. You got to help me."

"But you can't stay here. I got no room. All occupied. Nowhere for you to sleep."

The wan voice said: "That doesn't matter. I *don't* sleep."

"Eh?"

"I *don't* sleep. I haven't slept since they brought me back. I can sit here—till you can think of some way of helping me."

"But how *can* I?" He again forgot the background of the situation, and began to get angry at the vision of a dead man sitting about the place waiting for him to think of something. "How *can* I if you don't tell me how?"

"I don't—know. But you got to. You killed me. And I was dead—and comfortable. As it all came from you—killing me—you're responsible for me being—like this. So you got to—help me. That's why I—came to you."

"But what do you want me to do?"

"I don't—know. I can't—think. But nobody but you can help me. I had to come to you. Something brought me—straight to you. That means that you're the one—that can help me. Now I'm with you, something will—happen to help me. I feel it will. In time you'll—think of something."

Nameless found his legs suddenly weak. He sat down and stared with a sick scowl at the hideous and the incomprehensible. Here was a dead man in his house—a man he had murdered in a moment of black temper—and he knew in his heart that he couldn't turn the man out. For one thing, he would have been afraid to touch him; he couldn't see himself touching him. For another, faced with the miracle of the presence of a fifteen-years-dead man, he doubted whether physical force or any material agency would be effectual in moving the man.

His soul shivered, as all men's souls shiver at the demonstration of forces outside their mental or spiritual horizon. He had murdered this man, and often, in fifteen years, he had repented the act. If the man's appalling story were true, then he had some sort of right to turn to Nameless. Nameless recognised that, and knew that whatever happened he couldn't turn him out. His hot-tempered sin had literally come home to him.

The wan voice broke into his nightmare. "You go to rest, Nameless. I'll sit here. You go to rest." He put his face down to his hands and uttered a little moan. "Oh, why can't I rest?"

Nameless came down early next morning with a half-hope that Gopak would not be there. But he was there, seated where Nameless had left him last night. Nameless made some tea, and showed him where he might wash. He washed listlessly, and crawled back to his seat, and listlessly drank the tea which Nameless brought to him.

To his wife and the kitchen helpers Nameless mentioned him as an old friend who had had a bit of a shock. "Shipwrecked and knocked on the head. But quite harmless, and he won't be staying long. He's waiting for admission to a home. A good pal to me in the past, and it's the least I can do to let him stay here a few days. Suffers from sleeplessness and prefers to sit up at night. Quite harmless."

But Gopak stayed more than a few days. He outstayed everybody. Even when the customers had gone Gopak was still there.

On the first morning of his visit when the regular customers came in at mid-day, they looked at the odd, white figure sitting vacantly in the first pew, then stared, then moved away. All avoided the pew in which he sat. Nameless explained him to them, but his explanation did not seem to relieve the slight tension which settled on the dining-room. The atmosphere was not so brisk and chatty as usual. Even those who had their backs to the stranger seemed to be affected by his presence.

At the end of the first day Nameless, noticing this, told him that he had arranged a nice corner of the front-room upstairs, where he could sit by the window, and took his arm to take him upstairs. But Gopak feebly shook the hand away, and sat where he was. "No. I don't want to go. I'll stay here. I'll stay here. I don't want to move."

And he wouldn't move. After a few more pleadings Nameless realised with dismay that his refusal was definite; that it would be futile to press him or force him; that he was going to sit in that dining-room for ever. He was as weak as a child and as firm as a rock. He continued to sit in that first pew, and the customers continued to avoid it, and to give queer glances at it. It seemed that they half-recognised that he was something more than a fellow who had had a shock.

During the second week of his stay three of the regular customers were missing, and more than one of those that remained made acidly facetious suggestions to Nameless that he park his lively friend somewhere else. He made things too exciting for them; all that whoopee took them off their work, and interfered with digestion. Nameless told them he would be staying only a day or so longer, but they found that this was untrue, and at the end of the second week eight of the regulars had found another place.

Each day, when the dinner-hour came, Nameless tried to get him to take a little walk, but always he refused. He would go out only at night, and then never more than two hundred yards from the shop. For the rest, he sat in his pew, sometimes dozing in the afternoon, at other times staring at the floor. He took his food abstractedly, and never knew whether he had had food or not. He spoke only when questioned, and the burden of his talk was "I'm so tired."

One thing only seemed to arouse any light of interest in him; one thing only drew his eyes from the floor. That was the seventeen-year-old daughter of his host, who was known as Bubbles, and who helped with the waiting. And Bubbles seemed to be the only member of the shop and its customers who did not shrink from him.

She knew nothing of the truth about him, but she seemed to understand him, and the only response he ever gave to anything was to her childish sympathy. She sat and chatted foolish chatter to him—"bringing him out of himself," she called it—and sometimes he would be brought out to the extent of a watery smile. He came to recognise her step, and would look up before she entered the room. Once or twice in the evening, when the shop was empty, and Nameless was sitting miserably with him, he would ask, without lifting his eyes, "Where's Bubbles?" and would be told that Bubbles had gone to the pictures or was out at a dance, and would relapse into deeper vacancy.

Nameless didn't like this. He was already visited by a curse which, in four weeks, had destroyed most of his business. Regular customers had dropped off two by two, and no new customers came to take their place. Strangers who dropped in once for a meal did not come again; they could not keep their eyes or their minds off the forbidding, white-faced figure sitting motionless in the first pew. At mid-day, when the place had been crowded and latecomers had to wait for a seat, it was now two-thirds empty; only a few of the most thick-skinned remained faithful.

And on top of this there was the interest of the dead man in his daughter, an interest which seemed to be having an unpleasant effect. Nameless hadn't noticed it, but his wife had. "Bubbles don't seem as bright and lively as she was. You noticed it lately? She's getting quiet—and a bit slack. Sits about a lot. Paler than she used to be."

"Her age, perhaps."

"No. She's not one of these thin dark sort. No—it's something else. Just the last week or two I've noticed it. Off her food. Sits about doing nothing. No interest. May be nothing—just out of sorts, perhaps. . . . How much longer's that horrible friend of yours going to stay?"

The horrible friend stayed some weeks longer—ten weeks in all—while Nameless watched his business drop to nothing and his daughter get pale and peevish. He knew the cause of it. There was no home in all England like his: no home that had a dead man sitting in it for ten weeks. A dead man brought, after a long time, from the grave, to sit and disturb his customers and take the vitality from his daughter. He couldn't tell this to anybody. Nobody would believe such nonsense. But he *knew* that he was entertaining a dead man, and, knowing that a long-dead man was walking the earth, he could believe in any result of that fact. He could believe almost anything that he would have derided ten weeks ago. His customers had abandoned his shop, not because of the presence of a silent, white-faced man, but because of the presence of a dead-living man. Their minds might not know it, but their blood knew it. And, as his business had been destroyed, so, he believed, would his daughter be destroyed. Her blood was not warning her; her blood told her only that this was a long-ago friend of her father's, and she was drawn to him.

It was at this point that Nameless, having no work to do, began to drink. And it was well that he did so. For out of the drink came an idea, and with that idea he freed himself from the curse upon him and his house.

The shop now served scarcely half a dozen customers at mid-day. It had become ill-kempt and dusty, and the service and the food were bad. Nameless took no trouble to be civil to his few customers. Often, when he was notably under drink, he went to the trouble of being very rude to them. They talked about this. They talked about the decline of his business and the dustiness of the shop and the bad food. They talked about his drinking, and, of course, exaggerated it.

And they talked about the queer fellow who sat there day after day and gave everybody the creeps. A few outsiders, hearing the gossip, came to the dining-rooms to see the queer fellow and the always-tight proprietor; but they did not come again, and there were not enough of the curious to keep the place busy. It went down until it served scarcely two customers a day. And Nameless went down with it into drink.

Then, one evening, out of the drink he fished an inspiration.

He took it downstairs to Gopak, who was sitting in his usual seat, hands hanging, eyes on the floor. "Gopak—listen. You came here because I was the only man who could help you in your trouble. You listening?"

A faint "Yes" was his answer.

"Well, now. You told me I'd got to think of something. I've thought of something. . . . Listen. You say I'm responsible for your condition and got to get you out of it, because I killed you. I did. We had a row. You made me wild. You dared me. And what with that sun and the jungle and the insects, I wasn't meself. I killed you. The moment it was done I could 'a cut me right hand off. Because you and me were pals. I could 'a cut me right hand off."

"I know. I felt that directly it was over. I knew you were suffering."

"Ah! . . . I have suffered. And I'm suffering now. Well, this is what I've thought. All your present trouble comes from me killing you in that jungle and burying you. An idea came to me. Do you think it would help you—I—if I—if I—killed you again?"

For some seconds Gopak continued to stare at the floor. Then his shoulders moved. Then, while Nameless watched every little response to his idea, the watery voice began. "Yes. Yes. That's it. That's what I was waiting for. That's why I came here. I can see now. That's why I had to get here. Nobody else could kill me. Only you. I've got to be killed again. Yes, I see. But nobody else—would be able—to kill me. Only the man who first killed me. . . . Yes, you've found—what we're both—waiting for. Anybody else could shoot me—stab me—hang me—but they couldn't kill me. Only you. That's why I managed to get here and find you." The watery voice rose to a thin strength. "That's it. And you must do it. Do it now. You don't want to, I know. But you must. You *must.*"

His head drooped and he stared at the floor. Nameless, too, stared at the floor. He was seeing things. He had murdered a man and had escaped all punishment save that of his own mind, which had been terrible enough. But now he was going to murder him again—not in a jungle but in a city; and he saw the slow points of the result.

He saw the arrest. He saw the first hearing. He saw the trial. He saw the cell. He saw the rope. He shuddered.

Then he saw the alternative—the breakdown of his life—a ruined business, poverty, the poor-house, a daughter robbed of her health and perhaps dying, and always the curse of the dead-living man, who might follow him to the poor-house. Better to end it all, he thought. Rid himself of the curse which Gopak had brought upon him and his family, and then rid his family of himself with a revolver. Better to follow up his idea.

He got stiffly to his feet. The hour was late evening—half-past ten—and the streets were quiet. He had pulled down the shop-blinds and locked the door. The room was lit by one light at the farther end. He moved about uncertainly and looked at Gopak. "Er—how would you—how shall I—"

Gopak said, "You did it with a knife. Just under the heart. You must do it that way again."

Nameless stood and looked at him for some seconds. Then, with an air of resolve, he shook himself. He walked quickly to the kitchen.

Three minutes later his wife and daughter heard a crash, as though a table had been overturned. They called but got no answer. When they came down they found him sitting in one of the pews, wiping sweat from his forehead. He was white and shaking, and appeared to be recovering from a faint.

"Whatever's the matter? You all right?"

He waved them away. "Yes, I'm all right. Touch of giddiness. Smoking too much, I think."

"Mmmm. Or drinking. . . . Where's your friend? Out for a walk?"

"No. He's gone off. Said he wouldn't impose any longer, and 'd go and find an infirmary." He spoke weakly and found trouble in picking words. "Didn't you hear that bang—when he shut the door?"

"I thought that was you fell down."

"No. It was him when he went. I couldn't stop him."

"Mmmm. Just as well, I think." She looked about her. "Things seem to 'a gone all wrong since he's been here."

There was a general air of dustiness about the place. The table-cloths were dirty, not from use but from disuse. The windows were dim. A long knife, very dusty, was lying on the table under the window. In a corner by the door leading to the kitchen, unseen by her, lay a dusty mackintosh and dungaree, which appeared to have been tossed there. But it was over by the main door, near the first pew, that the dust was thickest—a long trail of it—greyish-white dust.

"Really this place gets more and more slap-dash Just *look* at that dust by the door. Looks as though somebody's been spilling ashes all over the place."

Nameless looked at it, and his hands shook a little. But he answered, more firmly than before: "Yes, I know. I'll have a proper clean-up to-morrow."

For the first time in ten weeks he smiled at them; a thin, haggard smile, but a smile.

THE GOLDEN GONG

The friends of Tommy Frang, if asked what sort of fellow he is, will tell you that—oh, he's just an ordinary, likeable, middle-aged fellow; no nonsense about him. But if you press them for any distinguishing characteristic, they will admit that there is just one thing about him that puzzles them; that is, that he can never pass a gong in a hotel or private house without furtively striking it and listening to its note with an air of awaiting a revelation. As an adult and a man of orderly and sensible habits, he has confessed that the act is futile and that he expects nothing from it; it has become a perfunctory habit, like Samuel Johnson's habit of touching all the posts in Fleet Street. But it is a habit which some inner and regrettably capricious force will not allow him to break; its roots are set too deep in reality and significance. They are set in the only essential reality—the reality of childhood. As we grow, we learn; but the things we truly know, the things that are the core of our being, are the things we have never learnt—the things we knew when we scarcely knew that we were alive. We do not believe these things. We *know* them. Here is what Tommy once knew about a gong.

When he was ten years old, Tommy was living in Limehouse, in one of those streets which housed an overflow of the Chinese from their two main streets—Pennyfields and the Causeway. These Chinese, as a sprinkling of foreigners in a street of Londoners, stood out and caught his young attention and held it. He fell into a way of shadowing them, and following them into their own streets. He was by circumstances solitary and by nature shy. He could not readily get on with his schoolmates; he was so much quieter and older of character. It was therefore natural that he should turn from those of his own age to grown-ups; natural, too, that after a time his shyness should drive him from the grown-ups of his own people to those of another race. From following the Chinese into their

own streets he came to be noticed by them, and he found that among
them he could be at ease. He found that his shyness passed without
comment or was accepted as characteristic of the English boy. He found
that he was not judged or compared or put at a loss by them. In these
streets he felt free from the demands of inhibitions and contemporary
standards. He was accepted as himself, with the result that among them
he was not shy. And there were no nagging or harassed or exasperated
people here—no complaining voices or harsh gestures. All was cool and
suave and imperturbable.

So he came to spend all his spare hours among them. He wandered
along their streets, and hovered about their shops, and soon made
friends with them, and was given the entry to their rooms. As a small
child, regarded casually as an adopted mascot, he was allowed to go
where he would, in and out, upstairs and downstairs, and to sit among
them without rebuke.

In a short time he knew more of the Chinese and their ways than he
knew of the ways of the people of his own streets. He liked their ways.
He liked their faces, and he liked their high voices, and liked to hear
them talk in their bubbling Cantonese. It sounded to him more like
comic songs than serious talk. He became wise in the affairs of the colony. His real life became identified with it, and the daily life of his own
home was no more than a background to it. He knew the names of a
score of them and their characters. He knew who were generous and
who were mean; who were prosperous and who were poor. He knew
who liked whom, and who hated whom. He knew where they came
from and where, at some fortunate time, they planned to go. And he
heard stories—casual stories of business and trouble, of death and revenge, and strange happenings in far-away hills—anecdotes of everyday;
but to him they were more wonderful and terrible than anything in the
Arabian Nights or Gulliver. Before he was nine he knew much more
about China than his school-teacher had even read. He could not relate
or compare this knowledge. It was pure and barren knowledge, akin to
the cramming of a dull student, without utility or significance. But he enjoyed possessing it and enjoyed adding to it.

At half a dozen shops and two or three lodging-houses he was admitted with smiles, and of all these places his favourite was a little store

in the Causeway. He grew to love this narrow street. It is a bitter-smelling street. Its air holds the true smack of Asia; the spirit that lives in it is radiant, gracious, delicate and utterly unhuman. But to the boy it was a street of human delights. It was so different from the streets of his regular life that he could not perceive its grotesquerie and its chill; he could see it only as a street that he would like all streets to be. Very little ever happens in this street, but it is a street where anything, however fantastic, *might* happen. It is the right setting for the odd and the peculiar, and if it be approached in the right temper the odd and the peculiar will sometimes emerge from it. It was something of this sort that Tommy's temper struck from it; something so odd and peculiar that it coloured the whole of his life.

Every evening after school he would wander into it and make for the little store, and there he would prowl about a more enchanting and bewildering Wonderland than any Christmas Bazaar he had ever seen. It was so enchanting that it became a worry to him. His mind was agitated by the thought that he might have to go away, or the shop might be shut up, before he had made full exploration of all its massed delights. It was an Ali Baba Cave. There were ginger jars of all colours, and banners with precepts inscribed in gold. There were curious foods and exciting sweets. There were tea-pots in scarlet cradles. There were boats and towers and houses in ivory and coral and soapstone and crystal. There were exquisite trifles in jade. There were paper lanterns with green dragons and yellow lions and purple serpents. There were gay vases and fearful masks and brilliant boxes. There were coloured tea-chests. There were red papers bearing queer drawings and signs which the boy studied stroke by stroke. There were mis-shapen musical instruments, of one and of twelve strings. There were idols and dolls and love-amulets, and fly-whisks of blue and yellow. There were little tobacco pipes and gorgeous water-pipes, and the tiniest tea-cups. All the exhibition junk that white visitors might be expected to buy.

But its chief glory was hidden upstairs.

Its chief glory was a huge golden gong.

Tommy had made many visits to the store before he discovered the gong, but once he had discovered it, he could not keep away from it. Against its glory all the assorted treasures of the shop shrivelled into the ordinary. It was a more desirable toy than any of the things he had ever coveted—bicycles, kites, trains, pistols, magic-lanterns, humming-tops, boats. It was more gorgeous, more exceptional, inexhaustibly interesting, more—or so it seemed—more alive and responsive.

It hung in a frame of red wood in old Foo's private room, and it was the king of the room. Indeed, it was the room. It claimed all the light and seemed to claim all the space. There were other things in the room, but under the august gleam of the gong they did not dare to assert themselves. All that the visitor saw was the gong. It was of a rich autumn gold, and its face was damascened with dragons and lilies and peacocks. In that small room it appeared three times larger than it was; it seemed to be trying to burst out of the room in fierce resentment at the confinement in an attic of such blaze and power. But when it was made to speak there was nothing of anger or resentment in its tones. In its tones, which circled the room like visible rays of liquid gold, rang a memory of all sweet things. They held honey and cream and wine. They held the dark reek of laudanum. They held plaintive song. They held porcelain and amber, velvet and silk and pomegranates. They held figs and lotus seeds; purple rugs and pearls and roses. They held ambrosial herbs. They had the roundness of ripe plums. In the moment of percussion its golden throat opened in a plush roar that evoked images of the opulent and the sumptuous, of the Violet Town and the Forbidden City and the Temple of Heaven. As this plangent tone rippled and declined, it evoked the suave and the perfumed, until its last tremblings dissolved into whispers of fleeting and fantastic forms so fragile that nothing palpable could illustrate them.

But behind all these ideas, and perceptible only when its last vibrations had perished, hung a hint of the uneasy; an image of something desiccated and austere and terrible. Not of anger, but something colder than anger, a disembodied potency as abstract in its action as the sea.

Something of this Tommy perceived, because he often told old Foo that it wasn't an ordinary gong; it was a magic gong. Each time he played upon it, which he sometimes did for an hour—old Foo was serenely tolerant of noise—he was aware of indulging in a secret delight; a delight which he not only could never bring himself to share with another, but could not even mention to another. It was *his* gong and *his* delight. Nobody must know about it. He hugged it as closely to himself as a sin. He did not know why he should have this feeling, and being ten years old he was not concerned to question it. At that age, feelings are feelings and experience is experience, to be taken as literally as food. But he did know that often, when the gong had trembled into silence after the mightiest blow he could give it, he too was trembling. He did know that the sonorous waves of its voice awoke in him strange emotions which until then had been sleeping unknown to him. They stirred in him ideas of cruelty which were as instinctive as his personal horror of cruelty. Its veiled utterance of the spectral and the forbidden fascinated his essential human side while it repelled his healthy animal side. In its reverberations hovered the spirit that hovers in the Causeway—radiant, gracious, delicate and utterly unhuman. They held echoes of all the stories he had heard in the quarter, and they put into his mind all manner of ideas. Some of them he felt were wrong and some of them he did not understand; but all of them, as they touched his mind, left a thrill. Sometimes these ideas were warm and pleasant; often they were cold and demoniac.

It was because of this that the word "magic" came to him when talking to Foo. Not only were there magical things in its music; it *looked* magical. In the evenings, as he entered the room, it hung in the dusk like a great yellow face on which the fall of light and shadow made the features. It looked to him as the Face of God might look. He amused himself with the fancy that it *was* a god—his god. Very soon he became its devotee. Often, when he had wished that something pleasant might happen, or something unpleasant not happen, he had added to his nightly prayers a promise to God that he would do something specially pleasing to God if God would look after this little matter for him. If God would grant his prayer, he would go to church three times every Sunday, and stop using bad words, and give all his foreign stamps to the boy next door. But he had never noticed any response to these generous offers of his, and now that he had the gong he ceased to add his personal pleas to his formal parrot-prayers. He took them to the gong. He made it the repository of his secrets and his hopes. If he did not actually pray to it, he told it what he wanted, and as it was a heathen god he felt relieved from any necessity of making it rash promises. Without talking to it he told it all about himself. He would sit before its great gold face and commune with it. He told it things that he would never have whispered to a living person. He told it all the things that itself had evoked in his mind. All his imaginings, commonplace and queer, he poured into the rippling waves of its music. He invented little mad stories for himself and the dragon and the peacock which decorated its face; stories that delighted him and, at the thought of their becoming known to others, gave him a hot sense of shame.

Now, on a certain night, after he had played many times upon the gong, he sat before it and begged it to grant him his dearest wish. He begged it to use its power to let him find a friend. A real friend. Somebody he could trust and who would trust him; somebody he would like and who would like him; somebody who would understand him and whom he would understand; somebody he could send little presents to, which would be treasured; somebody who would mean Everything to him. He did not firmly believe that the gong could give him what he wanted, and he did not disbelieve. His attitude was as open as that of the people in Sunday-morning church reciting the Lord's Prayer. His praying to the gong was something he liked doing; a thrilling ritual; and he did it with fervour.

Well, he had made this prayer for a real and perfect friend nine times when, on a certain marvellous night, the gong answered him. He was playing with the gong as usual, and was standing as it were in a shower of golden sound, when he became aware, through the greater sound, of a tiny rustling and of an instant warmth in the room. He looked round, and there, on the bottom step of the stairs leading to the second floor, stood a young woman—a young Chinese woman not much taller than himself. Her face was round and of the hue of apricots. Her eyes were long. Her lips were red and smiling. She wore a long, full-sleeved jacket of bright green silk, sprigged with pink flowers, a black silk skirt, and an amber scarf. Her flat black hair was dressed with a green comb.

Tommy stared. His first look was enough to fill him with a dumb sense that he was in the presence of beauty; and thereafter he stared. He had never known that anybody so lovely as this lady lived in that house. He knew the two men-lodgers, but he had heard no word from Foo of a lovely lady. He concluded that she must be the wife of one of the lodgers, and that she seldom went out, or perhaps had arrived that day on one of the boats. But her clothes. He had never anywhere, even in this queer street, seen such gorgeous and fantastic clothes. The men wore English lounge suits or jackets and trousers of canvas or dungaree, and the only two old women of the quarter he had seen wore black English costumes. Perhaps this was the special indoor costume of a very well-off lady, or perhaps she was giving a party, and this was evening dress or fancy dress. He did not know, and it was only a tiny corner of his mind that was debating the matter. The main part of his dazed being was absorbed in looking at her and in returning her smile. He did not find her grotesque, as other boys might have done; he found her lovely, and he found himself tingling with a warm-cold thrill at sight of her.

For some throbbing seconds they stood thus while the last ripples of the gong's voice died on the air; then she left the stairs and came into the room. She pushed the door behind her and came towards him and looked down at him. From out of her long sleeve came a slim hand. She put it gently on his head, and moved his head backward, so that he stood looking straight up at her. With the touch of her hand a new thrill went through him—a thrill of contentment and warmth and intimacy. From the moment when he heard the rustling of her skirt the little incident had taken but a few seconds; yet he felt that he had been a long time with this strange lady; that he knew her and that she knew him.

So they stood, each looking at the other, and to Tommy this looking was as though they were talking. One or two words were, indeed, spoken, but after that they lived in silence, since neither knew the other's tongue. She touched herself with a gesture that seemed to him as sweet as her smiles, and said: "Sung Sing." She pointed to him and questioned with her face. He said: "I'm Tommy." She said: "Tohme," and he smiled. He said: "Sung Sing," and she smiled. In a corner, at right angles to the gong, was a shabby old divan. She put an arm about him, and led him to it, and sat down, and held him before her so that his face was level with hers. She looked at him with gentle, rapt eyes. She seemed to be worshipping him. Then, from the folds of her jacket she brought out a little box of soft Chinese sweetmeat. She broke a piece and put it in his mouth. It was a luscious sweet, rich with flavours new to him. This little touch having made them familiar, he reached out to the box, broke off another piece, and did as she had done—put it in

Sung Sing's mouth. She laughed as she took it, and he laughed, and from the moment of their mutual laughter all that he did was impulsive. He was no more self-conscious or shy than the rowdiest of his school-mates. He existed in a kind of electric daze. When she took one of his hands and stroked it, with an air of benediction, he moved close to her knees and put up his other hand and stroked her face. He did not know why he did this ; he did not even know that he was doing it. He only knew that bliss had come to him, and that the touch of this lovely lady's face to his hand went through him like—like—he could think of nothing then to liken it to, but later he found the word music.

And then he was no longer aware of time. It was only when he noted that the room was growing darker that he found himself in her arms and sitting on her lap. She was crooning to him and caressing him and smiling to him, and his face was resting on her shoulder in such content as he had never known. Not until the room was quite dark was he recalled to his other life, and then he knew that he must have spent four hours there, that he would be late home, that there would be questions and nagging. He moved reluctantly from her arms. Nothing now was less inviting than his home and his other life, but that life had fixed its peremptory de-mands upon him, and his obedience to them was automatic. He would have liked to stay with her for ever, but he knew that he dare not.

He got up and pointed sadly to the window and the door, and Sung Sing nodded. She bent to him and softly kissed his cheek and pressed her face to his, and he returned the kiss many times, fervently and inno-cently. She stood back from him for a moment or so, holding both his hands. Then with a little laugh she opened the door, and he went out. On the landing he turned and smiled. He made some clumsy signs by which he tried to convey that he would return next evening. She seemed to take his meaning; she nodded and smiled and waved a little hand. He reached his home in a mood of sadness, bewilderment and ecstasy. He answered the challenges of his doings by involved lies about having gone for a walk and got lost. He did not know that he was speaking the truth.

That evening was the opening for him of the richest and most beautiful experience of his life. Nothing of it can be recaptured by words or by hints of words. Its essence was the poetry behind the poem; the unsayable. He knew then what he has never known since—complete harmony with life. His hours with Sung Sing were a realisation of all that we attempt to convey in the worn word paradise; our *selves* being nothing but ourselves. Every little act in that room, every tiny movement of her hands, every little thing that they did together, he remembers clearly today. Each act and movement seemed to be charged with a separate life and significance. He can recall today every evening of the many evenings he spent with her, and can recall everything that was done, minute by minute, in each evening. It was like a recital of music in which each little motion was an instrument, each minute a stave, and each evening a sonata.

There was the melting silk of her jacket and the warmth of her body. There were her liquid endearments—her whisperings in Chinese answering his whisperings in English. There was the touch of her hand on his, and their communications by hands and smiles. And there were her long eyes looking right into his. This was their closest communion. They would sit in this manner by the half-hour, until his whole being was resolved into his two eyes, and those two eyes were living their life in the lake of Sung Sing's eyes. He never troubled to wonder whether any of the queer things done in that room were right or wrong. It was all so blissful and perfect, and seemed so natural, that so dull a question never entered his mind. Years later he viewed the matter with his adult and informed mind, and judged it, and having judged it was moved to wonder why and for whom ethical standards were introduced to the world.

Throughout that winter this secret and bizarre love affair persisted. He cherished it as a fearful joy. He lived only for the evenings. During the dull day he cheered himself by anticipation, and the moment school was over he would race to the Causeway. If, by some family circumstance or enforced duty, such as running errands, he could not go there after school, he would make a furtive bolt from the house in the evening. On three occasions, when affairs prevented a visit, and he had no chance of slipping out unseen, he climbed at his eight-o'clock bedtime out of his bedroom window, regardless of reprimand or punishment. And as soon as he was in old Foo's room, he would bang on the gong, and bang and bang, until Sung Sing came down from upstairs and they resumed their strange communion.

But beauty cannot live with us for ever. Beauty visits us, but, lest we

282   THOMAS BURKE

forget its wonder in its familiar presence, it will not stay. It comes like the rose and passes like the rose, and we are fortunate if it leaves us the dry perfume of pot pourri.

It did not stay long with Tommy. Before he was eleven it was gone, and it went as instantly as it had come.

He was passing through Foo's shop one evening and about to slip upstairs, when Foo spoke to him.

"You like very much my gong—hee?"

"Yes. I love the gong. But I love the Chinese lady better."

"The Chinese lady?"

"'M. Sung Sing."

"Sung Sing? Oh." Foo turned to look at a friend who was sitting in a corner, drinking tea, and the friend returned the look with a screwing of the eyes.

"Yes—the Chinese lady that lodges upstairs. She's lovely."

Foo looked at the friend again. "Sung Sing. Oh, yes." He turned to the counter and re-arranged some of the boxes. "Oh, yes. You have been playing in Sung Sing's room?"

"No. I haven't been to her room. She's upstairs on the second floor. I haven't been there. She comes down to see me in the room where the gong is."

"Oh, yes. I see. I understand. Yes. . . . Are you going up to talk to her now?"

"Yes. She always comes down when she hears me."

"Ah. Yes. I will come with you. I have a message for her."

"Oh. . . . Alright."

Tommy had not anticipated this. He did not want old Foo pottering about while they were together. Sung Sing meant nothing to him unless he could be alone with her. He hoped old Foo wouldn't stay long over his message.

As they reached the first floor, he turned to Foo. "You going up to her?"

"No. I will wait here until she comes down."

"Oh. . . . Alright. She'll be down when she hears me play the gong." He went into the little room, took up the gong-stick, and gave the gong a valiant bang. "She'll be down in a minute, I expect."

Foo moved to the middle of the room, and stood with his face towards the door. Tommy attacked the gong and set the room ringing. Between each stroke he turned to the door. But Sung Sing was not so prompt that evening.

"Funny. She always does come at the first sound." He stopped banging and turned to Foo. "She isn't afraid of you, is she? You said you'd got a message for her. What sort of message? You haven't had words, have you?"

"Words," in Tommy's world, were the euphemism for quarrel or row, and "words" were weekly happenings in every house that entertained a lodger.

"No. We have had no words."

Boom! Boom! Boom! "She doesn't owe you for rent, does she?"

"No. She does not owe me for rent."

"Funny, then. Wonder why she doesn't come. Perhaps she don't know it's you. Perhaps she heard you come up, and thinks it's someone else. A stranger." (Boom! Boom! *Boom!*) "Which is her room upstairs?"

Foo made no answer; he was still looking at the door.

"Shall I go up and see if she's in?"

"No. I do not think you should go up. If she does not wish to come it would not be po-lite to dis-turb her."

Boom! Boom! Boom! The room was filled with such crashing roars of golden music that the air seemed alive with them. The vibrations were like powerful personalities in too small a space; they seemed, by their impact, to be trying to annihilate the old man and the boy.

"Perhaps she's ill?"

"No, I do not think she is ill. Indeed, I know she is not."

"Then I wonder what's keeping her. She always has come down other times. Perhaps she won't come while you're here. Perhaps if you go away she'll come. Then I can tell her you've got a message for her."

Old Foo stood immovable. "No. It is important that I should see her as soon as she comes."

"Then why don't you go up and see what's keeping her?"

Foo did not answer. Instead, he moved to the divan and sat down. Then he beckoned to the boy. "Come here."

Tommy went to him.

"Tell me—how long have you been meeting Sung Sing?"

"Oo, some munce now. A long time."

"Ah. Yes. And you like her?"

"Oo, I do."

"She was very nice to you?"

"Oo, lovely."

"She used to tell you Chinese fairy-tales, did she?"

"No. She couldn't speak English. She used to—" And then Tommy, who knew that he could speak freely to old Foo without being laughed at, told him all about the loveliness of Sung Sing, and her wonderful clothes, and all—or not quite all—about their meetings and what they did, and about her sweet ways with him.

Foo listened with gravity, and when the tale was ended he sat for a space in meditation. Then he put his hands on Tommy's shoulders and looked at the boy. Then he spoke.

"Listen, boy. I will tell you why the Chinese lady has not come this evening. You were quite right. She has not come because I am here. And because—because there is no Chinese lady."

"But that's silly. I—"

"There is no Chinese lady here. There is no Sung Sing here. There is no Chinese lady living here at all. There has not been ever a Chinese lady living here. There is no person named Sung Sing in the whole of this quarter. There are four Chinese ladies in this quarter—all very old. There is no Sung Sing. There never was a Sung Sing."

"Don't talk silly. I *know* she lives here. I've seen her dozens and dozens and thousands of times."

"I do not disbelieve that you have seen her. But she is not here. She is not at all. She does not—does not exist."

Tommy stared and frowned, and debated this statement. Old Foo was off his nut. He was talking nonsense. He admitted that Tommy had seen her; yet said she didn't exist. He must be cracked. Or else he was using the wrong words, and didn't know. Or perhaps he had private reasons for saying that she didn't exist. Perhaps she'd run away from somewhere, and he was keeping her hidden.

"You can't say she doesn't exist. Because she does. I know. She *is* here. She *is*."

Foo ignored the passionate assertion. Very quietly he said: "She is *not* here. She never was here."

For a long time Tommy would not have it, and he battered old Foo with a monotonous, "She is. She is. She is. She is."

But when, hopeless of convincing the old stupid, he studied the old stupid's face, he had to acquit him of private designs or of misunderstanding. He knew that old Foo was not really stupid, and he knew that he did not lie; when he wished to avoid lying answers to questions, he kept silence. So at last, dimly, and without full comprehension, he began to realise that it might be as Foo said; that she was not really there; that she was there only for him. He was not alarmed or dismayed by this idea; living so much alone and in imagination, the unusual was not so disquieting to him as it might have been to others. Indeed, Foo's explanation only made the affair more thrilling, more personal. If she really didn't live in that house, and if nobody else had ever seen her, then she must be something to do with the marvellous gong. He didn't know what or why or how, and was too bemused by the adventure to inquire. It was enough that she was real to him, and that she belonged only to him and would come only to him. He had only to call her by the gong, and whenever he was alone she would come.

With that decision fixed in his mind, he stopped arguing with old Foo, and left him sitting by the gong, and went home.

He never saw Sung Sing again.

Having missed Sung Sing that one evening, by Foo's intervention, he could not go fast enough next evening to the shop. He raced to it, and without so much as a greeting to old Foo he slipped through the shop and upstairs.

A few seconds later he came down. His eyes were wide. "Where's the gong?"

Foo said tonelessly: "I have sold the gong."

"*Sold* it?" It was a squeak.

"Yes. I sold it this morning."

"Who to? Where's it gone? Why—"

"I do not know. I sold it to a merchant at the other end of the town. He bought it for a customer."

"But why did you sell it, Mister Foo? Why did you? *Why?*"

"I was tired of it. It was not a good gong."

The boy stood like a statue, staring at nothing, hands limp. Somewhere, deep within himself, he was realising his first grief—a grief more poignant than any he knew in later life. He had seen paradise, and was being turned back to an earth without light. The gong was gone, and with it, he knew, was gone Sung Sing and all the loveliness of the past months. Blood and breath had been taken from him in one sudden stroke. He might continue in this other world; he might grow up and be a man; but he felt that without his gong he would no longer be alive in it. The gong and Sung Sing were his bread and his wine; wanting them, he would have no place and no life in either world.

He leaned his arms on the counter, and stared at a Chinese tea-chest. He had no will to leave the shop or to stay; he could only stand and stare in dumb misery, and he stood like this until, on an entrance of customers, old Foo gently edged him out. Out in the street he hovered restlessly for some minutes, nursing a wild fancy that Sung Sing might appear in the street or be seen in one of the houses. But he knew that she wouldn't, and at last he crawled home and hoped that he would die.

That is why, to-day, in middle-age, he can never pass a gong without furtively striking it and listening to its note with an air of awaiting a revelation. How many hundreds of gongs he has heard, he does not know; but none of them has had the note of the golden gong or anything of its properties. At least, he says not. But it may be that one of them *has* had the note. It may be that one of them was that very golden gong itself; and that it wasn't a magical gong at all. It may be that it was just an ordinary gong, and that the magic was in Tommy. It may be that he is to-day so deaf with the world's talk, so enclosed in the house of civilisation and tuned only to that house's vibrations, that there is no open window, no key-hole even, through which its golden notes can reach him, or the face of Sung Sing reveal itself.

The young days of every man are marked by a time when he is really born, when the thread that links him with elsewhere is irrevocably snapped and he is left with a sense of loss which is healed only in random dreams. Some are fully born on their first day; some in their first year; others not for many years; and until that time they are children of the invisible. Tommy was born when he lost his gong, so, even if he did at last find it, it would now have nothing for him.

BIBLIOGRAPHY

"The Bird." In Burke's *Limehouse Nights*. London: Grant Richards, 1916. New York: Robert M. McBride Co., 1917.

"The Tablets of the House of Li." *Cosmopolitan* (May 1926). In Burke's *East of Mansion House*. New York: George H. Doran Co., 1926. London: Cassell, 1928.

"The Bloomsbury Wonder." London: Mandrake Press, 1929. In Burke's *Dark Nights*. London: Herbert Jenkins, [1944].

"The Hands of Mr. Ottermole." In Burke's *The Pleasantries of Old Quong*. London: Constable, 1931. Boston: Little, Brown, 1931 (as *A Tea-Shop in Limehouse*).

"Desirable Villa." In *The Pleasantries of Old Quong* (q.v.).

"The Secret of Francesco Shedd." In *The Pleasantries of Old Quong* (q.v.).

"The Yellow Imps." In *The Pleasantries of Old Quong* (q.v.).

"Miracle in Suburbia." In Burke's *Night-Pieces*. London: Constable, 1935. New York: D. Appleton-Century Co., 1936.

"Yesterday Street." In *Night-Pieces* (q.v.).

"Funspot." In *Night-Pieces* (q.v.).

"Uncle Ezekiel's Long Sight." In *Night-Pieces* (q.v.).

"The Horrible God." *Evening Standard* (London) (7 December 1934). In *Night-Pieces* (q.v.).

"Father and Son." In *Night-Pieces* (q.v.).

"Johnson Looked Back." In *Night-Pieces* (q.v.).

"Two Gentlemen." In *Night-Pieces* (q.v.).

"The Black Courtyard." In *Night-Pieces* (q.v.).

"The Gracious Ghosts." In *Night-Pieces* (q.v.).

"Jack Wapping." In *Night-Pieces* (q.v.).

"One Hundred Pounds." In *Night-Pieces* (q.v.).

"The Man Who Lost His Head." In *Night-Pieces* (q.v.).

"Murder under the Crooked Spire." In *Night-Pieces* (q.v.).

"The Lonely Inn." In *Night-Pieces* (q.v.).

"The Watcher." In *Night-Pieces* (q.v.).

"Events at Wayless-Wagtail." In *Night-Pieces* (q.v.).

"The Hollow Man." In *Evening Standard* (London) (5 December 1933). In *Night-Pieces* (q.v.).

"The Golden Gong." In *Thrills,* ed. [John Gawsworth]. London: Associated Newspapers, 1936.

ABOUT S. T. JOSHI

S. T. JOSHI is the author of *The Weird Tale* (1990), *H. P. Lovecraft: The Decline of the West* (1990), and *Unutterable Horror: A History of Supernatural Fiction* (2012). He has prepared corrected editions of H. P. Lovecraft's work for Arkham House and annotated editions of Lovecraft's stories for Penguin Classics. He has also prepared editions of Lovecraft's collected essays and poetry. His exhaustive biography, *H. P. Lovecraft: A Life* (1996), was expanded as *I Am Providence: The Life and Times of H. P. Lovecraft* (2010). He is the editor of the anthologies *American Supernatural Tales* (Penguin, 2007), Black Wings I-II-III (PS Publishing, 2010, 2012, 2013), *A Mountain Walked: Great Tales of the Cthulhu Mythos* (Centipede Press, 2014), *The Madness of Cthulhu* (Titan Books, 2014–15), and *Searchers After Horror: New Tales of the Weird and Fantastic* (Fedogan & Bremer, 2014). He is the editor of the *Lovecraft Annual* (Hippocampus Press), the *Weird Fiction Review* (Centipede Press), and the *American Rationalist* (Center for Inquiry). His Lovecraftian novel *The Assaults of Chaos* appeared in 2013.

Printed in the USA
CPSIA information can be obtained
at www.ICGtesting.com
CBHW071543240724
12106CB00008BA/395

9 781614 982159